quiver & quill

A TENEBRA CITY MONSTER ROMANCE

TENEBRA CITY SERIES
BOOK 1

A. M. KORE

copyright

Copyright © 2021-22 by A. M. Kore.
All rights reserved.

Note: This is a work of fiction. Unless otherwise indicated, all the names, characters, businesses, places, events and incidents in this book are either the product of the author's imagination or used in a fictitious manner. Any resemblance to actual persons, living or dead, or actual events is purely coincidental.

Written by A. M. Kore

Cover Design Consultation: Kyleigh Wentworth (@wentdesigning)

Editing: Meg (@opalescent4026)

acknowledgments

Quiver & Quill began as a tribute to the mothman, but continues as a love letter to my readers.

Thank you SO much for supporting me on this journey to #pegmothman2k21 and beyond.

This special edition is for you <3

contents

I: The Odyssey	1
II: Pandora's Box	13
III: Sour Grapes	24
IV: The Labyrinth	38
V: Dionysian Frenzy	46
VI: Panacea	58
VII: Forbidden Fruit	73
VIII: The Descent	87
IX: The Second Circle	99
X: Beware of Greeks Bearing Gifts	112
XI: The Sword of Damocles	127
XII: Theogony	138
XIII: The Sphinx	146
XIV: Heliacal Rising	159
XV: The Agora	172
XVI: The Seer	185
XVII: Compendium	198
XVIII: A Judgement of Paris	207
XIX: Modern Prometheus	222
XX: Gorgoneion	237
XXI: Ode to Demeter	248
XXII: Midas Touch	259
Epilogue: Elysian Fields	270
Bonus Content: To a Flame	279
About the Author	289
Also by A. M. Kore	291
Thank You!	293
Special Edition Content	295
The Golden Bough	297

"To Demeter."
Hesiod, the Homeric Hymns, and Homerica

And now tell me how he rapt you away to the realm of darkness and gloom, and by what trick did the strong Host of Many *beguile* you?

i: the odyssey

WELCOME TO EVENTIDE FALLS UNIVERSITY, you thought to yourself while staring at the gnarled clocktower, recognizable from all of the cheery informational pamphlets with blocky letters and smiling faces, *where the only thing stranger than its monstrous student body population was the fact that its mascot is an emu.*

Feeling somebody — or some*thing* — bump your shoulder, you immediately shuffled aside and lowered your gaze. You were still a bit intimidated by your new cohort. A mumbled apology died on your lips as your eyes met two violet ones narrowed in a glare, a pair of ivory fangs flashing at you menacingly as their owner brushed past you with a haughty sniff.

Offering the person a meek smile, you quickly scuffled away, cursing at yourself for already making a terrible impression on what you guessed was one of your fellow students by planting yourself in the middle of the cobblestone sidewalk and blocking foot traffic. You couldn't really afford to piss *too* many people off here; EFU was actually rather small, boasting only a few thousand students to its Eventide Falls campus. Its 'monstrous student body' wasn't actually in reference to the numbers of its scholars, but to their natures. EFU's students were monstrous.

Literally.

You threw a last wary glance over your shoulder at the snippy vampire before continuing on your merry little way to the campus library, fingertips subconsciously drifting to your neck as you walked on.

You'd been in Eventide Falls, the town that your university was named after, for about a week now, having settled into your cozy little one-bedroom apartment near campus upon your arrival. While you were no stranger to co-mingling with various other species, EFU was *much* more diverse than the university you'd attended for your undergraduate studies, which had been primarily human. Your own hometown had been pretty unassuming and had virtually no diversity at all, so you had purposely chosen your undergrad so you could see more of the world and dip your toe into the realm of variety.

From the looks of things, if your undergrad had been a puddle, EFU was an ocean... and you were now waist-deep in it.

Though on the smaller side, EFU was well-known for its liberal arts programs. The acclaim of the business school in particular was what had attracted you to applying to their graduate program; you remembered being impressed by the post-degree employment rates, as well as their placement services when it came to large corporations.

You loved the fast pace and bright lights of a city, but after enduring four years of smog and traffic and blisters from running up and down city blocks, you were ready for a change. An added benefit of EFU was that it was located in a much more quaint town with cute little cafes and steeples and lore of its own. Plus, it was decently far from where you had grown up, and you had been making it your personal mission to get the hell out of Dodge and your overly-critical parents ever since graduating high school.

You took the steps to the library two at a time, feeling proud that you were only *slightly* winded when you got to the top. Approaching a copper statue, you paused briefly to regard it a little more carefully.

Kronos the Emu, the plaque stated as your gaze moved upwards to rest on its beak, a bit faded due to hundreds of hands rubbing it for good luck. Underneath the moniker was the university's official slogan: *tempus edax rerum*.

Time, devourer of all things, you remembered as the translation from the school's website. A bit bleak, but whatever.

You weren't quite sure why a university with such an *interesting* population would have opted for a mascot as mundane as an emu; some of the student forums had explained simply that it was because "emu" was one letter away from "EFU," while others spun some fantastical tales that you didn't even remember.

It may have had something to do with keeping things a bit more fair; perhaps it would have been offensive to the other species if only one was chosen to be glorified, or maybe it could have been offensive to the species itself. You recalled looking at another university in your application process where the mascot was a kraken.

Actually, you *had* met a kraken before, but only once. He was a nice fellow whose peculiar orange eyes were the only things that betrayed his origin: you'd only ever seen him in his human form. You wondered how he might have felt about a caricature of his kind sprinting up and down a field and waving a towel in helicopter motions to pump up a roaring crowd.

Regardless, Kronos the emu was here to stay, and his topaz eyes — the only non-copper part of his effigy — shimmered a bit menacingly as you resumed your little journey. You hoped that flicker meant that you had passed his inspection and the spirits of Kronos past wouldn't try to haunt you and peck out your eyes right before your next big exam, as student superstition might suggest.

Kronos the Emu himself was one of the charming quirks that had initially drawn you in, the mascot becoming much more endearing to you after having discovered that he was named after the father that Zeus and his brothers so kindly overthrew. This may have paid homage to the annual harvest festival the town celebrated in the fall, the scythe clutched in Kronos' copper beak tipping you off to such a suspicion.

You had read that on some occasions, handlers paraded an actual emu around campus to boost morale during finals, which was kept at a local farm. As the current resident emu was male, he was naturally named Kronos, but there had been female emus in the past that were named Rhea after his consort. In your research, you had discovered that this was rather clever: apparently, a *rhea* was also a species of large, flightless birds related to ostriches and emus.

You would have appreciated the complicated homage to Greek mythology behind it all a *bit* more if not for the fact that the subject of mythology itself was currently a festering thorn in your side.

With a dramatic sigh, you placed your hand on the heavy door leading into the library. The dark wood was smooth under your fingertips as it creaked and groaned while you heaved it open, practically having to put your entire shoulder into the effort.

While you were enrolled in the business program, the university required that its students take at least one elective in a topic unrelated to their major each semester. Due to some mix up with your personal email address, you had gotten this memo a little late, so most of the easier electives were taken by the time you signed up. You had no beef with mythology itself — you actually did find the topic *kind* of fascinating— but rather with the fact that the reviews for the course warned of how *difficult* it was.

So much for being able to just focus on your business courses and coasting by on an easy pass/fail elective.

You had been able to snag the last seat in the class; as wary as you were with the difficulty level, something told you that it was the *lesser* of two evils as the remainder of electives were for advanced physics and calculus. Admittedly, you had no interest in digging the graphing calculator you had paid way too much for in high school out of the depths of your childhood bedroom.

You'd also have to face your parents for that and the very notion made your blood curdle more than the image of Kronos pulling an Oedipus and pecking out your eyes.

Telling yourself just to '*think positive!*', you approached the large wooden desk situated in what must have once been the narthex — the library itself had been converted from an old church building — and cleared your throat politely.

"Uh, hi!" you greeted, giving a small wave to the petite girl situated behind the desk. She glanced up at you from the magazine she had been looking at. The bubble she had blown from the pink gum she was chewing burst with a sharp *pop*. "Oh! Wait, do I know you?"

Something about her shimmery translucent wings looked familiar. You tilted your head slightly, trying to remember where you might have seen her.

"Yes!" Her voice was high-pitched and bubbly. She snapped her magazine shut, bounding to her feet and leaning over the desk towards you. "We're neighbors! You live in the building next to mine." She extended a delicate hand, the skin covering her arm an interesting pale shade somewhere between a lilac and a periwinkle, which complimented her darker lavender hair. "I'm Efficlair," she said confidently, "Efficlair Arden. You can call me Claire. Or Effie!" She fluttered her lashes playfully. "I'm your resident manic pixie dream girl."

You laughed at her enthusiasm and the self-appointed moniker, introducing yourself as you shook her hand. You'd met a few fairies at your undergrad; they either tended to be very sweet or very snooty. You were glad that Effie — you decided that Claire wasn't *nearly* as fun of a nickname as her personality deserved — seemed to be of the *sweet* variety, all smiles and sparkle and sunshine.

"I'm your *resident boring human*, I guess," you returned with a grin, removing your hand from hers to heft the strap of the messenger bag a bit higher on your shoulder. "Nice to officially meet you!"

"Oh, *pish*!" She waved off your self-dig, shaking her head as she did so. "Not boring to me! I'm glad to have met you. "*Oh!*" Her rosy eyes brightened. "We should get coffee sometime! I know a cute little cafe right by campus. The owner is a bit of a troll — *literally*. He's a literal troll. *But*, he's sweet and he makes the best scones. Seriously, they're *aaah-may-zing*! The blueberry ones are my favorite. No! The *strawberry* ones. No! The *cranberry* ones..."

You could only stare at Effie as she continued to ramble on about scones, the tips of her wings twitching in excitement as her one-woman show launched into its entr'acte. At least she was self-aware; *manic pixie dream girl* was an apt description for her contagiously chipper character.

"*Definitely* the blueberry," she finally concluded with a determined nod, apparently choosing to forgo a curtain call. Maybe this was just the intermission. "The blueberry scones are my favorite. *Any*ways, we should *definitely* go." She clapped her hands happily, but then suddenly wilted. A sheepish smile crossed her face. "Ah, I've done it again, haven't I?"

"Er—done what?" you asked, feeling about ten steps behind her as you struggled to keep up.

"I've wasted your time!" she fretted, to which you waved your hands at her. She threw the back of her hand against her forehead in lament. "I'm *so* sorry!" With a sigh, her shoulders slumped as she collapsed back in her chair before she abruptly brightened again. "Anywho, I'm sure you didn't come to the library to learn about scones!" She removed her hand from her forehead to clasp it together with the other atop the desk, straightening her back as she gave you her best matter-of-fact look. "What can I help you with?"

"Um." You blinked again, trying to remember what the hell you were here for. Effie was like a whirlwind of emotions and your brain felt a little bit muddled as it was caught in the gale. "Oh, yeah." You reached into your bag to pull out a piece of paper, unfolding it and smoothing the creases on the desk before swiveling it so Effie could read it. "I'm looking for one of *these* books"—you tapped at a title on top of the list—"for an elective I'm taking."

"Oooh!" she squealed, unclasping her hands to clench them into fists. She shook them in front of her face giddily. "Is this with Professor Dulcis? I'm *so* jealous! I tried to get in, but there were no seats left. Now I have to take *anatomy*." She stuck her tongue out in distaste. You recalled that course also being on the list of ones you had firmly wanted to avoid.

You merely nodded, not having the heart to tell her that you had quashed her dreams by taking the last seat. With a dreamy sigh at your fortune, she quickly opened a drawer to take out a simplistic map of the first floor of the library. Also retrieving a pen from the same drawer, she clicked it a few times before circling a section towards the back of the building. Picking up the page, she waved it a few times so the ink would dry before offering it to you.

"They should be in this section!" she stated with cheerful triumph. She pointed over her shoulder. "Just follow this aisle and you'll be right there!"

You thanked her and took off with a wave, shooting her a thumbs up when she chirped at you not to forget your promise to get scones with her as you continued on with your task. With your head down, you studied the lavender circle — that girl *really* knew how to pick a color and run with it — trying to figure out if you were in the right vicinity. The syllabus had given you a few options as to which book you would be required to bring to the first day of lessons, so you hoped at least *one* of them would be in stock. You mentally kicked yourself as you should have asked Effie to look up the titles so she could tell you *exactly* which ones were still available, but you had been too distracted by her musings.

Fuck. Now you really wanted a scone.

"Stupid mythology," you grumbled to yourself miserably. Anything that came between you and a good snack deserved to be on your bad side. You heaved another sigh at your lament, taking a sharp turn around the bookshelves. "*Oof!*"

You staggered back, rubbing the tip of your now-smarting nose where it had collided with the person in front of you. Great, this was twice in one day where you hadn't been paying attention. The monsters were going to hate you!

"I'm really sorry," you apologized, crouching to lift the paper you had dropped. "I should have—"

"Been more aware of your surroundings? Or more considerate, perhaps?"

You gaped at the clipped, snobby tone before a flash of hot annoyance surged through your veins. Sure, maybe you'd been a bit *distracted* lately, but what was it with people and not considering your apologies? Did they think you were running around just looking to throw yourself into people for shits and giggles?

"Listen, buddy," you grumbled, standing up to poke a finger into his chest. "I *said* I was sorry!"

As you tilted your head back to look at your apparently affronted victim, the pieces of your mind you fully intended to give to him shattered in surprise.

He would have been handsome if not for the expression of absolute loathing on his face. His body, rigid with vexation under your accusatory index finger, was lithe and firm. You could see tufts of gray fuzz poking through the top of his crisp white shirt where the first two buttons were undone. The same shade of gray was apparent on his forearms, which were exposed as his sleeves were cuffed smartly to the elbow. The hair atop his head was longer and darker; it was seemingly held back by something, though a few tendrils escaped to fall into his face over the square frames of the glasses resting against surprisingly sculpted cheekbones.

He gave off the air of a person who really just couldn't be bothered. The expression *'no fucks given'* immediately came to mind, but somehow even *that* seemed beneath him. Something about him told you that you should be kneeling on the floor in front of him, apologizing for even breathing the same air as he did.

Looming aura aside, the most striking aspect wasn't the fact that this infuriating man seemed to be covered head-to-toe in gray fuzz, nor was it the presence of the silvery wings that furled imposingly over you, but the realization that behind those frames, two almond-shaped scarlet eyes were narrowed at you.

"Are you quite finished accosting me?" With the tip of a claw, he pushed his glasses down to look over at the rims at you, gaze flat as he frowned pointedly at your finger. He spoke in a lilted tone, an accent you couldn't quite place. Holding back a squeak as you remembered what you were doing, you drew it back to your chest as if he had burned you.

"I didn't *accost* you," you protested with a huff, glaring at him in return. "Now, just take my apology and be done with it."

A single antenna quirked, reminding you of how one might arch a brow as he said, "No."

"Whatever." You rolled your eyes. This man — *moth... mothman?* — was quickly becoming your least favorite of the handful of people you had met, and you'd come across a few gems. Pivoting on your heel, you turned to walk away from the hoity-toity bastard, only to hear his accented voice calling out after you.

"If you are looking for texts on mythology, you are going the wrong way."

You froze with a curse, planting your foot to turn around once again. You marched back towards him. You'd love a scone right about now if only to drag down the front of his stupidly immaculate shirt. Except then you couldn't eat it and that thought made you sad.

But if you had *two* scones...

"How do you know I'm looking for those books?" you demanded, still scone-less and pissed off. He had the gall to smirk at you, what looked like a tapered fang poking out from his pillowy upper lip as he did so.

"I am *literate*," he stated, "and you have a list. I managed to glance at it when you so kindly *attacked* me."

"I didn't *attack* you!" You whisper-screamed, not wanting to get thrown out of the library for shrieking like a banshee at strangers in the aisle.

But officer, you'd tell the security guard if somebody actually put in a complaint about your screeching, *this guy's a real asshole!*

He gave you a dismissive shrug, choosing to ignore your dissent as he asked, "You are taking mythology?"

"I thought you were *literate*," you returned, waving the paper in his face. "Do you think I'm just looking for textbooks on the subject for *shits and giggles*?"

The next look he gave you was dry. "Some people may find it interesting."

"Interesting, *schminteresting*," you scoffed. "It's just an elective. I didn't even want to take it..."

You couldn't stop the absolute word vomit from escaping as you bemoaned your frustrations about a class you hadn't even started yet to a complete stranger. Effie had seemed rather envious of you, and you remembered how your counselor had told you how lucky you were to get into the class when you had registered. You didn't *feel* so lucky, especially when your GPA might be at risk for suffering with how unnecessarily difficult the forums and reviews made the class seem. You pictured some crotchety old man wagging his finger at the front of the room as he droned on and on about some obscure minor god whose name you would never be able to remember.

"...and I bet the professor is a real *jerk*!" you finished with another huff, paper scrunched in your hand as you folded your arms over your chest. One of his antennae twitched again as he regarded you in silence.

"You do not know who your professor is." It was a statement and not a question, but he still sounded a bit incredulous. When you shook your head, his lips twitched. "Perhaps he would have *reason* to be with such a stubborn student. You do not seem to want to give the course a fair chance."

"I came here to study *business*," you said, unable to stop the defensiveness that you knew was creeping through. "It was either *this* or spending my mornings agonizing over string theory or dissecting frogs. Frogs are gross and why spend all that time on a *theory*?"

He looked reproachful and you felt as if you might have been in for a lecture. "Theories are the foundational building blocks of modern science! The claim that the sun is the center of the universe is a *theory*—"

"Whatever!" you quickly interjected, raising your brows at him. Was this guy some kind of mad scientist or something? Either way, you didn't want to get into quantum mechanics. "Mythology isn't as bad as the other options were, but it still isn't what I'm here for!"

His eyes narrowed further. "You make the field sound like a waste of time."

"It *is* a waste of time!" You scowled at him. "For me, at least. Business is *practical*! Some of the myths and legends are cool and all, but what use do they have in the real world?"

The corners of his lips quirked downwards, his already guarded expression becoming even more closed off. It suddenly felt as if you were in a vacuum with the way the air stilled as if affected by his very demeanor. He gave you a chilly look before finally saying, "Everyone is entitled to their opinions, I suppose. I wish you luck in this course; I daresay you may need it." He stepped to walk away from you before he paused, turning slightly to peer at you over his shoulder. "As for use in the real world, you might want to reconsider that point."

"What do you mean?" you asked, still a bit flabbergasted by this whole encounter.

"It seems like some mythological legends are words made flesh. For example," he drawled, the ice in his tone becoming much more biting, "you may very well be a *harpy*."

You gawked at his wings when he finally left you alone, feeling your temper rise. You'd heard of harpies before, and although your knowledge on them was limited, you knew enough to understand that him calling you one wasn't a *compliment*.

You would spend the rest of your day fuming about this, cursing this mysteriously maddening stranger into oblivion as you picked out your book and made your way back to your apartment. You texted Effie about the bizarre encounter after having exchanged numbers on your way out the library, cackling at the array of emojis and memes she sent back to egg you on. And the next morning, when you finally walked into the very classroom that might become your hellscape, you were still pissed.

The lecture hall was large and arranged almost like an amphitheater. Squinting at the figure in front of the blackboard, you walked down the steps, wondering if you should sit in the front or somewhere in the middle. You would have no shot of being able to see anything all the way in the back.

As you got closer, you realized that something about the back facing you seemed familiar as the figure continued to write on the blackboard. You froze mid-stride, blood rushing in your ears at the familiarity of the wings and tilt to the antennae, forcing your classmates to walk around you with sleepy grumbles of complaint.

Professor Gideon M. Dulcis, the board read as the instructor finished his elegant scrawl with a flourish. As he turned around, clapping his hands together to dispel the chalk from his hands with a puff of white dust, those same vexatious eyes narrowed at you once again, glowing ominously like two rubies nestled in a bed of ash.

ii: pandora's box

AS YOU SLUNK deeper and deeper into the too-hard wooden chair you'd finally managed to lower yourself into, you quickly learned three things about the not-so-nutty professor standing in front of the room throughout the course of his lesson:

First of all, his class required mandatory attendance. That meant that you'd get to see his brooding and stern face in the wee hours of the morning three days a week, which you had discovered when he had actually gone through the motions of *taking attendance*.

Attendance, as if his lecture hall was full of elementary schoolers!

Never mind the fact that you felt every bit as small as one when you raised a shaky hand once he had called your name.

Secondly, he had a brusque, no-nonsense attitude. You'd gleaned this from the fact that he hadn't bothered in going over the syllabus at all as *most* instructors did on the first day of class, instead launching right into the lesson. At least he hadn't delved into the dreaded icebreaker — you weren't sure how many more times you could argue that you needed more specifics about the duel at hand in order to choose if you'd rather be a *shark* or a *lion*.

Third most, for such an ass, he had a pretty *nice* one himself. This was an observation that hadn't come as quickly to you as the first two, but an important one nonetheless. Equally — if not *more* — important was the knowledge that you'd need to try your best to quash this train of thought before it left the station, else you might forget that he was about to become the bane of your existence.

Luckily, you were able to text all of this — save the last bit — to Effie on your laptop; if the infuriating mothman had a shit list, you were definitely at the top of it, and you didn't think whipping your phone out in the middle of his drawling would do much to help your cause.

You could practically hear her squealing as the little dots indicating she was typing danced across one side of your screen. The other side was dedicated to your attempt to take notes, but you were too frazzled by the whole situation to pay much attention. Usually a pretty gifted multitasker, you were finding it a *bit* harder than normal, especially when Effie — saved in your phone as *Manic Pixie Dream Girl* — was just encouraging you to be, well, incorrigible.

"At least he's hot*,"* was what her message said when she finally replied. You pictured a dreamy look on her pastel face as you stared at the chat bubble. *"Why do you think that class is so hard to get into?"*

You frowned at her words, wondering how the fuck to respond to that. It felt like the entirety of the EFU student body had been in on this little secret, while *you* were the only one *dumb* enough not to look up the professor's headshot ahead of time before registering for the class. You'd researched literally *everything* else, but not this tidbit.

What that ass do, Prof? you mused to yourself, scoffing at the utter ridiculousness of it all. *Nothing but hold a stick up it, apparently.*

As you glanced around the room, you could see that your fellow students, male and female alike, seemed to have hearts in their eyes as they watched the lithe form of Professor Dulcis move back and forth across the board, an open book nestled between his palm and elbow on one arm. The other was extended with a piece of chalk in hand as he rapped it against the matte black surface he had been writing on for emphasis on whatever he was saying.

You really *should* have been paying more attention, but between your ire and the way the muscles in his forearms rippled at the movement that you could clearly see as he was wearing his sleeves cuffed at the elbows again, you really weren't retaining much.

Having gone back to glaring at Effie's texts, you nearly jumped out of your seat when you heard your name — your *last* name — being called, head snapping up so quickly that you swore you heard the crack all the way down your spine. Those two piercing red eyes were focused intently on you, and when you looked around the room again, so were hundreds of *other* pairs. A few looked a bit hostile, especially the sanguine ones on what you suspected was another vampire chick.

Were you *really* about to go fists-to-fangs with somebody over this guy? Your fingertips flew up to your neck again.

"I'm sorry?" Your words were more of a squeak as you felt yourself hunching in your chair just a little bit more.

Wait, what were you *doing*?

You were much more resilient than this; it would take much more than a few dozen — or *hundred* — piercing stares to shake you! Where was the person who kicked and clawed their way out of their hometown to pay their way through undergrad, where they were amongst the top in the class? Why were you so flustered by this stupid moth?

More determined now, you straightened in your chair, lifting your chin slightly as you cleared your throat to ask, "Could you repeat the question?" You paused, then decided to add a bit abruptly, "Please."

Even from a few rows back, you could hear Professor Dulcis sigh in response, placing his book on the lectern near his desk. With his now-free hand, he nudged his glasses upwards to pinch the bridge of his nose between his thumb and index finger in clear irritation, and you fought the urge to grit your teeth in response.

Hey, you're at least being paid to be here, buddy! you were tempted to shout in retaliation. You briefly considered chucking your laptop at him, but it had cost you a pretty penny and you were rather fond of it.

That exasperating man made something as mundane as adjusting his glasses look elegant when he pushed them back into place with a clawed pinky before rapping his piece of chalk against the board again. In the motion, you noticed how his fingernails looked perfectly manicured, filed and shaped to precise points. Everything about him was absurdly poised and aristocratic; almost slightly feminine, even, though he exuded such an aura of haughty confidence that it only made him seem that much more intimidatingly powerful.

You suddenly realized he seemed to have five fingers on his hands like you did, but you tried not to fixate on this confrontation of similarities as you squinted at the single word he was pointing to. *Metamorphoses*.

"I do not like to repeat myself," he warned, tone firm. You caught yourself just before you were about to roll your eyes; that probably wouldn't have gone over well. "But I will, this *once*, for the sake of continuing the lesson." He paused and you wondered if he was waiting for you to say something about how grateful you were. You didn't. "Who penned this?"

You sat back in your chair, folding your arms across your chest. *Phew* — you had been prepared for a more difficult question, but like the good little student you were, you'd done the required reading the night before. Your response was easy. "Ovid."

One of his antennae twitched as he regarded you silently for a beat, the inner you mentally flipping him the bird in smug satisfaction. You could practically feel the air crackling with energy and you briefly wondered if it was the doing of some kind of witch or warlock in the room; they were a bit harder to spot than the vampire who was still glaring daggers at you. Eventually, he nodded, turning to pick the book back up again.

One point for you, zero for Professor Prick.

He continued on just as he had said he intended to, peppering students at random with a few more questions. When your biggest fan, the vampiric diva who seemed intent to make it her personal mission to kiss this man's ass with a vigor that you had never seen before, was finally called on, you didn't miss the haughty little look she threw your way.

"Greece," she stated confidently in response to him asking where Ovid was born, simpering all the while. You couldn't contain your snort at her pompous attitude, especially when you knew she was wrong. Immediately, you felt her red eyes on you again. "Do *you* have something to say?"

"Uh, no," you responded, not quite sure how you kept getting yourself into these situations. If your mouth wasn't betraying you, it was your overly-expressive face. You would never be able to play poker professionally. She turned her pert nose up at you.

"Yes, *please*," you heard Professor Dulcis call from the front of the room. That prick. You turned your head to see him gesture to you almost sardonically. "Enlighten us."

At this, you did roll your eyes as you answered, "Ovid was *Roman*." You shrugged. "Last time I checked, not many Romans were born in Greece."

You probably didn't need to add that last bit, but with the way the vampire hissed at you, your derision was well worth it.

Two points for you, zero for both Professor Prick and Vampire Bitch. They could share their loss, for all you cared.

"Correct," he acquiesced, and didn't he sound just a touch impressed? "Although we could have done without the sarcasm."

You bit your tongue, giving a semi-apologetic shrug in response as he moved on to his next point. Placing an elbow on the desk in front of you and resting your chin on your fist, you decided to keep to yourself for the rest of the lesson, ignoring your not-so-secret anti-admirer still trying to will you into bursting into flames with the intensity of her gaze alone.

When class finally ended, you gathered your things and shoved them into your book bag, wanting to just get the hell out to meet

Effie for coffee like you had promised so you could continue your little bitchfest. You noted a few people staying behind, most likely wanting to introduce themselves *personally* to him — vampire included — before you whisked up the steps and out the door.

Except when you were about to leave the building, you paused.

Having learned from your past mistakes, you stepped out of the way of traffic and tucked yourself into a corner of the building's lobby, groaning to yourself. As much as you *wanted* to mock those students for sucking up, you recognized that you had somehow gotten to a really rough start with a professor whose class was already apparently hard enough before the lessons even began. It would probably be in your best interests to see if you could smooth things over to save yourself an even steeper uphill climb for the rest of the semester with this stupid elective.

Mind made up, you swiftly texted Effie to apologize in advance that you might be a little late, pivoting on your heel to march back to the lecture hall. You ducked around a corner when the vampire bitch and her crew exited the room — you weren't sure if you were equipped to take her and her entire coven on yet — waiting a few moments longer until you were sure the rest of his blatant admirers had cleared out as well.

Poking your head through the doorway to confirm that he was the only one left, you quickly made your way down the stairs two at a time, mentally hyping yourself up so you could just get this over with. His back was turned towards you as he worked on erasing the board.

You tried not to look at the way his gray slacks — a few shades darker than the fuzz that covered his forearms — strained over his butt. Moving your gaze upwards to avoid the temptation of staring, you were met with the sight of his wings, shimmering an interesting shade of lavender in the light that filtered in through the windows. They reminded you of monochromatic stained glass and you wondered if they felt as delicate as they looked; like silk stretched between delicate webs of soldered iron. Between those wings, you could see a hint of gray underneath his crisp, not *quite* opaque white button down shirt, which stretched across his toned shoulders.

You idly pondered if such shirts with slits for his wings were readily available on the market, or if he had to have them custom-tailored to suit his needs.

"You should refrain from antagonizing your fellow students."

You nearly jumped at the sound of his lilting voice, finally realizing the words were directed towards you after a few seconds, even though his back was still turned.

"Uh, what?" you returned oh-so-eloquently, a bit thrown off by his sudden statement. "How did you know it was me?"

The dumbfounded question was out of your mouth before your brain had time to play goalie, bouncing around in the large lecture hall and sounding extremely stupid to your ears. You could have cursed at how astonished you sounded.

"Violetta did not seem pleased at your attitude." He turned around, folding his arms across his chest as his ruby eyes met yours. "She was *very* insistent on letting me know that."

"Oh, was *that* her name?" you threw back flippantly, a little peeved that he was ignoring your question, as idiotic as it had sounded. You didn't know exactly who this *Violetta* was, but you could figure out he was referring to the vampire bitch using your context clues. "Well, if I don't show up to class one day and you hear that I was found in some alley with my throat ripped out, you might want to call her in as a prime suspect to the police."

He stared at you, not looking at all amused. The vision of you bleeding out against cracked asphalt may have been a *bit* macabre, you had to admit, but you had delivered it with a playful shrug.

Did this man have an ounce of humor in those wings of his?

Deciding that no, in fact, he did not, you held your hands up with your palms facing him in what you hoped he would interpret as a placating gesture. "Ok, noted, don't piss off my colleagues, got it." You arched a brow at him. "But, really, can you *blame* me?" Shaking your head suddenly, you quickly said, "Actually, don't answer that."

When he continued to stare at you, you gave him a sheepish smile, lowering your hands to instead adjust your bag on your shoulder. You curled them around the strap as you tried to lighten the mood, saying with a small laugh, "I can't believe I didn't catch your name yesterday!"

"I can." An antenna quirked. "I never dropped it."

What. The. *Fuck.*

Ok, you could work with this, you told yourself as you tried your best not to gawk at him. Resilience was key!

"Um, right." Your responding chuckle was humorless as you glanced down and shifted your weight uncomfortably from foot-to-foot, feeling your knuckles straining as you clenched the strap of your bag even tighter. Looking back up at him, you tried to stay chipper as you said, "I think we started off on the wrong foot." You held out a hand. "Professor Dulcis — er, Gideon — can I call you Gideon?"

"Absolutely not."

"*Fantastic!*" you chirped, noting how his eyes were narrowed at you again. He completely disregarded your offered palm, which you slowly retracted as your smile died. "Professor Dulcis it is, then!"

Dulcis. *Pleasant, sweet,* you recalled from the Latin meaning. How fucking ironic.

You opened your mouth to continue, but he held a hand out to stop you. Your teeth clacked together when you promptly closed it.

"I understand what you are trying to do," he began, tone a bit frigid, "and I *appreciate* it"—it sounded as though it physically pained him to say the word—"but such pageantry is lost on me. If you would like to make a good impression, simply apologize and stop disrupting my class."

"*Apologize?*" you repeated, your lip curling slightly at the prospect. "For *what?*"

He looked incredulous again, the expression similar to the one he wore in the library when you hadn't realized he was your professor. "For insulting my field of study, of course."

"Ok, I didn't *exactly* insult your class," you argued. You hadn't realized you had been wagging a finger at him until you followed his disapproving eyes to the tip of it, immediately clenching your hand into a fist and tucking it at your side. "It was just my *opinion*!"

He merely hummed at you, to which you wanted to throw your hands up in frustration. You imagined instead wrapping them around his fuzz-covered neck, watching in satisfaction as his hurried breath rushed between his lips in pants. Would his cheeks turn red, like a human's would, or the same delicious shade of lavender as the shift in his wings? Maybe he would like that, actually.

Fuck, where had *that* thought come from? You fought the blush at how your mind had strayed to that visual.

Wait, would *you* like that?

"What are you here for, then?" His voice jolted you out of your musings, and you were suddenly grateful for how it had yanked you back from the edge of oblivion. You squared your shoulders, blinking to dispel the sinful fog as you re-focused on him.

"I wasn't here to *make a good impression*," you snapped, tone a bit on the petty side, "I just wanted to make sure there wasn't any *animosity* between us."

He waved a dismissive hand at this, moving to pick up a few books that were resting on his desk. You watched as he stacked them neatly upon each other, largest book on the bottom and smallest on top. They seemed well-worn and ancient, as if Ovid himself could have written them.

When he was done with his little chore, he straightened to look at you once more, a few smoky tendrils falling over his forehead. "You are wasting your time, then," he returned finally. "Yours *and* mine." You felt the urge to tie his antennae together and pull in your annoyance at the way he was looking at you so coolly. "To state that there would be any animosity on my behalf is to suggest that I care at all, which I do not. If you are concerned about your grades, simply show up to my lessons on time and *do* try to keep up."

"I was doing a pretty good job of *keeping up* earlier," you protested, feeling your anger rise again at how he was just brushing you off.

"Those questions were elementary at best, it was not such a feat to respond correctly," he retorted curtly. Then, he feigned surprise, "Oh, were you looking for *praise*?" You felt yourself bristle at this. So what if you *were*? That dick. "You may have been right, then... your professor *must* be a *jerk*."

You glowered at him as he calmly stepped around you to exit the room. You wished you had the ability to cast curses or hexes or something. Maybe Effie had a friend that could jinx him on your behalf?

Was that legal?

Did you care if it *wasn't*, at this point?

When he was at the door, he paused. Too bad you had been rendered speechless by this encounter, otherwise this would have been the perfect opportunity to let him have it. But he turned his head slightly so you could see his profile and a single red eye over his shoulder as he finally called, "Your scent." You swore you saw one corner of his lips twitch slightly. "I knew it was you from your scent."

You stilled, flabbergasted again as you struggled to collect your thoughts. So he hadn't completely ignored your question, after all. You cleared your throat. "And what do I smell like?"

He stepped forward to open the door, turning to face you more completely. This time, you were able to clearly see an actual smirk on his face, a single fang glinting as he responded simply, "A harpy."

And with that, he closed the door behind him, leaving you standing at the bottom of the lecture hall with your jaw practically on the floor.

You felt your blood boiling as you managed to shut your mouth after a few beats, hands once again gripping the strap of your bag where they threatened to tear it in two.

Man, fuck that guy!

Not literally, though.

Well, *maybe* literally?

No!

You had to get a grip. He may have been *somewhat* attractive, but you had to remind yourself how downright, completely, absolutely, utterly *mean* and *unfair* he was being to you! He could go straight to the Ninth Circle of Hell. Or was it the Fifth, maybe? Which circle did pompous assholes with nothing better to do than pore over ancient textbooks and make your life a living nightmare go to, exactly?

Perhaps it *was* worth brushing up on the textbooks.

Ok, so one point for Professor Prick. You still had two, so you were technically winning, but you knew it would take much more to hold onto your lead. You seemed to actually be evenly matched.

You unclenched your fists from around your shoulder strap, instead gripping them in front of your chest in resolve. If he challenged you to keep up, you would show him keeping up; in fact, you would ace his whole damn course and make him see exactly who he was messing with!

This business major was about to become a bonafide expert in mythology. If he wasn't careful, maybe you would come for his job. Would serve him right, the oversized insect!

You made a mental note to start updating your résumé. You'd bet your left tit that you'd even give a better handshake than he could. Well, maybe your right one, just to be on the safe side; you'd always been much fonder of your left.

You'd show him how much of a *harpy* you could be; you were only getting started. Nodding to yourself in determination, you began your ascent up the stairs as your descent into what may have been madness commenced.

Sure, you would show him, but you just hoped you weren't about to open Pandora's box.

iii: sour grapes

LIFE HAD SEEMED SO simple two months ago, when you had just arrived at EFU as a fresh-faced graduate student, excited for all that lay ahead. Full-ride scholarship secured, all you would have to do was continue to ace your business classes from there on out, which was exactly what the trajectory had been looking like. The only way had been up, up, up — up you continued to climb.

Except now, staring at the two simple words glaring right back at you, stark against the crisp white papers that were slowly crumpling in your fists, you felt yourself falling down, down, down.

See me.

You were spiraling, the crimson ink reminding you of a certain pair of infuriating eyes.

Your business classes, luckily, had been going well so far; you'd had a few exams and the results for all of them were exactly what you had expected. What you *hadn't* counted on was this stupid mythology class taught by Professor Prick, King of All Assholes himself, whose preferred form of academic torture were essays as he, quote, '*liked to read premeditated matters of substance,*' end quote. From the reviews you had read, you knew it would be difficult... you just never imagined that you would be quite literally staring in the face of failure.

It was as if he were some harbinger of doom.

What would happen to you if you actually tanked this class? Sure, it was only one out of the five you were taking for the semester, but it could still result in your GPA taking a pretty decent hit. The terms of your scholarship were pretty rigid; you needed to keep an average of at least an A-, which seemed nearly impossible with the start you were off to.

At this point, you literally could *not* afford any failure.

The sound of your voice being called repeatedly made your head snap up, just as you heard Effie squeal, "*Breathe*, lady! You're turning more blue than I am!"

You took a deep, shuddering breath, looking right into Effie's eyes, pink and wide with concern. They grounded you, helping you to remember where you were. Then, you let out a groan.

"I'm doomed!" you exclaimed, your torso folding over your crossed legs as you hunched forward. You felt your essay being snatched out of your grip as a large, warm palm rested against your spine.

"You're not doomed yet!" another voice chittered cheerfully. "It doesn't exactly *say* that you failed anywhere. At least, not literally."

You nearly rolled your eyes at the optimism. Those damned fairies were basically cotton candy personified, and as much as you normally appreciated the pick-me-up, all you wanted to do right now was wallow in your own self-pity.

Which your merry little crew was simply refusing to allow.

When you lifted your head again, you could see that Calli — short for "Callista," because fairies also apparently loved their nicknames — was squinting at the paper, the tip of her turquoise tongue peeking between her lips as she scanned the front page.

You had met her through Effie, who had apparently clicked with her the first week of classes as they discovered they had both been members of the same sorority in their undergrad — *Phi Alpha Epsilon*

— albeit, at different schools. Where Effie was all pinks and bluish purples, Calli seemed to be right next door on the color wheel, her skin a shocking shade of nearly lime green. She claimed that when she was more "tan," she could supposedly blend right into the grass you all were currently resting on as you lounged in the quad.

"What is this, Schrödinger's '*F*?" you bemoaned, extending your hand and flexing your fingers at her in a grabby motion so she could return it to you. "I've simultaneously passed and failed until I walk into his office?" When you snatched the paper back, you frowned at the words again. "I might as well just be dead."

"Morbid, but whatever floats your boat," Calli sniffed, causing Effie to giggle like a chorus of tinkling bells. The hand on your spine lifted to awkwardly pat at your shoulder.

"S'not so bad," its owner rumbled from behind you, giving you another placating pat before the hand left you completely. "If you *did* fail, which I'm not saying you did"—you rounded to see that Greer, the minotaur you'd befriended in one of your business classes, now had two of his hands held up with his palms facing you defensively —"then it's just *one* essay, right?"

"I guess," you huffed, still wilting slightly. If you had wings like your fairy friends, they'd be completely drooping against the grass.

You felt a bit bad for being a party pooper on such a nice day; here you were, sitting with the two fairies, Sun and Sunnier, along with a minotaur who gave you the most *dad* energy you had ever experienced in a person who didn't actually have kids, and you were pouting the whole time.

How very human of me! you mocked at yourself.

In truth, the dread of failure was less potent than the trepidation of having to see the grouchy mothman alone again. In the past few weeks since your disastrous meeting in the library and first day of class, you'd done your best to fly under the radar and only speak when spoken to, half for your own sanity, and half for self-preservation. You still didn't like those looks of absolute murder the vampire bitch gave you.

Apparently, one of the things that vampires tended to perfect throughout the course of their very long lives was the art of holding a grudge.

Maybe you should start wearing scarves to class.

You weren't quite sure where it had all gone wrong; after vowing to ace this stupid elective you'd never wanted to take in the first place, you had studied your ass off and put way more effort than was probably necessary into the essay, yet you'd still apparently fallen short. Perhaps you should have groveled or something.

Although the more you thought about it, the less your scholarship seemed worth your pride.

"I guess I should go, then," you sighed, standing up and brushing the errant strands of grass off your jeans. Picking up your bag, you shoved your essay back into it with a scowl. You hoped he wouldn't take off additional style points for rumpled paper.

"Good luck!" Effie exclaimed, to which Calli and Greer echoed. "I don't know why you're so down in the dumps! I'd give my left wing to spend some time alone with that hottie."

"He isn't *hot*, he's *evil*," you retorted sourly, wrinkling your nose at her.

"The two things aren't mutually exclusive," Calli pointed out with a grin. "In fact, the whole evil *come-to-my-lair* aspect is kinda sexy, don't ya think?"

Effie nodded enthusiastically in agreement, but all a blushing Greer muttered out was, "No comment."

You would be so lucky to find a man half as loyal to you as Greer was to Silas, his half-orc boyfriend who visited on the weekends. You'd only met him a couple of times, but he made some damn good chili and the two of you had briefly bonded over your human heritage as his mother was human. You only wished that your family was as accepting of these kinds of interspecies relationships as Silas' and Greer's were.

In fact, you wished your parents were as accepting of literally anything.

This was pretty much the root of where all your stress was coming from now. Your parents had offered to help you pay for your undergraduate education with the stipulation that you went to a traditionally human university, which was exactly the opposite of what you had wanted. So, when you had chosen to go to the co-ed uni that you had ultimately obtained your Bachelor's from, that left you fronting the entire bill. The only way you were able to afford going to EFU was with this full scholarship, which was now ironically at risk because of a mothman.

In short, you had fought tooth and nail for the opportunity to experience a more diversified world with monsters, and boy, were you experiencing it. Talk about a full circle ending.

You gave your motley crew a half-hearted wave as you took off, practically dragging your feet as you trudged to Professor Prick's office — or his *lair*, as Calli had more aptly deemed it. It was luckily by the library, which was in the middle of the campus, so the walk wasn't too far but each step felt like you were on your way to the gallows.

This painted a vivid picture in your mind; you imagined the mothman dressed as an executioner, his usual white button-downs and gray sweaters replaced with a black rubbery poncho. Over his head would be a pointed hood, black to match the poncho, with two slits at the top for his antennae. Two more cut outs would be made at the front of the hood so his eyes could peek through, shining as scarlet as the blood that would drip freely from where your head had once been attached from your neck.

By the time you found yourself in front of his office door, knuckles poised to knock against the wood, you had worked yourself into quite the tizzy. With your breath once again coming out in panicked rasps, you debated just cutting your losses and running.

You didn't really *need* a Master's degree anyway, right?

Except it was that very moment where the universe decided to intervene on your behalf, and you could only blink dumbly as the door was yanked open, your fist now hovering in mid-air. As you lowered it, you slowly looked up from a knit sweater into the same carmine eyes you now spent most of your time cursing, which were narrowed down at you in turn.

"Were you planning on ever announcing yourself," he began in a drawl, "or are you content with simply haunting my hallway?"

Speak of the devil. *Harbinger of doom* was starting to feel more like it.

Your mouth snapped shut with a *click* — you refused to acknowledge the embarrassment at the realization it had dropped open — as you felt the heat of your anger begin to return. Like some kind of locomotive, the gears and pulleys in your psyche began to launch into action, picking up speed the more annoyed you got. You seemed to run on pure rage these days, your ire providing the fuel that stoked the engine of your very being, and while it may have not been such a sustainable fuel, it was better than feeling completely down on yourself the entire time.

"I'm not haunting your anything," you grumbled back in reply, fishing your now-wrinkled essay out of your bag to shove at him. You felt as though he were some kind of wicked conductor and this was your one-way ticket aboard the express train to Hell.

Choo choo, motherfucker. You wished they gave refunds.

"Ah, so you do sometimes follow instructions," he responded, gingerly pinching the crinkled pages between his fingertips as if anything less-than-immaculate might sully him. You swore a vein in your forehead twitched. He stepped aside, sweeping his arm theatrically from the doorway to the rest of his office. "Come in, then."

Giving him a mumbled "thanks," you brushed by him to walk farther into the room. If it hadn't been for the knowledge that it was occupied by the devil himself, you might have thought it was rather quaint with its walls lined with shelves upon shelves of ancient-looking leather books, vaulted ceiling, and dark wood furniture. There was even a nice circular window letting in an ample amount of sunlight, painting the space in translucent gold.

It actually seemed quite the opposite of what evil incarnate would choose to banish himself to, the professor's dark, cool-toned palette a stark contrast to the warm hues of his lair. You would have expected him to clash with it all, but when gently closed the door and then strode around you to lean against his mahogany desk, arms folded over his chest as he crossed one ankle over the other, he seemed more at home amidst the warmth than you may have ever been in one singular place.

"So..." you started, suddenly feeling awkward, like some kind of intruder into a world you had never actually been welcomed to, "I'm here about my essay."

His response was completely deadpan as he tossed the stack of creased papers that had once been your essay atop his desk. "Yes, I had managed to deduce that, actually."

You scrunched your nose at him, unable to stop the tart expression. He merely cocked an antenna at you, tilting his head to the side in question. Brows furrowing, you continued to stare at him for a few moments, before folding your own arms over your chest. You decided to be a bit more direct in your next approach.

"Did you fail me?" you blurted, the toe of your foot tapping at his floor.

He hummed at this, lips quirking in what looked like amusement. You clenched and unclenched your jaw, not thrilled at how he seemed to be enjoying your plight. What an asshole!

"If you did indeed fail, it has nothing to do with me."

You glared, moving your arms so that you could place your hands on your hips as you demanded, "What do you mean '*if*'? Did I fail, or didn't I?"

You felt the tell-tale twinge of a headache coming on, a subtle pressure beginning to build behind your eyes. At this point, you wanted to just learn what your grade was and move the hell on with your life so you could figure out what damage control you might need to do. Your shoulders tensed again, the earlier stress creeping back in as your initial anger slowly ebbed away into tiredness.

"Not exactly." His cryptic response made the fists you dug into your hipbones clench even tighter. Then, as if gauging your reaction, he quickly explained, "What I mean to say is that you may have earned the highest score in the class."

You felt your eyebrows shoot straight into your hairline.

"I don't think I'm following," you admitted, bringing a hand up to rub at your eye. Damn, you hoped that you still had some of that pain medication left. You should have restocked after your most recent studying bender; you had never been good at doing things in moderation as far as your grades were concerned. Realizing what you were doing, you dropped it again. "So I either failed or... have the best grade?"

"If you can convince me that your work has not been plagiarized, then the latter." He uncrossed his ankles to stand straighter and unfolded his arms to rest the heels of his palm against the surface of his desk. "If you cannot, then the former."

"Wait." You shook your head, a bit dumbfounded. "You think I *plagiarized* my essay?" You gaped at this; you'd never been accused of such a thing in your entire life! "So I'm being penalized because it was *too* good?"

"I am just doing my due diligence as an instructor," he said firmly. When you swore aloud, unable to stop the curse from leaving your lips, both his antennae twitched. "Language!"

"This is absurd!" you protested, not sure if you were still astonished or just enraged. Maybe a healthy bit of both. "And that's not just sour grapes! You know how much time I spent on this when I could have been sleeping? You can't possibly expect me to write another one!"

You were well-aware that your rudeness was bordering on the edge of inappropriate, but you were too peeved to care at this point. You watched as he held a single gunmetal hand up to staunch your additional objections.

"I never said I am tasking you with writing another one," he said firmly. "I have something else in mind." He frowned. "See it from my perspective: you delivered an entire *soliloquy* as to how 'frivolous' mythology is, yet you hand in an essay not only recounting Orpheus and Eurydice from *The Metamorphoses*, but comparing its variations across Virgil's and Plato's?"

"I told you that it was my opinion that it wasn't useful! That didn't mean I wasn't going to take this class seriously." You glanced around the room, trying to focus anywhere but on how intently he was looking at you. Following a beam of light, you noticed how it filtered through his delicate wings, refracting into streams of magenta and olive like some kind of prism. You remembered seeing only a lavender tint in the classroom, but they seemed to be so much more lively here. You shifted your gaze to a pile of books neatly stacked on the corner of his desk. "So what do you want me to do, then?"

In the silence, you heard the whisper of his clothing against the gray fuzz that covered his body as he shifted. "I have quite a demanding schedule when it comes to my lectures and grading papers. The Dean has advised that I procure some additional aid. I am proposing that is where you may be able to prove your knowledge."

"What?" You nearly gave yourself whiplash with how quickly your neck swiveled so you could look at him again. "I'm not even majoring in anything close to this! You want me to be your TA?"

He looked a bit disgruntled at your baffled tone. "You would not be teaching or grading," he replied, though you continued to look skeptical. "You would merely be helping collect relevant materials for my lesson plans. I never said you would be my 'TA,' just my assistant."

"Yeah, the word *'assistant'* is literally part of that abbreviation, dude," you retorted flippantly, ignoring the way an antenna twitched at how you had so casually addressed him. "Is this even allowed?"

"I already cleared it with the Dean." He shrugged. "She thought it might be an intriguing way to promote a more well-rounded curriculum."

"So let me get this straight," you tried again, feeling your head pulse, "you want me to be your *assistant*"—you made air quotes around the word—"to show that I didn't plagiarize my essay? I still don't see how that really proves anything."

"Fair point," he conceded, much to your surprise. "Think of it as extra credit, then. I will just pretend your first essay does not exist, and your assistance will make up for it. It will only be about an hour or so of your time a week."

"Well, fuck," you stated, trying to count how many hours that meant you would need to spend with him. EFU did much longer trimesters rather than traditional semesters like your undergrad had been, so it was only just nearing the last legs of the summer. It felt like you still had *forever* to go until final exams in the winter.

"*Language!*" he admonished again.

"That still doesn't seem like much of a fair trade," you argued, ignoring the stern look he was giving you. What was he, your *dad*?

"I am not sure you are really in the position to debate," he countered easily. You quirked a brow at him, any further arguments fizzling out on the tip of your tongue.

"Touché," you muttered, rubbing at your temples again. Forget headache medication, all you needed was a tall glass of approximately eight shots of vodka. "Ok."

"Ok?" he repeated dubiously, the abbreviation sounding oddly foreign as it left his lips. "Transparently, I expected more of a fight."

"Yeah, well," you gave him a dismissive wave, "I'm learning how to pick and choose my battles, I guess."

"Hmm." Head still slightly tilted, he looked a bit hesitant, but then gave a curt nod of assent. "Very good."

You tried not to think too much about how this slightest amount of approval sent a thrilling chill down your spine; it must have just been the headache and your tiredness.

While this definitely wasn't the development you had been thinking of, all things considered, you supposed everything could have gone much worse. This '*extra credit*,' as he had called it, sounded simple enough, and even if you had to spend a prolonged period of time with him, at least your grades would remain intact.

That was one less thing you'd need to worry about.

Straightening your back, you tried to dispel your fatigue so you could at least leave this conversation on your own terms. You extended your arm to offer him a hand to shake, reminded of the last time you had tried to do so on the first day of class. He had ignored the proverbial olive branch then, and you wondered if he would do so once more.

Had you made the same mistake twice?

You flinched when his eyes rested on your hand, the sear of his gaze nearly palpable where it scorched your flesh. Having half a mind to retract it, you could have fallen over in shock when his fingers suddenly curled around yours, long and tapered, like a master pianist. Despite his cool exterior, they were oddly warm, just like the environment he had somehow managed to create in his office.

"You won't be disappointed, Professor Pri—er, Professor *Dulcis*," you declared as you shook his hand firmly, managing to catch your slip-up before it was out in the open. If he took such offense to your *language* before, you didn't even want to think about the hellfire he would rain down if you ever made the mistake of revealing the fond little nickname you had thought up especially for him.

"That remains to be seen," he returned, and though you bristled at his vote of no confidence, you didn't detect any hostility in his tone. His grip was firm, the thin layer of fuzz on his skin reminding you more of silk than velvet. He dropped your hand first, pulling his hand back to tuck into the front pocket of his tailored slacks.

He paused, studying you for a few moments, before drifting by you once more to pull the door back open. As he gestured at the doorway, you took it as your clue to leave.

"You, uh"—you tipped your head to nod at where your essay was lying in state atop the glossy surface of his desk—"you can keep that."

His response was a soft rumbling sound, coming from somewhere within his chest. Something about it was rather soothing, reminding you of a hot mug of cocoa cupped against windburned hands. After a beat, you realized he was *chuckling* at you.

After another, you realized you didn't hate the sound.

"Thank you," he said a bit sardonically, dipping his head in feigned gratitude. His antennae bobbed at the movement. "Now, go back and get some rest. You are useless to me if you fall asleep on the job."

"It's only the afternoon!" you responded in a half-whine, turning back to face him once you stepped through the doorway. The corridor was much dimmer; had it always been this cold? "I still have so much to do and—"

He leaned against the doorknob, a small smirk on his lips as he cut you off to interject, "Maybe you would be less of a *harpy* if you were more well-rested."

"I—*hey*!" You wished you could stick your tongue out at him, but you figured that might set back what little progress you had managed to make thus far. "Isn't that a bit inappropriate?"

"Inappropriate?" he parroted, his voice dropping an octave lower. "I do not think you want to go there."

You nearly squeaked at the way his expression darkened slightly, taking a giant step back to distance yourself from him. There was that weird thrill again; perhaps you needed a nice tall glass of closer to ten shots of vodka rather than eight. Maybe you could take Greer up on his offer to treat you for having helped him study for the last strategy exam.

Professor Prick took one last long look at you before the hallway suddenly became much more gloomy after he promptly shut the door in your face. Sure, he may have been pretty hot — although you would probably never admit that to Effie — but he was still a Grade A, bonafide asshole.

You gave your eyes another second or two to adjust before you resumed your journey out of the building, not wanting to take a tumble down any flights of stairs. He probably would never let you live it down if he were the one to stumble upon your crumpled form, after all.

As you leisurely made your way down the hall, you stilled for a moment, realizing he had never given you any specifics as to what times to meet and when. You debated going back to ask him, but ultimately decided that you had endured enough for the day and you could always just email him.

You left the building in somewhat of a daze, still not quite believing your current predicament — if you could even *call* it that. On one hand, you hadn't failed, but on the other, you were encroaching into unfamiliar territory. You had always enjoyed a good challenge, but this one seemed a bit daunting. It was innocent enough on the surface, but there was still something about him that put you on edge.

In general, it was all disconcerting; like how strangely disappointed you had felt when that door had closed on you, as if he had enticed you by welcoming you into his forbidden world, only to cast you out the moment you had acquired a taste for it. There had been a sense of security that cocooned you in his office, and while you had started off on high alert, he had managed to make you much more pliable than you had thought you would be.

Sure, you chalked it up to exhaustion, but was that *really* the case?

Maybe he wasn't a full mothman at all; maybe he was part spider, and though you may have escaped from his web, you couldn't quite ignore the strand of silk that was wrapped around your wrist, tethering you back to him.

As you made your way across campus, shooting a quick text into the group chat you had with your three friends to ask where they were and if they were free, you saw that while it was still technically the afternoon, it was much later than you had thought it was. How much time had you spent in his presence?

You clenched and unclenched your hand where his fingers had

wrapped around yours, the ghost of them still whispering against your flesh. It was as though you were living your own personal Odyssey, his office having been like the isle of the lotus eaters that you had been dangerously close to succumbing to.

"I'm being stupid," you muttered to yourself.

You suddenly heard your name, lifting your head to see your friends waving at you from where you had originally left them. It was like nothing had changed, yet you knew you were on the brink of some kind of seismic shift.

They stood up to pepper you with questions about your meeting as you traversed the rest of the campus together. You did your best to explain while glossing over some of the parts that still had you reeling, not having the mental capacity to unpack all of it with an audience just yet.

The setting sun blazed hot and bloody against the horizon, fat and round like an all-seeing eye as you continued your trek. You didn't have the heart to reveal that deep down, you couldn't shake the feeling that you had just made a deal with the devil.

iv: the labyrinth

INFURIATING. Exasperating. Aggravating. Maddening.

You could rattle off a list of synonyms from 'A' to 'Z' for the concept of being *'downright annoying as hell'* for Professor Prick, King of Assholes, Patron Saint of Douchebaggery, and yet, none of them would be able to convey quite how absolutely irritating the man was to you.

Over the weeks you had spent in a little too close proximity due to your new arrangement, your annoyance had only grown. It wasn't necessarily his actions towards you — he was a perfect gentleman, after all — but rather, the irksome little quirks you had been able to pick up on.

For one thing, never had you met any singular being who dressed in such a bland color palette; the man must have sold whatever soul he may have once possessed for the uncanny ability to keep you eternally on edge in exchange for being cursed to a lifetime of solely wearing whites and grays and darker grays. It was as if he were so attached to the black and white media of yesteryear that he rebelled against all other more vibrant hues by shrouding himself in desaturated tones like some kind of specter of the silver screen, a crisp white button down always rolled up to his elbows serving as his uniform in pigment purgatory as he worked.

Apart from the lavenders and magentas and olives that you would refuse to admit that you stared at a bit longer than was entirely necessary whenever his wings would catch the light just-so in his office, the only noticeable color on his person was the vivid red of his eyes. They were always narrowed at you in some sort of scrutiny both in your time together and in the classroom.

Another thing you had noticed was his stupid drink of preference: tea. *Disgusting.* Though absurdly clean in all other aspects, at any given time he would have four or five cups in varying states of fullness scattered around his office, the scent of Earl Grey — his brew of choice — lingering in the air. It even seemed to seep into the pages of the books stacked neatly throughout the room, and if you made the mistake of drawing close enough, you were able to catch how it lingered on him as well. That, combined with the faint scent of leather and some subtle lemony floral note you couldn't quite place, made your head spin.

Not in a good way, you firmly insisted to yourself.

These observations aside, what absolutely took the proverbial cake for you was his attitude. The pretentious jerk would like tea, with how uptight and snobbish he liked to act towards you. He had recruited you as his assistant in order to help with his workload, yet he still insisted on micromanaging you to the point that you suspected you were actually just adding to the strain on his bandwidth. You often debated about the interpretations behind some of the works he included as part of his curriculum, parrying back and forth like two deranged ping pong players on crack until you finally snapped and asked why he even asked for your opinion in the first place, to which he would easily return that he hadn't. Then, like clockwork, you would gather your things to storm out of his office, but not before he wished you a saccharine good night as he called you a harpy.

For all of these things that you had managed to discover and learn about him, including the fact that he was apparently ambidextrous — because was there a single thing this man couldn't do? — which you had noticed when you realized he was able to write with a quill in his left hand just as easily as he was with his right, he still remained a mystery to you.

You had the suspicion he may have been part fae with how shady he had been when you had offhandedly blurted out the question of what the 'M' in his name stood for on an otherwise uneventful rainy day. He had merely shook off your inquiry, slyly pointing out that names had power and he wasn't about to grant you any more leverage that you didn't deserve. While that alone didn't necessarily confirm your hunch, his more human-esque face despite the wings and antennae, along with the slightly pointed ears that poked through his long hair, seemed like pretty good indicators.

Those details and the fact that he seemed to absolutely adore being cruel to you.

When you had asked Calli and Effie what the differences between fairy and fae were exactly, they simply responded that fae were *like* fairies, but with an agenda. Boy, did he have an agenda.

It was to make your life a living hell.

You guessed you could have always look him up online if you really wanted to find out more — the know-it-all acted like he had more than a few hundred years under his belt, so you wouldn't be surprised if you found out that was true — but you still had your pride and didn't want your search history to betray your curiosity. Besides, you were still trying to mend your dignity from when you had spent three hours rattling off all these observances to your dumbstruck friends, Effie finally breaking the silence to point out that not once had you stopped talking about him all evening.

Of course, you blamed him for that. It was entirely his fault that he irritated you so much that you needed to spend that long getting everything off your chest. Just as it was entirely his fault that you couldn't see a white shirt without noting that it wasn't as crisp as his were and his fault that your eyes automatically flitted to the tea selection in new cafes to see if they carried Earl Grey and his fault on why you found yourself mentally listing your debates in the shower to prepare yourself for an imminent verbal skirmish.

It was also his fault that you were currently on another terrible date.

After Effie had accused you of being *attracted* to him, you had started taking her up on her advice to put yourself out there and begin dating. You had also figured it would be a welcome distraction for you. Unfortunately, you had taken the quantity over the quality route, almost as if you were seeing people just to prove a point. To whom, you weren't sure; maybe to Effie and your other friends, maybe to yourself... maybe to the universe.

Either way, you had been on a slew of pretty shitty dates, the latest one you were doing your darnedest to escape from.

You had been to cafes and museums and parks and restaurants with orcs and cervitaurs and dragon shifters, yet you had felt no spark. They had all been perfectly pleasant; holding doors open for you, offering to pay when applicable, asking just the right amount of questions about your life and interests, but you always left your dates so bored. You knew they just weren't the ones when what you would look forward to most about the encounter was the knowing quirk of Professor Prick's lips and the glint of a tiny fang poking through whenever you trudged into his office the next day, immediately shooting him a warning glare not to ask about your dour mood.

You should have never admitted to him that you were seeing people, but you hadn't been able to muster any kind of proper excuse when you had needed to leave a few minutes early the first time. It didn't help that every time after that you purposely dropped hints just to see how he would react. Much to your chagrin, his unruffled countenance was not what you had hoped for.

Would it kill him to show any interest? Probably, that asshat.

Ugh. You and your big mouth.

Yet, as you turned into another dead end of the corn maze you had tried to lose your current date in, you would choose boredom any time over the feeling of fear that was beginning to creep up on you.

This time, you had agreed to go out with a werewolf that you had met at a farmer's market a week ago, and although he had kind of given you bad vibes at first, you compromised by suggesting you meet up at the upcoming Annual Haunt that marked the true beginning of fall. It was the traditional month-long harvest festival the town held every year with jack-o'-lanterns and bobbing for apples and haunted hayrides and the like, and it was cute and very public, so it had seemed like the safer bet.

Key word being *'seemed.'*

You had quickly realized about an hour into your date that you should have trusted your gut. Lowell — the werewolf in question — had started off *kind* of sweet at first, but was immediately a bit too touchy-feely for your liking, practically manhandling you from stall to stall. He had rapidly become almost overbearing and despite your best attempts to come up with excuses as to why you had to leave earlier than planned, he was having none of it. This was why you were currently trying to sprint through a corn maze to lose him.

Another key word being *'trying.'*

Promptly pivoting on your heel, you scurried through another set of twists and turns only to come up on another dead end. Chewing your lip in nervousness, you let out a soft curse. You were so stressed that you were almost tempted to bite your nails. "Fuck. Oh, fuckity fuck."

This was just your luck. Panic was beginning to set in that as much as you could try to evade him, as a werewolf, Lowell likely would be able to track you right down with his keen sense of smell. It didn't help that in your nerves, you had downed one too many alcoholic pumpkin ciders than you should have, nor did it help that your phone was currently dead.

Just like you pictured yourself being dead at the end of the night, your face plastered on a milk carton as you went missing after Lowell disposed of your broken body once he had torn your throat out with his giant canines for attempting to run away from him. You nearly whimpered at the grotesque imagery, unconfident as to whether or not you were being a tad overdramatic.

In a few hours — if you even had that many — it would become dark, and not only did that mean the chances of you finding your way out of here would become nearly zero, but you hated the dark. Your eyes widened when you swore you heard the crunch of a dried out corn husk underfoot, causing your heart to skip more than a few beats. You held your breath to try and listen more intently and when your ears were met with silence, you took that as your cue to sprint the fuck out of that corner.

Straight into what felt like a brick wall.

The scent of Earl Grey and leather and foreign florals enveloped you as you bounced back a bit, instinctively reaching out to grip at whatever was in front of you to prevent yourself from landing flat on your ass. Your fingers curled around a buttery fabric — leather, your frightened mind was able to recognize — just as you realized you knew that scent all too well.

Just as you knew the slightly accented voice that accompanied it.

"Are you quite finished accosting me?"

You would have come up with something snarky on how he needed to find some new material if you weren't so freaked out in your desperation to escape. As you looked up, expecting to see him leering down at you in such a state, you were a bit surprised to see that whatever he was about to say died on his lips as his eyes didn't narrow at you as they usually did, but instead slightly expanded in concern. Catching a fluttering movement out of your peripheral vision, you glanced at his wings.

Did they look slightly bigger than normal?

His tone immediately shifted, his subsequent question coming out much softer than the first. "What is wrong?"

"My date sucks," you responded quickly. Maybe it was the alcohol that was causing you to admit this so easily to him. You licked your dry lips and looked around, ignoring the odd sense of safety you felt when his long fingers curled around your wrists. "Trying to escape him. Kind of got lost."

"Did he do anything to you?" he half demanded, jostling your arms slightly to get your attention again. You looked back up at him, shaking your head. You noticed that his jaw, which had been slightly clenched, relaxed minutely at your action, as did the tips of his wings. His gaze, peering behind his usual frames, darted all over you, as if he were searching for something, before it met yours again. He let out a small sigh and gave you a curt nod in response. "Come along, then."

You didn't think to question where he was taking you or if he knew his way out of the maze, just allowing him to take one wrist in his hand and gently tug you along. Shoulders immediately relaxing in pure relief, you were thankful you had stumbled upon a familiar face, even if it was the one that had gotten you into this mess in the first place.

Oh, well. You could let him have it when you were out of this god-forsaken maze. You never wanted to see another ear of corn in your life.

Except when he led you around another corner, you were met with yet another familiar face. The one that you had been trying — and failing, apparently — to elude.

You let out a squeak of surprise, your free hand reaching out to grip at the arm Gideon was currently holding your other wrist with. Giving you a quick glance, he shifted slightly to step half in front of you, apparently quickly comprehending the situation. One of his wings seemed to curl back, as if it were gently hugging you from behind.

"Where didya run off to?" Lowell practically growled, sounding not at all pleased. Though he was currently in his more human form, you didn't like the way he cracked his knuckles in irritation. You were almost in awe as you saw Gideon's wings puff up in response, growing slightly larger than they had been before.

Wait, would Gideon be able to take a full on *werewolf*? He may have had tiny fangs of his own, but they were definitely no match for the giant ones that Lowell undoubtedly possessed, nor would his delicate fingers serve as any kind of weapon against a werewolf's sharp claws. As much as you blamed him for your plight, your mouth went completely dry at the thought of him being put in harm's way because of your inability to stick up for yourself.

The gears in your mind were practically showering the rest of the inner portion of your skull with sparks as you tried to think through this. Squaring your shoulders, you shoved Gideon aside, stepping around his wing to plant yourself between him and the fuming werewolf. You felt his hand grip at your shoulder, but you shot him a look of warning before looking back at Lowell.

"Man, this is so awkward," you said with a forced laugh, feigning a look of sheepishness as you rubbed the back of your neck. "I'm really sorry, Lowell. I wasn't paying attention and must have taken a wrong turn. I was trying to get back to you and stumbled upon my ex, isn't that crazy!" You jerked your thumb over your shoulder at Gideon. "He practically begged for me to get back with him and... well... I think I kind of owe it to him to give him a shot."

v: dionysian frenzy

YOU QUICKLY LOOKED BACK at Gideon expecting to see a look of shock, only to see that his face was totally impassive. When his eyes met yours, he nodded, easily snaking an arm around your shoulders to draw you closer to him. You tried not to acknowledge the way your heart thudded at the warmth that seeped into your skin.

"I could not let her get away, I am sure you understand," he announced to the werewolf, a bit too *theatrically* for your tastes, but Lowell seemed convinced at this display. He scowled, folding his flannel-clad arms over his broad chest.

"Are ya sure you wanna get back with an ex?" Lowell asked, voice gruff. "He must be a jerk if ya broke up in the first place."

"Oh, he *is*," you agreed enthusiastically, to which you felt said jerk stiffen beside you. You looked up at Gideon with what you hoped Lowell would interpret as a love-struck expression on your face as you continued emphatically, "But he's my jerk and I miss him!"

Maybe you should quit business school to become an actress from how Lowell seemed to take the bait. He snorted at your insistence. Giving Gideon one last overly-sappy smile, you looked back to the unamused werewolf, who was now shaking his head in disappointment.

"Whatever, I guess," he muttered, mud-colored eyes narrowing as he met Gideon's ruby ones peering behind their usual frames. "What a waste of time."

"Sorry," you apologized again, shimmying out from under Gideon's arms to grasp at one of his hands instead. "I guess this is our cue to leave, then!"

You turned one way, only for your arm to nearly detach itself from your shoulder when Gideon tugged you in the opposite direction. You then remembered you had no idea where the hell you were going. Giving Lowell one last too-friendly wave, you let Gideon tote you out of the small clearing in the maze, half in shock and half smug that your last-minute plan had actually worked.

You didn't realize that you had been holding his hand the entire time he led you out of the maze until you finally let go of it once you were staring at the parking lot of the town hall building, fighting the urge to sink to your knees to kiss the gloriously un-hay-covered sidewalk. Punching the air in relief, you turned to him with a grin on your face, only to see him staring at you with one antenna quirked.

"Your *ex*?" he questioned sardonically. You recognized that look on his face; it was the same one he gave you whenever he was in disbelief at whatever you had just said, head slightly tilted as his mouth lifted slightly at one side.

Your cheeks quickly heated with embarrassment, but you refused to give him the satisfaction of letting him know that.

"I saved your ass!" you exclaimed defensively, jabbing an index finger in his direction. "He's a werewolf! He could've ripped us both apart!"

"I seem to recall that I was the one who saved *your* 'ass,'" he sniffed dryly, folding his arms across his chest as he said the word a bit distastefully, "and I could have easily taken him."

As your eyes followed the movement of his hands tucking under his elbows, you finally registered what he was wearing. The material that you had initially clenched in your hands was part of the black leather jacket he currently wore. The dichotomy between the piece of clothing and his usual impeccable nearly glowing button down shirt underneath was almost too much for your slightly inebriated mind to handle. Another marked difference was his dark gray hair, which was usually pulled back into a low bun at the nape of his neck, hanging loosely around his shoulders. Your mouth nearly went dry again.

Realizing you were staring, you muscled your brain back into action to grumble, "This is the weirdest theoretical pissing contest I've ever witnessed."

Giving a slight huff at that, he dropped his arms to step closer to you. Too close, your mind screamed as you had to tilt your head back to gape up at him. "I believe," he began, dipping his head slightly to peer down at you, "the customary response to someone coming to your aid is '*thank you*,' little harpy."

With a *harrumph*, you quickly turned around, the pink on your cheeks no doubt deepening into a bright red at the proximity to him. You then bit out a clipped, "I'll thank you when you stop being so annoying!"

"Stubborn, as always," you heard him sigh. You peeked back at him to see he was shaking his head. "Now, which way do you live? I am taking you back to your place of residence."

"I only live a few blocks from here. I can take *myself* to my '*place of residence*'," you insisted, trying to mimic his posh accent as you repeated his oddly formal way of speaking and moved to step away from him. You felt his hand on your shoulder once more, jerking you to a stop.

"I am not leaving until I see you safely behind a locked door." Feeling another hand land on your other shoulder, you were suddenly spun around to face him. You would have argued, but your protests died when you saw how stern he looked.

Was he *worried* about you?

Scrunching your nose at how ridiculous that thought was, you stared at him for another second or two before rolling your eyes.

It was clear this would be another battle of wills, and as much as you would have loved to spend the rest of your evening locked in yet another debate with him, all you wanted to do was to collapse on your couch, charge your phone, and let your friends know that you survived a disastrous date. You could figure out whether or not it was worth telling them who else you managed to come across once you weren't so flustered.

"Fine," you acquiesced, dragging a hand down your face. "Can we walk, though? I don't want you to bother wasting gasoline." You then paused, peeking at him through the gaps in your fingers as you realized you didn't actually know where he lived. "I'm assuming you drove, that is?"

"In a way," he responded cryptically. He then gestured towards a nearby vehicle and yet again, your mind short-circuited.

You gawked at the sleek lines, chrome pipes, and glossy black finish, not quite sure you were believing what you were seeing. It glinted in the dying sun, devoid of any kind of speck of dirt or dust.

"You have a *motorcycle*?" you finally managed to ask, still shell-shocked.

You could already feel the headache setting in at the level of mental gymnastics you had been forced to go through today, not quite being able to connect the dots between the prim and proper professor who taught mythology during the week and the apparent biker who wore black leather jackets and tore up the asphalt like hell on wheels on the weekends.

"My own form of rebellion," he mused in reply. When you wrenched your head away from the motorcycle to look at him, you saw that his lips were quirked as if in recollection of some inside joke you weren't privy to. He didn't seem to feel the need to elaborate further, and you didn't have the energy to pry.

"Never pegged you for the motorcycle type." You took a step closer towards the bike as you admitted this. Tilting your head when you saw a scrawl of words in lustrous letters the same shade as his eyes, you read: *alis volat propriis.*

"It is a hobby of mine," he replied before you could ask what the words meant, glancing up at the setting sun. "Shall we start walking before it becomes completely dark?"

You nodded, tilting your head in the direction of your apartment as you began moving. This time, he allowed you to lead, and if someone would have ever told you that your asshole of a professor would be walking you home after a date gone sour, you would have told them right back to seek professional help immediately.

"Is that the only one you have?" you asked after a few steps, strolling at a comfortable pace by his side. Though the silence wasn't entirely awkward, you craved the distraction of conversation, otherwise you may have been prone to overthink this entire situation.

"Yes," he responded, facing forward. You were able to trace the outline of his profile at this angle, seeing the sharpness of his jaw and how his straight nose sloped downwards only to angle slightly up at the tip, shadows on his high cheekbones from the glasses that rested on its upper bridge. The delicate point of it almost mirrored the point to his tapered ears. "I built it myself with spare parts. It is a common interest I share with a... *friend.*"

He said the word strangely with a bit of hesitance, almost as if tasting something for the first time and debating whether or not he enjoyed the flavor. Even from this angle, you could see the area between his brows furrowing.

"I didn't know you had *friends,*" you teased, latching onto this observation. He quickly turned his head to look at you, the motion causing a few errant strands of hair to fall into his face. Your fingers twitched as you clenched your hands into fists to stop yourself from entertaining the urge to tuck them back behind his ears. You wondered if they felt as silky as the fuzz that covered his arms.

You stumbled over your own two feet the second that thought crossed your mind, murmuring an embarrassed *"thanks"* when he swiftly moved to grip your shoulders to prevent you from face-planting.

He frowned at your clumsiness once he steadied you again, hands hovering for a moment longer until he was sure you were stable. "I suppose *friend* is a generous moniker. Eden is more of a person I have begrudgingly *accepted* as being present within my life." He shrugged and you thought of how strange the casual gesture looked on him. "He is an absolute menace, quite frankly. Most incubi are."

"I guess that's one thing you have in common," you laughed, marveling at how strangely easy it was to talk to him. "Oh! This is me."

You realized that you were standing in front of the brownstone that housed your apartment, the walk being much quicker than you had anticipated. Glancing at the glass doors that led into the small space the listing had dubbed a foyer, you climbed up two steps before turning to thank him for walking you home, only to pause.

Instead, taking one step down again, you asked, "Why were you in the maze in the first place?"

As much as you were thankful for the coincidence of coming across him there, the camp and crowds of the Annual Haunt didn't seem super characteristic of him. For one thing, there were definitely too many colors for his liking, and for another, he seemed to prefer his solidarity. You could tell this from the way the tension seemed to leave him when the last of your fellow students left the lecture hall, as well as how much more at ease he was when it was just the two of you in his office.

"You did not 'peg' me as the festival type either, I presume?" You could have been chilled at how easy it was for him to practically read your mind at this point, but you just gave him a small, patient smile. "I was volunteering."

You opened your mouth to ask him to elaborate, but he read your mind again, beating you to the punch to continue, "Part of the proceeds go to the town library. They have been holding this festival for over one hundred years, and for the past fifty or so that they have included the maze, it has been the same every year. I was taking one last sweep through prior to leaving to make sure nobody was lost." An antenna twitched. "Obviously, I managed to come across a certain disoriented *harpy*."

You shot him a glare at the annoying nickname before rolling your eyes good-naturedly as you acquiesced, "Yeah, I know. Not my best moment I guess."

"Has anybody ever told you not to indulge before entering a maze," he asked, "or is that another one of your first date tactics?"

You flushed again, looking down at your shoes to kick an imaginary rock aside. The whole thing still felt really stupid. Maybe this was a sign to pump the breaks on your rapid dating for the time being.

He must have felt the awkward shift as you heard him begin to say, "I did not mean—"

"Yeah, you're right," you quickly interjected, cutting him off. For some reason, the thought of an apology coming from him felt even more embarrassing. Wanting to change topics, you thought of something to joke about. "Would have been more fitting for me to be stuck in that labyrinth with a minotaur than a werewolf, huh?"

You had figured referring to one of the books within *The Metamorphoses* that he loved teaching so much would have been a great way to get back to that effortless conversation you had enjoyed earlier, but you instantly realized you had made a mistake. Instead of simply appreciating your jest, you watched his countenance change as he slipped back into full lecturing mode. The leather jacket almost seemed to fade away, replaced with one of his gray knit sweaters as he lifted one arm in the air, index finger pointed to the sky as if he were standing at attention behind his lectern.

"That is a common misuse in our modern vernacular," he began, tone lilting as you bit back a groan at the impending lecture, "but, in fact, 'labyrinth' and 'maze' are *not* synonymous. Rather, there is a distinct difference between the two. A *maze* contains much more complexity with various paths to take and directions, while a *labyrinth* is unicursal with only one path to the center. Recall in book eight of *The Metamorphoses* where Ariadne…"

Your eye twitched as you felt yourself completely detach from his droning, managing to catch the words 'Theseus' and 'thread' before you mentally checked out.

This was why you couldn't have nice things, you told yourself; he only ruined them with his stupid superiority complex.

Instead of listening to his impromptu lesson, you stared at him, taking the opportunity to study him under the guise of paying attention. When you filtered what he was saying out —not a small feat, to be sure — you supposed he wasn't *too* bad.

Maybe Effie was onto something.

Even from your position one step up from the sidewalk, he still loomed over you, allowing you to see the sharpness of the edge of his jaw and how the shadows from the glow of the streetlamps overhead managed to soften the cut of his high cheekbones. You could appreciate the perfect mirror symmetry of his antennae, as if he purposely held them poised at matching angles to an exact degree. His eyes had the tendency to somehow glow even more luminous behind his sophisticated frames whenever he spoke of a topic he was particularly passionate about, and his lips…

You licked your own as your eyes settled on his, a darker gray than the rest of his face. They had a faint lilac tint to them, soft and plush and well-proportionate to his delicate features. The longer you continued to stare at these traits, the more convinced you were that he *had* to be part fae, especially with the spell he seemed to have been wrapping around you.

Completely entranced, you weren't sure if the beguile was due to this enchantment or some kind of Dionysian frenzy as a result of your "indulgence," as he had put it, but you couldn't bring yourself to care. Instead, you were too intent on watching those lips move, wishing they would stay still long enough for you to fully admire the slight cupid's bow that dipped into his upper lip.

If only he would stop talking. If only he would just be quiet. If only he would just...

"*Shut up*," you breathed, reaching out without a second thought to grip the edge of his open jacket and yank him towards you.

The feeling of his lips meeting yours wasn't an explosion of fireworks; rather, it was like free-falling into a vat of molasses, slowly drifting to a stop as the world froze and blurred around you. He immediately stiffened at the contact, lithe body going rigid at your touch, before fingertips were suddenly woven into the hair at the base of your head, pointed nails scratching pleasantly at your skull as he tugged ever so slightly to angle your face more so his frames were out of the way. His wings seemed to grow again, edges curling around you in a secondary hug.

There was the faint realization that the buzz that thrummed through your veins wasn't from the spiked cider at all as an arm settled onto the small of your back, pressing you closer than you thought was humanly possible. But you weren't dealing with a *human* exactly, you remembered as a thin tongue swept against your lips, greedily darting between them and unfurling once you parted them with a soft groan.

If you were hungry for him, he was ravenous, taking his fill and nearly leaching you of your soul as his tongue swept over yours, practically wrestling it into submission. All of it you gave freely, twisting the buttery leather of his jacket in one hand, uncaring of the way the zipper bit into your palm. You moved to grip at his shoulder for balance with the other so you wouldn't tumble down the step.

With the way you were caught in his grip, you doubted he would ever let you topple over in the physical sense; in all other senses, you were both careening over the edge as pulsing warmed pooled in your lower abdomen.

You felt his hair whisper against your cheekbones as he slightly pulled back to tease your lower lip between his tiny fangs, the sudden burst of pain quickly transforming into darts of pleasure that seared its way down your chest into your very core. The hand at your skull seemed to chase the current, dropping to dance against your heated abdomen before shifting to grip at the swell of your hip as the other remained iron-clad on your lower back. Then he was lifting you slightly until your toes were no longer touching the step. Your yelp turned into a sigh as he swallowed your surprise with his talented mouth and you shivered at the brief wonder of where else you could put it to use.

Gideon tasted of Earl Grey, notes of bergamot and citrus blooming on your tongue when his own swept in again to resume your dance with a pleased hum. Maybe the tea wasn't *so* bad, you thought, melting further into him, his chest rumbling in approval in response.

Perhaps you could learn to appreciate the brew.

Through the syrupy bliss, you could vaguely register alarm bells sounding in your sluggish mind. Wait, when did you start thinking of him as *Gideon*? He was Professor Dulcis. No, he was Professor Prick! King of Assholes! Patron Saint of Douchebaggery!

With a start, you realized the liquid haze cocooning you wasn't molasses after all, but congealed nitroglycerin, and you were dancing dangerously close to lighting the fuse.

Gasping in shock at your actions, you abruptly pulled back, head spinning as the blur gave way to the kind of acute clarity that made your teeth hurt. The halted world seemed to begin turning again with a vengeance, your surroundings crashing back into place with a cacophony of shapes and sounds as you were once again back on the step. Suddenly without the shadowed warmth of his wings around you, the golden light of the street lamp you both had been standing under was too harsh, making you wince at its brightness, just as the cool night air was nearly glacial, causing your breath to freeze into jagged crystals in your lungs.

"I shouldn't have done that," you finally managed to breathe, cheeks aflame with embarrassment as you stared down at your feet. "*We* shouldn't have done that."

You felt his hands leave you carefully, as if he were afraid you would bolt as you took another backwards step up from him to gain more distance. You didn't trust yourself to be so close to him.

Your chest heaved, partially from the effort of wrenching yourself away from him and partially from the effort of the kissing itself. You could have blamed a lot of things for this slip up; the volume of your frustrations at him finally bubbling over and being displaced into another outlet, the alcohol for your lowered inhibitions. But you weren't really that intoxicated, and weren't drunk actions sober thoughts?

You didn't allow yourself to contemplate that any further.

Instead, you looked up to see he was staring down at you, a kind of apathy staining his face that made your heart ache. You marveled at how quickly he was able to slip that mask of indifference back on, though it didn't completely hide the hard set to his jaw, nor did it do anything to conceal the slight dust of lilac on his cheeks that tinted his ashen skin. His wings seemed slightly smaller again, both antennae stiff atop his hair, which was somehow perfectly smoothed back into place. Not even his glasses were a hint askew.

"It is already forgotten," he stated coolly after a few beats, inclining his head slightly to your front door. "I believe you said this was your home, so I have fulfilled my purpose. Have a pleasant rest of your evening."

On any normal occasion, you would have sniped at him not to order you around to have a pleasant rest of your *anything*, but these circumstances were far from the ordinary. You gave him a stiff nod, the movement jerky and disjointed as if the joints in your neck were slightly rusted together. The way you turned away from him felt like an out of body experience, as if some other force were piloting your movements.

You must have completely blanked out as the next time you blinked, you were already in your apartment and staring down at where you had kissed him perched on the bottom step under the streetlight. Your own fingertips grazed your lips where his had met yours, slightly swollen and still tender from where he had caught your bottom one between his teeth. You remembered the feeling of weightlessness from when he had lifted you from the step and how it impossibly fit with the accompanying feeling of being completely grounded as he held you against his form.

You staggered back from the window at this, hands clasping at your too-hot cheeks as you willed yourself to forget. It would do neither of you any good to revisit this with your current arrangement; you were still his assistant and his student and he was your professor, and as much as you had gone and almost mucked it up, he was willing to forget everything and move on.

Giving a nod of resolve, you launched into action, first plugging your phone in so it could charge enough for you to let your friends know that you were alive. You could take it one day at a time, remaining cordial with him and sticking strictly to topics related to his lesson plans. All you had to do was survive the rest of the semester. You were proud of your professionalism, so this would be a breeze for you. Perhaps you could start with a cold shower...

If Gideon —no, *Professor Prick* — was anything, he was definitely a man of his word, so if he said it was already forgotten, it had definitely already been forgotten.

Except while part of you was relieved, the other part was disappointed, and you didn't know which one would win out against the other.

vi: panacea

OVER THE NEXT week since your disastrously incredible kiss, the weather grew chillier as a cold snap rolled through the Eventide Falls. The garnets and topazes and citrines of the leaves of the lush trees that lined the town and its eponymous university still blazed brightly like in the peak of fall, but the way your breath puffed in front of your face in crystallized clouds as you scurried around campus was more reminiscent of the throes of winter.

You *hated* the cold. Absolutely despised it. You could appreciate the glittering vista of a fresh snowfall, but that serene view lasted for all of three seconds before something came along to disrupt the pristine picture. It didn't help that in the past week, Professor Prick's attitude towards you had mirrored the shift in weather and you found yourself constantly shivering in more ways than one.

That kiss was like the proverbial elephant in the room. If the elephant in question were hot pink, had ten limbs, were strung trunk to tail in twinkling Christmas lights, and had a flashing neon sign hanging from one of its tusks. You skirted around each other like two magnets, except it felt like the universe was purposely trying to force together the same poles.

How easy it would be for one of you to flip around to attract instead of repel. Except you didn't want it to be *you* to bend again.

You never thought you would miss his condescending smirks or haughty tone as he contradicted or corrected you, nor would you think you would yearn so much for the narrowing of his scarlet eyes during one of his infamous impromptu lectures. The silent treatment was something akin to torture for you, and in the weeks and months that you had known each other, the sound of his voice had apparently somehow become some kind of drug that you had become addicted to. With the way he had only been speaking to you when absolutely necessary for the past week, he had basically forced you to quit cold turkey — emphasis on *'cold'* — and it was a marvel that it had only taken you that short of an amount of time to crumble.

Despite also never having been a morning person, you looked forward to his morning classes, if only to hear him speak at length, even if you had to share the experience with hundreds of other students in the lecture hall. The illogical side of you could have sworn that the vampire bitch had been mocking you from across the room, despite the fact that she could have had no way of knowing exactly what had transpired.

Your friends, however, had been quick to catch on to your more-fidgety-than-usual attitude, sensing you had been leaving out bits and pieces when you had finally charged your phone enough to get on a group video call and divulge all about that stupid date of yours. Greer wasn't usually one to pry, his silent sentinel style being one of a keen observer, but Calli and Effie sometimes seemed to share the same brain cell. This single brain cell had somehow been able to read between the lines and was subsequently intently hyper-focused on getting all the details.

You had initially debated whether or not to tell them, but you had remembered that once hearing that admission was the first stage to recovery; what *exactly* you were recovering from, you weren't sure, but you weren't sure your conscience could bear the secret much more anyway. So, you had blurted out the kiss, throwing your hands over your burning cheeks as Calli and Effie squealed in excitement. Except you must have looked absolutely anguished afterwards, because they had quickly stopped mid-screech to ask what was wrong.

It was nearly impossible to explain why exactly nothing could come of this. Sure, there was the whole frowned upon student-professor thing, but you were two consenting adults and it wasn't necessarily forbidden. Your response to the barrage of questions from your two fairy friends had just been a repeated chant of "it just can't happen," and while Greer had seemed perfectly satisfied with that answer, Calli and Effie weren't. They had finally relented after you had begged them to drop the topic, asking for them not to bring it up again unless you did first, and although the crestfallen looks on their colorful faces had suggested disappointment, they hadn't skipped a beat into planning your next shopping excursion.

You were thankful for the boundaries you were able to set with your friends. You weren't sure how much additional strain you could take when it came to this; not because you couldn't bear the embarrassment of your actions, but because the more you thought about it, the more you also questioned why nothing could happen.

Long story long, you had been spending the last week attempting to distract yourself from thinking about it and him, which was easier said than done — and it hadn't even been that easy to say in the first place. To ward off the lingering thoughts of the heat of his hand gripping your hip and the taste of bergamot and citrus, you had dove headfirst into the rest of your business studies with an aggression that would have been frightening even to you — had you possessed the headspace to be more self-aware. You had spent your nights holed up in the library, ignoring the texts and calls of your friends telling you to take a break and join them. You thought you had even caught Professor Prick frowning at the purple bruising under your eyes from lack of sleep, but it must have just been a trick of the light.

All in all, it wasn't necessarily surprising when you had woken up with a bit of a scratchy throat the day prior, and now as a raging fever took hold, you couldn't help but begrudgingly admit that your friends may have been right.

"I *told* you so!" Effie exclaimed, causing you to wince and immediately turn the volume down on your phone. She was currently with Calli and Greer in your favorite cafe, The Abridged Bean, which was owned by that troll who made great scones she had told you about upon first meeting. "Ow—*hey!*"

"Are you sure you don't want us to bring you anything?" you heard Greer cut in. Though they were only on speakerphone so you couldn't see them, something told you that Greer may have just elbowed her.

"No thanks," you muttered for what felt like the millionth time, wanting to just wallow by yourself so you could atone for your own stupidity. "I have a bunch of stuff here."

That was a lie, but *they* didn't need to know that. At some point, you would peel yourself off of your now-sweaty covers and trudge down to the general store a few blocks from your apartment to get some medicine, but all you wanted to do now was nap in hopes that your pounding headache would subside. You screwed your eyes shut, the sparse light that filtered in through your translucent curtains becoming nearly blinding.

"I was just kidding." You could practically hear the pout in Effie's voice as Calli snickered softly in the background.

"Guys, let her get some rest!" Calli then interjected. There was some kind of scuffling sound, as if somebody was sliding the phone across the table. "Feel better!"

Your response to the echoed well-wishes from the other members of the group was a cough as they ended the call. With a groan, you blindly groped for your pillow, finally clumsily bumping against it and clutching it with weak fingers to drag over your head.

Luckily, it was Saturday, so you really had nowhere to be. You could nap for a few hours before throwing on the darkest pair of sunglasses you owned to venture out into the sunlight. Maybe this was how vampires felt; if so, no wonder that Violetta vampire chick was such a *See You Next—*

Oh, fuck!

Your eyes shot open as you abruptly sat up in bed, letting out a string of curses as the action caused a flurry of knives to pierce your brains as you suddenly remembered that you did, in fact, have somewhere to be, and that was in Professor Prick's office. Today was the day you were supposed to help him prep for one of his off-campus lectures that would happen on *Tuesday*, and as you fumbled around for your phone to squint at the time, you saw that you had been due there two minutes ago.

Great minds must have truly thought alike, because you were sluggishly trying to bring up the contact card for *Professor Prick* when an incoming call from the devil in question lit up your screen. Slumping forward, you accepted the call and held the phone to your ear.

"Where are you?"

You would have rolled your eyes at the demandingness of the inquiry if the action wouldn't have been so painful. For as much as he could drone on and on in his lectures, it was interesting where he chose to get straight to the point and not mince his words.

Would spending an extra two seconds wishing you a 'good morning' really have killed him?

Except you didn't have the energy to snark with him about this, instead bending to cough into the crook of your elbow before saying, "Sorry, I—" Another cough interrupted you. Taking a shuddering breath, you cleared your throat and tried to continue. "Be there in ten."

You pressed a button to put your phone on speaker and carefully sank to the side, curling your knees to your chest. As your eyes drifted shut, you tried to muster the strength to get up and dress so you could make your way to campus. While you felt pretty shitty, incurring the wrath of a certain grumpy professor seemed much scarier than the prospect of contracting pneumonia.

Maybe you should have told him *fifteen* minutes, not ten. Despite the fog settling over your brain, it painfully whirred back into motion as you tried to piece together the appropriate timelines.

It normally took you ten minutes to get from your apartment to campus, but that was from the door on the street to the library. You should have also added on an additional three to get down the stairs, and maybe five more to get from the library to his office. But that was his office building, so another four would probably be necessary to account for those stairs. Ah, but you hadn't gotten dressed yet... so you would most likely need another ten just to accomplish that, eight if you hurried. Yet none of this was accounting for the fact that you were sick in the first place, so what multiplier should you apply on top of it all for a buffer since you were slower than normal? One point five? *Two*?

"Are you quite alright?" he suddenly asked, the question throwing a crowbar in the spinning gears of your mind. His words had also ceased your fumbling within your calculator app as you tried to blearily add together these minutes with one eye open. It was probably a good thing, too, because when you opened the other eye to blink down at the screen and saw that your math somehow added up to a total of seven hours and forty eight minutes needed to walk from your apartment to campus, you realized you must've miscalculated somewhere.

"Just peachy," you responded; you had wanted for it to come across as your usual sarcasm, but even to your ears the words sounded flat and tired. You sighed, imagining his antennae twitching to attention at your uncharacteristic tone.

"You are ill," he stated slowly, to which you wanted to respond, *No shit, Sherlock!* But you didn't, instead just nodding. It didn't occur to you that he wasn't actually able to see your confirmative gesture until he was speaking again. "What are your symptoms?"

"Um." You coughed once more, brows knitting together. Symptoms, symptoms... what were symptoms? That was a big word. It had more than one syllable. That was also a big word. Oh, yeah! "I dunno. My head hurts, and"—another cough—"*that*."

"Are you feverish?" He sounded tense, but you weren't sure why. Was he stressed that he lacked your assistance for this lecture? You immediately felt guilty. You were never one to be a flake.

"No," you lied, "I'm fine. I can—"

"You most certainly are *not* fine," he insisted. There was some kind of metallic clinking in the background, like the jingling of keys, and then what sounded like wood scraping against wood. "What did I say about detesting liars?"

You shrugged, again not necessarily cognizant of the fact that he couldn't see you, muttering something unintelligible before he said, "Stay there. I will be there shortly."

Humming at this, you finally were able to utter a brief, "Okey dokey," but he had already ended the call. Falling back against your pillows, you closed your eyes again, trying to mentally will away your headache.

You must have fallen asleep, because a sudden insistent knocking caused you to jolt and the implication of his words finally sank in.

He had said he was coming to your *apartment*. And now he was here. At your apartment. Which you were currently in. Because it was your apartment. Where you now *both* were. At your apartment. That he had said he was coming to.

"Oh, fuckity fuck!" you cursed, nearly rolling off your bed in surprise. You managed to somehow catch yourself, flinching at the pain still blooming in your skull as you gingerly stepped onto the floor. You grimaced at the way the cold wood felt against your bare feet.

Practically tilting sideways, you steadied yourself and paused to catch your bearings. Even though you felt a sticky sheen of sweat on your forehead, your apartment felt absolutely frigid. You reached down to wrap half of your comforter around yourself, throwing it over your head like a hood as you stumbled out of your bedroom. You heard the *thunk* of your phone hitting the ground as the other end of the blanket trailed off your bed and rippled to the floor behind you like a cape.

Your short journey from your bedroom to your front door felt like it stretched across continents as your hand finally rested on the cool brass knob. Peering through the peephole, you took in his slightly distorted image. He was wearing his usual white shirt, though an unbuttoned peacoat was thrown over it. The color was slightly darker than the pair of graphite-colored tweed pants that covered his legs. When your eyes swept back up, you could see that his sooty hair was neatly pulled back with only a few strands escaping and a plush black scarf was wrapped around his neck, the stark contrast making his already light gray skin seem even paler.

You stepped away from the peephole and swallowed, grimacing as the rasp in your throat as you debated whether or not to let him in. He had the audacity to look straight off of a ready-to-wear early winter runway, while it would be an insult to all of gremlin-kind to compare your current appearance to one of them.

Hearing the soft rap of his knuckles against your door again, you looked at your ceiling, as if some greater power might swoop down to help you. Except no higher being came down to save you from your plight and instead, you had the misfortune of noticing a suspicious-looking water stain that would, from there on out, plague your existence in this place. You made a mental note to call your landlord at some point.

With a little internal pep talk, you finally opened the door, not sure you had the strength to shimmy down the fire escape and run away from him after all. You stared at each other for the briefest of seconds as you noticed the brown paper shopping bag nestled between the crook of his elbow and his side and a to-go coffee cup clenched in his opposite hand while he simultaneously silently took in your current ridiculous garb.

It's called fashion, asshole, you could have grumbled. *Look it up!*

An antenna quirked at you as you then stepped aside, sweeping your arm to the side in a gesture that was meant to welcome him in.

You could feel the weight of his crimson gaze searing through your comforter as you turned from him to close the door, swiveling again to stand awkwardly in front of him.

His presence in your humble apartment made it seem that much smaller, especially with the way his wings brushed your furniture. You half expected them to leave a magical silvery sheen behind, a tad surprised when they didn't.

"May I?" he tilted his head towards the battered coffee table you had rescued from a flea market and you nodded, watching as he carefully set the bag down on its scuffed surface. He kept the cup in one hand, eyes darting around as if searching for something. "You do not happen to have a coaster, do you?"

You blinked owlishly at him in response, which he must have correctly interpreted as an emphatic *no*, his wings only bristling *slightly* when he was forced to rest the coffee cup directly on top of the table. Opening your mouth with the intention of asking him what was in the bag, your question was replaced with another hacking cough so rough it caused your eyes to water. You wondered whom, exactly, you had pissed off to earn such strange and unusual punishment.

Which circle of Hell was *this*, exactly?

Before you could contemplate any further, you felt him tug your makeshift hood off of your head. The resulting protest on your lips died as the back of his hand was suddenly placed against your forehead. Unable to help yourself, you leaned into the warm silkiness of his skin, eyes drooping as his chest rumbled with his hum of disapproval.

"I knew you were lying," he murmured, the quirk of his antenna mirroring that of his lips, despite his clear displeasure. Yet, even with your sickness clouding your mind, you could recognize that his eyes weren't narrowed at you in criticism, but what instead looked to be some kind of concern. When you let out another cough into your comforter-clad elbow, he moved to rub soothing rhythmic circles onto the middle of your back, patiently allowing you to sag against him as you wheezed.

It dawned on you that the way he moved about you was with complete confidence, as if he didn't need to second guess any of his actions.

It also dawned on you that you liked this way more than you probably should have.

Finally able to catch your breath, you shuffled back slightly to jut your chin at the items he had brought. "What are those?" Then you stilled, realizing you hadn't seen him with any kind of additional bag. You doubted that the volumes he owned would have fit in the brown paper bag on the table. "Where are the books?"

"The *books*?" he repeated, his other antenna swiveling as he tilted his head. He looked confused. "What books?"

You returned the look of confusion. "Aren't you here so I can help you prepare for your lecture?"

The staring at each other commenced again. You were a bit bewildered, not sure why he looked so perplexed. Why else would he currently be standing in the living room of your apartment, allowing you to cough and hack all over him?

"You are ill with a fever," he began, purposely saying each word one-by-one as if he were thinking through some kind of ancient paradox, "and you think I am expecting you to *work*?"

"Um, yes?" you responded, your nod subsequently causing your brain to bounce around in your skull again. Hiding a wince, you watched as he disentangled himself from you and took a step back, folding his arms across his chest.

"I have come with medicine," he stated, shaking his head at you, "not quite panacea, but it should suffice."

You ogled at him as he stepped towards the coffee table, bending down to reach into the bag and procure two plastic bottles, one red, one orange. He held the red up, the liquid sloshing inside as he tilted it to peer at the label. Then he did the same with the orange, but its contents were pills that rattled with the movement.

"These should be safe to take together, according to the pharmacist," he explained, taking one last glance at the labels before looking back at you. "This one"—he shook the red bottle—"is for your cough, while this one"—he shook the orange bottle—"is for your fever and your headache." When you merely blinked again, he looked back at them in contemplation. "I opted to go the pharmaceutical route as that is what most humans are partial to, but if you do not feel better, I do know a rather talented witch..."

"Wait, sorry." You brought a hand to your sweltering forehead, not sure if you were actually awake or if this was all some elaborate fever-induced hallucination. "You came here... to bring me *medicine*?"

"And hot chocolate," he replied easily, gesturing towards the cup. "I know you do not like coffee, and while tea is definitely the more effective option"—he gave you a stern look—"I know you do not care for that, either."

"And hot chocolate," you murmured dumbly, parroting his words as you dropped your hand. While he no doubt knew your distaste for tea from the way you would pull a face whenever he drank the stuff, you couldn't even remember when you had mentioned not really liking coffee. You only really drank it when you needed to cram for finals.

Ignoring your dumbfounded gaping, he unscrewed the red bottle, its cap acting as a tiny cup as he broke the safety seal and carefully poured the thick syrup out. He did so with complete precision, only stopping when the curve of the liquid — the *meniscus*, you idly recalled from science class — was at the indicator line. You wondered if *'chemist'* was on what you imagined to be the very lengthy résumé of his.

He held the cup out to you, then hesitated.

"I assume you have not taken anything yet." It was less of a question and more of a statement as you shook your head to confirm his supposition. You winced at the ache the jostling movement caused.

"Have you at least been hydrating yourself?" When your response was another stare, he sighed. "Right, of course not."

"I *just* got out of bed," you said a bit defensively, though you didn't fight him when he moved to maneuver you around the cramped space so he could settle you on your couch. He handed you the medicine, crossing his arms tightly across his chest, tapping a clawed finger impatiently and pursing his lips strictly when you stuck your tongue out at the viscous liquid and scrunched your nose.

"You are drinking all of that right now," he ordered, voice strangely dropping half an octave as he did so. For some reason, the firmness in his tone sent shivers down your spine as you automatically moved to obey him, tilting your head and throwing the liquid back quickly like the shots you had opted to take to get through your undergrad. You grimaced at the artificial taste, but didn't miss the nod of approval he gave as you handed the cup back to him. "Good girl."

If his earlier command had made a shiver crawl down to your toes, his latter statement made a bolt of lightning sizzle right back up as you felt your cheeks heat at the praise. You were glad that you were most likely already flushed from your fever, otherwise he may have caught your blush.

You put up no fight at all when it came to taking the pills, in part because you knew they were tasteless, but also because you just wanted to please him again. Your brain must have been completely fried at this, but you could ruminate over these thoughts when the sides of your skull decided to stop playing pong with it. The hot chocolate you chased them down with tasted a bit funny at first mixed with the lingering aftertaste of the cough medicine, but the warmth blissfully soothed your raw throat.

After taking a few more small sips, you noticed that the bag still looked to be full. You stilled, lowering the cup from your lips to rest in your lap. "Please don't tell me you brought something else."

He chuckled at you, turning to dip his hand into the bag. When it reemerged holding a bundle of celery, you wondered just what the hell was in this *'medicine'* he had given you. You must have really been hallucinating.

"I—ah—read something about chicken soup and its correlation with human illness," he replied, earlier confidence tinged with a bit of sheepishness. "I looked at the ones in the supermarket, but they all seemed to be extremely high in sodium and preservatives..."

"Alright." You hunched over, tucking your cup of hot chocolate between your legs as you rested your elbows on your knees. "Let me get this straight." Dragging a hand down your face, you said with measured pauses, "You left your office — went all the way to the pharmacy — then to the supermarket to get me medicine and make me soup? And you... don't want me to work?"

"Actually, I ventured to the supermarket first, but semantics, I suppose." Your mouth must have dropped open because suddenly his fingertips were under your chin, gently pushing it back shut. "I just realized it was rather rude of me to presume you would allow me the use of your kitchen. I will tidy up after myself, of course." He tilted his head towards it. "May I?"

You could only give him the start of another dumb nod before you stopped. "Don't you... have other things to do? You know, better, more *productive* things?"

He frowned at this, halting for a moment as if carefully choosing his words. Then, he replied, "Well, you are no use to me dead, so one could argue that this is considered productive."

Biting back a retort, you merely dared to roll your eyes, at least content that the medicine he had brought seemed to be doing the trick so fast. Your headache was quickly abating, only a dull throb now instead of a piercing roar. Your cough had also lessened significantly.

Maybe he wouldn't need to contact his witch friend, after all.

"...Can I at least take your coat?" you asked a bit lamely, because for as bizarre as this whole thing was, you were still for some reason concerned about his comfort.

"No, stay where you are," he responded, shrugging it off with absurd grace and draping it over an arm. Unwinding his scarf from his neck, he then carefully wove it around yours. You caught a whiff of Earl Grey, leather, and that lemony floral again — a scent that was so distinctly *Gideon*— and subconsciously snuggled into the soft cashmere. "Just tell me where to place it."

You pointed to a chair by the door, tired eyes trailing him as he moved to drape the peacoat carefully over its back. Maybe you should add a coat rack and coasters to your list of things to buy so he wouldn't have more grounds to judge your humble abode. However, that assumed he would be returning to said humble abode.

Was that wishful thinking? Or part of this fever dream?

He returned to pick up the paper bag before whisking it away as you watched him place it on your countertop from over the back of the couch you were situated on. Managing to find a glass in your cabinets, he swiftly procured a cup of water for you with an unspoken order to drink it, tucking your comforter around your form before returning to his task at hand.

Where you usually made a ton of noise, pots and pans banging and clanging together as you worked in a flurry, his movements were more poised and practically soundless. Even as he moved around, trying to figure out where everything was, he looked perfectly natural flitting around, cuffing his sleeves a few rolls higher than his elbows.

The sight of him chopping vegetables in your little kitchenette was the very picture of surrealism. You didn't have any clocks around, but if you did, you imagined they might be in various stages of liquidity, draped at odd angles as they melted all over the rest of your furniture. You could only blink as the image got stranger and stranger, hearing him hum softly to himself as one antenna swayed subtly like a conductor.

It was decidedly *Gideon*, not Professor Prick that was currently the centerpiece of this odd work of art.

You made a note to check those bottles again, still not entirely convinced he hadn't drugged you or something. If this was, in fact, a hallucination, at least it was turning out to be a rather pleasant one. If it wasn't... well, you could cross that bridge when and if you got there.

You must have really been sick, because amongst the medicinal haze of your mind, your most intelligible musing was that you had never before in your life wished to come across a bridge as much as you did now.

vii: forbidden fruit

IT WAS UNCHARACTERISTICALLY warm for the end of fall despite the recent cold snap, yet Professor Prick had gone back to his post-kiss frigid self the moment you had started feeling better.

He had spent the better part of last week by your side in your tiny apartment, filling in the empty spaces between when your friends visited you. It had just been a nasty cold, yet he had hovered around you with such intent that you had almost been convinced you were dying.

When you hadn't been awake, throwing back cough medicine and allowing him to spoon feed you his homemade chicken noodle soup — *good* soup, you had to admit — pink elephants danced behind your eyelids as you dozed. It was as if your subconscious had been trying to remind you of how strange it was that your professor, the man who you had all but thrown yourself at and who you were convinced hated you, had been playing nursemaid while you sneezed and coughed all over his immaculately-pressed shirt.

Over the course of the four — or was it *five*? — days that he had come and gone from your apartment, you had managed yet again to pick up three more things about him:

First of all, he was apparently a vegetarian. You had learned this upon asking why he hadn't made himself any soup, to which he had responded that he didn't eat any kind of meat or fish. The latter was actually one thing that you had confessed you actually had in common; fish grossed you out, too.

Secondly, you may have harbored feelings for him. Other than pure annoyance, actually. The armchair psychologist in you had been trying to convince yourself that the kiss had just been a strange form of redirected frustration, but the more time you had spent with him as he had chastised you for being impatient and burning your mouth on soup — you had snarkily retorted that you were getting mixed messages as he had all but demanded that you finish it — the more you found yourself just wanting to kiss him again. Not just to shut him up, even, but because you desperately wanted to taste bergamot and citrus and decide once and for all if Earl Grey really wasn't your thing.

Finally, in perhaps the most bizarre realization of all, you had discovered that despite your earlier contemplations of whether or not you had been hallucinating, this very much had *not* just been a dream. The presence of his black cashmere scarf, which you had gotten dry cleaned because you hadn't trusted yourself to wash it yourself, was physical proof of his existence in your apartment, like a specter made flesh.

This last realization was a tad unfortunate as it gave your second one much more weight; had everything just been a dream, you may have been able to sit yourself down and rationalize that *dream* Gideon was not the same as *real-life* Gideon, but when they were one and the same, your argument about why you shouldn't be attracted to him fell apart.

None of this mattered, though, because a week after you had recovered, marking two weeks after the kiss-heard-around-Eventide-Falls-but-only-really-to-you-actually, you were back to your usual program, attending classes during the day and acting as his assistant after hours while he did his best to ignore you and you did your best to not feel so upset about it.

You let out a groan, flopping back against the blanket that Calli had brought. Due to the warm weather, you and your friends had decided to spend part of your weekend lounging in one of the campus quads, trying to get as much sun as you could before the winter set in.

"I'm an idiot, aren't I?" you asked aloud, throwing an arm across your eyes. It could have been a rhetorical question, but as they had given you the floor and you had just spent the first few hours of your time together divulging all of this to them, you fully expected a response. Which you got.

"Definitely *not*!" Effie exclaimed. You dropped your arm and instead used it to prop yourself up an elbow, seeing her clench two periwinkle fists in determination. She had a dreamy, far-off look in her pink eyes, as if thinking of another idea for those novels she kept starting and not finishing.

"He forreal has the hots for you," Calli stated with a matter-of-fact nod, wings fluttering as if nodding on their own to agree with her. You rolled your eyes and let out a huff at this, blowing a few strands of hair out of your face as you sat up fully again.

"Yeah, right," you grumbled, throwing your arms up in the air theatrically. "Then why is he icing me out?"

Both Effie and Calli shrugged simultaneously, then instantly swiveled their heads to look at Greer, who innocently sipped at his blueberry smoothie through a striped red and white straw. He paused, lowering the drink from his lips while his marble-like eyes darted back and forth between their expectant gazes.

"Why are you looking at *me*?" he asked, licking his lips with a blue-tinted tongue. One of his furry ears twitched, a gold hoop glinting slightly with the movement. "Stop that!"

"Well, you're a guy, aren't you?" Calli sniffed, sounding almost accusatory. "Can you translate for us?"

"You're also the only one of us in an actual relationship!" Effie pointed out cheerfully, bending over to grasp his knee. "Help us, Greer! You're our only hope!"

Despite your exasperation at the way a certain professor was acting towards you, you couldn't help but giggle at the sight of two fairies needling a smoothie-drinking minotaur, watching as Greer swatted Effie's hand away.

"I dunno!" he retorted gruffly, giving you a look that screamed '*SOS!*' He errantly reached up and rubbed one of his horns, which he had the tendency to do when he felt a bit overwhelmed by the attention.

"Alright, alright," you interjected, waving your hands to distract them from him. He gave you a grateful nod as he went back to drinking his smoothie. "Maybe I'm just looking too into it and he was just being nice or something." You sighed. "This sucks. I feel like I'm in middle school again."

"No way, lady!" Calli shook her head vigorously. "Just being nice is shooting you a text to say he hopes you feel better... not going out of his way to buy you medicine and literally make you soup!"

"She is so right," Effie agreed, that dreamy look on her face again. "That's boyfriend behavior right there! He wants to wife you up for sure!"

Scrunching your nose, you pulled a face at her dramatics as you said, "I think that's a bit overboard..."

"Actually," Greer butted in, tilting his head thoughtfully as he lowered his drink again, "I think they're kinda right. Well, maybe not the 'wife you up' part, but he did seem to go above and beyond..."

"See?" Calli looked triumphant, green wings puffing up behind her. "He has feelings for you!"

"I still think that's just wishful thinking," you bemoaned, watching as Effie reached into her bag to pull out a narrow can of sunscreen. You looked up to see that the sun had actually been replaced with thick cloud cover over the course of the morning and arched a brow at her.

"Most people are at a greater risk of getting sunburn on a cloudy day," she stated, seeing your inquisitive look while she held out the bottle to Calli and shook it. "Would you be a gem and spray this on my wings so I don't burn to an absolute crisp?" She then turned back to you. "Maybe he's drawn to you like—"

"I swear, Effie," you said, quickly cutting her off, "if you finish that statement with *'a moth to a flame,'* I will start a sunscreen company of my own, raise enough capital to commence hostile takeovers of all the remaining companies in the industry to establish an absolute monopoly, destroy my mega company and all the sunscreen products before the government can catch wind of it, and then punt you straight into the sun!"

Greer chuckled just as Effie pouted, Calli smirking behind her as she generously doused Effie's wings in the spray, reaching behind her to lightly coat her own for good measure. You lifted your arms above your head and stretched, pulling out your phone from where you had been sitting on it to look at the time.

"Well, I should go and finish studying for that exam we have." You stood up, glancing at the sky again before saying, "It looks like it's going to rain anyway. You may have wasted that sunscreen."

"Yeah, same," Greer said, standing up as well. He handed you your bag, picking his smoothie up. "Although you seem to know your stuff." He shook his head. "I hate statistics."

"*Too-da-loo!*" Effie called, wiggling her fingers at the both of you. "Glad we're not in business courses, eh?" She elbowed Calli in the side, who nodded.

You gave Greer a sympathetic look before waving at the rest of them, having offered to help him study before, only for him to insist he was more efficient studying on his own. Hauling the strap of your bag over your shoulder, you dropped your phone back in one of its pockets and began making your way to the library, trying your best not to think too much about Professor Prick and his conflicting messages.

That asshole.

When you heard your name being called, you considered it a

distraction; however, turning to face a certain werewolf, you immediately saw that it wasn't so welcome. Lowell, who you had thought you had seen for the last time in that stupid maze — not a labyrinth, Professor Prick had insisted — was striding towards you, cocky grin on his face. You tried to summon your best polite smile, one that you tended to use during interviews.

His sneering question as he stopped in front of you immediately had it faltering. "Where's ya boyfriend?"

Your mind stuttered for a minute. Not even a hello to start things off? This guy was a piece of work!

"Uh." You cleared your throat to buy yourself an extra moment or two, awkwardly shuffling on your feet. "I'm on my way to see him right now, actually!" You sounded overly cheery in your lie, but the deepening of his scowl suggested he was still buying it. Your performance in the maze had been pretty convincing, after all.

"Still together then, huh?" He took a step forward, causing you to flinch. You quickly nodded, trying to subtly look around. For some reason, the campus looked like a ghost town, although from the few drops that started pattering against the sidewalk, that could have been attributed to the weather.

"Yu*p*," you responded, popping the 'p' as you gingerly took a step back to create more distance. You didn't like how he was peering at you, teeth flashing in probably what he thought was a nice guy smile, but really just made you feel like you were a slab of meat.

He ogled at your bare legs and you cursed your past self for deciding it had been warm enough to wear a skirt. Judging from the rain and the way the temperature had dropped more than a few degrees, hindsight told you that you really should have looked at the forecast, although it still wouldn't have been astute enough to warn you it would be cloudy with a chance of *douchebag*.

You tried to tug your skirt over your kneecaps self-consciously as the rain began to pick up. With a lame attempt at a laugh, you gestured vaguely at the sky. "I should go, you know, before it really starts coming down. It was, uh, nice seeing you again."

Although he didn't necessarily deserve your civility, you had seen and read enough about men like him to know that the act of being courteous could be considered self-preservation. Except while you tried to pull away, you felt grimy fingertips curl around your wrist in a nearly bruising grip, yanking you back.

You immediately started to panic, mind flashing through a bunch of different scenarios. *Option A*: you could try to flee, but considered he seemed much stronger than you, you probably had no chance at breaking away. *Option B*: you could try to fight, but weren't sure if he'd be quick enough to stop your kneecap to his groin or block the heel of your palm pushing his nose upwards. *Option C*: you could call someone, but your phone seemed out of reach, and who would you call that could come quick enough to help you, anyway?

Just as you were mentally hyping yourself up to go with Option B and attempt to ram his own nose into the organ that would be too-generously called a brain, his fingers were suddenly no longer digging into your skin. In fact, the rain had stopped completely.

You blinked, finally catching a whiff of Earl Grey and leather, and nearly threw yourself into the arms of the man who had once again been in the right place at the right time to assist you.

Gideon looked absolutely livid, eyes practically glowing in red fury as he glared at Lowell. His gray wings quivered slightly, antennae rigidly standing at attention as he did so. He quickly handed two things to you and you automatically took them, glancing up to see that one was an umbrella, which he had been holding over your head, and the other was a steaming cup of what you suspected to be tea.

"What do you think you are doing?" he demanded, taking a step towards Lowell once his hands were free. Lowell, surprisingly, retreated in response.

Though Lowell was all muscle and seemed to have the body proportions of a refrigerator, there was something terrifyingly efficient about Gideon's taller, lither form. You recalled having been worried for his own safety in the maze, scared that he wouldn't be able to hold his own against a werewolf, but seeing him now with his wings puffed out and his fingertips looking much sharper than you remembered, it dawned on you that he was very much a predator in his own right.

"Er—" Lowell raised his arms up, two palms facing outwards as if in surrender. "We were just talking!"

"Bullshit!" you called out, giving Lowell a glower of your own as you felt much more emboldened by the safety of Gideon's presence. Gideon glanced back at you as you shook the umbrella angrily. "This guy can't take a hint!"

"I didn't realize she was still dating ya, bro, I swear!" he exclaimed, giving you a pleading look over Gideon's shoulder. You scoffed at this.

"I literally just told you I was on my way to his office!"

"Office?" He frowned, shaking his head. "Ya didn't say nothin' about an office. Wait." It was nearly comical how you could practically see the steam coming out of his ears as his mind struggled to whir into action. "You're dating a professor?"

"Yes, is that a problem?" you retorted, patience wearing thin. You shuffled forward, thrusting Gideon's tea and umbrella back at him. Having every intention of now fully committing to Option B as originally planned, you moved to roll your sleeves up. Gideon, who appeared to sense your aim, shoved the umbrella back at you and threw an arm around your waist to tug you closer to his side.

"Come on, he's way too old for ya, then!" Lowell protested, making you wonder just how deep the stupidity went. He motioned toward you, but you felt Gideon's chest rumble as he practically growled at him, stilling him instantly. "Let's grab coffee, my treat!"

"She does not like *coffee*," Gideon snapped, holding you back again when you made to lunge forward with a forceful *Yeah!*

Sliding his arm across your lower back to clasp your hand in his, he gave Lowell a look so icy that your own blood nearly froze over. "If you ever so much as look at her again — no, if you so much as *breathe* in her presence again without her permission, I fully intend on hunting you down and doing with you whatever she deems fit." Then, his lips twitched into a cruel smirk. "Based on her current sentiment towards you, I have reason to believe you will be pleading for much more than a simple coffee date"—he tilted his head almost innocently, one antenna quirking as he did so—"and who would I be to deny her every desire?"

If your blood had frozen at his earlier countenance, that last statement had practically shocked it into a boil as you felt him tugging you along, his umbrella clasped dumbly in one of your hands as he led you away from Lowell's sputtering form. Everything else forgotten, you hyper-focused on his words, wondering just how much of a lie they were.

Was that really just an act for your benefit, or could this reverie have the chance to be *real*?

You were so caught up in your musings that you didn't realize he had somehow brought you to his office until you found yourself sitting in a plush leather chair, umbrella no longer in your grasp. Gaping slightly, you took in the familiar surroundings of his tidy shelves and books and empty teacups, flushing in embarrassment at the way you had completely spaced out.

He looked unaffected by this, simply holding a hand out to you. You stared at it for a moment before his eyes flitted pointedly to your thin jacket, which was dampened from the rain. Your mouth opened slightly in understanding as you shimmied to remove it and held it out to him. He deftly placed it on the coat rack by his door, removing his own dry one. Stepping forward, he bent to drape it around your shoulders, the faint scent of Earl Gray and leather flittering around you before dissipating as the expensive fabric settled.

Then, he strode towards his desk. Picking up his paper cup, he turned to face you and leaned against the desk's wooden surface, one ankle crossing over the other. He took a measured sip.

You simply stared.

The only sounds in the otherwise quiet space were the ticking of the ancient grandfather clock in the corner of the room, the rain gently splattering against the circular window, and your own breathing as you continued to watch each other without speaking. He took shallow, regular sips, as if timing himself down to the second, while you did your best not to fidget, gripping at the lapels of his peacoat to draw the material in tighter.

Attempting to divert your attention, you fixated on the feel of the fabric. The outer cloth was slightly scratchy, most likely some kind of wool blend, while the inside was lined in satin. You immediately recognized it as being the one he had worn to your apartment last week, the image of it draped over the chair in your living room burned into your brain. That also reminded you that you still had his scarf, having procrastinated on returning it to him, despite the fact that you had seen him multiple times since recovering from your little cold.

You thought of how caring he had been with you while you were sick, similar to how he had acted when he had just draped the coat around you moments ago. This only made you more confused, because now he was acting like he didn't have a care in the world, just as he had acted right after your kiss.

Oh, your *kiss*.

Feeling your cheeks heat again, you swallowed a squeal, this train of thought very much not helping you out when it came to occupying your mind with other things. It was one thing to obsess about it in the comfort of your own home, but to do so in his presence felt absolutely taboo.

Don't think of the kiss, you chanted to yourself. Don't think of the kiss. Don't think of the kiss. Don't think of the—

You suddenly sneezed and he was somehow much closer to you than seemed physically possible when it came to closing the short distance, holding out a pristine white handkerchief. Hesitantly, you took it, catching the monogram 'GDM' in shiny crimson embroidery in one corner as you dabbed at your nose and sniffled morosely.

He sighed. "What are we going to do with you?"

You felt your eye twitch at this. Oh, so he wanted to *care* again?

You weren't sure how much more of this weird *hot-then-cold-then-hot-then-cold-then-UGH, whatever!* behavior of his you could take. He reminded you of the pendulum on his grandfather clock, swinging back and forth between moods, while you for some reason felt the need to continue to chase him to and fro, never quite able to catch up before his temper shifted again.

You knew you should just cut him off at this point; it wasn't healthy for you to continue to pine for a man who would never give you the time of day, but the human part of you wanted some kind of closure. Or at least an explanation. It would have been so much easier if he just stayed with the persona that clearly completely loathed you.

What made it so difficult to walk away was when he was feigning concern, just as he was now, bending over again to feel your forehead.

"What is *wrong* with you?" you suddenly exploded, his coat sliding down your back as you let go of it to bat his hand away. You clenched your fists on your lap as straightened his spine.

"Whatever do you mean?" Though the question was calm, you could see the slight clench of his jaw and the subtle twitch of one of his antennae.

"Cut the bullshit, Gideon!" His eyes widened minutely at your outburst before instantly narrowing once more. "And don't go all *'language'* on me!" you quickly interjected when he opened his mouth to chastise you, completely butchering his accent when you attempted to mimic the lilt to his voice. "Stop acting like you care!"

"Of course I care," he insisted, frowning at you. "You are my—"

"Your *what?*" you snapped, interrupting him again. "Your student? Your assistant?" You shook your head. "Is that all I am to you? After we—"

"After we *what?*" It was his turn to cut in, voice dropping lower. His tone reminded you of the chilly one he had adopted when speaking to Lowell, a touch of ruthlessness to it. "What, exactly, did we do?"

"Stop with that melodramatic bullshit!" you snarked. "Is that from your moth half, or your *fae* half?"

"How did you know I am part fae?" He seemed surprised at your inquiry, the tips of his wings fluttering slightly as he bristled.

"I am *observant*," you returned in the same dry tone he had used when he had once told you he was literate. "Stop trying to change the subject. You know exactly what we did!"

"Use your words, then, harpy," he said, spreading his arms wide as if in invitation.

With a frustrated snarl, you stood up, poking at his chest with your index finger. "Damn it, you asshole!"

"Language."

"I don't give a fuck!" You huffed, giving him another jab. "We kissed, remember? Or do you not, after all?" You scowled, fighting the urge to rip your hair out. "This is all so stupid! Ugh, of course you don't remember—"

"*You* were the one who said we should not have done that," he reminded you, and it took you a second to recall that you had, in fact, said those very words. Your mouth snapped shut as you blinked at him. "Clearly, I would have been holding you back from your various conquests."

"W-Wait a minute!" you spluttered, pulling back to wave your hands around in protest. "What do you mean 'conquests?' They were just innocent dates!" You glared at him. "I shouldn't have to defend myself, anyway! I can go on as many dates as I want!"

"I was not accusing you." He shrugged nonchalantly, but you still noted the tension in his jaw. "It is none of my business who you choose to cavort with."

"Damn straight!" you exclaimed, practically snorting at this. "None of it mattered, anyway! Obviously you see how it went with Lowell." His eyes seemed to darken at the mention of the werewolf. "I've been so distracted lately that I had thought it would be a good idea to put myself out there..."

"And I became part of your failed experiment, it seems," he stated dryly, causing you to wince at his tone.

You gawked at his misinterpretation, wondering how the hell you ended up in these situations. Screw business, maybe you needed to pick up an extra communications class or something.

"No!" Wringing your hands together, you chewed on the inside of your cheek in distress. "There was no experiment and you certainly weren't part of it! I don't—I *can't*..." You trailed off, struggling to find the words. Then, you said almost helplessly, "None of them are right for me."

He stiffened at your admission. A strange look crossed his face, mouth contorting ever so slightly before he pursed it into a thin line. "Because they are not human?"

You gaped at him, heart stuttering into overdrive right before you decided to cut your losses and throw caution to the wind. "No, you absolute prick," you hissed, stabbing his chest with your finger again, "because they're not *you*!"

Not quite sure what you had just done, your every instinct told you to flee the premises as you turned to run out the door, but he seemingly had other plans. He finally gripped your wrist to wrench you back to him, your body thudding against him as he wrapped his other around your waist.

Gone was the facade of indifference from before; the look he gave you now promised destruction, as if he wanted to sear you from the inside out with your stuttering heart boiling within your chest, and you found yourself craving the burn. He looked like desired to destroy you; to shatter you into a million tiny pieces, and you would let him if only for the thrill of having him pick them back up again.

He gave you one last calculating glance, as if daring you to break away, but you held your ground, slightly tilting your chin up haughtily. When he finally swooped to claim your lips, it was all iron and teeth, your fingers greedily grasping to find purchase in his once-immaculate shirt as you hungrily took everything he offered. There was no doubt that his shirt would be thoroughly wrinkled and you errantly wondered if he would be cross with you.

Almost more excited by the prospect of his ire, you nipped at his bottom lip as he had done to you under the streetlamps, a bead of crimson welling up where you'd nicked his supple ashen flesh like a bloody pomegranate seed. And when the tip of your tongue darted out to lap at it, you felt him stiffen, finally yanking himself back to look at you.

It was unfair how perfect he looked. Though his shirt was now slightly rumpled as you had suspected it would be, glasses a tad askew, his eyes blazed like the hellfire you knew he had every intention of consuming you with between the smoky tendrils of his hair.

"I should punish you for that," he uttered, tone as dark as the sooty fuzz that covered his arms. Even his wings, fluttering behind him, seemed to be a few shades deeper.

"Then do it," you challenged, moving your hands up from his chest to circle around his neck. You hiked a leg up slightly, resting it against one of his thighs.

"I do not think you know what you are asking for," he warned, but you felt one of his hands encircling your ankle. His fingertips ghosted against the skin of your calf, causing you to shiver as they tracked closer to your center. The trailing stopped when he gripped your thigh, squeezing slightly so you could feel the pinpricks of his nails on your bare skin as he pushed your skirt aside. A telltale hardness pressed into the thigh you kept between his legs, while your own core throbbed in response.

"I'm not asking anymore." You licked your lips, aching with the lingering aftertaste of him, like the most forbidden of fruit. You found you did have a taste for Earl Grey, after all. Then, you tilted your chin upwards again in resolve. "I'm demanding it."

viii: the descent

"YOU ARE A HARPY, AFTER ALL," he muttered; had you been in a lucid state of mind, you may have been offended, but all you could focus on was the heat of his hand and how you wanted it to keep moving closer, closer, closer, caressing the contours and curves of your body like an artist searching for his masterpiece within clay.

You felt completely vulnerable under the weight of his gaze as he swept the pad of his thumb in a wide arc, caressing the edge of your underwear. This made you inhale sharply, while he kept a tight fist on his control as he watched you. Everything about him was always so severe; his high cheekbones, sharp-edged jaw, perfect arch to his antennae atop his head. You wanted to soften him. You wanted to be the one to make him come undone. You wanted to see those ruby eyes flutter shut as he did so. You wanted to—

But *oh*, he was doing all those things to you instead. You somehow found the strength to grip onto him when his clever fingertips found their way under the thin fabric, yanking him downwards so you could bury your face in the juncture where his neck met his shoulders. You could have sworn you heard him hiss ever so slightly when your nose brushed the pointed tip of his ear, but you were too focused on your desire to touch him to appreciate the sound. Sliding your hand down from his neck, you moved to tug at the buckle of his belt.

"No." The word was soft, but undoubtedly a command. You stilled, pulling back to peer at him in confusion. Quicker than you could blink, he turned you around so you were facing away from him, splaying a hand across your stomach while the other snaked its way back under your skirt again. "You *demanded* punishment, remember?"

You felt him walking backwards with you, stopping when the back of his legs hit his desk. He let out an appreciative hum, nipping at your ear with his tiny fangs when you whimpered at the feeling of his fingertip teasingly circling around your core. "I meant what I said earlier, and I am a man of my word. I fully intend to indulge your desires."

Leaning backwards, he used one of his thighs as a stool of sorts, hoisting you atop of it while your legs splayed apart on either side of him. He continued his circling with his digit, like a tiger stalking around its cage, inching closer and closer to the center, more heat blooming in your abdomen with each pass. You let out a groan of frustration, tilting your head back against his chest as you panted at his ministrations.

"I can already tell how wet you are for me and I have not even been inside you yet," he murmured, dragging the tip of his slightly upturned nose down the column of your neck to stop at where it met your shoulder. He took the skin there between his sharp teeth, suckling gently before releasing. He chuckled at your moan as your eyes drifted half-shut, stopping his movements just when you felt you could become completely lost. They snapped back open at this as you feebly tried to turn your head to look at him, but you could only manage tilting it back. "Good, now that I have your attention, I have a few rules. You will listen, yes?"

You nodded earnestly, to which he gave a sly smile. He resumed, his deft fingertip finally slipping into your inner folds, continuing its steady circuit, though it seemed like he was purposely avoiding your clit.

"Use your words, harpy," he ordered gently, the same instruction he had given you moments before under entirely different circumstances. Your mind struggled to will your tongue into action as you tensed when his finger dipped even farther inside you.

"Y-Yes," you managed to stutter, tilting your head back down to rest it against his chest again. You felt it rumble beneath you as he hummed once more, seemingly pleased by your response.

"Good girl." The praise, coupled with the addition of a second finger nearly had you reduced to a puddle of a human being, but his teeth against your neck made you jolt back to attention. "Number one: you will watch your language. As much as I appreciate that smart mouth of yours"—he finally brought his thumb into the mix to rest against your clit—"there is a time and a place, and now is neither of them. Number two: you will not move. I will place you exactly where I want you, and that is where you will stay." As if to emphasize his point, the hand on your abdomen was suddenly on one of your kneecaps, pulling back to open you even more for him. "Number three: you will come first." Alright, you definitely liked the sound of that. "But only after I tell you to."

"Fuck," you whispered, not sure you would be making it out of this alive.

"Already breaking my first rule, I see," he said with a dramatic sigh, "I suppose you will have to atone for it, then."

You couldn't find the means to ask what that meant as you growled in frustration when he pulled his hands away from you. Almost sensing your protest, he nipped at your jugular to still you. You felt him leaning backwards as you remained splayed open on his lap and heard the soft rumble of a drawer opening before the warmth of his chest was once more at your back.

When his arms encircled you again, you saw he was holding a glass file in one of his hands. You squirmed a bit, only for his other hand to clamp on your knee, firmly opening your legs even wider across his thigh. He hummed nonchalantly, letting go of your flesh to bring the file to the tips of his claws and slowly drag the file over his nails.

You were soaked, basically spread as far as you could go while creating a wet spot on the expensive fabric of his pants… and the man was giving himself a manicure?

"Easy, harpy," he warned preemptively, his breath warm as it fanned the shell of your ear. His chin rested on your shoulder as he worked, pulling the file in curved, methodological strokes rather than jerky sawing motions. He did so with purpose, maddeningly slow as you fought to keep your legs kept open for him. "This is for your own good, you know."

Rather than the distraction allowing you to calm yourself, it only made you chew your cheeks in anticipation, your eyes following the sweep of his motion. The subtle texture of his tweed pants under your overly-sensitive skin felt like sandpaper as you watched him finish with his index finger, only to move to his middle, stilling after the nail there was filed down too. He hummed again as if in thought and you nearly wept in agony when he continued with the rest of the fingers on his hand. You practically heard the smirk in his voice when he mused, "Better do all of them, just to be on the safe side."

This was where you died, you thought to yourself, expiring due to sexual frustration while your professor merrily did his nails.

After finishing one hand, he switched to the other, carefully placing the file down and holding his hands next to each other to make sure his claws, now much shorter and blunter than they had been, were perfectly even. You fought with yourself when he procured a cloth from somewhere and carefully wiped the dust from under his fingertips with scrutinizing precision, wanting to verbally tear him a new one, but unsure as to if that would just cause him to delay more out of spite.

You closed your eyes and tried to count to ten to ground yourself, still resisting the urge to take matters into your own hands and seek your own pleasure against his thigh only to half-sag in relief when the warmth of two fingers returned, finally fully dipped into your wet heat easily with no resistance. Your eyes snapped open as his thumb worked tiny, languid circles around your clit as his index and middle fingers pumped slowly. His pace was maddening, keeping the pressure building within you at a dull roar as he took his time with you. The hand holding your jaw dropped to your stomach once more, dancing across your flushed flesh as if you were an instrument he was about to compose his fugue on.

"P-Please," you begged, wanting — needing — more from him, greedy as you were. You felt him smile against your neck.

"Well, since you asked so *nicely*."

A third finger was added, working its way into you to join the others. He alternated between pumping and twisting now, every so often making a beckoning motion towards your front that made you swear you could see the constellations he often waxed so poetic about, all the while teasing your little nub with the tip of his thumb. Even after filing his nails down more, he was careful about the remaining slight sharpness of his digits, positioning them so that he wouldn't puncture you, the tips leaving a pleasant scratching sensation to an itch you never knew you had.

He slowed to a near stop, the change in his motion nearly causing you to launch yourself onto the floor in frustration. A whimper left your lips, hissed between clenched teeth. An antenna twitched at the noise as he pumped more lazily now, curving his fingers as if searching for something. When the hard press of his fingertips hooked against a particularly sensitive area just under your belly button, you let out a barely muffled cry, your thighs quaking.

"So sensitive," he murmured appreciatively, thrusting his fingers shallowly before purposely hooking them again. You let out another keening whine as he stilled, pressing into that spot again with more pressure. "Squeeze."

Huh? You could only focus on the constant warmth of his fingers fitting perfectly curved so deep within you, as if they had carved out a special spot of your flesh only he knew how to find. When he repeated the word again, you finally understood its meaning; understood what he was asking of you.

You struggled to regain control of your body, weakly clenching around him. You had to hold your breath in the effort as you were feebly unable to hold your squeeze.

"You can do better than that," he admonished wickedly, pressing those maddening fingers even harder. His touch was bordering on pain, though part of you almost wanted him to follow through — to make your vision burst white in a shower of stinging sparks.

Your breath came out in pants, disappointed in yourself and wanting so *desperately* to please him. Sucking in some more air, you held it, straining to clench him once again and holding it. He hummed his approval, the unspoken praise like champagne bubbles fizzing straight to your head as he resumed his previous pace once more.

He played you like a harp, a tightening feeling in your abdomen winding more and more taut under his skillful hand. But just as you were about to reach the swell of a crescendo, feeling your walls beginning to flutter around him, he completely stopped. You would have protested if not for another impossibly quick shift in positions leaving your mind spinning as you looked up at him, realizing he had somehow placed you back on the surface of his desk while your legs dangled off of it.

The sheen you left on his fingertips was enough to make you blush as you watched him bring those three digits into the light, smirking wickedly down at you as he asked, "Are you enjoying your punishment?"

You merely nodded dumbly as you rested against your elbows, flushing more at the sight of him bringing his fingers to his plush lips, parting them slightly. A long tongue darted out, uncurling to wrap around them as he tasted them — tasted *you* — and you were fascinated at the display. That tongue had been in your mouth; you remembered the feeling of it twisting against your own, but you hadn't been able to appreciate the look of it then. It was a dusky purple, a bit thinner than a human's and clearly *much* longer.

"Normally I do not make it a point to play with my food before I eat it," he stated, his voice causing you to look up from his mouth to his glowing eyes, "but I could not help it before I devour you."

Positioning himself closer between your legs, he lifted your ankles, quickly removing your flats from your feet. Then, he reached forward, lifting you by the hips so he could shimmy your underwear down your legs. Folding the dampened cloth with exaggerated slowness, he winked at your glower, placing it neatly on a nearby leather chair. He grasped at your ankles again, hosting them upwards to rest your heels against the edge of his desk. Leaning forward, he placed a kiss to your inner thigh as he pushed the fabric of your skirt upwards so it pooled around your waist.

"Gideon," you began, not sure what else to say or what else to beg. He looked up at you, tendrils of hair teasing the delicate skin of where you were splayed open for him.

"I like the sound of that," he admitted, voice a bit husky as his tongue darted out once more to lick at his mouth. "My name on your lips." You shivered at this, causing one of his lips to twitch. "Just as I would like the taste of you on mine, straight from the source. May I?"

Leave it to him to be polite. You started to nod, but remembered how he had liked you to use your words, instead giving him a curt, "Yes, please."

He ducked his head once more and wound his fingers around your ankles, grin apparent on his lips as he bumped your clit with the tip of his nose before gently taking it between his teeth. The tips of his antennae brushed against your clothed stomach as he did so. He then hummed, the action sending reverberations straight through the sensitive little nub to join where the rest of the liquid heat was pooling once more within your lower abdomen.

Then, abruptly, he removed himself from you.

You could have cried at the loss of contact, but he merely

removed his hands from your ankles, reaching out to gently push you backwards so that your back was flush against his desk. Reaching behind his head, he undid the little leather strip that held his hair in a bun at the nape of his neck, the sooty tendrils falling around his shoulders as he carded his other hand through them. Then, he gripped at your wrists, maneuvering them so that they were crossed over your head atop his desk, using the piece of leather to tie them together.

"Rule two," was all he said, tightening the knot pointedly before resuming his previous actions. You had to think absurdly hard to remember what he was even talking about. Oh, yeah, you weren't supposed to move.

That was easier said than done when he was sucking at your clit again, causing you to swallow an abrupt gasp. You chewed on the inside of your cheek as you tried to ground yourself with the feeling of his pointed nails digging shallowly into the skin of your ankles, but when you felt his long tongue curl around the nub and *pull* ever so slightly, you couldn't help the low moan that escaped you. He immediately paused, tongue retracting from your clit to look up at you.

"A bit uncharacteristically quiet, are we?" he asked playfully, nipping at your inner thigh again. Despite the situation, you still blushed.

"Shut up!" you snapped, lifting your head to give him a glare for good measure. He chuckled, tilting his head up to drag his tongue slowly from near your kneecap and down your inner thigh back to your clit as you gave another sharp intake of breath. "You're such an" —you had every intention of berating him for being so infuriating when his tongue wrapped around you again, giving you a much firmer tug that caused your head to fall back again with a moan—"*oh!*"

"*That* is more like it," he pulled away to mumble and you had to fight with the urge to clobber him so you wouldn't move your wrists. When he made another humming sound, you couldn't help but whimper, telling yourself that if he did this more often, he would have every right to be as aggravating as he was with you.

Sucking at your clit gently while his tongue worried its way around it, he gave one last draw before you felt the tip of it curl against your entrance. You immediately stiffened at the sensation as it slowly entered, circling around your inner walls as it did so. You had never felt something like this before; it was as if he were trying to taste every part of you on the way in, swirling like water down a drain as it unfurled within you.

While Gideon's tongue wasn't thick by any means, it well made up for its lack of girth in its length and dexterity, curling and uncurling as it pumped inside of you. It left you the feeling of being *almost* full as you squirmed and panted with the effort of not moving your wrists. You wanted to grab at him and wind your fingers through his hair and tug him closer, *deeper* into you.

"Gideon!" you cried out again, tears practically pooling in the corners of your eyes when one of his hands left your ankles so his thumb could circle your clit again. You tense again, feeling the cord within you continue to tighten. You were so *close*.

He must have sensed this too from the way his hand on your other ankle tightened in warning as he stopped again. Pulling his tongue out of you with a soft slurping sound that would have made you squeak in embarrassment if you weren't so worked up, he let go of your ankle so two of his fingers could replace it as it curled and disappeared back behind his lips. He had two hands on you now; one still teasing your clit, the other pumping into you cruelly as he frowned at you.

"Rule three, remember, darling?" he mocked, giving a particularly brutal thrust of his fingers. You groaned, unable to stop yourself from surging forward to grasp at one of his forearms. Forgetting all about the leather that he had tied around your wrists, you heard it snap, flinging off somewhere into the room as your fingers curled around his skin.

"Oh, dear, that was my favorite one," he pouted, stilling in his movements. You must have looked like a mess with the way he looked at you almost sympathetically, eyes glossy with unshed tears while your face flushed with the effort.

"Please, Gideon," you pleaded, letting go of him and falling back with a swallowed curse when he thrusted and *twisted* at the same time.

"Very well," he said, bending again. He curled his fingers in a beckoning motion, pressing against a particular spot that had you keening. "But only if you ask nicely again."

"Please," you pleaded, dangerously close to babbling, "can I—"

"*May* I," he corrected with another devilish curl of his fingers. You closed your eyes, swallowing thickly to try and remember what to say.

"May I please come?" you finally managed to say, opening them again. You saw that his own eyes, intently trained on you, weren't *just* red. There were an abundance of brilliant flickers within them like you had just tapped into a plethora of ores; coppers, golds ran under their surface, and even deeper yet, lay the rich veins of rubies and garnets and beryls. With all of this, you were the fly caught in amber, and while you felt your hair plastered against the dampness of your forehead, you knew the rain was now not to blame.

"What is my name?" he asked, pressing his thumb a bit harder into your clit. "Say it."

"*Gideon*," you hissed, watching him duck closer to you again.

You felt his breath fan across you as he said, "Good girl. Now string the whole phrase together."

Replacing his thumb with his mouth, his tongue curled around your clit once more as he sucked it into his mouth. You could have sobbed at the sensation, but as determined as you were, you forced your brain to do its job.

"May I p-please come, Gideon?" you asked breathily, to which he hummed in what you considered his approval. He added a third finger again just as you gasped, feeling that cord tightening and tightening and tightening. The pressure grew almost unbearable as you felt the heat flare, and just as you thought you may never reach the peak as you climbed and climbed and climbed, another curl and twist of his fingers combined with his tongue tugging at your clit made the string within you snap.

He quickly removed his fingers from you, but you didn't have time to bemoan their absence as his tongue immediately delved in, coaxing you through the crest of your orgasm. He kept one hand on your clit, teasing it between his fingers as he lapped at you, tongue resuming its curling and uncurling motion within you. Your hands moved as if on their own accord from where you had been grasping at his arm to weave through his hair, gently scratching his skull while doing your best to be careful of his antennae as you mewled for him.

He faltered slightly at this, but didn't cease his movements, the resulting rumble seeming more approving than reprimanding as he slowly brought you down from your high. Your knees were shaking now as you realized you had somehow managed to keep your ankles locked in place despite the fact that his grip was no longer on them, your toes curled over the side of his desk in your release.

When you finally felt completely spent, twitching every now and then in the wake of your orgasm, he slowly withdrew his tongue from you, but not before giving you one last lewd lick. He straightened, grinning at your bewildered expression as his tongue darted out to clean his fingertips and his lips.

"Oh," you managed to say after a beat, chest still heaving as you tried to catch your breath. You should have been tired, but the slightly lavender flush to his cheeks once again had you wanting more.

Now that you had acquired a single taste for him, would you ever have enough?

"Yes, *oh*," he mimicked, reaching down to place one arm under you to snake across your lower back, the other supporting the back of your head as he gently lifted you into a sitting position. He brushed his lips across your sweaty forehead. Your eyes drifted shut.

"That was—"

"Was?" Your eyes opened again at the amusement in his voice. Removing one hand from the back of your head, he brought his thumb to your lower lip, pressing the sharp tip of his nail into it, not enough to break the skin, but enough to make you wish that he would. "*Was* would suggest that we are finished."

Your heart stuttered in excitement as he loosened his tie with his other hand, pulling it through the loop of his collar. Removing his thumb from your lip, he made another show of rolling it up gently, placing it on top of where he had put your underwear. Then, he removed his glasses and you were more in wonder of how they hadn't fogged up with his ministrations than how he intended to see without them. When he moved to finally unbutton his shirt, you reached out to stop him, wanting to do that part yourself.

"Allow me," you offered, though the dolt in you still managed to fumble with the first two buttons as he laughed. You pouted at him, tugging at his shirt probably a bit harsher than necessary. "So, we're not done, I guess?"

"Oh, no," he said, fingertips resting at the hem of your own shirt. You fought a grin, but it quickly faded when you saw the wicked gleam in his eyes. His wings shimmered various shades of magentas and olives as they twitched behind him, as if sharing in your anticipation. "We have only started the descent. Your punishment is just beginning."

ix: the second circle

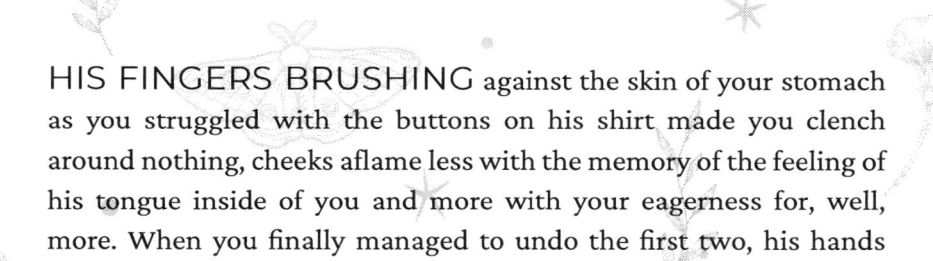

HIS FINGERS BRUSHING against the skin of your stomach as you struggled with the buttons on his shirt made you clench around nothing, cheeks aflame less with the memory of the feeling of his tongue inside of you and more with your eagerness for, well, more. When you finally managed to undo the first two, his hands were suddenly on yours, stopping you.

"I feel a bit foolish for not bringing this up earlier," he admitted, reaching out to tuck a strand of hand behind your ear, "but we need to discuss protection..."

"Oh!" You felt a bit sheepish, wondering if he thought you threw yourself at every half-cryptid with wings and antennae that looked your way. "I'm on the pill!" you blurted, smiling bashfully at your sudden outburst. "And I'm STI-free, if that's also what you're asking?"

"Wonderful," he said, leaning forward to brush his lips against your hairline. "As am I. STI-free, I mean. Although..." He looked thoughtful for a moment. "I suppose you could say I am on my own form of birth control. Fae have the ability to choose when they want to be fertile. We are also immune to most human infections." He shrugged. "One perk from that accursed side of my family, I suppose."

You noticed the way his lips seemed to twitch down at the mention of his fae ancestry, but didn't comment any further as he continued, "I just wanted to be certain you were fully certain of this. I trust you, of course, but needed to ensure you had my full transparency."

"Gideon," you began playfully, gripping the lapels of his shirt to yank him closer to you, "is this the part where you try to scare me off and warn me that I'm making a mistake?"

You leaned into his palm when he slid the hand near your ear down to cup at your jawline, sweeping his thumb across your skin to rest against your jugular. "On the contrary, little harpy, I believe you may be past the point of being scared off," he responded. "Rather, you are the sort who enjoys a challenge, and I intend to give you one."

Using his index and middle fingers, he slowly trailed his hand from your jaw down the front of your shirt. Your breath hitched when he moved between the valley of your breasts, abdomen twitching as he grazed your bellybutton. When he reached the waistband of your skirt, the hem still pooled around your hips, your legs spread slightly on their own volition, as if no longer connected to your brain.

A single antenna twitched at this as he smirked, one tiny fang peeking out from his lips. Apparently getting the hint, his hand returned to its previous position that had you reeling before, his thumb pressed to your clit while two of his fingers dipped inside you.

"Still so ready for me," he mused, spreading his fingers in a scissoring motion. You reached out to grip at his arm again, brow furrowing at the pleasant jolt the action sent through you. "I will admit, I did not imagine the events of my day would unfold like this. I had meant to quickly pick up some tea on the way to my office, but a certain harpy got in the way of things…"

You knew he was speaking, but you couldn't bring yourself to expend the additional energy to actually process his words, your brain too focused on the way he had added a twisting and beckoning gesture to his motion. Each circle of his thumb around your clit felt like the crank of the wheel that cord within you was wrapped around as it began to be pulled taut once more.

Then he stopped and you could have reached over to grab his discarded tie to throttle him with it.

"Now let's get back to it, shall we? My routine was interrupted earlier." His tone was chastising as he looked at you impassively, as if his fingers weren't currently buried in your cunt while you mentally cursed at him to move again. "So now you will sit here while we get some work done."

"*Work?*" you repeated, tongue feeling too large in your mouth. That wasn't what you had in mind. You let out an audible whine, dropping your hands back to the desk. "But it's my day off!" You purposely clenched around him, but stopped when his thumb pressed into your clit in warning.

"You demanded punishment," he said simply, "I am simply complying."

You glared as he removed his hand from you, nonchalantly reaching into his pocket for a handkerchief. He considered it for a second, eyes sliding to his fingers before he pocketed it again, instead choosing to clean them with his tongue. He locked eyes with you as he did so and you silently fumed, jealous of the treatment they were getting.

That should have been *you*.

As he casually moved around the room to collect some of his ancient texts without seemingly a care in the world, your glare turned into more of a gape as you were left confused. How the hell had you gone from being splayed across his desk so deliciously to sitting on top of it with your legs spread while he refused to touch you? What was the purpose of him asking about protection if his ultimate intention was to use you as a dripping paperweight?

"Come here."

You must have spaced out because he was no longer traipsing around his office, but was now behind you. Looking over your shoulder, you saw that he was seated in the large leather chair behind his desk, mindful of not crushing the wings behind him. You noted the books spread across his desk near where your palms were resting on its surface.

With a scowl, you hopped off his desk, doing your best to straighten your more-than-rumpled appearance as you stalked over to him. You stood in front of him, arms folded over your chest, nearly falling over in surprise when he said, "Remove your skirt."

You recognized it as an order, but tilted your head at him. "I—I thought you said you wanted to work?"

"We *are* working," he insisted. "I have selected the works we will be going over. You will read to me while you sit."

"What the actual fuck, Gideon?" you muttered, uncaring of the way his antennae quirked at your use of profanity. You leaned against the edge of his desk, waving a hand in the air dismissively as you rolled your eyes. "Yeah, yeah. Rule three, or whatever."

"That was rule *one*," he corrected, looking not at all pleased. "Now, will you be a good girl and come and sit for me?"

You wanted to snip at him and ask 'or what,' but when his hands purposely moved to unclasp his belt buckle, you suddenly understood that he may have had a much different idea of *sitting* than you had originally interpreted. Watching as he then undid the top button and slowly eased the zipper down, he slid the expensive material down just enough to reveal the cause of the slight bulge you had felt earlier.

Though you weren't sure exactly what you were expecting, you also weren't sure what surprised you more: the fact that Gideon apparently liked to walk around *commando*, or the fact that he possessed some kind of slit that his cock was tucked away in. Your eyes widened in fascination at the latter, eyes glued to how it sprang to life, no longer hindered by the fabric.

Despite your fascination with him, you clearly hadn't done your research of half-mothman anatomy, and you certainly had never seen anything like this before. A bit of a darker gray than the rest of him, his cock flushed lilac towards the tip. Curving slightly forward, it looked disproportionately long and when he brought his hand closer to guide it through his zipper, you could see that even his fingers, which were much longer than yours, didn't quite close over its full girth.

You hadn't realized you were biting your lip at the whole display until a pang of pain shot through it, causing you to release a shaky breath. Stepping forward to get a better look, you noted the way it was slightly feathered at tip with small, pointed ridges patterned throughout its length. You reached out, quickly meeting his eyes for approval, hiding a grin of excitement when he gave you a curt nod.

When your hand replaced his, his cock jumped in your hand, though he made no noise. You found that the ridges weren't sharp at all, but instead had more of a cartilage feel to them, giving way to your fingers. It was covered in short, dense fuzz, so fine that you couldn't see it earlier; it felt like satin and as you swept your thumb over the tip, you collected a bead of pre-come that welled there. You were mesmerized to discover it had almost a pearly sheen to it; pinks and ceruleans and lavenders swirling around in its opalescence.

You wanted to sample it —to see if it tasted like the rest of him, all bergamots and citruses and leather and floral, but as you pulled from him to do so, he grabbed at your wrist. Seemingly still able to read your mind, he said one word. "Later."

"I'll be good," you managed to say after a beat, the warmth pooling in your abdomen beginning to simmer at the feel of him alone.

"That is what I like to hear," he murmured, gently pulling you closer to him. "Do you trust me?" When you nodded, he let out a pleased hum. "Good. Now, turn around and do what I asked you earlier."

It took you a second to remember just what he was referring to before you quickly complied, swiveling to face his desk and shimmying your skirt down your legs. You were tempted to kick it off into oblivion, but thinking of the look of disapproval he would undoubtedly give you, you instead folded it carefully, placing it off to the side. You hoped that would earn you a few brownie points.

Which you could then cash in for... *things.*

You jumped slightly when his hands were at your hips, sharp points of his fingertips leaving shallow indentations in your skin as he guided you backwards. And when you felt the tip of him nudge against your entrance, you practically moaned at the sheer anticipation alone.

You let him guide you, pulling your strings like a master puppeteer as he eased your legs open, the head of his cock teasingly spreading you apart. He lowered you down slowly, as if afraid he would break you; from how impossibly girthy even just the *beginning* of it felt, this may have been a completely valid fear, but your last coherent thought was how much you *wanted* him to shatter you.

"You are doing so well," he crooned. "So warm." You felt the tip of his antennae tickle your ear as he moved your hair out of the way. He bent to press a kiss to your shoulder, one thumb reaching forward to circle your clit once again as his other hand continued to act as a lead. Your head tilted backwards to rest against his chest, each little ridge acting like markers to show how far he was sinking into you as you panted, wondering how much longer it would be until your head was completely under water.

"Breathe," he had to remind you as you finally bottomed out, fuller than you could have ever dreamed of, his thumb ceasing its circling. Your resulting intake of breath was somewhere between a high keen and a stuttering gasp as he gently pushed you forward to hunch over the top of his desk.

From this angle, you could feel a slight bulge of him in your lower stomach. He pressed his palm against it, rubbing at your skin appreciatively as your eyes nearly slipped shut, your walls fluttering around him at the pressure. Your head felt fuzzy with him and the ache, while the only indication he was as affected by this as you were was the slight flexing of his hand before it rested once again on the expanse of your thigh.

"Now," he began; you almost felt him more than you heard him, the rumble of his voice sending reverberations straight to your core as you tried not to clench too much around him, "I have prepared these texts for you…"

"*Oh,*" you breathed when he reached around you to open one of the books, the motion causing his dick to slide ever so slightly within you. The feathered tip seemed to flare with the drag, scraping down your walls in a way you never knew you needed. He was saying something to you again and you struggled to focus on the blurry words on the page opened before you.

"Same rules apply," he stated, antennae tickling your neck as he dipped to trace the shell of your ear with his nose. You shivered. "I will not repeat them. I trust you remember them."

"Y-Yes," you half-lied, quickly having learned that he wanted your voice. His chest rumbled pleasantly at your answer, shooting more vibrations up and into you.

"Good." He tapped the page in front of you and you blinked, forcing yourself back into literacy to try and make sense of the words under his fingertips. "When you finish this passage, I will allow you to come. If you stop, I stop. Understood?"

"Yes, Gideon," you responded, almost crumpling at the pad of his thumb against your sensitive nub again. You leaned heavily on your elbows, trying not to completely melt.

"Then begin."

You bit back a curse when his thumb started moving, his other hand still resting on the bulge he had created within you. Afraid your hesitance would cause him to pause, you narrowed your eyes at the page, skimming it quickly and recognizing it as one of the Homeric hymns; specifically, the passage where Demeter confronts Persephone about her time spent in the Underworld.

"S-Surely you have not tasted any food while you were below?" you began, shuddering at the way his thumb applied slightly more pressure, "Speak out and hide nothing, but l-let us both know. For if y-you have not, you shall c-come back from loathly Hades—*ah!*"

You hissed when the palm on your stomach snaked under your shirt to rest on your breast, feeling the prick of his fingertips on your nipple. When he rolled it between them, you paused, another jolt sizzling all the way down to pool in your core. He immediately stilled, causing you to choke back a sob.

"You were doing a lovely job." You heard the frown in his voice as you whimpered, blinking rapidly to try and refocus on where you were.

"...F-From loathly H-Hades," you continued, fists clenched atop his desk in determination, "and l-live with me and your father, the dark-clouded Son of Cronos and b-be honored by all the deathless gods." You tried to ground yourself by focusing on the way his zipper was cutting harshly into the swell of your ass as he resumed his ministrations, coupled with the strain of him seated within you. "B-But if you have t-tasted food, you must go back a-again beneath the secret p-places of the earth, there to dwell a third part of the seasons e-every—*hah*—year: yet for the t-two parts you shall be with m-me and the other deathless—*oh, gods!*"

You were on quite the roll when he suddenly decided to give a shallow thrust, every single word flying from the page as you were forced to grip the edge of his desk to keep yourself from fraying. The drag of him was almost painful in its overstimulation, the flare of his cock and those ridges hitting all the parts within you that you never knew *existed*.

Needing more of the addicting friction, you scrambled to find your place again, picking up where you left off before he could still to reprimand you, "B-But when the earth shall bloom with the fragrant flowers of s-spring in every kind, then from the realm of d-darkness and gloom—*mmf*—thou s-shalt come up once more to be a wonder for gods and m-mortal men."

"You are so *close*," he breathed into your ear, and while he may have been referring to the passage, you both knew he words rang true in more ways than one.

You sucked in a sharp breath before tears were in your eyes. You bent forward at a harsher thrust, the head of his cock creating a suction-like effect in the abrupt movement. "Gideon, please! I—I *can't.*"

You waited for him to mock you as he stilled; you waited to hear the cruelty in his voice as he reminded you that he was punishing you because *you* had asked — no, *demanded* — for it, but you were met with silence as his hands fell from you. You realized you were trembling now, arms shaking as your hands ached in the white-knuckle grip you kept at the edge of his desk. The words swam in front of you and you knew you would never be able to continue.

As if sensing this, he gently slid out of you, pulling a strangled, guttural moan from the back of your throat. Clenching your eyes shut, you felt yourself being turned around and pushed onto his desk. When you opened them again, he was hovering over you, staring down at you with the kind of hunger that your most sinful imaginations couldn't even dream of.

He brought a hand up to cup your chin, thumb sweeping up to press against your bottom lip. He tipped the claw into your teeth, beckoning for you to open for him. When you did, he slid it further into your mouth, compressing your tongue with it.

"If you cannot read, then we must occupy your mouth in other ways, hmm?" His tone was teasing, but there was a hint of darkness in it as he pressed your tongue down further, dipping his pointed nail into it in warning. The prick sent goosebumps down your arms. "*Suck.*"

It was a command. Desperation to please him took hold of you again as you carefully closed your lips around his thumb, your cheeks slightly hollowing at the suction. He smirked at you, tips of his wings fluttering as if in proud approval.

"Now, allow *me*," he intoned, thrusting back into you with a fierceness that stole your next breath. You felt your heart stop and stutter all at once, mouth dropping open around his thumb in a silent scream at the sensation. Not wanting to disappoint him, you quickly latched on again as he ground into you, leaning forward to catch the skin of your neck between his teeth as he finished the passage. "And now tell me how he rapt you away to the realm of darkness and gloom, and by what trick did the strong Host of Many *beguile* you?"

He looked every bit the god of the Underworld himself with the way his hair spilled over his shoulders like a dark curtain, his wings fanned out behind him in a canopy of solidified smoke. Scarlet eyes glowing in the shadows he created over you, he pulled back to watch your face as he thrust into you once more. You choked on another moan while you struggled to suck on his finger, feeling as though the room was beginning to boil around where he slid against you as you continued to grip onto the edge of his desk.

He was the ivy and the balm all at once, creating the itch and then soothing it with each drag of his length. He suddenly pinched your chin, which caused you to open your mouth. Voice raspy, he commanded as he withdrew his thumb, "Let me hear you."

"N-*Now* you want to h-hear me?" you were somehow able to snark, just wanting to be able to finally relish in the feel of him without having to work for it. "I—*oh*"—you sucked in a breath between your teeth when he pushed your shirt up to tug a nipple between his teeth—"I t-thought I was a *harpy*."

"You are," he replied, dragging a fang across your chest to capture your other in his mouth. You gasped, removing your hands from his desk to rest against the back of his neck. "Loud and overbearing, but I never said I disliked it. I have been itching to see how rapacious you could be and I am not disappointed." He gave another sharp thrust, making your toes curl as his ridges stuttered against you. "I have every intention to *sate your greed*."

You clenched around him in response, greedy, of course, for more. He let out the beginning of a groan, the rest of it muffled when his mouth was on yours, swallowing your own cry as he rolled your clit between his fingers. Reaching backwards with his other hand, he guided each of your legs farther around him, leaning forward to angle you more sharply.

You hissed at the new tilt and the way his teeth nibbled at your lower lip, his prehensile tongue taking the opportunity to sweep into your mouth when your lips opened in another gasp. You had thought you could feel all of him before, but the way he was bending you now gave you such an acute clarity that you could practically count every nub and ridge as they bumped within you.

The heat was almost unbearable now, completely overwhelming and all-consuming as you felt yourself about to burst into flames. Your head fell back, lips unlatching from his as you struggled to breathe again.

"G-Gideon, Gideon, *please*," you chanted, your drunken mind unable to form any other words. His chest rumbled at this as he chose to respond by thrusting harder and deeper. Removing the hand from your clit, he used both of them to hike your knees higher up on his torso, somehow spreading you even wider for him as you let out a loud, strangled cry.

"Beautiful," he said, leaning forward slightly to create even more of an angle. You cried again at this, the tip of his cock now positioned perfectly against a spot in you that made your veins hum. Your face must have betrayed this as his eyes narrowed at you, honing in on that spot and purposely hitting it on each beat, the flared head simultaneously creating a maddening sucking sensation with each pull, only to ram at it again. Snaking an arm around you, he held you to his chest as you gripped at his upper arms.

One more thrust and he said your name; not 'harpy,' but your actual name, and the crimson flames lapping at your core blazed white, your very consciousness ripping apart as the tight coil finally snapped. You felt yourself quivering around him, hearing him grunt as he picked up his pace. His thumb worked at your clit again, cresting you higher and higher over the peak of your release, only to ease you into another climb as he showed no signs of relenting.

Finally feeling yourself crash again, you felt his hips stutter, the head of his cock seeming to quiver and flare within you like an umbrella as liquid heat seeped within you at his own release. Your hair blew back slightly from your sweaty forehead at the current his wings created as they pulsed shallowly behind him.

He'd ruined you, you thought as your chest heaved, trying to breathe around the feeling of him continuing to languidly pump within you. He'd completely obliterated and shattered you for anything else, and like many fae, he seemed to like jagged, broken things with sharp edges.

Finally slowing, he eased you back onto his desk, panting slightly as he leaned over you. With a shaky arm, you reach out to tuck his sooty locks behind a delicately pointed ear. He kissed the inside of your wrist in response, removing an arm from where it had caged around you to capture the hand in his.

"How do you feel?" he asked a bit breathlessly. You smiled in smug satisfaction that despite his usually impenetrable facade, he was at least showing some signs of fatigue.

You sucked in a breath, waiting a few moments for your heartbeat to become a bit steadier before answering, "Fine." Understatement of the century, but you had to wait to suck in another breath to be able to speak again. "I-I think I ruined your shirt." You licked your lips, brows furrowing as you tried to regain control of your mind. "And maybe your pants."

He pulled back slightly to give you a bewildered look, one fang poking out from the twitch of his lips as you giggled at him. He shook his head in amusement, ducking forward to press a kiss to the corner of your mouth. You swatted playfully at his antennae, scrunching your nose when they tickled at your forehead.

"You may be the death of me yet, little moonflower," he sighed, finally moving to ease out of you. Still overly-sensitive, you flinched at the graze, relaxing again when he fully unsheathed himself.

"I thought I was a harpy?" you managed to reply tiredly as he turned away from you. You heard the sound of a zipper and of his belt buckle jingling before he was back in front of you, handkerchief back in hand. You moved to sit up to take it from him, but he shook his head at you, ignoring your proffered palm.

"That, too," he murmured as he began to clean up the mess you both had made. Despite the fact that he had literally just been buried inside of you and his tongue probably knew you much more intimately than you would ever know yourself, you still blushed at this. You jumped at the first pass of the soft material against you, feeling his palm press to your inner thigh to sooth you. "You may also make a convincing Persephone now."

"I think you're mistaken," you replied, relaxing into his touch. "I have a black thumb." You paused. "*And* if you're implying that me being Persephone makes *you* Hades, well, that and the fact that I'm not your niece."

He stilled at this, staring at you for a moment before tilting his head back to laugh, the sound full and rich and oh so warm. You couldn't help but grin at the sooty waterfall of his hair falling back over his shoulders and the way both his antennae and his wings quivered at his mirth. When he looked back at you, the flickers in his ruby eyes dancing in amusement, you couldn't help but feel that maybe there was some merit to his comparison.

Except if you were actually Persephone, you would have been smart enough to consume more than a few pomegranate seeds. But as you found yourself face-to-face with the gates of the Second Circle of Hell, still drunk on the heady smell of Earl Grey and leather and now *moonflower* — the foreign floral that you couldn't quite place earlier, but finally recognized — you couldn't help but hope there would be more opportunities to indulge.

x: beware of greeks bearing gifts

IT WAS a good thing that you had already been thoroughly prepared for your exam because you definitely hadn't done any studying, despite that having been your original plan.

By the time you both had emerged from his office, you, a bit wobbly-legged; him, as infuriatingly immaculate-looking as usual, night had fallen. He had insisted on driving you home, failing to hide a smug smirk as you practically swayed on the spot after hopping off of his desk. In the process of him escorting you to your apartment, you had discovered that in addition to fixing motorcycles, he also had a penchant for restoring vintage cars.

You had also discovered that you had no idea what the hell to make of anything.

Gideon had dropped you off with complete innocence, as if he hadn't just spent the past few hours practically rearranging your insides and having you contemplating whether or not eternal damnation was really all so bad. He had exited the car to open the passenger side for you, walked you all the way into and through your building to your apartment door, and simply bent to kiss you on the forehead before leaving with a small departing wave. You had stood staring at your then-empty hallway in utter shock for a solid five minutes before turning and promptly rounding up all your friends for an emergency group video call.

Your eardrums had ached for no less than half an hour at the squeals of Effie and Calli after you gave them a much watered-down version of what had happened, Greer going into full on dad-mode and telling them to shut up to gruffly ask if you had used protection. After your cheeks had heated and you had given him a rather vague answer that seemed to satisfy his inquiry, you had then divulged the strangeness of the whole drop-off situation. Effie and Calli had seemed to think that the whole thing was rather romantic in an old-fashioned way, while Greer had begrudgingly grumbled that at least he had seemed polite. You imagined Gideon and your friends meeting for the first time and the sullen Greer extending a solid arm to give him the handshake test.

If you would even get that far with him.

Despite the fact that none of your friends had shared your same concerns, now, almost two weeks later, it was as if everything and nothing had changed. He was being completely professional in class, which was to be expected, but he was also being pretty reserved when it was just the two of you in his office, which wasn't exactly what you had anticipated. It felt as though he had brought back that hot pink elephant in the room, all ten limbs waving to you while the Christmas lights twinkled as its neon sign swung back and forth on its tusk, except the hot pink elephant had also invited its lime green glow-in-the-dark buddy.

And now you were stuck with two imaginary elephants, one scrambled mind, and a half-moth-half-fae asshole of a professor who didn't seem to want to touch you with a ten-foot pole, despite having literally screwed his tongue so far deep within you that you had rivaled the most expensive telescopes with the amount of stars you had been able to see that day.

It did nothing to aid your cause that whenever you were in his office, you couldn't help but stare at his desk. You flushed deeply at the image of him completely ripping you apart and putting you back together again on top of it. You supposed you could have initiated a conversation about it yourself; various ways to do this cycled through your mind as you question how you could address the topic.

Maybe you could take a more direct approach: 'Hey, cool sex, right? We doing that again, or what?'

Maybe you could ease into it: 'You know what I really would enjoy? A cup of hot cocoa and your dick in my mouth.'

Maybe you could sneak it on the heels of another question: 'Could you please pass me that book and fuck me seven ways from Sunday again while you're at it?'

Despite your dramatics, it wasn't as though he completely stayed away; lingering touches here and there, a simpering gaze... maybe 'not touching you with a ten-foot' pole wasn't entirely accurate. Maybe it was more like three feet. Semantics aside, your beef with the annoying man was that even if he was giving you some kind of attention, it was nowhere near the kind you wanted. Except the more you thought about it, the more bitter you became that he could also bring it up.

The more pragmatic side of you told you that you were two rational adults and if you were the one with the problem — clearly he seemed to be of the opinion that everything was just hunky-dory — it was on you to do yourself a favor and bring it up to resolve the matter. The more insecure side of you told the pragmatic side that it could suck it, somewhat afraid that maybe you would learn that Gideon regretted the encounter, despite how eager he had been in the moment. Had you pressured him into it? Or even worse... had he just been using you to scratch a temporary itch?

Effie and Calli would remind you that if he really wasn't interested, he would be ignoring you completely. You had first-hand experience on what it felt like for him to ice you out, and while you could admit that this was definitely different, you were still confused. The only thing that was saving you from fully obsessing over it was the fact that you had a bunch of additional exams coming up in your business courses to distract you. Which was also why you were currently hunched over your coffee table when you should have been asleep hours ago, poring over a textbook in the faded yellow light of your living room as you sat on the floor to study.

You stared at the words on the page, trying to make sense of this particular case study on fraud. It described how a publicly-traded olive oil company was able to commit fraud and lie about its supply to shareholders by adding water to its tankards so that they would appear full as the oil would float to the top. Your stomach growled at this; you had skipped dinner in favor of your studies and would do unspeakable things for some pasta right now. Maybe even a nice tall glass of wine.

Unfortunately, wine reminded you of a *certain* professor's class as you had just gone over one of the three Homeric hymns about Dionysus, which led you to think about the hymn he had made you read after hours to Demeter about Hades and Persephone. This led you to remembering the feeling of being seated on his cock while he had forced you to read for him and the delicious stretch and drag of those ridges biting into your walls in the best way, your stomach bulging slightly from the forward curve of it while he—

You yelped as a shrill ringing sound jarred you from your musings, drool nearly having dripped onto the pages of your textbook as your mind clouded over with the memory. Shaking your head, you finally realized that the sound was coming from your phone, which was basically screaming at you from across your coffee table. You clumsily grasped it, almost knocking over the shitty cup of coffee you had brewed yourself to try and stay awake.

"I had a thought."

No sooner had you accepted the call than you heard the familiar voice of a certain Professor Prick coming from the other end of the line. You gaped at the device in surprise, brain still a bit sluggish as it both grappled with lack of sleep and tried to recover from the heat of your recollection.

"Huh?" His words had barely registered as you blinked, the blue light from your screen nearly blinding. "Gideon, it's"—you squinted at the tiny numbers in the top left hand corner of your cell—"nearly 3AM."

You sounded more surprised at the time, having completely lost track of it, than he was. "And?" He sounded impatient and you imagined him tapping his foot at you. Then, there was a pause. "Oh." You rubbed at your eyes, picturing his wings bristling as he let out a *harrumph* sound. "I forgot about human sleeping schedules." There was another pause, before he half-demanded, sounding rather cross now, "Why are you picking up the phone at this hour?"

"I didn't know who was calling!" you exclaimed defensively, glowering at the screen as if it were his face. "I thought it was an emergency or something!"

"It did not *sound* like you were sleeping," he muttered. You could have asked him what the hell sleeping exactly sounded like, except he was already moving onto his next question. "If you had recognized it were me, would you have still picked up?"

"We are not having this conversation right now," you grumbled, a bit snarky. You were tired and needed to finish this chapter and very much did not need your mind to lose focus by wandering back to your little escapades. "I wasn't sleeping, actually."

"But it is *'nearly 3AM,'*" he echoed, the way he said this allowing you to practically hear the air quotes. "What on earth are you doing awake?"

"Studying," you bit out, irritation rising. Between your hunger and lack of sleep and the fact that you were being distracted and cock blocked by the very cock you wanted, you were getting really cranky. "Or at least I was."

"Studying," he repeated again, sounding dumbfounded. You bit back a groan, resisting the urge to slam your forehead repeatedly against the table you were stooped over. "And do you plan on sleeping any time soon?"

"No," you retorted, the word clipped. You heard him hum, though it somehow sounded disapproving to you.

"Very well," he responded after a moment. "I will be right over."

"Fine." You flipped a page in irritation, just wanting to get back to your work. "See you soon." Then, you hung up, grumbling to yourself.

Wait, what?

You froze, another page halfway through being flipped when you finally registered what he had said and what you had said in return. Swearing under your breath, you rubbed your temples, still not sure how the fuck you got yourself into these situations. You wondered if half-praying mantises existed the same way half-moths did. You once watched a show about how females of certain praying mantis species bite the heads of their partners off during sex and briefly regretted not being one. If you had decapitated a certain Professor Prick, it would have saved you a lot of trouble.

Maybe you could ship him a crate of mothballs and it would have the same effect.

Not sure if it was worth calling him back since you knew he wasn't easily swayed once his mind was made up, you stood up to pour yourself more tepid shitty coffee in your kitchenette. You hated the stuff, only reserving it for studying binges like this, but it did the job — sort of. You were somewhat still awake, after all.

Padding back to your living room, you unlocked your front door with a sigh, figuring it would save you from having to stand up again. You folded your legs under you when you returned to your makeshift desk, lowering yourself to the floor with an ungraceful grunt as you flopped against the front of your couch. Closing your eyes briefly, you tilted your head back to let out a deep sigh before opening them to hunch over your book again.

Before long, you heard a muffled rapping at your front door. You called out that it was open, rubbing your aching temples again tiredly as you heard the click of the knob turning. Steeling yourself, you craned your neck to look at him, feeling your heart thump as you watched him close the door behind him.

He was dressed as usual, all sharp lines and pressed to perfection; crisp shirt, dark slacks, peacoat. Did this man ever dress *casually?*

Entering with his signature flourish, he quickly shrugged off his coat, draping it over the chair it had occupied the week when you had been sick. His ruby eyes lingered on the scarf — *his* scarf — that was still draped over one of your other chairs, freshly dry-cleaned and lying almost in state as you continued to procrastinate on returning it to him. One antenna twitched, but he made no comment on it as he turned to you.

Instead, he started scolding you. "It is extremely unsafe to leave your door unlocked as such at any time of day, but especially at night."

Narrowing your eyes at him, you wondered how he would react if you gave him the finger. His wings would probably flutter indignantly at that as he frowned at you, chastising you for your crude gesture. He would get really annoyed if you cursed at him. Maybe so annoyed, in fact, that he would force you to sit on his—

Damn, you really needed to stop that.

You tried to will away your impending blush, instead noticing he had apparently come bearing gifts. You spied another steaming to-go cup in one hand while there was some kind of maroon fabric draped over his other arm, a folded paper bag clutched in that hand's grip.

"What's that?" you asked, ignoring his chiding as you waved in his direction vaguely. He stepped forward, turning to walk into your kitchenette to place the paper bag on your counter before walking back to you.

"Scones and hot chocolate," he responded, bending to put the cup in front of you. Before he did so, he reached into his back pocket, pulling out a coaster — the man fucking brought his own *coaster*, apparently having learned from his week spent playing nurse that you didn't and would never own any — setting it underneath the cup on the table's surface. Then, he swiftly unfolded the material draped over his arm, draping it over your shoulders while you gawked at him.

"You brought me a blanket," you said slowly, fingers coming up to grip at the edges of the warm fabric, "and snacks?" You felt like you had just stepped into the theater of the absurd. "What bakery is even open at this hour?"

"I remembered your apartment being a tad drafty and it is getting colder." He shrugged, straightening slightly. You bemoaned at how the artificial light of your apartment did his wings no justice, the appendages seeming too dull, the usual silvery sheen flattened to a gloomy iron in this tiny space. It also cast strange shadows across his high cheekbones, making them appear much harsher. "No bakery is open, actually. I made these scones earlier today and the hot chocolate was easy enough to whip up." You continued to stare at him in silence, causing him to quirk a confused antenna at you. "Apple cinnamon. They are your favorite, are they not?"

You could only continue to gawk at him. Yes, you had definitely stepped into the theater of the absurd, and you somehow found yourself as the reigning primadonna, star of the show. You must have prattled to him at some point about that cafe that Effie liked so much; blueberry scones may have been her favorite flavor, but apple cinnamon was yours, and Gideon managed to not only *remember* that, but also bake a batch for you.

You tried not to think of how cute he might look in a frilly apron.

Finally yanking your eyes away from him, you moved your stare to the cup of hot chocolate he had set by your book. You gripped at the blanket, which felt by far like it could be the most expensive thing you currently owned, the gears in your mind grinding into motion. You couldn't help but be a bit suspicious at this; you had gone from being courteous to each other at best, to you practically jumping down his throat, to him outright ignoring you, to him giving you the best orgasms — yes, plural — in your life, to him being somewhat detached again, and now he was in your living room, at nearly 3AM, bringing you hot chocolate, scones, and blankets.

Make it make sense!

You looked back up at him, eyebrows furrowing as you did so. Maybe he was just interested in some kind of platonic friendship, after all. Sure, the sex had been mind-blowing — to you — but maybe to him it was just something that happened. You didn't know much about fae, but from what you'd heard, they could be fairly promiscuous, so perhaps to him, nearly folding you in half over his desk wasn't much to shake a stick at.

You tried not to dwell on the dull pang of hurt that went through you at the thought.

Allowing yourself to consider this briefly, you wondered if you could do platonic. You hadn't exactly started off as friends first, and although you may have had your differences, you actually enjoyed spending time with him. Your other option was to just end things and go back to being strictly whatever it was that you were with him before, but for some reason, the thought of that made your chest ache even more. You remembered debating walking away from it all when you had been sick, and it would have been much easier back then than it was now.

You heard him clear his throat politely, calling your name to get your attention. You had apparently zoned out again, doing your best impression of a sunfish as you struggled to wrap your mind around everything. Quickly rubbing at your eyes, you shook your head at yourself, patting a couch cushion by your shoulder. "Do you, uh, want to sit down, or something?"

He gave a curt nod, settling himself by you and crossing one ankle over the other in that aristocratic way of his. His posture was perfect, although you supposed it had to be in order for him not to completely crush his wings behind him. With a tilt of his head, he gazed over your shoulder at your open book, leaning forward to peer at it. You caught a whiff of Earl Grey as he did so, eyes nearly falling shut as you recalled the taste of him on your tongue.

"This is what you have been studying so feverishly about?" he asked. His surprise wasn't unkind or condescending; rather, it seemed innocent. "You seemed fully confident about this material the other day."

You remembered ranting to him about the topic the other day and half-bragging about how you had bested a cocky cervitaur in a classroom debate over it. You supposed you did seem confident, but with your scholarship always at stake, you couldn't take any chances.

With a shrug, you reached over to close your book, knowing for certain there was no use continuing with his arrival and your fatigue. You probably looked like the walking dead right now, red-rimmed eyes potentially rivaling even his. His that actually weren't behind their usual frames.

"You aren't wearing your glasses," you observed aloud, brows furrowing as you remembered that he had also taken them off before completely *devouring* you, as he had put it.

"I do not tend to wear them at night," he said simply, straightening his back again.

"Don't you need them to see?" The question sounded extremely dumb to you the second it left your mouth, but you were too tired and curious to care.

"Not exactly," he returned, the corner of his mouth quirking at you. "Things are more... muted at night. My glasses are not for distance, they are to tone down everything else." He brought a delicate hand up to his chin, pointed nails brushing against his sharp jaw as he looked thoughtful for a moment. "Moths can see ultraviolet rays. My eyes are very sensitive to light in general."

"So it's like you're basically wearing sunglasses all the time?" Another dumb question, but now you were definitely intrigued. "How are the lenses so clear? They look like regular glasses to me."

"Magic," he said, and it took you a moment to realize that he was being completely serious. "My—er—*friend*, I supposed I am calling him now, knows a witch. The one I had mentioned when you were ill."

Your eyebrows must have been shot into your hairline as you nodded, trying to let it all sink in. There was a lot to this world that you didn't know, you realized. As much as you kicked your own ass trying to keep your scholarship, you were glad that you had gone against your family's approval and cut your ties with them to move to a more diverse town. Everything was so much more exciting here. You wanted to learn more.

You wanted him to teach you.

"Huh," you said finally, mulling this information around in your brain. "The incubus?" He gave a nod at your venture, though he looked a bit hesitant in doing so. "Will I ever meet him?"

You suddenly felt shy at the question, biting the inside of your cheek after asking it. Were you being too bold to assume he might want to let you into his little bubble? But he just chuckled, waving a dismissive hand at the thought. "Gods, I hope not. More for your sake than mine." He cocked his head in consideration. "Actually, for my sake, too."

You weren't sure what to make of that response, but were just pleased that he hadn't outright blown you off. "He doesn't seem so bad," you said, trying to sound casual. "You both like fixing motorcycles and cars. You said that was something you have in common."

He nodded again, reaching out absentmindedly to brush a tendril of hair that had escaped from your braid off your shoulder. The sharp tips of his fingers ghosted against the lush material of your blanket, the gentle touch making you shiver. He frowned at this, seemingly misinterpreting the reaction as you being cold, gripping at the extra material pooling over the floor to fold over your back to create another layer.

"We do," he responded when he was finished, though he didn't completely withdraw his hands from you. Instead, he played with the end of your braid as he spoke. "It is a hobby I have had for a while. Grease. Manual labor." A smile tugged at his lips, but it had a strange hint of bitterness to it. "Everything my grandmother hates."

This was the first time that he had mentioned any kind of family to you, and as much as you wanted to ask the flurry of millions of questions that instantly flew around your head, you got the sense that this might have been a sore subject. You opened your mouth to say something only for a yawn to interrupt your train of thought. You were barely able to get a hand in front of your mouth to cover it.

"You really should sleep now," he admonished, though his tone was much gentler than it had been on the phone with you. You grumbled nonsensically in return, looking back at your closed book.

"I need to study," you insisted, reaching out to it again. His hands left your braid to close around your wrists, stopping you. You couldn't stop your peeved scowl. "Did you come here to sabotage my mission or something?"

"If ensuring you get some rest is considered *sabotage*, then yes, I suppose so." You rolled your eyes at him as you reached forward to grip at the handle of your coffee cup, grimacing as you took a sip of the bitter, now-cold liquid. His eyes trailed your every movement, more like a hawk than a moth. "What is that?"

"Coffee," you responded, your nose still scrunched at the aftertaste. You set it back on the table, instead picking up the cup of hot chocolate he had brought you. You practically sighed in contentment at its warmth seeping through to your hands.

You heard him hum in response, looking back to see his antennae quirking at you again. The tips of his wings quivered as he innocently asked, "Can I have a taste?"

"You don't like coffee," was your snide response as you arched an eyebrow at him.

He gave you a hard look, apparently not impressed by your stubbornness. "Neither do you."

"Fair, but I am the one cramming for exams." You shrugged, too tired weary to care about his sudden fascination for the drink.

Sweeping an arm towards the table, you muttered, "Knock yourself out."

Rather than *knocking himself out*, as you had told him to, he nearly knocked *you* out with your shock alone as he suddenly took your cup of hot chocolate from you and bent down to brush his lips against yours, giving an appreciative hum as he did so. You felt his tongue dart out to sweep at your mouth, darting inside when your lips parted in shock. The feeling of it curling against your own tongue sent a jolt straight down into your abdomen, causing it to clench when you remembered just how it had once furled deep within you somewhere else.

He pulled away as abruptly as he had ducked in, leaving a whimper to fizzle on your lips where the taste of bergamot and citrus crackled. A single fang poked out as he smirked, stating matter-of-factly, "I suppose I could become partial to coffee."

You didn't have time to even process this before he was placing your cup down and reaching out to pick you up, blanket and all, with surprising strength and nestle you close to his side, one of his wings folding slightly around you almost protectively. "Maybe I should read for you, then."

One long arm extended, gripping at your book to pull it onto his lap. He somehow managed to open it exactly to the page you had been staring at before you had shut it. Giving you a cheeky look, he intoned, "You read so *prettily* for me before. It is only natural that I return the favor, hmm?"

Screw your impression of a sunfish; you were now doing the world's best damn impersonation of a lead balloon hitting a power line as your brain sparked and fizzed when your neurons crossed. You were reeling now, no longer feeling like merely a star in the theater of the absurd, but a one-woman act entirely. You tried to backtrack on everything so far; how you had gone from being courteous to each other at best, to you practically jumping down his throat, to him outright ignoring you, to him giving you the best orgasms — yes, plural — in your life, to him being somewhat detached again, and now he was in your living room, at nearly 3AM, bringing you hot chocolate, scones, and blankets, kissing you and reading to you as if it were the most innocent thing in the universe.

He cleared his throat, beginning to read from your textbook. Although your mind was still recovering from your shock, your body must have been on autopilot, betraying you by burrowing into his warm side instinctively. In response, his wing curled even more around you as he extended an arm to grip at your blanket, neatly tucking it tighter around you without so much as faltering a world.

Maybe your coffee hadn't been doing its job, you thought to yourself as you felt your already struggling mind slowing to a sleepy stop. You barely registered the sensation of his shoulder pressed against your cheek as your head apparently lulled against him, the deep rumble of his lilting voice acting as a lullaby. His wings were softer than you had imagined, cocooning rather than caging you against him and enveloping you in additional warmth as he crooned on.

This man might be the death of you yet; or at least the death of your scholarship. You apparently were never able to get any studying done because of him, although you had to admit you were probably being overzealous in your efforts, anyway.

You burrowed in closer, feeling the weight of his arm joining his wing to wrap around you as he drew you in. As you felt yourself drifting off, surrounded by the cozy smell of Earl Grey and leather and moonflowers, your brain gave a last mental hypnic jerk as you realized that just as you suspected, you would never be able to walk away.

You were human.

You were greedy.

You wanted *all* of him.

It was almost a blessing that you were so spent given the overwhelming burden of your confusion. It would have been too easy for your more lucid mind to spiral, trying to connect the dots and make sense of his actions and mixed behaviors towards you. You wondered if he was just being as old-fashioned as Effie and Calli had suspected in his reservations towards you, or if this was maybe his last hurrah; his parting gift before he ripped you out of his life by the roots, as if you had been the seed that turned his world into an unweeded garden.

You didn't have much time to brood about this as the sound of his voice quickly pulled you under, dragging you deeper and deeper into the suspiciously saccharine warmth of his abyss. Maybe he wasn't the gatekeeper of the Second Circle after all, but of the Eighth, and he was about to introduce you to Geryon, the personification of fraud.

Beware of Greeks bearing gifts, the saying went. Except it wasn't Greeks that the Trojans should have been afraid of, but moths. More specifically, moths that were also half-fae with burning red eyes, silky wings, and a searing touch that reduced you to a simpering puddle of liquid explosive, only to ignite you once more with a single sweep of his skilled tongue.

xi: the sword of damocles

WHEN YOU HAD OPENED your eyes the next morning, you had fully expected to be alone with a strange crick in your neck from falling asleep at such an odd angle. Instead, you had found yourself draped comfortably across the length of your couch, head resting on a pillow Gideon had procured from somewhere and placed on his lap, one of his clawed hands rubbing soothing circles into your lower back while the other had held your textbook aloft as he had continued to read silently to himself.

Upon sensing you were awake, he had carefully extracted himself from you, setting you upright so he could heat up the scone he had baked for you previously. Then, while you had munched on it, still a bit overwhelmed at the situation and at the fact that it might've been the best damn thing you'd ever eaten, he'd peppered you with questions about the case studies in your textbook, having apparently also perused your notes for good measure. Finally satisfied with your answers, he had declared you fit for your exam, scolding you once more for your destructive studying regime and your poor sleeping habits.

Apparently, he had conveniently glossed over the fact that he had *also* forgotten about healthy human sleeping schedules since he was the one who had originally called you in the first place.

You had stared at him, watching the twitching of his antennae as his finger wagged at you. While you had felt a vein in your temple throb during his lecture, all you had wanted to do was grab him by the collar of that still somehow perfectly crisp shirt and kiss him.

You hadn't, though. Instead, your brain had once again short circuited, its momentary lapse allowing your mouth free reign. In its autonomy, it had blurted a question out of nowhere, surprising the both of you.

"Would you like to have dinner with me tonight?"

And that's why you were currently peering in your bathroom mirror, trying to get your hair to cooperate while your hands shook with nerves.

"You look ah-*may*-zing!" Effie gushed, perched cross-legged on the closed seat of your toilet. Her wings shimmered as they tittered behind her, as if to agree with her statement. You sighed, gripping the edge of your sink as you bent forward to stare at the tarnished silver drain.

You weren't sure what exactly had possessed you to ask him to dinner. Maybe it had been just the result of sleep-deprivation, or maybe it had been the desperation of you trying to cling to the vestiges of this fanciful dream. You had immediately steeled yourself for rejection when his eyes had widened slightly as he had looked every bit as taken aback as you were, but instead, the tips of his wings had twitched as he had rumbled his acceptance.

His response may have been slightly hesitant, but you tried not to think *too* much about that as you continued to primp and preen.

You were thankful Effie was your neighbor and was free, having practically flown through the window to your apartment when you had finally called an hour prior. After Gideon had left sometime after lunch following his impromptu mock exam, you had spent the rest of the afternoon grappling with whether or not you should cancel. You prided yourself on being bold when it came to matters of business, not one to back down in the classroom and always having the data to back up your strategic claims, but there was no analysis you could run in this situation to make yourself feel the slightest bit better.

Sure, you had spent a lot of alone time with him, but this was different. This was more like a *date*, at least to you, without the pretext of studying or illness or coursework to muddy the waters. You had paced back and forth, chewing at your fingertips without realizing it, a habit you thought had been forced out of you in middle school. When you had looked at their jagged edges, sighing at yet another thing you would have to fix before seeing him, you had finally managed to figure out the root of your anxiety. Now that the waters were no longer cloudy, you were afraid of what you would find once you peered into them.

You knew that clarity could sometimes be so cruel.

Gideon had insisted he knew a place in nearby Tenebra City, and although Greer and Calli hadn't been free to come over, when you had told them in your group chat that the restaurant he had mentioned was some place called *Cielo*, you could barely get a word in text-wise as they had all but blown up your phone. Greer, whose texting habits reminded you more of a gruff grandpa than a young minotaur enrolled in graduate school with his few-word answers, had suddenly seemed to come to life, composing paragraphs about the menu and food pairings. Although Calli was nowhere near the foodie Greer was, her texts practically screamed at you from how rapidly she had sent them, apparently having quickly searched all about it as she enthused about how apparently exclusive it was and how there was a waiting list to get reservations.

Gideon definitely hadn't mentioned *that*, simply instructing you to dress a little fancier than usual. Effie was doing her best to hype you up, assisting in picking out a dress with you and making suggestions on how to do your hair and makeup. Peeking at the frosty edges of your window, you knew it had definitely started growing consistently colder, but you figured you could just throw a jacket over your outfit. You also still had his scarf.

That remembrance made you tense again, knuckles going white as you gripped the edge of the porcelain harder.

"I don't know why you're so jittery!" you heard Effie call. You looked up, seeing her wings flutter in her reflection. They glittered pink, the rosy color exactly matching her eyes as she gave you a cheerful grin. "It's just dinner with your boyfriend!"

"My—" You paused, looking back down into your sink. My *boyfriend*. You rolled the word around in your mind experimentally, picturing Gideon's face along with the moniker and found that it made your heart skip a beat. With a pang, you wondered if you would ever be able to call him that as you sighed. "He's not my boyfriend, Effie."

"*Yet!*" she chittered with a giggle, ever the optimist. You didn't have the heart to contradict that statement, turning fully to see that those stars were in her eyes again as she overly-romanticized your life in that way of hers. Maybe fairies possessed some kind of gene that allowed them to be unfailingly hopeful. Maybe the tint of her eyes was truly the same one she viewed the rest of the world with.

You opened your mouth to retort, but heard your phone vibrate, the sound oddly grating against the surface of your sink. Quickly swiveling to catch it before it could teeter over the edge and clatter against the tile of your floor, you saw that the screen had lit up to show that he had texted you that he was here. Eyes widening, you turned to look back at your appearance in the mirror.

"You're perfect, you're beautiful, you look like a model," Effie babbled, waving her hands animatedly at your form. Giving her one last withering look, you heard her call, "Go get 'em, tiger!" as you quickly exited the bathroom, picking up your purse and keys in a flurry as you shrugged on your coat. Your eyes lingered on the scarf draped over your chair as you chewed the inside of your cheek, debating whether or not to take it and what he would think if he saw you wearing it.

Deciding you would rather spare yourself the lecture you knew you would get if he thought you weren't dressed adequately warm enough, you grabbed it, wrapping it around your neck as you scurried out the door.

Gideon somehow looked more formal than usual, dark gray slacks replaced with black, his peacoat open to reveal a matching blazer underneath atop his signature white button down. He was leaning against the passenger side of the same car he had driven you home in once upon a dream ago, looking up at the sky almost appreciatively.

The glossy obsidian exterior of the vintage vehicle looked flat in comparison to the gleam of his wings. They almost seemed to wink at you as you bounded down the front steps leading into your apartment building, your shoes clattering noisily against the stone. Your feet stumbled on the last step, as if shocked in their own memory of the kiss you had once shared there, and as you careened into his arms, you found that the way he stared down at you was not dissimilar to how he had been looking at the heavens.

You tried to still your heart, telling yourself that you were only seeing things.

He dipped his head in acknowledgement at your embarrassed mumble of a *thank you*, opening the door after he managed to right you on the sidewalk. His eyes slid to your — *his* — scarf, one antenna twitching as he did so, but he otherwise said nothing as he ushered you into your seat, gently closing the door behind you with a soft *thump*.

Though you had come across its name in your initial research for EFU, you had never actually been to Tenebra City before. From the refresher research you had done prior to Effie stopping by your apartment, you knew that it wasn't too far away from Eventide Falls. As you gazed out the window, you watched as the rolling hills of the heart of your sleepy town gave way to dense forests, trees blurring together into a murky wall as you drove on. Some kind of classical music droned in the background of your journey as neither of you said anything, but Gideon seemed content with it as he hummed to himself, one antenna swaying in tempo to the counterpoint of the melody.

By contrast, you were trying your best not to fidget, having to sit on your hands to resist the urge to chew at your fingernails again. A feeling akin to dread washed over you, reminding you of one of the more recent lectures Gideon had given on Damocles, who had been able to taste the luxury of the life of a king at his master's insistence. You recalled how Damocles had gleefully indulged in lavishment, only to realize that his king had hung a razor-sword from the ceiling, suspended only by a single strand of horsehair as it loomed over Damocles' head.

You were beginning to realize that perhaps the Sword of Damocles wasn't just applicable to a man in a legend sitting on a golden couch who would learn that fortune doesn't come without a price; perhaps it could also extend to a person sitting in the passenger's seat of a car, anxious at the feeling of impending doom accompanying a desire just outside of reach.

The shrill ring of a phone savagely hacked through the silence like a rusty blade, startling you from your doldrums. You looked away from the window to see Gideon frowning, giving you an apologetic look as he accepted the call and put it on speaker so he could drive unhindered.

"Good evening, Eden," he greeted, sounding more strained than anything. "What do you want?"

The resulting laugh from the other end of the line reminded you of molten sugar before it solidified into hard candy; cloying, yet dark and smooth all at once. "Gideon," the voice rumbled, sending a delicious chill down your spine. You frowned at yourself, not sure what prompted such a reaction. It was as if your body were responding all on its own. "Always so to-the-point. I thought *I* was the businessman here."

"I am on my way to dinner." Gideon's words were clipped, each delivered in a punctuated staccato. You noticed that his antennae twitched in irritation now, the movement more terse than their usual playful sways.

"Ah." The word sounded like it was meant to be in response to a revelation, but Eden didn't actually seem the least bit surprised. "With your human?"

You tensed at this, feeling Gideon's eyes rest on your profile briefly before returning to the road. You were curious about what he would say, having to stop yourself from craning in your seat to hear him better. After a beat, he bit out, "She is not *my* human."

Something about that deflated you.

The two exchanged barbs for a short while longer, though you were too peevish at the response to pay much attention. You trained your eyes on the vista as the forest finally gave way to a clearing, seeing a long bridge leading into Tenebra City's Sapphire District stretched out in front of you, shadowy arches nearly purple against the darkened sky. The inky skyline of the city on the other side of it looked practically alive, lit windows of its skyscrapers blinking and twinkling. A halo of light surrounded them, blanketing the view in a glowing fog. You knew the phenomenon was due to light pollution, but something about it was almost magical, making it look like the city was its own little planet, ascending into the heavens.

While your eyes had widened at the sight, excitement poking through the gloom you had felt, Gideon's reaction was entirely the opposite. He went more rigid the closer he drove into the heart of the city, tips of his wings almost standing at attention. Part of you was paranoid that you might have had something to do with this, but you forced yourself to hone in on the flicker of your enthusiasm if only to give yourself room to breathe.

Soon, he was parking outside a behemoth of glass and iron, holding the door open for you once more as he pressed his keys into the hands of an awaiting valet. He ushered you into the building, one wing curling around you to shield you from the bite of the wind that was much stronger here than it had been in Eventide Falls. The Diamond

District was supposedly known for its high-end restaurants and corporate zeniths and you barely had time to gawk at the characteristic glitz of the sparkling marble lobby as you were led to a glass elevator.

You were tempted to risk fogging the spotless glass and press your face against it as you looked out to the cityscape. Cars and people began to look like little ants the more you climbed, the elevator ascending so high that your ears popped. If you squinted, you swore you could see the curvature of the Earth from this vantage point. At the very least, you could begin to make out each of Tenebra City's districts, nestled like the jewels they were named after in an elaborate crown. The lush green spaces of the Emerald District blended into the urban sprawl of the Ruby District's brownstones, while smoke from the various industrial plants of the Sapphire District curled like sooty ribbons into the night sky.

It was amazing to see the descriptions of your quick internet search come to life and though you couldn't see the remaining Garnet District from this angle, you wondered if Gideon would ever bring you there.

When you turned back to him, you saw that he was watching your reactions intently. You flushed, feeling sheepish at seeming so uncultured, but allowed him to guide you out of the elevator to stop in front of a podium, which was manned by a snobbish-looking, willowy elf wearing a stuffy tuxedo.

The man looked up, apparently instantly recognizing Gideon as his sharp eyes brightened. He dipped his head as he greeted him. "Master Dulcis. Welcome."

Master? The title sounded strange to you, but maybe that was just how they referred to patrons at these kinds of fancy restaurants. The man's sophisticated accent sounded a bit fake to you, as if it were something he could turn on and off at will, and you flinched when his gaze slid over to you, a dark eyebrow arching slightly in curiosity as it fell on your hapless figure.

You looked up at Gideon's profile to see that his jaw clenched in response, wings going slightly rigid before he relaxed, giving a serene smile. It looked practiced, but somehow not forced, though it didn't extend to his eyes. Both fangs flashed as he did so; you could only think of how strange this looked while he exchanged pleasantries with the elf, finally tugging you alongside him as the maître d' personally showed you to your table.

Had you been less overwhelmed with your own emotions, you may have had the mental capacity to fixate on how the widened eyes of the patrons trailed him, heads bowing to murmur to the rest of their party as you both passed by. While you normally felt like you stuck out like a sore thumb in Eventide Falls, you felt completely invisible next to him here. You weren't sure what to make of this, although you supposed being invisible was better than being scrutinized, which was clearly what the elf was doing to you.

Trying not to make eye contact with anybody, you glanced around the interior of the restaurant to take in your surroundings so you could give your friends the full report. You noted the rich, plum-colored linens that blanketed the round tables, which were spaced far apart in a circular grid. The entire floor plan of the restaurant was circular with floor-to-ceiling windows, perched so high on top of the skyscraper that it felt like you were above the clouds themselves, the glow of the city beneath providing more illumination to the space than the small tea candles glinting within the votives they floated in. You felt Gideon put an arm around your shoulders as you both followed the elf, who was droning on about something that you didn't understand.

When you arrived at your table, he held your coat for you so you could slip out of it, giving him a tight smile when he handed it to the maître d'. You then unwrapped your scarf from around your neck, not missing the way he smirked slightly when you handed it to him as well. Before you sat down, you also noticed how his gaze roamed your figure. It wasn't in a lascivious way as Lowell had done, which had made you feel like some kind of trophy; rather, it was as if he was turning the object Lowell had made of you into a work of art.

You wondered if this would be the last time he would visit the museum.

"You look lovely." His voice was low as he complimented you, removing his own coat to hand to the elf. You blushed in response, thanking him while he guided you into your chair, moving to his own once you were seated. When you looked back at the elf, you saw that both his eyebrows were raised, as if to say, *Really?*

Fighting the urge to stick your tongue out at him, you were thankful when another waiter — an orc — walked up to stand next to the uptight man, smoothly handing both you and Gideon menus. You thanked him, giving the elf a steely glance of derision before he bowed to Gideon, stiffly turning to walk away with the orc.

Able to relax slightly without his judgmental glare, you held the menu, squinting at the words that were clearly in a language you didn't know. You swore you felt his eyes flickering to your stubby nails, which you had hurriedly filed and painted over in an attempt to make them not look so ragged. You placed your menu down with a *snap*, giving him an unsure smile.

"I, erm, don't really know what to get," you admitted, drumming the table with the blunted ends of your nails. Realizing what you were doing, you quickly clenched your hand into a fist. He tilted his head at you, laying his own menu down as one of his antennae quirked. "What do you usually order?"

He rotated his menu so that it was facing you and tapped at an entree that looked like gibberish to you with a sharpened claw. Your nose scrunched as you tried and failed to make sense of it.

"I'll have what you're having, then," you said after a moment, waving your hand nonchalantly as you chuckled a bit awkwardly when you looked back up at him.

"Would you rather not have something with meat in it?" he asked, tipping his head to the side. Then, one corner of his lips quirked. "I know fish is strictly off limits."

"It is," you agreed, a bit surprised he remembered how grossed out you were by it. You were pleased about it until that nagging voice within you told you not to get too smug; the man just had a remarkable memory. By contrast, you had almost forgotten he was a vegetarian. Resisting a sigh, you shrugged. "That's ok, I'd like to try what you're getting." You slid your fist across the table, choosing to sit on both of your hands again, uncaring if that was proper etiquette or not. "If *you* like it, it must be good."

His chest rumbled at this, eyes glowing brighter than the candle floating between the both of you. You felt yourself leaning forward at this, drawn in by his gaze as it held your own. When his mouth opened to say something, your breath caught in anticipation, but the spell was broken when your orcish waiter returned.

You sat back in your chair, letting Gideon place your order for you, a curt edge to his smooth voice. When the waiter pivoted smartly to walk away again, Gideon opened his mouth again, only to be interrupted by the sound of his phone ringing. With an apologetic smile, he motioned to silence it, only to go rigid at the name flashing on the screen. He closed his eyes, muttering under his breath.

"This is extremely discourteous of me," he began hurriedly, opening them again, "but I must take this call. It is my grandmother and—"

"No worries," you insisted, lifting your hands from underneath you to wave in front of your face. "Take it, please. I completely understand. I don't mind."

Swiftly accepting the call, he rose, gaze lingering on your face before he disappeared farther into the restaurant with the device held to his pointed ear. Your shoulders slumped as you looked around the room only to see that without the presence of Gideon distracting the rest of the bystanders, dozens of shrewd eyes were now trained on you. Some of them held curiosity, but most looked cynical, as if they could see right into your very soul where your insecurity took root.

You felt yourself sink further into your chair, deciding that being invisible had definitely been preferable. Especially when you met the six-eyed gaze of a rather voluptuous-looking spider demon who only smirked condescendingly at you when she saw you wilt.

xii: theogony

BY THE TIME Gideon returned a short while later, you were staring at the candle in the middle of the table, suddenly finding the way it floated atop the water filling the half-empty votive very interesting as you held the stem of the wine glass the orc had brought you sometime earlier in a death grip.

You had tried to occupy yourself by trying to listen in on conversations around you, catching a rather hushed discussion about what sounded like some kind of dragon mafia lord in the city. That had sounded interesting until you were on the receiving end of a glare at your rudeness, which had caused you to turn into yourself after giving an apologetic smile to the table. While seating himself, Gideon mumbled a stream of apologies as another waiter then appeared, holding various plates in his numerous arms.

You picked at your food in silence, looking up every so often to see Gideon was doing the same. Despite the attention he garnered here, he seemed to fit right in among the sophistication and splendor, the way he held his fork even so absurdly elegant that you could only be reminded of how much you didn't belong here. And certainly not with him.

Feeling your appetite sour, you placed your utensils down, haphazardly tucking a strand of hair behind your ear. You glanced up and noticed the way his eyes followed the movement, sweeping over your jawline and the shell of your ear. You could almost feel his phantom touch, causing you to shiver. He immediately frowned.

"Are you sitting under a draft?" he asked. "Would you like to trade seats with me or change tables?"

"No!" you blurted, not wanting to be a burden. You then lowered your voice, cognizant of the hushed sounds of the restaurant, its patrons not speaking above a whisper as the clinking of silverware accompanied the croon of a violin somewhere in the background. "I mean, no thank you, it's lovely here. I'm not cold."

His eyes narrowed slightly at you before he rose, swiftly removing his blazer and being mindful of his wings as he did so, crossing the distance around the table to you in one long stride. He placed it over your shoulders before returning to his seat, the whole action so quick that you barely had time to close your fingers around the fabric before he was sitting again.

You felt all those eyes rouse like vipers from their dens at the sudden movement, piercing into you as you pulled his blazer tighter. Bemoaning the fact that Gideon no longer seemed to cloak you from their notice, you suddenly realized why they were staring. They weren't considering you as an independent entity; rather, they thought of you only as an extension of him, as if you were some appendage that clearly festered and would need to be removed to stop the infection from spreading.

From how uncomfortable Gideon looked, antennae rigid, wings stock-still behind him, you could tell he was as cognizant of this as you were. Then, it hit you — the explanation for your feeling of dread earlier. Gideon had agreed to have dinner with you not because he enjoyed your presence, but because he was going to break up with you. This whole charade was to give you closure, to show you *why* he had to do what he was about to do and *how* you didn't fit in his life.

She is not my human, he had admitted to the incubus that might have been the closest thing he had to a friend, for all you knew.

It was as if this was exactly what the voice within you had been trying to tell you, except its words had been muffled by the thick sheet of ice it had been trapped under. This whole time, it had been pounding and pounding at the barrier, finally able to break through and dousing you in a spray of frigid water when it sprung free to deliver the final blow. The effect was akin to taking your salad fork and stabbing it into your heart, twisting it savagely like a bushel of overcooked spaghetti.

You rose abruptly, the silverware clattering on the table as you did so. The soft music suddenly felt like an orchestra rushing through your ears. You could barely hear yourself speak. "I need to use the restroom."

Removing his coat, you didn't give him time to respond as you nearly sprinted to the restroom, numbly following the signage to locate the facilities. You lucked out, finding that the room had individual stalls equipped with their own sinks and mirrors as you shoved yourself into one, fumbling at the latch to lock it behind you.

The lighting in here was much better than your shitty, tiny bathroom, you noticed with a bit of chagrin, your eyes looking slightly crazed and sad as you gazed at your reflection. You instantly knew that what you were feeling wasn't just related to your situation with Gideon; this was the result of suppressing the feeling of abandonment when your parents had rejected your wishes to go out into the world and Gideon's own rejection was the icing on the proverbial poisoned cake.

Your parents had offered to help you pay for your undergraduate education only because you knew it came with the expectation that you would find a decent husband there. The list of *traditional human universities* they had chosen for you had been meticulously crafted; they had wanted you to settle down with a richer man, wanting to elevate their statuses even further.

Your family wasn't necessarily loaded, but your father's business ventures had been lucrative enough to put you at eye level with the feet of the upper crust, and now that your parents had caught a glimpse of that world, they wanted *in*. They had intended to bum-rush the door, using you as a battering ram to do so.

Ironically, they would have been ecstatic to see you now, sitting amongst who you suspected may have been society's elite in a restaurant fancier than you could ever imagine. The only thing wrong with this picture in their eyes would be that the man who had brought you here was entirely *not* human. *That* would disappoint them, just like they had been purely disappointed when you had instead expressed your desire to go off into the world and reject the little box they had been trying to put you, scoffing when you had insisted you could be successful on your own. You had thought that your father would be pleased at your suggestion that you could take over the family business; rather, he had looked downright contemptuous, completely livid that you had even entertained yourself capable of it.

Your way of coping with the fact that they had basically disowned you was to pretend they didn't exist, as if ignoring a blister would make it go away. This was the real reason why you never told your friends about your scholarship; why they thought you were just obsessively competitive. The logical side of you knew that they wouldn't judge you, but the more dominant side of you, the one still groveling in the insecurity they had thrust upon you, was fearful that speaking about it would give the situation more truth.

This method had worked well, until suddenly, it didn't. Now, the wound had ruptured, and pure vitriol filled your veins as the memories flooded back.

You hadn't necessarily realized this when you were younger, but having been on your own for a decent amount of years now, you acknowledged that they had possessed a nasty habit of setting aspirations for you that would always be impossible to meet. They had expected you to somehow manage to marry your way into the tight inner circle without spending the time and money to even prepare you for it, a notion you had been reminded of earlier when you had stared at the various silverware in front of you at the table, not sure which one to pick up first. In a way, you supposed that you had disowned them as much as they had done to you, and you weren't entirely regretful of it.

You were proud of yourself. You had funded your own way through your undergraduate studies and were now doing the same in your graduate studies. You had found your own friends, carving your own life in Eventide Falls. The future was promising, and it was one you had created for yourself.

Still, you weren't fully certain why you were so hung up on Gideon. Maybe it was because he hadn't been part of the plan to prove your worth, more to yourself than your parents. Maybe it was because you had craved adventure, and right when you were staring it in the face, it was rejecting you in the form of glowing eyes and quivering wings. Maybe it was just simply because you *cared* for him and the thought that he didn't feel the same for you saddened you; it was another reminder that you weren't good enough, just like your parents had said.

You yearned for him. You wanted to know more about him and his hobbies; what exactly made his antennae twitch and his wings quiver the way they did. Maybe you should have heeded his warnings, after all; you had acquired an initial taste, and just as you had suspected, partaking in the fruit of the Underworld was keeping you there. Except you weren't actually trapped; you had closed those gates behind you of your own volition.

"I'm so fucking stupid," you muttered to yourself, slowly drawing your hand away from your mouth after you realized you had been chewing on your thumbnail again. You pressed it against your palm, curling your fingers around it and squeezing to suppress the sting of biting too deep into your nail bed.

This wasn't like you and it felt unfair to Gideon to lump him in with your shitty parents. It was your own fault that you had tamped these emotions down, letting them build unattended until the pot finally bubbled over, scalding you in its wake. Gideon not caring about you had nothing to do with the people who had rejected you, and if he truly felt that way, his feelings were completely valid and you would just need to deal with them.

This felt like your own personal Theogony; your adult, independent self had been built from the Chaos, and now you had to choose who to align yourself with. Something about your father reminded you of Kronos himself — not the emu that served as your school's mascot, but the father of Zeus — and you wondered if his reservations about you taking over his business weren't because he thought you would run the business into the ground, but the exact opposite. Maybe he was afraid you would excel, doing a much better job than he would ever be able to do, and that made him fearful.

When you peered back into the mirror of the stall you were occupying, the person in front of you looked more like *you*; determined and resolved. Unlike your father, you didn't feel the need to sit at the pinnacle of society; you would be satisfied with your own humble abode, one that you had built with your own ambition. With your time spent amongst various species, you had learned that humans weren't so different, contrary to what your parents thought. In fact, humans might have been the most monstrous of them all, but regardless of how many limbs or eyes or other appendages another being may have possessed, anybody who judged you without knowing you could go fuck themselves.

Pleased with your little pep talk, you punched the air, feeling hyped up again. Gideon ending things — whatever, that meant, exactly — would hurt, but you had to rip the metaphorical bandaid. Maybe the Sword of Damocles had been dangling over your head, but you had seated yourself on that golden couch; this was the nightmare of your choice, and you would be loyal to it. This meant no more skirting around the bush; you would confront him head-on, process those emotions with an absurd amount of scones and potentially alcohol while you sobbed to your friends for precisely three hours, and then you could get back to the program of kicking ass, keeping your scholarship, and showing Professor Prick exactly what you were made of. If he thought you weren't good enough for him, he could go fuck himself, too.

With one last fist pump, you emerged from the bathroom with your head held high, ready to flip off the entire restaurant if you had to. Maybe you could even take on that spider bitch — ok, maybe that was *too* ambitious. You could start with the elf bitch, instead. You could probably fold that willowy bastard like a lawn chair, pointy ears and all.

The eyes didn't land on you until you were in much closer proximity to the table you had fled from, as if Gideon had some kind of sphere of influence that made you become visible again. They seemed expectant, trailing you as you drew closer to your destination. With a squeeze of your fist, you continued on, lifting your chin haughtily.

If they wanted a show, you would give one to them.

Ignoring your abandoned chair in favor of marching right up to him, you stood in front of his seated form, moving to fold your arms over your chest. You tucked your fist underneath an elbow. "What are we doing, Gideon?"

Although the demand was vague, the way he looked at you suggested he knew exactly what you were asking. He stared at you hard, the cut edge of his jaw sharpened even more by the tension he clearly held there. You could see the flickers in his crimson eyes, molten specks of golds and coppers bubbling to the surface, rippling and roiling as they held yours. The contrast with the veins of silver in his wings was remarkable as they shimmered as if inlaid with opals and moonstones, seemingly possessing their own life in the dim candlelight of the restaurant.

It was in that moment that you finally understood how dragons could be so transfixed with their hoards of gemstones.

He finally stood, surprising you for a moment. You had half expected him to protest that you hadn't finished your now-cold meal, but instead he was collecting his blazer from the back of your chair, murmuring something about how the dinner would be covered on his tab. Then, he extended a clawed hand to you. You stared at it for a moment, chewing the inside of your cheek.

You weren't sure what this would lead to. It could be the beginning or the end, but either way, you needed to find out. You caught a glimpse of the flicker of candle, still bobbing within its half-full votive. Swallowing thickly, your eyes met his once more; as you squared your shoulders, you placed your palm in his.

xiii: the sphinx

YOU WERE GOING to kick his ass, you told yourself, fists clenching and unclenching while you tried to ignore the throb of where you had chewed your nails to stubs. You were going to kick his ass, ruffle his wings, and maybe tug at his antennae for good measure. Then, you would wrap his scarf around his own neck and choke him with it, cursing a certain asshole all the way to the moon and back.

Ever since you'd first run into the insufferable man in that accursed library, it felt like you had been trying to solve some impossible riddle, but instead of the body of a lion and the head of a falcon, the Sphinx you were currently facing resembled a moth with fae ancestry. You weren't sure what, exactly, he had been protecting, but it sure did piss you off. Forget the plague of Thebes; you were currently dealing with the plague of Professor *Prick*.

Gone was the frigid chill of the nerves you had felt on the journey to Tenebra City; that ice had thawed as fire took its place while you did your best to act like your own personal hype team. It was inevitable that Gideon was going to drive you back to your apartment to end whatever strange fling you were currently having, and although you had made peace with it, you were never one to go down without a fight.

You may have been trying to play offense with the shield you used to protect your own emotions, but you could deconstruct that later over a quart of ice cream or something.

The car was completely silent this time. Gideon had forgone music entirely, the only sound being his uncharacteristic occasional tapping on the steering wheel with the pointed tip of his index finger. You were still working yourself up, fortifying your full debate strategy with a full-on SWOT analysis to figure out how to take him on. By the time you were satisfied with your assessment of both of your strengths, weaknesses, opportunities, and threats, the car was slowing to a halt.

Except you looked up to find that you were very much *not* stopped in front of your apartment.

So caught up in your introspection, you hadn't been paying much attention to much else. Rather than seeing the familiar, cracked sidewalk and flickering yellow light of the lamppost outside your apartment building, you were met with a thick wall of trees as the car had pulled to the side of the road.

Your brows knit together in your confusion, though you felt even more perplexed when you turned from the window to look at the man you had been willing to spontaneously combust by sheer mind power alone. Even in the dimness, you could see from his profile that his jaw was still clenched and his wings had a tense rigidity to them, but there was something different in his ruby eyes than irritation. Something like... fear?

"Did we break down?" you asked suddenly, voice sounding thunderous in the stillness.

His grip on the steering wheel tightened briefly before he relaxed again a moment later. The lights from the dashboard reflected strange pixelated shapes in his glossy red eyes. You watched his antennae droop slightly as he let out a soft sigh. "No, we did not."

Eye twitching in irritation, you looked back and forth from him to the forest beyond the passenger's side of your window, not really liking where this was going. Your mind spun into overdrive, previous bravado forgotten. Had he gotten as pissed off with you as you had been with him? Was he having the same ideas that you were?

You were fully convinced that it was ok for *you* to want to choke him, but for him to want to do similarly to you just seemed unfair.

You slumped in your seat, back sliding against the buttery leather as you burrowed your nose into his scarf that was still wrapped around your neck in what was your best impression of a turtle trying to go back into its shell while trying not to hyperventilate. Did Eventide Falls have a serial killer? You tried to rack your mind, but didn't remember seeing anything like that on the news; in fact, one of the things you had come across in your research was how *safe* the town was supposed to be. A minute sense of relief washed over you.

Unless you had the honor of being the very first in his burgeoning career. They could call him the *Eventide Falls Exterminator* and your name would forever be tied to his. Grainy low-quality photos of you would flash on a screen years from now whenever they finally did some kind of documentary about him and how it had been the perfect night for a murder with the way the full moon kept slinking behind the swarthy blanket of clouds.

You hoped they at least picked some flattering angles. You should have left some kind of stipulation about that in your will.

Wait! You didn't even *have* a will! You couldn't die... you weren't legally ready for it! Not that you really had anything of worth to distribute to anybody, but still. It felt careless to get murdered now when you hadn't been able to plan for it. How *unprofessional* would that look to the employers who would never get to hire you?

You whimpered.

"Are you quite alright?"

The sound of his voice made you shoot straight up in your seat as you leaned away from him, the interior board of the door digging uncomfortably into your back through your coat. You could practically see your crazed expression in the glow of his eyes, tinted red like you probably would be while steeping in a puddle of your own blood in a few moments.

You could try to make a run for it, but you were more scared of running through the darkness of the woods than you were of dying at his hands. There was also no feasible way you would be able to fight him off; those claws may have looked innocent compared to Lowell's, but they were still *claws*. His wings were another factor in this. You weren't sure if he could necessarily achieve flight, but they had to be good for something.

Maybe you should start praying. To what, exactly, you weren't certain. You might as well have called upon Kronos the emu at this point. If he could help students ace their exams, how good was he at getting them out of murder situations?

"I don't like guns!" you blurted, cringing at the shrill of your own voice. You swallowed thickly, hoping he would at least be merciful. "At least use a knife or something. A sharp one!"

"To do what, exactly?" he asked slowly, the tips of his antennae lowering as he frowned. When you scrambled against the door again, they stiffened in realization as incredulity took hold. "You think I desire to *murder* you? I would not dream of it." He was completely taken aback, though he suddenly looked thoughtful. "Well, at times, I suppose I do find myself rather—"

"Hey!" you interjected, not at all liking where this was going. You glowered at him. "Not helping your case!"

"This is completely absurd," he scoffed. At least some of his earlier tension seemed to have dissipated. "I should have suspected something was awry when you were being so peculiarly quiet. How did you manage to come to *that* conclusion?"

"I don't know!" You held your hands up defensively, scowling at him. "I guess I'm just a little bit on edge, ok? Between my exams and that disastrous dinner and the fact that you're about to break up with me, maybe my imagination is running wild! What would *you* think if you were a passenger and found yourself stopped at the edge of the woods in the dark with—"

"Break... up with you?" He said the words with marked exaggeration, as if he didn't know what they meant. His eyes narrowed and you suddenly felt extremely self-conscious.

"Ok, ok, maybe that's not the best term," you said quickly, scrambling to explain yourself. "I know we're not, uh, *together* or anything, so I guess that's not the right way to say it."

He was silent again, considering this as he tilted his head at you. A single pointed finger tapped at his chin with one hand as brought the other up to curve under his jaw. Studying you for a moment longer, he then posed, "And the concept of me 'breaking up with you' is upsetting to you?"

"No shit!" you shot back, ignoring the way his eyes darkened at your curse. "Do you know how confusing this has been for me?" If you had been standing, you would have stamped your foot. "One minute you're all over me, the next you're refusing to touch me, the next you're holding me while I fall asleep! Those are mixed messages, Professor Dulcis!"

"Professor Dulcis?" he parroted, sounding not at all pleased. "You have not referred to me as that since—"

"Since what?" you demanded, nearly hissing at him in your ire. "Since you stated your intention to *sate my greed*"—your tone was mocking as you quoted him—"and have all but fucking kicked me to the curb since?"

"I never intended—"

"Then what did you intend?" You were past the point of letting him get a word in, cutting him off to throw your arms up in the air dramatically. You winced when your hands hit the roof, but otherwise continued with your theatrics, exclaiming, "Enlighten me, oh great *Sphinx*!"

Though he obviously wasn't privy to your earlier musings, the way his antennae stiffened suggested he understood the meaning behind your allusion. He said nothing, though, his lack of response cutting surprisingly deep.

Instead of chastising you for your use of expletives, he removed his glasses, setting them down in the cup holder between the two of you. Pinching the bridge of his nose between his thumb and index finger, he sighed.

You fidgeted in your seat, biting on the tip of your thumb while he remained that way for a few more seconds as if debating with himself over something before he abruptly moved to turn off the ignition. Then, he unbuckled his seatbelt and opened his door, ducking as he exited the car so that he wouldn't catch his antennae or wings on the roof.

When his door shut with a muffled *thud*, your eyes trailed his figure skirting around the front of his car before he stopped in front of your door. He opened it, extending a hand to you like he had done in the restaurant earlier. "I am not going to murder you, little harpy," he said, voice gentle, "but you may very well be the death of me."

This was the second time he had said that to you. You blinked at him, gaze sliding down to give his light gray palm a hard look as you chewed the inside of your cheek. When you looked back up, you saw that he was completely still, as if he were holding his breath.

"This is the fucking *weirdest* breakup I've ever experienced," you grumbled with a huff, feeling your anger ebbing as you reached to unbuckle your own seatbelt while muttering to yourself about how ridiculous this all was. Turning back to him, you gripped at his hand, trying not to let yourself be too thrilled about the feeling of his long fingertips closing over yours. "If you promise you're not going to murder me, will you at least explain why you're leading me into the woods at this hour? A bit suspicious, isn't it?"

He hummed at this, pushing your door shut behind you. Bending slightly, he let go of your hand to wrap his scarf a bit tighter around your neck before taking it again and leading you forward. Normally, you'd downright hostile at anybody who tried to lead you into the dark, but for some odd reason, you felt perfectly safe with him. Even if he was on the precipice of becoming the Eventide Falls Exterminator.

"I would like to show you something," he responded as you stepped into the tree line with him, squeezing his hand a bit tighter when the thick canopy of leaves completely cut out what little moonlight had escaped from the cloud cover by the side of the road. You were all but blind, yet he seemed to know exactly where he was going.

It was eerily quiet as you continued through the woods, the crunch of frozen leaves under your shoes making your footfalls sound like they belonged to some giant beast rather than a human of your stature. By contrast, Gideon moved like some kind of spectre; smooth and silent, as if he were one with the shadows that regularly haunted the trees. As your eyes adjusted to the darkness, you could just barely make out the outline of him; the tips of his antennae, the impressive span of his wings, shimmering slightly despite the lack of light, as if lit from within.

Maybe he wasn't one with the shadows, after all; maybe he was one *of* them.

This would be one hell of a story, you thought to yourself, hoping again that you might live to tell it. It may have been a slight overreaction on your part to think Gideon was planning to murder you in a forest — he would more likely poison your hot chocolate or something as that was much tidier and a little more sophisticated than downright brutality — but there was something different about his behavior that still seemed off to you. It was the nervous twitch in his antennae and the minute vibrations in his wings that were throwing you for a loop; the Gideon you knew was completely poised and always assured.

This one seemed almost... human.

Before you could dwell on that realization, you noticed that there was a soft glow coming from in front of him, the starkness of the light cutting around his inky figure and completely flattening his silhouette. You had to squint to protect your eyes from the sudden intrusion, his hand tightening around yours as he led you into the mist.

Then, as quickly as everything had gone black when you stepped into the forest, everything went white when you stepped out of it.

You blinked rapidly, trying to force your eyes to adjust again. As your pupils slowly equalized themselves, you found that you weren't seeped in white at all, but instead a light, powdery blue. It settled closer to the ground, clinging to the damp grass like evaporating snow as it swirled around your feet. Lifting your head from it, your breath caught at the sight in front of you.

The vision that greeted you was otherworldly; that forest Gideon had brought you through must have been a portal to some different plane entirely, the mundane giving way to something completely captivating. The fog dancing around your ankles made you feel like you were standing on a cloud, though from what you were seeing, you didn't doubt that perhaps this is what Olympus may have looked like.

Whereas the moon had largely been hidden by the clouds when you had left the car, it was fully visible here, almost as though the clouds were now afraid to touch it. It illuminated the clearing you now stood in, which was perfectly surrounded by a dark ring of trees, as if stitched by the gods themselves and held aloft in the middle of a heavenly embroidery hoop.

As you dropped Gideon's hand to step forward, you watched the mist spiral in lustrous eddies, as if glitter was caught suspended among its droplets. It became thicker the closer you drew to a rushing stream, whose bright blue waters reminded you of liquefied lapis lazuli. When you toed the edge of it, peering down, you could see a myriad of pebbles, though the way they shone back at you made them look more like pearls than stone.

Your eyes followed the length of the stream, resting on a roaring waterfall that tumbled over an inky cliff. The light of the full moon refracted with the spray it threw as the rush collided at its base created a lunar rainbow, though the colors weren't what you would have expected to see in such a phenomenon. Instead of reds and oranges and greens, the hues were all cool tones, showing a fuller spectrum of blues and purples than you knew even existed.

Even the air itself seemed different here, the puffs of your breath expelling in front of your face instantly condensing into clouds of diamond shards, as if physical proof of the magic invading your lungs. When you turned back to look at Gideon to see that he had moved forward to join you in the center of the clearing, finally remembering he was the one that had brought you here, you found he had been touched by the same spell.

Through the silken mist that blanketed the ground, you could see pinpoints of brighter light, some tinted blue, others gold. Yet none of these earth-dwelling stars could compare with how luminous Gideon looked, the silver veins in his wings glowing of their own accord. The magentas and olives and turquoises that you could sometimes see in the lighting of his office were also more pronounced here, rippling like prismatic shards of crystal as they gleamed. Even his hair, which was normally dark and sooty, had some kind of shine to it, as if the cuticle of the strands could not completely hide the light of the cortex within.

Gideon was radiant; he looked less like a fallen angel and more like a fallen constellation, though you had never seen an assortment of stars as colorful.

His eyes shone a brilliant crimson as you stepped towards him, the flecks of copper and gold roiling beneath their surface becoming more pronounced the closer you got. You reached out once you were within arms-length of him, capturing an errant silken tendril of hair between your fingertips.

"What *is* this place?" you asked, voice in a mere whisper. You were afraid to speak any louder, as if the sound of your words would ripple the puddle this fantasy was suspended in and everything would fade away. He looked down at you, bringing his hand up to curl his fingers around your wrist.

"Eventide Falls," he replied after a heartbeat. The response made you arch a brow, but your gaze drifted from his face to settle on the glow of his wings. From the research you had done prior to moving here, all the sources had explained how the town was named after a mythological waterfall, although you should have known that Gideon would find a way to bring these stories to life. "The town's namesake, of course. And mine."

Your eyes snapped back to his at this. You were able to see the way your nose scrunched in your reflection in those ruby orbs in your bewilderment. "*Eventide?*" you repeated, cocking your head slightly. "Your last name is *Dulcis*, isn't it?"

"It is," he confirmed with a nod, "a surname inherited from my father and his father before him. Eventide was my grandmother's maiden name." The way he said the word was with a bitterness that didn't seem like it belonged here, but you made no comment on that. Instead, you listened as he continued, "My grandmother's family founded this town. She believed it was my father's birthright. Now that he is gone, by extension... it would be mine."

He guided your hand to rest against his chest with one of his own, bringing the other up to run the pad of a fingertip along your jaw. You shivered at the flutter of his touch and at the intensity within his eyes. "My grandmother is extremely opinionated. She thinks my current profession is...frivolous." You winced at the humorless laugh that then fell from his lips, remembering how you had said something similar to him on your first meeting in the library. "She would like nothing better for me to return to my roots, restore the family name to what it once was, whatever that means." He shook his head.

"Why are you telling me this?" you asked gently, gripping the thick fabric of his peacoat between your fingers. He applied slight pressure to your wrist, squeezing it as if to ground himself, before he allowed his grip to go slack. "Why did you bring me here?"

"I am gifted at many things," he stated, the flicker of his usual haughty self making you smile. "Courting is not one of them."

"Courting?" you repeated, stunned. You blinked, not sure if you were hearing him correctly. "I thought I wasn't your human. I thought you didn't care." You couldn't stop the acerbity from seeping into the words you threw at him and instantly regretted saying them; you hadn't expected them to be like a boomerang, coming back to smack you in the face a few seconds after you'd said them.

"Did not... care?" Now he seemed stunned. "How could I not care when I had brought you all those things?" You gaped at him, knowing instantly he was talking about bringing you scones and hot chocolate and blankets. "I am part fae, remember? Fae do not give gifts without any reason." He then looked a bit more grim. "Fae also have... possessive tendencies," he admitted, eyes dropping down to where he was still gripping your wrist as if to prove a point. "It is a trait I fear I have inherited from my father. I did not want to scare you..."

"How could you scare me?" you asked, eyebrows shooting nearly into your hairline. "Didn't I fully consent to this? Didn't I tell you explicitly that I wanted this when we—"

"That was *physical*," he interjected with another dismissive shake of his head. "I brought you here to explain, to tell you what you might be getting into. I have never shown anybody this before. It might be the only thing that was wholly determined mine, and I so desperately wanted to share it with you. I so desperately want—"

He suddenly looked unsure, the expression markedly foreign for a man whose usual confidence always edged on arrogance. "I want *you*. I want more than just to want you. It is entirely selfish of me." He shook your wrist slightly as he curled the hand resting on your jaw to capture your chin, nudging it upwards as if hopeless for you to see. "I am from a long line of fae on my father's side. I am thirteenth of my name, with all of the curses befalling such an unlucky number. Like my father and his father before him and every other Gideon prior, I am doomed to abandon everything I hold dear—"

"Gideon, wait," you implored him, your hand darting out to remove the one he had resting against your jaw. You placed it on his chest over his heart, right next to where he was holding your other against his coat. "Isn't this a self-fulfilling prophecy then?" You extracted your hands from him to grip at his shoulders, squeezing them so that he would pay attention to you. His wings glittered with the slight jostling movement. "You were trying to abandon me *then* to save yourself from abandoning me *now*?"

"Not myself, I was trying to save *you*," he insisted stubbornly. You fought the urge to roll your eyes at how he was trying to revert to this whole *god of the Underworld* act as you slid your hands from his shoulders back to his chest. "But I just cannot stay away. I am like a moth to a—"

"Don't say a flame." Your nose scrunched again as you cringed internally, remembering how you had threatened Effie when she tried to insinuate this exact thing. "Then don't stay away. I can make my own decisions. I demanded you to touch me before, remember?" You allowed a playful smirk, despite the intensity he was trying to make of the situation. "I'm not sure if this was your way of trying to scare me off, but it definitely didn't work. You were right; I *do* like a challenge, and if you would deny me the challenge of proving to you that you aren't cursed like you say you are, you really aren't a man of your word!"

He stared at you, scarlet eyes blown wide at your words. His mouth dropped slightly agape, the ivory tips of his fangs practically glowing with the rest of him. You felt him go stiff under where your hands were resting on his chest, his antennae following suit.

"You called me a Sphinx earlier," he finally intoned, voice dropping low, "I have a riddle for you after all. What is a trumpet that does not make a sound, that dies in the light of day, only to come alive again in the dark of night?"

You couldn't respond, simply captivated with the sparkle of his eyes and how they seemed to trap your living body, just as they were able to capture your reflection in their depths. You felt the weight of one of his hands rest against the small of your back as he moved an arm around you, while he lifted the other to tuck a strand of hair behind your ear, caressing the shell of it like you had hoped he would back in the restaurant. Finally shaking your head, you cleared your throat to speak, knowing he would want you to say it out loud. "I don't know."

"A moonflower," he answered. "I am inexplicably drawn to you, not like a moth to a flame, but a moth to a *moonflower*. You, little harpy, are that moonflower. It thrives in the darkness, and perhaps, in your insistence"—his long tongue darted to sweep across his lips as an eerie hunger sharpened the glint in his eyes—"perhaps you shall, too."

xiv: heliacal rising

YOU PRESSED INTO HIM, fisting the fabric of his jacket in your grip. You never did like the dark, but the kind of darkness he was referring to excited you, gathering a pool of want in your abdomen much warmer than any jacket could provide.

"You wish to pursue this relationship further?" he asked, voice low as he bent his head down at you. You bristled at this, feeling like it was all a bit redundant after what you had talked about. He gently tugged on the strand of hair he had tucked behind your ear. "Darling, do not give me that look. I need your words, remember?"

Trying not to pout, you nodded before giving him a verbal confirmation. "Yes, Gideon, I'd like to *pursue this relationship further*." You couldn't help but mock him slightly as you said that last part, one of your hands trailing from the lapels of his coat down to his pants. Feeling him stiffen, your fingertips continued their descent before you stopped at his buckle, playing with the polished edges of it. "Although you *did* lie to me before."

He pursed his lips at you, his eyes shining bright in his dusky face like twin blood moons. "A bold claim," he said, dipping his head farther. His voice was husky, his usual lilt replaced with a rasp that curled around you like smoke.

"In your office, when you took me over your desk"—you tugged at the buckle to punctuate the word—"I wanted to touch you. You promised me later, and later never came." This time you did pout at him, giving his belt buckle another tug. "That makes you a liar. Unless later... is *now*?"

You weren't sure why you were being so bold; maybe it was your body seeking warmth in the cool night air and knowing it would find it in him. Maybe it was the magic of this otherworldly clearing that held you steadfast in its grasp. It felt like the clouds caressing your ankles had invaded your mind, filling it with a dense fog and he, a colloid in the mist, beckoned to you like a siren in the deep.

"I am no liar." His tone was one of stubbornness. "But if we continue in this way," he began, a warning edge to his strained voice, "I fear you may not... like what you see."

"I've seen it all before, haven't I?" you retorted, a bit haughtier than you had originally intended. His antennae were at full attention now, the tips of his wings quivering slightly as a tendril of his hair brushed against your forehead. His responding silence was nearly deafening, your curiosity suddenly piqued.

"Not *all* of it," he admitted after a beat, though he made no moves to extract you from him, instead choosing to close more of the distance and brush his lips near the corner of your mouth. You wanted to grab him by the collar and slide them more fully over yours, as if you were starving and the taste of him was the only ambrosia that could soothe you.

"Will you show me?" The question was a mere whisper as you stood still, your eyes sliding halfway shut when his other arm moved to join its twin at the small of your back, pulling you flush against him. You felt his wings curl around you as well, fluttering against your shoulders. He tilted his head, nipping at your bottom lip like he had once done under the paltry light of the streetlamps. Back then, the action had caused a dart of pleasure to sizzle down to your core. Now, in the brilliance of this fantasy world, the sear was even more pronounced.

He worried at your lip again, swiping the tip of his tongue against it to soothe the sting only to pull back when you sighed into him. "Perhaps, if you ask nicely." His almond eyes were hooded now, the red there glowing through waxing crescents. "Unless you are demanding it again."

You wanted to blush at the memory of your previous boldness, yet chose to repeat what you had said then. "I'll be good." You slid your hand from the buckle to rest lower against his crotch, feeling the bulge you knew would be there. "Will you please show me, Gideon?"

His lips were on yours again, drawing a wanton moan from your mouth like sucking venom from a wound as he unwound his arms from around you to remove his coat. While you worked on shedding your layers and your scarf in frantic, jerky movements, his were much more fluid. He broke from you briefly to lay his coat on the ground before undoing the buttons on his shirt.

Your own coat discarded, you took the opportunity to step forward, pushing his hands aside to undo the buttons yourself. His breath came out in quick, shallow pants as you brushed the fabric away, allowing him to step back to carefully shrug his wings out through the slits in the back of it.

You knew Gideon wasn't human, but this fact had never been more made apparent than when you were staring at his naked torso, his upper half bathed in nothing but moonlight. Though lithe, he was clearly toned, the subtle musculature of his chest cutting into a sharper V-shape closer to his groin. The fuzz there was thicker and darker than what covered him everywhere else except for his face.

When he stepped back towards you, you caught the glint of where his wings splayed impressively behind him, shimmering like specular hematite in the blue glow of the field. He must have removed the usual leather band he kept his hair pulled back in as it now spilled over his shoulders in sooty waves of silk, a few strands hovering around his face as if the laws of gravity did not apply to him. Somehow, if it was later revealed that they didn't, you wouldn't be surprised.

You couldn't help but think again that you didn't belong here; this place was somewhere that you had happened to stumble upon and you had intruded on its splendor. Gideon took the place of some deity guarding the meadow and now that you had entered into his domain, he would make you pay for it. Except he would never need to *take* anything from you; you would give him anything and everything you gave, you gave wholeheartedly.

Your hands fell back to the buckle of his pants as he tugged you into him again, giving a soft groan when you purposely rubbed your side into the bulge there. He absolutely devoured your mouth, lips working against yours as if reciting some kind of prayer as you finally managed to undo his belt and tug his zipper down, hand sliding against him immediately after. You bit back a giggle at the discovery that yet again, he had chosen to go commando, but were unable to contain your gasp at the tip of his cock nudging against your palm. He swallowed the sound, his hand sliding to grip at your waist as you drew away to look more fully at him.

The lilac-flushed tip fully emerged from the slit that contained it, unhindered by the fabric of his pants as more of his cock was revealed. As you coaxed it out, it jolted in your hand, the rest of him tensing as you ran your fingertips over the slight upwards curve near its base. Giving him a questioning look as you continued to palm it, you lowered yourself to your knees when he gave you a hesitant nod of approval.

It amazed you that his cock had fit inside you, though you remembered the bulge it had created in your stomach when he had finally seated himself fully. You weren't able to fully wrap your hand around it and that definitely meant you wouldn't be able to take him in your mouth. Had you been able to afford jaw realignment surgery, you may have considered attempting it, but ever the adaptable one, you decided to try another tactic. Now that you were closer to him, you could see that there were two additional smaller slits a bit higher up on his groin, which you hadn't been able to see in his office. You weren't sure what they were for, but now didn't seem like the time to ask.

You gripped him a bit more firmly, pulling your hand to follow the curvature of his cock while your other slid in underneath to grip at its base. You watched him as you slowly pumped him, your hand catching every little ridge, while simultaneously squeezing. Your body practically hummed at the way his antennae twitched and how the tips of his wings quivered in their own response. Shifting to widen the distance between your knees to rest more comfortably against the damp ground, you bent forward to taste him, only to pause.

You remembered the way Gideon's come had beaded on the feathered tip, shining like a pearl with its sheen of pinks and lavenders and turquoises in the light of his office. Here in the darkness, it not only shone, but it *glowed*, soft and luminescent like his wings. You were completely enraptured by it, feeling the warmth of your own need pulse much hotter in your desire to taste him. You dipped your head, sweeping your tongue over the droplet.

Bergamot and citrus exploded over your tastebuds as you greedily lapped at him, his cock jolting to attention again. You swirled the tip of your tongue around the feathered edges of its head, the ripples tickling you as you did so. When you gripped him tighter, simultaneously pulling upward again with your other hand as you moved to take his tip more fully in your mouth, a clawed hand was suddenly in your hair, making you halt.

It did not escape your notice that he had been keeping his nails much shorter lately.

"Do you want me to stop?" you asked, voice a bit raspy as you pulled away from him in puzzlement. He looked like a phantom looming above you, the glow of his eyes seeming even more pronounced now.

"No," he was able to bite out after a moment, hair swishing like smoky curtains when he shook his head. "It is just... I"—he took a deep, shuddering breath, as if trying to collect himself—"I fear I may lose control of myself if you continue in this way."

"That's the *point*, Gideon," you said playfully, ducking again to press a quick kiss to his lilac tip. He groaned at you, dragging a hand down his face as he muttered something to himself. "You said you would show me. I thought you were a man of your word—"

Quicker than you could register it, you suddenly found yourself on the ground, the familiar silken feel of the inside of his peacoat brushing against the bare skin of your thighs as your dress hiked up around your waist. It took your brain a moment to process the change in elevation, mind spinning in the abrupt movement and with the scent of him invading every last crevice of your head.

"I am a man of my *word*, little harpy," he intoned, his knee rubbing insistently against your crotch as he knocked your legs wider. "If you are so insistent on me showing you, I will, but I want to be inside you when I fully lose myself."

Gathering both of your wrists in one hand, he guided them to hold above your head, the other lowering to press against you. Taking a leaf out of his book, you had also decided to forgo underwear, something that apparently greatly pleased him when his fingers met no resistance, dipping to work you open. He hissed at your hushed whimper, giving you a sharp look of warning when your hips bucked upwards in response to his touch.

"Rules?" you panted, remembering how he had so liked rubbing them in your face before. He shook his head, but his lips twitched in a smirk.

"No rules, not tonight." Then, he looked more serious. "Except stay still," he commanded, bending his head to nip a fang against one of your kneecaps. "Just watch."

It was hard to *just watch* when he was working a second and third finger into you, keeping his thumb pressed against your clit as he splayed them apart like a trio of scissors, twisting and curling them like his tongue had once done. You bit your lip, a particular press against your walls combined with the swirl of his thumb on your clit causing another ragged moan to fall from your lips, though the more worked up he made you, the more relaxed he seemed to get.

His shoulders drooped, tension leaving his wings and antennae as he concentrated on your reactions to his ministrations, moving his other hand from your wrists to splay flat against your abdomen. You felt that coil within you beginning to build again, but just when you felt like it might snap, your walls beginning to flutter, he eased on his pace, shifting from pointed pumping to a more delicate caress. You felt drunk on him, the scent of Earl Grey, leather, and moonflowers seeming suddenly much more heady.

He then shifted, allowing you to catch a glimpse of his bottom half. You would have wondered when he had managed to step out of his pants during all this if not for the silvery tendrils that you finally noticed were curling upwards. You had thought they may have wisps of smoke until one furled closer to you, looking decidedly solid. With a gasp, you moved your hands from above your heads to grip at the wrist of the hand that was twisting inside you, needing him to stop so you could wrap your mind around what you were seeing. You didn't care that you may have been breaking his order to stay put at this point.

"What"—you let out a pant, trying to draw in a deeper breath as you attempted to will your brain back into basic function—"are *those?*"

He moved the hand resting against your abdomen to grip at one of your kneecaps, his thumb rubbing soothing circles against your skin as you stared. The tendrils, four in total, looked almost like tentacles; they were slightly narrower than his cock and much longer, spiraling lazily towards the sky from behind him. You dug your elbows into the fabric of his coat, hoisting yourself upwards to get a better look.

Though they were lighter than his cock too, they seemed to be covered in the same satiny fuzz. Unlike his cock, however, there were no ridged nubs; instead the span of them was smooth, the girth denser towards their base and more tapered at the top. Those tips twitched in your direction when you spoke, as if recognizing the sound and looking at you.

"When I am in more in *control*"—he said the word pointedly, carefully studying you as he spoke—"I am able to retain more of my fae ancestry. When I am not, my... other tendencies tend to emerge." He lifted his hand from your knee, bringing it up by his face. A tendril wrapped around his wrist, slowly curling around it like a snake. "These are my coremata." He tilted his head, gauging your reaction. "Are you afraid of them?"

You nearly forget that his fingers were still buried within you until he moved to extract them, but you gripped his wrist harder to stop him. Shaking your head swiftly, you extended your other hand in a gesture for him to help you sit up more, but instead of him offering an arm to you, two of his tentacles — no, his *coremata* — moved to wind around your lower back. You tensed briefly before allowing them to assist you, guiding you into a seated position. When he finally removed his hand from you, you would have protested if not for another one of his corema taking its place.

"They can be quite useful," he stated almost playfully, apparently pleased that you weren't headed for the hills at the sight of them. You could only nod dumbly, the grind of the appendage against your clit sending sparks all the way through your core into maybe your soul itself. It felt similar in firmness to his cock, but it was much more nimble; something you discovered when it made a rippling motion, sending a wave of knobby bumps across your clit.

It seemed to have a mind of its own and while it wasn't penetrating you yet, the stimulation you were receiving from the pure friction of it rubbing against you was enough to have you feeling that coil tighten again. You closed your eyes, focusing on the way his other two coremata held you upright while rubbing against your skin. One of his hands was brushing your hair away from your forehead, the other dragging a pointed fingertip down from your neck to circle around one of your nipples while the fabric of your dress did nothing to assuage the sensitivity.

You could have wondered where the fourth went before you felt it join the other one rubbing insistently against your clit. They seemed to wrap around each other, creating a spiral that stuttered along your opening, their tapered tips rolling your clit between them. You whimpered, feeling a hot flash of *something* as your head dropped backwards, the coremata at your back not letting you fall.

"Please, Gideon," you managed to whimper. Your hands — where were your own hands? It took you a second to take stock of your own limbs, your body apparently no longer your own, finally regaining enough control of your extremities to grip at his shoulders. "I need—*fuck*!"

You couldn't help the curse at the feeling of his fangs pinching the skin of your neck as he tipped forward to suckle the skin, tongue lapping over the prickles to soothe the bite. You shuddered as the corema undulating across your core pressed more firmly against you, nearly letting out a sob when he simultaneously dragged another claw across your chest from one nipple to the other.

"What do you need, sweet moonflower?" he crooned. You felt him smirk into your shoulder as you gripped him tighter.

"*You*. Inside." You sounded entirely dopey, but it was a wonder you were able to speak at all at this point. He pulled back from you, swooping to place a rather chaste kiss against your lips before nodding.

While the corema at your clit still rubbed against you, the two that had been holding you upward moved away from your back as he gently pulled your arms upwards. He leaned forward, nimble fingers quickly yanking the zipper of your dress down before he was guiding the fabric over your head, carefully folding it once it was free of you and putting it off to the side. Then, he was guiding you back down, pressing kisses all over your bare shoulders and breasts as he laid you against the fabric of his coat with such tenderness that you could have cried.

You were reduced to nothing but putty in his hands, the ache in your abdomen throbbing for more of him. When you felt the feathered tip of his cock nudge against you, you sighed in relief, bringing shaky hands up to circle around his neck. He dipped towards you as he pushed forwards, capturing your mouth in his and swallowing another gasp when he gave another thrust.

Those nubs on his cock caught each and every part of your walls, branding them as they dragged against you. While his hands cradled the back of your head like claw-tipped pillows, you felt two coremata brush against your nipples, the other two supporting the small of your back as they angled you more into him.

As he rocked into you, even your feeble brain was able to register how different this time was from your encounter in his office. Back then, he had downright fucked you; it was completely primitive, all heat and vitriol and aggression. This was much more tender; Gideon was clearly in no rush, taking his time to allow you to feel the stretch and the burn as his tongue swept into your mouth, engaging it in a waltz instead of a twisting battle of submission like had done before.

A roll of his hips as he languidly pumped into you had your head falling back as you let out a moan, the feathered flare of the tip of his cock creating that suctioning feeling within you again. You shivered as he adjusted his grip on you so that only one hand was holding your head, the other trailing down and down and down. The tip of his sharp nails scorched through the valley of your breasts and past the coremata rubbing against them. It finally stopped at your clit as you felt him take the sensitive nub between his thumb and index finger, rolling it with slight pressure as you bucked into him, your stomach bulging and jumping where he was buried inside you.

"You take me so beautifully," he breathed, though the words were half lost on you. Your eyes must have been blown wide, the light of the meadow much more vibrant now. The glow of his wings also seemed to have increased in luminosity as they gently surged above you, blanketing you from the pale shine of the moon.

It felt as though you were ascending, every bump and drag of his cock, the brush of his coremata against your pebbled nipples, and his fingers playing with your clit guiding you upwards and upwards. Even the tips of his hair brushing against your overly-sensitive skin had you reeling, vision fading from a soft powdery blue into a brilliant white.

Then he said your name and the white burst pure around you, a feeling of liquid warmth surging through you. You were fluttering, matching the quiver of his wings as you chased your release in the light of a dying star. He was easing you into and through your orgasm, slowly rocking deep within you to guide you through it like Charon ferrying your recently departed soul across the River Styx.

You felt the rumble of his chest. He was saying something to you, but you were too far gone to comprehend the words while you continued to ride the waves of your release. As he gently guided you down from your high, thrusts slowing as you twitched around him, your sight began to return to you, although white spots still danced in your vision like dust motes.

You blinked, the blurry picture of his face finally solidifying in front of your eyes again. His mouth was still moving, but it took you another moment longer before your hearing returned. You registered the feeling of his hand smoothing your hair back from your now-sweaty forehead and the way his lips quickly pressed against yours once more.

When he drew back from his kiss, you realized that the dust motes had settled onto his hair, suspended in the inky strands like fallen stars. Except they weren't dust motes at all, you recognized — they were *snowflakes*.

"I-I like your coremata," you were able to say after another few moments of trying to control your breathing, though the words still sounded a bit too breathy. He laughed at this, the sound deep and rich. It sent vibrations down where his chest was pressed to yours all the way through where he was still seated in you, causing you to wince.

Noticing this, he immediately stopped, gently moving to pull himself out of you. Your breath caught as he did so, letting out a soft hiss when the flare of his tip bumped against your clit. He smiled an apology, though your attention immediately went to the feeling of the rush of his hot spend seeping out of you instead.

He bent to reach around you into one of the pockets of his peacoat, extracting a handkerchief with a familiar red monogram on it. As he began to attend to you, mindful of your sensitivity as he gently wiped away where his release had mixed with yours, you couldn't help but notice again how it glowed, coating the silky material as he continued his work. You also noticed that his coremata had apparently disappeared.

"I'm naked," you blurted suddenly, dumbly, only just remembering how he had helped you remove your dress. Given that the temperature was apparently low enough for it to snow, you should have been shivering. Except you felt completely content, entirely comfortable as you rested upon the fabric of his coat. You hoped this didn't mean another dry-cleaning bill.

He paused to shoot you a look that said *no shit*, but you ignored it, instead moving to tug at a tendril of his hair. "Aren't you afraid I'll get sick again?" you teased, your voice no louder than a whisper. You moved your hand from his hair to trace the pointed tip of his delicate ear before he captured your wrist, brushing his lips against the inner side of it. His antennae twitched at his, eyes taking on an eerie glint as they narrowed at you, studying your face.

"I am *always* concerned for you," he responded finally. He somehow managed to locate his scarf, reaching to grip at it. He wrapped his around your neck, hands moving to cradle your jaw when he was done. "But this time, I shall keep you warm."

The first snow of the season twinkled around you like diamonds, making you feel like you were among the heavens themselves.

Maybe he *was* some kind of deity and he had brought you with him, toting you through the heliacal rising so you could take your place with him amongst the stars. And as his wings curled around you to shield you from the crystals of snow, you knew that Gideon, true to his word, was no liar.

xv: the agora

YOU DREAMED OF A PALE MIST, of a blue-tinted glow and a lunar rainbow. You dreamed of the quiver of silver wings, of shining red eyes among the twinkling spatters of stars. Most of all, you dreamed of a searing touch brushing against your skin, working you up and up and up until your body was bursting into white flames on the end of a moonbeam.

Except when your eyes opened, lips already parting in a silent gasp, you realized the latter was not a dream at all.

Your groggy mind was still able to recognize Gideon's featherlight touch, one hand circling your clit almost lazily while the weight of his head pressed against your chest as he rolled a nipple between his teeth, long tongue wrapping around it to tug gently. His other hand was tangled within your hair, tips of his clawed fingers scratching pleasantly at your skull.

You had a hard *no* about kissing in the morning; even though the phenomenon of morning breath seemed to be too commonplace to plague the likes of Gideon, you were self-conscious about your own. He had insisted that you were being silly when you had admitted this, but respected the boundary nonetheless. Something you *did* say you were partial to, however, was being woken up in this particular manner with his mouth occupied *elsewhere*, and Gideon was all too happy to take advantage of that.

Because Gideon didn't require much sleep, he was already awake before you were. As the days rolled on following your tryst in his meadow, he had woken you like this quite often. You remembered feeling like you had been at the gates of the Second Circle of Hell after you had slept with him that very first time in his office; now, wrapped in the heady scent of him, the smoky wisps of Earl Grey and moonflowers curling around your tongue, you knew you had fully stepped into that realm's inner depths.

When you came off of the crest of the wave he had eased you onto, your blurry surroundings began to come into focus. Your body twitched in the wake of the afterglow as you felt the soft rumbling of his pleased hum. Blinking a few times, you finally managed to squint at his face, half-curtained by tendrils of sooty hair, ruby eyes alight with mirth as a single fang poked between his lips as they quirked in that roguish smirk of his. He hadn't even put on his glasses yet.

"Good morning," he said once you were somewhat lucid, the honey-smooth lilt of his voice tinged with a delicious morning rasp that had heat pooling within you once more. He pulled away from you to make enough room for you to give a languid stretch atop his massive bed, though you immediately reached out to grip at his silken nightshirt to tug yourself closer to him after doing so.

"It's too early," you grumbled into his chest, grinning at the feeling of the wings accompanying the arms that automatically circled around you in response. His body rumbled again at his chuckle.

"It is not," he countered. You could already picture the way his antennae were twitching at you. "The market has been long open."

"Do we *have* to go?" The question was more of a whine as you tried to burrow farther into him, rubbing your toes into his strong calves. They were covered in the same silky fuzz as the rest of his body, but you hadn't been able to appreciate how toned they were until you'd finally gotten him to drop those tailored pants of his. Maybe you could one day convince him to give shorts a try, though that didn't really seem like his aesthetic.

"This was your idea, little harpy," he returned, rubbing small circles into your back while he gently peeled you away from him. When you only glared, one of his antennae arched. "Do not give me that look. It was your idea and you know it."

"I thought I was a moonflower," you pouted when he moved to sit up, tugging you along with him. Disentangling yourself from him so you could stretch your arms above your head, you tipped forward to yawn into his shoulder.

"You are a moonflower when you make that most *exquisite* face, quivering around me seated deep inside of you as you take me so prettily," he crooned, the way he dragged the tip of his slightly-upturned nose from the shell of your ear down your jawline making you shiver. His words sent another pang of longing straight to your lower abdomen, having you thirsting for more even though he had just brought you release. "But right now, you are being a bratty little harpy, sulking in my sheets while I attempt to indulge one of your other desires." He pushed you back slightly to give you a peck on the nose, a slight tinge of mintiness to his breath. "Now, go get ready. I have to make a few calls, but I will have your breakfast waiting for you."

You stuck your tongue out at his wings when he turned his back to you after rising from the bed, but gave another stretch before much less gracefully clamoring out of the covers. Even if you felt like being lazy, you had to admit it was much more pleasant to wake up in Gideon's apartment, fun little morning routine aside; whereas your floors were always like ice, his were pleasantly warm under your bare feet. As if terrified for you to get sick again, Gideon kept his apartment toasty warm, almost overwhelmingly so. At one point, you had to request for him to actually turn the heat down, saying it felt like you were in a sauna.

Even though you were no longer in that meadow with Gideon,

enamored with the spectacle of the soft glow of the moonflowers and of his wings, the image of him so sharp and vivid amidst the blurry spray of the lunar rainbow from the falls, the dream just continued. It hadn't taken you long to tell your friends that you and Gideon were now an item. Though begrudgingly happy for you in that overprotective way of his, Greer had been disappointed that you were unable to report back on the food at Cielo, but Calli and Effie were markedly much more thrilled to hear about the development.

Effie's face had absolutely screamed *I told you so* at the news, but she squealed equally as loud in delight as Calli had, clapping her hands all the while enthusing about how jealous she was that you were dating a *smoking hot professor*. Calli had wriggled her eyebrows at you the whole time while Greer had continued to bemoan how you hadn't even taken *one single lousy picture* of your dish. He was almost offended when you had admitted you didn't even remember what you had ordered.

The *smoking hot professor* in question, not that you would tell him that Effie had deemed him as such as you didn't need his ego to inflate even more, was ever the practical one, insisting on 'doing this right.' He had cleared everything with the Dean, arranging it so a colleague would grade your essays to ensure there would be no conflict of interests in the grading system. You appreciated the gesture and were actually secretly thrilled at this; if anything, Gideon would show the opposite of favoritism, only being much harder and more critical of your writing. Maybe this colleague would give you a fucking break for once. You were already dealing with enough after-hours lectures as it was.

As you brushed your teeth in a bathroom that was probably the size of your apartment with some kind of fancy toothpaste whose name you couldn't even pronounce, you never realized you would be so absolutely smitten with the concept of the mundane. Despite his own perfectionist tendencies and flamboyant ways of going about things, Gideon's matter-of-fact efficiency did wonders to keep you grounded. The antics of Calli and Effie definitely kept you amused, but you needed the more sensible minds of Greer and Gideon to keep the balance.

You were still equal parts eager and equal parts nervous to bring the two worlds you had so carefully curated in Eventide Falls together. You might need to give Gideon a pointer or two on how to give an adequate handshake in order to impress Greer. Although knowing him, the insufferably gifted man, he would probably excel at that already.

The notion of a found family was something you hadn't realized could actually exist. Sure, you had made friends in your undergraduate studies, but you hadn't managed to forge anywhere near as deep of a connection with any of them. If you would've told your past self that it would take two fairies, a minotaur, and a half-moth-half-fae professor as the cherry on top of your jubilant sundae, she would've snorted right into the whipped cream.

You were constantly ignoring that traitorous voice in the back of your mind telling you that you didn't deserve all of this and they'd only walk away from you. Your parents had done quite the number on your psyche, but the support of Gideon and your friends kept those thoughts at bay. It almost surprised you how much you and Gideon had in common in that regard; though he didn't make it a habit to speak of his grandmother much, you were able to gather from one he'd told you that she was just as critical as your parents were.

He hadn't yet broached the subject of his parents, but given his allusion to his father being gone and having never mentioned his mother, you assumed she also may have passed. You also had been avoiding divulging more about your family, still a bit worried to speak about the whole thing, but you knew that you would someday, just as you hoped he would reveal more of his past to you. All you wanted to do right now was focus on living in the present, and possibly the future you could have with him.

After taking a quick shower and patting yourself dry with what may have been the softest towel in existence, you set it back on its heated rack, folding it so the red monogram was fixed just so in the way you knew Gideon liked it. His over-the-top precision may have been a tad aggravating at times, but you would humor him since you were so appreciative of his attentiveness. Attentiveness that you were extremely thankful for when you dressed and exited his bedroom to patter down his iron staircase, finding a steaming cup of hot chocolate and a plate of freshly-baked scones waiting for you on the stainless steel island of his industrial kitchen. In place of a coaster, there was a note with an elegant scrawl tucked under the mug: *do not burn yourself.*

You rolled your eyes at him, but instantly cursed when you nearly scorched your mouth at your first sip. Wincing, you set the mug back down to come back to later before grabbing a scone to take with you as you wandered around the space. You'd been spending a decent amount of time in his loft with him, but hadn't necessarily explored. The warm brick and neat eclecticism had somewhat surprised you at first; you had been expecting a clinical-looking, completely modern box of grays and blacks, only to see various colorful bobbles from his apparent many travels placed precariously on shelves. You noticed that the shelves were very high up; he was much taller than you for sure, but they were much too high even for his reach.

But the more you took in his dwelling, the more it made sense, especially when you thought about what his office looked like. On the outside, Gideon may have been all hard lines and prim edges, but you were beginning to understand that once you got past his proper exterior, he was more akin to the frame of stained glass hanging by the floor-to-ceiling windows of his living room, throwing arcs of jewel-toned light into the rest of the expansive room.

Chewing on your scone while being mindful not to leave crumbs, you trailed a hand over the back of a caramel-colored couch, the leather smooth and buttery under your fingertips. You stopped at a vintage record player, its dark wood exterior glossy and polished. Noticing a stand right next to it, you put your scone in your mouth to hold between your teeth so you could use both hands to thumb through his records.

Just like he organized the books in his office, his records were organized by genre and by title. They were meticulously arranged so that they were all facing the same way and although they must have been old, you could see that they were well cared for, noting the corners of the sleeves were still crisp. You smiled to yourself when you ran a finger across the edges of a section of old crooners, recognizing a few of the titles yourself, but paused when you grazed a more colorful chunk. Taking a record and pulling it out, you peered at the group of leather-clad human men standing together, tongues out while they flipped off the viewer with their hair teased to high heaven.

"Not what you were expecting, I gather?"

You nearly dropped the record and choked on your scone as you turned to see him leaning against a chair, his arms crossed as he watched you with a sly grin. He was dressed in his usual ensemble, except he now had a gray cashmere sweater over the top of his button down. He was also wearing his glasses again and had your mug of hot chocolate in one of his hands.

Taking the scone out of your mouth, you gave him a sheepish smile and held the record up. "I dunno," you said with a shrug, "I mean, the classical music and jazz made sense... never took you for the *hair metal* type."

"And this breaks the mold that you had assigned me to?" he inquired, seeming more curious than bitter as he uncrossed his arms and strode forward to take the record from you. You nodded and he hummed, seemingly pleased with your response.

"You are a riddle, wrapped in a mystery, inside an enigma, Professor Dulcis," you announced dramatically, finishing the rest of your scone in a few quick bites. He handed you your mug of hot chocolate, which you gingerly took.

"You burned yourself." His eyes lingered on your lips before they met your own as he stated this rather than asked it. Ignoring the face you pulled as you scrunched your nose at him, he then said rather airily, "It is *Doctor* Dulcis, actually."

"Seriously?" you blinked at him, taking a tentative sip as you did so. He nodded and you took another sip after you found it was no longer molten hot. "Doctor of what?"

"Oh, a few things," he waved his hand flippantly. "This and that. Titles are cumbersome, though. It is much easier to just abstain from using them than to have to explain."

You wondered exactly what *this and that* actually meant, but figured you could hold your questions for later as you finished the rest of your hot chocolate. Briefly, you recalled one of the first conversations you'd had with him about *string theory*, of all things, and wondered if quantum physics was anywhere within his portfolio. You left him to walk back to the kitchen and place it in the sink, returning to see that he was already wearing his coat and had yours draped over his arm while he waited for you by the private elevator. He also held his scarf and what looked like a pair of gloves.

"These are for you," he said, holding up the gloves after helping you into your coat and winding his scarf around your neck. The fact that you wore it so often was something that neither of you had ever really addressed, but you always noticed how his eyes seemed to linger on it nestled against your skin every so often.

You thanked him, allowing him to slide them over your hands as you fought the urge to roll your eyes at his overprotectiveness. His penchant for giving you gifts had once made you a bit uncomfortable, but you had just learned to accept that it was one of his preferred methods of showing affection. After all, fae, he had once told you, did not give gifts without reason. "What about *your* hands?"

He held his hands up, which were covered in a fine layer of gray fuzz. "I have my own set of built-in ones, I suppose you could say."

You smiled at this, taking one of his uncovered hands in his as you pressed a button on the elevator. His primary love language may have been gift-giving, but you were much more into physical touch, though he seemed to have no problems in that department either. He also seemed to always know exactly what you needed, wrapping an arm around your shoulder to tug you into his side once you were into the cold morning air outside of his building.

Gideon lived pretty close to the center of Eventide Falls, though his apartment was on the opposite side that yours was. The location was extremely convenient as you only had to walk a few blocks to get to the market that the town held every weekend.

"Any other fun facts you'd like to tell me?" you asked teasingly, elbowing him in the side as you strolled along the sidewalk. It was cold enough that you could see your breath and though he was wearing a coat and had the added benefit of an extra layer of dense fuzz to keep him warm, a lilac blush colored his gray cheeks. He had tied his hair back, but a crisp breeze ruffled the strands that framed his face, as well as the tips of his antennae.

His glasses flashed when he inclined his head down to smile at you, but you noticed it looked a bit forced. An antenna twitched as his brow bone knit together, as if debating something, but then his face was impassive one more. "Well," he began, hand tightening around yours as you drew closer to the crowds within the market, "you already know about my penchant for motorcycles and vintage cars. I like to travel, as you may have noticed." He looked thoughtful for a moment. "I also like to collect quills." As he said this, you remembered seeing an assortment of them displayed on his lofty shelves. He lifted his shoulders before lowering them again. "I am not that interesting, I suppose."

You arched a brow at him in disbelief at that last statement. You wholly begged to differ; Gideon was probably one of the most interesting people you had ever and would ever meet, but you could debate that with him until you were red and he was purple in the face. Feeling his fingers squeeze yours again, you noticed that had gone rigid, tips of his wings and his antennae on high alert just as he had been in the city. Even as early on as him saving you in the maze you knew he preferred solidarity, but you were beginning to realize that his distaste for crowds may have been deeper than you thought.

It humbled you that twice he had gone out of his comfort zone just to humor you. Gideon possessed a deep sense of duty; when you had stumbled upon him in that stupid maze, it was because he had been volunteering on behalf of the local library, and you wondered if he felt the same sense of duty towards you now. As you remembered the confrontation with Lowell and allowing him to cart you out of the maze, you also recalled a similar conversation you had had with him about his motorcycle and how you had admitted you never thought he was the 'motorcycle type.'

A riddle, wrapped in a mystery, inside an enigma, indeed. That may have even been an understatement, as theatrically cliché as it was; you never would have thought that a man who solely dressed in a black-and-white color palette and brought his own coasters to places would have the kinds of interests that he so clearly did, but the phrase *don't judge a book by its cover* instantly came to mind.

As you perused the stalls, you sidled closer to him, feeling a bit bad that he still looked so uncomfortable. Thinking again about his quill collection, you thought to share your curiosity to distract him. "Why are your shelves so high up?"

He blinked, looking confused for a second, before understanding what you were talking about. "Ah. A few of the items displayed there are rather priceless and would be quite inconvenient to go about replacing, naturally." The tips of his wings fluttered slightly as if to prove a point as he then said, "The slightest breeze could jostle them out of their perches. They are more out of the way in their current positions."

"What's it like having wings?" you asked, enjoying the way they caught the morning light. You wondered if it was inconvenient to always have to be mindful not to crush them or close doors on them or something.

"What is it like *not* having wings?" he postured, tone playful instead of unkind. As if he could read your mind again, he then said, "They are a part of me. I often forget I have them, honestly."

"I wish *I* had wings," you said a bit mopingly, touching the wing of a hummingbird depicted in a wind chime at the stall you were currently stopped in front of. It was made out of stained glass, reminding you of the panel in Gideon's apartment, but the colors were all wrong.

"I like you just as well without them." He ducked to press a kiss into your hairline, making your face instantly heat in a blush. The shopkeeper, a dwarf woman with deep set lines in her face and a billow of white hair that looked spun into floss, seemed to melt at this, her kind eyes going misty at the gesture. You could only flush deeper as you waved at her, tugging Gideon along with you.

You really did love physical touch, but physical touch in *public* was still something you had to get used to. Yet again, Gideon surprised you, seeming unbothered about openly displaying his affection even in the crowds he hated so much.

As you continued to walk, he appeared to relax, though you knew from the angle of his antennae that he was far from being completely tranquil. Just as you had seen in Cielo, you began to notice how others — especially those with clear fae ancestry from their similarly-pointed ears — observed him. He paid them no attention, completely focused on asking you questions and pointing things out to you, but you saw how they looked at him almost reverently. Remembering how he had told you that his grandmother's side of his family had lowkey founded the town, you wondered if this had anything to do with that.

"Have you come across anything that interests you yet?" The question was more of a murmur as he reached over to wrap the end of the scarf that had apparently been dropping off your shoulder more tightly around your neck with the hand that wasn't in yours. You shook your head, though a sign for The Abridged Bean caught your eye. The cafe was already in the center of town, but it looked like they must have set up a little pop up counter for the market.

Without warning, you made a beeline for the queue, tugging him to stand beside you behind a faun wearing a red scarf. He must have noticed you looking intently at the assortment of scones even though you'd just had one, wings bristling slightly. You hid your grin, squeezing his hand.

"Yours are better," you insisted, snickering when he sniffed at that, "but you know I'm always hungry. Effie couldn't make it today either, so I figured I'd bring her back some!"

Though he gave you an innocent *I have no idea what you're talking about* look when you tried to soothe his ego when it came to his baking prowess, he seemed to preen at your praise. You stepped forward as the line continued to move, humming to yourself and swinging your joined hands back and forth as you waited.

"Hey, didn't you say there's a word for this in Greek?" you asked suddenly, nose scrunching as you tried to remember it. "The market, I mean. Angora?"

"*Agora*," he corrected. You instantly tensed, regretting asking as the shift in his tone suggested he was about to launch into another impromptu lecture. "Angora is a type of wool." As his back straightened and both his wings and antennae went more rigid, you swallowed a groan. He pointed an index finger upwards. "The *agora* was much more than an open air market, however, and was also an arena for business and politics. The literal meaning can be translated to 'gathering place' or 'assembly.' There is also a phobia, *agoraphobia*, wherein the afflicted becomes anxious in unfamiliar environments or where they perceive that they have little control..."

As he droned on, you couldn't help but think that maybe Gideon was one of the sufferers of that particular anxiety disorder. Even though you weren't necessarily dating him for the after-hours lessons, he finally looked perfectly at ease as he continued his little sermon in an even, measured tone, the slight flicks of his antennae and tips of his wings the only things betraying how excited he was to be telling someone all of this. You merely smiled and nodded, offering hums at certain parts where you knew he had purposely emphasized because he thought them particularly interesting. It was only until you were at the front of the line and having to order your scones where he stopped the knowledge spill.

Despite you insisting you could pay for your own scones, he gave you a scathingly cold look to stop you, pulling out his wallet to cover your purchase and leaving a rather generous tip before he carted you away. You at least had managed to snag the bag, insisting you carry it yourself.

"Gideon." You tugged at his hand, getting him to look down at you once you were back on the sidewalk out of the crowd. "Thank you." You shook your head when he moved to wave his hand nonchalantly. "Not just for the scones. Or even for the gloves and the blanket and everything else." You let go of his hand to instead hug his arm, careful not to drop the small paper bag that held your most recent purchase. "For everything. For bringing me here and showing me Tenebra City and the meadow. For allowing me into your life." You swallowed, suddenly feeling very small and shy. "I—*ah*—sometimes have a hard time expressing my thanks, but..."

"You are most welcome, my moonflower," he interjected, cutting you off when he could tell you were faltering. You tipped your temple against his arm, smiling at the moniker.

"I thought I was only your moonflower when... well, *you know*." You lowered your voice and wriggled your brows, not wanting to say it aloud since you were in public, even if the sidewalks weren't as crowded as the market was.

He tipped his head towards you almost conspiratorially. "Trust me, darling, I call you that merely in anticipation of when we return to my abode." He pushed you gently forward, ignoring your *eep* and corresponding deep blush at the suggestive tone of his voice. "Now let me carry your scones, you insatiable little harpy."

xvi: the seer

"I'M NOT sure how the fuck you talked me into this," you panted, head still a bit muddled from the myriad of stars he had just made you see. At this point, you could have filled a small galaxy with what he had put you through, yet he still seemed intent for more.

Not that you would complain, but damn. A girl had to catch her breath.

"Language." You felt a nip at your shoulder as his hands tugged at the silk tie he had wrapped around your eyes. "You did not seem to mind as much when my head was between your legs and—"

"Alright, alright!" You blushed, grasping for him blindly. You were sitting atop his bed, needing to hold onto something to keep you from completely folding over. His chest rumbled, the sound of his laugh accompanying the vibrations. They shot straight down your abdomen into your core and down further, causing you to twitch and swallow a weak moan.

It was a normal weekday night and you should have been studying, but instead, he had decided to put you through an impromptu *marathon* of sorts. "How can you have this much energy?" you whined, taking a deep gulp of air in an attempt to catch your breath. "It's like you're—"

"*Inhuman?*" You heard a smirk in the offered reply, feeling the tip of a fang trace the shell of your ear. You groaned, finally managing to seek out an arm and cling to it. "Divine, is it not?" You scowled in what you assumed was the direction of him, grip tightening on his arm. "This is a tad reminiscent of King Phineus as referenced in the tale of the Argonauts." He sounded thoughtful and you let out another groan, knowing the lecture that would follow. "He is tormented by harpies... an irony that is not lost on me, although *you* are the one who currently cannot see."

"And whose fault is *that?*" you snapped with a huff, just wanting him to get on with it. He had promised you something and now, greedy as you were, you were impatient for it. You felt his hand grip your jaw gently in warning before it slid down the length of your neck and down your chest, moving to cup one of your breasts. Your breath hitched as you leaned into him, nearly growling in frustration as he just left it there without doing anything.

"Phineus, however, chose his blindness." Though he kept them more filed down than when you had first met him, you still felt the minute prick of the tip of one of his claws stinging a nipple, the warmth of his tongue immediately sweeping over it to soothe the bite. You gripped his arm tighter, a hot surge of longing making your core clench. He released it with a wet *pop*. "He had the gift of prophecy and chose to forgo physical sight in exchange for something much more *powerful*."

The pressure of one of his thumbs suddenly on your clit made you jolt, a shudder ripping down your spine as he captured your bottom lip between his teeth, nibbling at the flesh as you panted against him. He pulled away, dragging a fang down your jaw to rest at the junction where your neck met your shoulder. "In exchange for your loss of sight, I intend to fully compensate you. I would like to try something. I came upon the most *fascinating* concept... I wonder if you would humor me."

"Gideon," you managed to say, feeling your grip on his arm weaken at his ministrations on your sensitive nub. You leaned into his shoulder as that strange haze settled within your mind once again, and although you were beginning to have trouble gathering your thoughts, you knew you above all wanted *more*. You needed him inside of you again, feeling like you might fly apart if he didn't do something soon. "As long as you make me feel like *that* again, you can do whatever the fuck you want." There was another sting as he nipped at your earlobe in reprimand. "Alright sorry, sorry. Rule two, I remember."

"Rule *one*," he corrected, but sounded pleased. You could have sobbed as his hand pulled away from your clit, but it was soon at your other breast to join its twin. Two *other* smooth appendages suddenly were under your arms, lifting you and turning you; the motion was slow, but you still felt a bit dizzy as two more settled around your hips, the heady scent of Earl Grey, leather, and moonflowers accompanying them. You tried to count the touches fluttering about you: four wriggling coremata, two strong arms, one weeping cock, and a partridge in a pear tree.

Must have been your lucky day. You hit the fucking — literally — *jackpot.*

"Describe what you're doing," you said softly, a bit desperate. You recognized you were sitting atop of his strong thighs, the muscles rippling underneath you as his cock jumped against your stomach from where you straddled him. You felt the ridges grind against your skin. "*Please.*"

"I will not need to describe anything," he rasped, voice suddenly sounding much darker, "you will be able to feel all of it and know exactly what I am doing to you." You let out another moan at the feeling of his thumb returning to your clit, rubbing lazy circles against it. "Although since you asked so *nicely*, perhaps I shall indulge you."

"Please," you whispered, feeling his coremata lifting you slightly as his thumb continued its pace. Your hands managed to find his shoulders, digging into the velvety skin as you felt him adjust under you.

"I wish to see how many of my coremata can fit within you." His mouth was near your ear again, breath fanning against it. You heard a hunger in his words, an eagerness that made your heart lurch just as you felt yourself clench in tune to the rhythm of his thumb. You weren't sure if he had turned up the heat of his apartment again or if it was just the result of the exertion, but your body felt absolutely aflame, sweat already pooling at your temples. "You look so pretty taking one... you would look absolutely ravishing taking two. Or three. Or perhaps..." He pressed against your clit a bit harder, the sudden pressure causing you to let out a high keen, "*Four.*"

Your mind seemed to refuse to even try and imagine the feeling of *four* of those silvery appendages curling within you, though your walls quivered in excited anticipation. Since he had first shown you his coremata, he became less self-conscious about them. He didn't use them often during sex, but when he did, you were always a happy camper. He hadn't yet slid more than one in you at a time, though.

You faintly recognized that you were being lifted once again before you felt the tip of one of them brush between your legs. You stilled, feeling Gideon's other hand rest upon your thigh and begin to rub small, comforting circles to match the pace of his thumb against your clit. When the corema began to push forward, his lips were on yours in a gentle kiss, swallowing your gasp.

"Relax, darling," he murmured, voice like honey as his thumb applied a bit more pressure to your clit, as if to distract you. With a tiny nod, you tried your best to unclench your muscles, feeling a bit of smug satisfaction when you felt the rumble of his pleased hum. "Just like that. So good for me."

This had you melt even more and when more of his corema sank into you, you didn't tense. Instead, you leaned forward, trying to take stock of the rest of his appendages again. Ok, one hand on your thigh, one on your clit, two by your hips, the third very obviously within you... and the fourth?

Where was the fourth?

You didn't have much time to dwell on how the fourth corema was MIA as the sensation of the one seated inside you twisting stole all rational thought. You groaned, head falling against his shoulder. One of his hands slid up from your thigh to rest against your abdomen, pushing slightly against it. The skin felt too tight under his touch, and as he swept his thumb over it, the fullness made you quiver again.

It was borderline uncomfortable, the pronounced weight of it pulsing within you practically making you delirious as you felt yourself stretch and strain around him to accommodate it. Its undulating motion was relentless while it rippled and roiled, massaging you more open for him. You felt the urge to shift your hips, but there was nowhere to go; nowhere to escape from the sensations tearing through you.

You were probably drooling against him, but he didn't seem to care as he continued his ministrations, peppering your neck with innocent kisses as if the rest of him wasn't working to completely debauch you. Unlike Gideon's dick, his coremata were completely smooth, though they still managed to create a dragging sensation by twirling and knotting within you. Another twist and surge of his corema basically ripped your release from you, a pitched moan muffled by his shoulder escaping your mouth as you fluttered around him in surprise at your own orgasm.

"Beautiful," he crooned as the fourth corema made itself known again, brushing your hair back to bare more of your neck. It then wrapped around it, squeezing slightly. It wasn't enough to inhibit your breathing, but just so that you could clearly feel the weight of it. "Are you ready for a second?"

You weren't sure what possessed you to attempt to nod your head as you panted against his skin, but you did, and you could practically see his antennae twitch in your mind. You felt the soft breeze of his wings quivering as the coremata at your hips readjusted you, one leaving your skin to brush against your entrance. His thumb left your clit to brush downwards, massaging where his other corema was pressed into you, and you realized he must have been using your own wetness to ease the second corema's passage.

His thumb returned to your clit when the second dipped into you, your mouth dropping even farther open. You let out a strange sound that was somewhere between a moan and a hiss, unable to stop your body from tensing. You already felt so *full*.

"I—" You licked your lips, brow furrowing at the fullness. "I d-don't think I can."

You felt his lips press against your scalp as the second coremata paused. "You can, little moonflower," he insisted gently, and for some reason, you found yourself believing him. Even reduced to a pool of your former self, you trusted him. "You have done so superbly, thus far. You make me so proud. Just relax. *Breathe*."

But oh, there was your desire to please him again. In that moment, you would be willing to do anything to get that rumble of approval that would bubble from his chest, imagining the glow of pride in those eyes you couldn't see. Though a quiet whimper escaped your lips, you attempted to hone in on the way he was now rolling your clit between his thumb and index fingers. His other two coremata had left your hips to massage your breasts, while his other hand still rubbed against your abdomen, which you suspected must have had a slight bulge to it. Even though you couldn't see it, the image of it in your mind excited you.

When he began moving again, the first retreated just as the second continued its advance. You lightly pressed your teeth into his shoulder to bite back a choked sob. You felt like you were beyond bursting at this point, but somehow the sensation of being utterly filled and strained seemed so *right*, like you were always meant to take him like this.

Gideon had once told you that his coremata were sensitive in the way that a limb was, but not necessarily in the way a sexual organ was. This was a blessing and a curse as it essentially allowed him to do whatever he wanted to you without pause, although from the way his cock, which was fully out of his slit, jerked against your stomach again, he must have been getting aroused by the sight of them disappearing within you. You wished you could see his face, wondering if it was colored lilac in a flush, just as you wished you had the strength to reach down and take his cock in your hands to run your fingertips over the sensitive ridges and the flared, feathered tip of its head.

You pressed your teeth a bit harder when the second pushed in more. Gideon's body tensed under you, his mouth finding the junction of your neck to suck at your heated skin. A bead of sweat rolled down your face as you nearly sighed in relief when the coremata stilled within you, eyes falling half-shut behind your blindfold. Then, they popped right back open, going wide as dinner plates at the feeling of his coremata shifting and wrapping around each other to intertwine.

"*Oh!*" was all you managed to exclaim, the cry whistling between where your teeth met his shoulder. You shuddered, not sure if the tightening coil within you at this point was your desire or his coremata sliding in a spiral around each other to bump and drag at your inner walls. You could feel their slightly pointed tips slithering around you in a helix as if searching for something, and when one managed to hook at a particularly sensitive spot, you jolted, letting out another cry. The pull of Gideon's lips marked his smirk against your neck while the other corema joined its twin to almost savagely press against that spot as you cried again.

That was enough to rip another orgasm for you, the tips of the coremata continuing to piston against their new discovery as their bases twisted and contorted around each other. Somehow, the feeling of being beyond full was stretched even more, so overwhelmingly so that you thought you were being consumed from the inside out. Though your body trembled, your walls were nearly unable to flutter around him in your release due to the lack of room. You ground your eyes shut, rubbing your forehead into his shoulder as you tried to stay conscious, a strange cloudy haze beginning to cloy its way through the edges of your already fragile lucidity.

Just as you thought you were coming down from your high, another sharp twist and pull and drag would have you on the ascent yet again, mind cursing Gideon with the swears your mouth was unable to form. Finally, mercifully, the coremata began to slow, the gentle rubbing of his thumb against your clit guiding you downwards.

"Two it is then," he sighed mournfully as you continued to twitch under his electric touch. "A pity. Oh, well. Perhaps one day we shall try for four."

You must have not been as lucid as you had originally thought because suddenly you felt very *empty*. You realized that he had managed to pull both coremata out from you, your entrance quivering around utter nothingness. He must have *also* managed to make you completely depraved because you still wanted him, the feeling of your own wetness dripping from your core a reminder that you were no longer full.

"M-More," you gasped into his shoulder. You felt the silk sheets of his mattress underneath your hands, where they now hung limply by your sides. You counted two coremata back at your hips, sliding against your skin with a telltale dampness. The ones at your breasts had been completely forgotten about, though they still rubbed circles into your pebbled nipples.

"Say please." His command was mocking, but there was a tenseness to it that suggested that maybe he wasn't completely immune to what he had done to you. You licked your dry lips, brow furrowing as you tried to will your brain back into motion.

"*Please*," you were able to finally say after a moment and a few more pants. His hand slid across your abdomen to rest at your waist, the other leaving your clit to join it at the other side. Then he was pushing you back from him, the two coremata at your breasts sliding upwards to keep you from completely slumping. "W-What are you doing?"

"Did I not tell you that you would feel it?" he asked with a sardonic sigh, though you knew he was only teasing you. "Very well, I shall tell you in a moment."

You felt a third corema wrap around your neck again, slightly lifting your head up. His forehead was then pressed against yours as his hands trailed down your side to rest against your thighs, pulling your legs a bit wider around him. You recognized the feeling of the feathered tip of his cock as it slithered down your stomach, causing you to hiss when it bumped against your overly-sensitive clit and dragged down your entrance, where he paused.

Had you possessed the strength, you may have tried to lower yourself down to take control of your own pleasure. Luckily, his coremata were soon doing that for you, the one around your neck keeping your head in place as your spine arched when you finally felt the flare of him begin to drag into your walls. He sank in little by little, allowing you to adjust this time as you blindly searched for something to hold onto. You recognized the little ridged nubs scraping against you, but when you felt something *else* there, your brain stuttered to a complete stop.

"W-What?" was all you could inquire, your eyes torn between squeezing shut or widening even more at the foreign sensation. He felt even *girthier* somehow, something you hadn't thought possible.

"So *tight*," he purred, sounding absolutely smitten. Had you possessed more of your faculties, you may have smiled in delight at his reverent tone. "That, my moonflower, is the feeling of one of my coremata wrapped around me. Intriguing, is it not?"

Intriguing. That was one way you could put it, though you may have used *another* word for it if you were more capable of thought. The way his corema wrapped around his cock almost made it segmented, forcing you to expand as he sank into you ring by ring, the spiral bumping against your clit the more you were lowered upon it. You felt him tense when you clenched again.

He stilled momentarily before you felt his hips begin to move, the coremata at your waist assisting his hands in moving you up and down while he thrusted. The thrusts were shallow, as if he were trying to let you get acclimated with the new sensation of his corema wrapped around his cock, though the flared tip still created that pleasing sucking feeling you liked so much. The corema around your neck squeezed gently as you felt his lips moving against your own while you babbled nonsensically against them.

You realized that as he was thrusting into you, he was simultaneously working you lower and lower; although you must have been completely drenched by now, the friction was still mind-blowing as the coil within you began to wind around itself again. You were starting to wonder if you would be able to see straight after this, even once he removed this infernal blindfold.

You were beginning to feel so impossibly full again, the skin of your stomach stretching taut once more from where he was seated within you. A strange anticipation began to take hold as you questioned how much more there was left to go; surely, he was almost fully there?

Except a rather large bulge stuttering against the already straining entrance to your core had your brow furrowing again. It took you a moment to process what it might have been before you remembered how long Gideon's coremata were; it felt like he had almost wrapped one around the same section once or twice, creating a knot of sorts at the base of his cock.

"If only you could see yourself now, little moonflower." His temple was now pressed against the side of your head, the corema against your neck still holding it upright. "You look absolutely *magnificent*." Though his words seemed even enough, it sounded like he was almost gritting his teeth and you could hear his breath beginning to come out in much harsher huffs. "Your lips are parted in the most delectable way. Your skin is flushed the most exquisite shade of red from your hair all the way down to your toes. I can *feel* them curled around my back even if I cannot see them, just as I can feel you quivering around me so *sinfully*."

You arched your back in an attempt to take some of the pressure off, but when you did so, the movement caused you to open even more to him. It was enough so that the knot he had created finally slipped within you, allowing him to be fully sheathed in your warmth. His resulting groan had you clenching even more, the sound so wickedly rich that it was almost tangible, curling around your tongue like melted chocolate.

You were beginning to lose track of his other appendages again, fully focused on the drag and the fullness of him pumping into you. You tasted bergamot and citrus as his tongue swept across your lips, mouth parting to allow it access while the pinpricks of his fingertips made you cognizant of where they were squeezing into the side of your thighs. One corema still wrapped around your neck to hold you steady while the other two must have still been at your waist.

As white began to creep into the edges of the darkness the blindfold had forced upon you, you registered sharper pinpricks at your thighs. Gideon's thrusts became more fervent, though the drag of his cock within you was still forceful and intense. When he gave a particular roll of his hips that allowed the knot to twist within you as the tip of his cock snagged against somewhere deep, your darkened vision exploded into the kind of brightness that made your head throb.

You didn't recognize the sound of your own moan, which Gideon seemed to enjoy from the ever-increasing tempo. You were only able to choke out a long, sustained breath, the bumps and ridges and feathered head of his cock mercilessly ravaging your inner walls as he continued to plunder you through your orgasm. You heard the flutter of his wings behind him as he moved. Finally, just as you thought you would cease to exist, his hips gave a few quick stutters before he was moaning your name into your own mouth, sweeter than anything you had ever tasted as you felt a rush of warmth as he spilled within you.

The sharper pinpricks turned into more of a squeeze as you were suddenly clamped flush against him. *Claspers*, you recognized, remembering how he had first shown them to you after your time in the meadow. They were hidden behind those two additional slits you had seen higher up on his groin. They would leave bruises on your skin, something you once had to convince Gideon you *liked* after he had freaked out about it the first time, nearly flying out the window for some kind of salve when he had realized what he had done. Now, he liked the slightly purple splotches they left just as much as you did.

Though his claspers holding you so tightly against him no longer allowed him the space to thrust, he continued to roll his hips, dragging his cock languidly as his hot release still pumped within you. You convulsed around him again, having him hiss as you felt another torrent of his release coat your inner walls, though the knot he had created with his corema allowed none of it to escape.

It felt like you had died a small death, though you finally felt completely satiated. You felt the corema around your neck give you one last squeeze before it slid away, the ones at your side also retracting as you slumped forward. He pulled his lips from yours.

"Such a good girl." The sound of his voice was like a lullaby as you sank into him. You no longer felt his claspers at your thighs; instead, his hands were lifting you upwards again as he carefully pulled out of you. "Easy there, darling. That's it."

You whimpered at the drag, but gave a blissful sigh when it was over, though the hungriest part of your mind still mourned the loss of him. Even though you were empty, you still felt yourself twitch and quiver and you jolted when the light touch of the silk handkerchief between your legs as he gently swiped against you, the action coupled with your sensitivity causing a bolt of electricity to fizzle back to your core. He must have recognized this as he guided your head back to his shoulder, your eyes fluttering shut beneath your blindfold as he used his other hand to rub your back while murmuring words you couldn't even register into your ear.

You didn't attempt to hide your tired yawn, fully spent and not even sure what time it was. You felt the slide of your blindfold coming away from your skin as the hand on your back moved up to remove it while he warned, "Keep your eyes closed. Open them slowly so they may adjust."

You grumbled at this, not sure you would be able to even open them at *all*, instead burrowing your nose into him. You inhaled, the scent of him swirling around your head like incense. Once he was done cleaning you up, you felt his arms caging you as he delicately guided you to lie against him atop his bed.

You snuggled into his chest, throwing a leg over his thigh to pull yourself closer to him. He gripped at it, his other arm snaking under your head to curl against your upper back.

"Phineus was right," you said after a while, though the words came out in more of a slur in your exhaustion. "That was a fair trade." His chest mumbled as he chuckled, causing you to press a sleepy smile into his skin.

"I had intended for you to take all four," you heard him say, fingertips brushing at your thigh. You giggled at how he seemed to bemoan this, though his fingers suddenly curling to squeeze at your skin had you pause. "You think I am jesting, little harpy? I assure you; one day, you will take them all."

He then pressed a kiss against the crown of your head, humming to himself innocently as he stroked your skin as if the concept of taking all four coremata at once wasn't simultaneously terrifying and thrilling you.

That motherfucker.

Ah, well. You burrowed into him, allowing yourself to begin to doze off. Too bad you weren't actually a seer like King Phineus; you would love to know if that would ever come to fruition.

Although he knew it as well as you did… you were never one to back down from a challenge.

xvii: compendium

THE MONSTER in front of you was not unfamiliar. Taller than any human man, its thin, papery skin was pulled so tight that veins of arteries and cords of muscles could be visible underneath its surface. It was crafted with the intent of being beautiful, yet its lustrous black hair and pearly white teeth could not make up for the watery, sunken eyes, nor could they mask the overall air of death the creature brought.

Out of your peripheral vision, you noticed a dark object slinking towards you. With a squeak, you slapped away the gray claw-tipped hand reaching for your popcorn. You turned your head away from the silver screen to glare at a pair of glowing red eyes.

"I told you to get your *own*," you huffed, pinching a piece between your thumb and index finger to hold out to Gideon when he only narrowed said glowing red eyes at you. He merely scoffed in response to your meager offering. "Don't make me say I told you so!"

"I did not wish for a whole bucket to myself," he retorted, lifting the arm he had resting across your shoulder to flick at the shell of your ear. "I assumed that getting you the *family* size meant you might have been willing to share. Clearly, I was mistaken."

"Well, you know what they say about *assuming*," you chirped, yanking your hand back to toss the spurned offering back into your mouth. You chewed and then grinned at him. "You make an *ass* out of you and—*hey*! Stop that!"

You erupted in a flurry of giggles when his arm slid down to tickle at your sides, trying not to launch the bucket of popcorn off your lap as you tried to swat his fingers away. It would serve him just *right* if you got melted butter all over his leather seats and pristine floors, but you decided you'd like to live to see another day.

"Fine, keep your hoard, harpy," he said with a smirk, though it seemed somewhat forced. It looked more like a tightening of his lips across his teeth, no tell-tale crinkle by his eyes or fang peeking through to seem genuine. He pulled his hands from your side to settle an arm around your shoulder again.

You stuck your tongue out at him before looking back at the movie you were watching, but couldn't help but glance at his figure out of the corner of your eye every so often. The family-owned Sundown Diner in the center of town hosted drive-in movie nights here and there to capitalize on its late hours of operation — appropriate considering the family in question was one of *lycan* nature — so when Gideon had asked what you wanted to do over the weekend, that had been your suggestion. Continuing to munch on a handful of popcorn, you then remarked after a few seconds of watching the monster flail in front of a pillar of fire, "Undead monster terrorizing a village doesn't really scream *super festive,* huh?"

Winter was just beginning to wrap its icy fingers around Eventide Falls, so the fact that the movie being shown was an old black-and-white rendition of *Frankenstein* didn't seem all that seasonally appropriate. You would have to look at the Sundown's upcoming schedule to see if they were planning to show pictures more to the tune of jingle bells and snowmen and less to rotting flesh and gore.

You waited for Gideon to contradict you and say that Frankenstein's monster was not, however, considered undead at all, but merely an *assortment* of body parts, but he only chuckled. The somewhat flat sound was accompanied with a half-hearted lifting of his shoulders rather than a rumble of his chest.

"No," he agreed a bit detachedly after a beat, the reflection of the blazing fire dancing in his glossy eyes as the old audio crackled with static while the music swelled dramatically, "it does not."

You gave him an odd look before shrugging and looking back down at your popcorn. You thought something might be off, but weren't sure if you were just over-thinking things. Knowing neither of you were really paying all that much attention to the movie, you tried another topic of conversation.

"I'm going to start applying for internships soon," you supplied casually, shaking your bucket of popcorn to more evenly distribute the butter. Scrunching your nose at how soggy the popcorn looked, you decided against burying your hand in it. You should have requested for them to go light on the butter at the concession stand just as he had suggested, but you would never admit that to *him*. "I did some research earlier before you picked me up. I think I found a few companies I'd like to apply to."

Not only was the internship a requirement for your program, but the extra cash along with the needed experience would be nice. You had a decent amount saved from past part-time jobs, as well as the undergrad tutoring you'd started doing lately, and your rent wasn't too expensive, but you were beginning to feel a tad anxious about your financial buffer wearing a smidgen too thin. There was no way in heaven or hell or anywhere else on earth or in the afterlife that you would even consider contacting your parents even in the most desperate situation, but ever the planner, you kept a five-layer contingency plan in place to avoid getting close to that.

"Really?" He was looking down at you much more intently. So that *did* get his attention. Dragging a pointed fingertip along your jawline, he tucked a strand of hair behind your ear. "Eden owns a rather large enterprise in Tenebra City, you know. I am sure if I inquired about it that he would—"

"No thanks," you interjected quickly, blushing a bit at your sudden outburst. You knew exactly where he was going with this and while it was really considerate of him, you'd never even met Eden and you weren't about to have Gideon feel indebted on your behalf. "Not that I'm not grateful. It's—I just..." you sighed, fidgeting with the cardboard rim of your bucket, "I want to do it on my *own*, you know?"

That was also the truth. While you considered yourself an opportunist, you didn't necessarily like the concept of anything being handed to you. You wanted to be able to look at your résumé and know that you had landed those jobs on your own, and although business may have been all about networking, you wanted to do that by yourself, too.

You half expected for him to protest; to give you a condescending look and tell you that you were being foolish by turning down the offer. He might scoff and tell you how much time you would save by just accepting or how unlikely it would be to even get an interview, never mind obtain an offer. These were all things your parents would have done and said, at least. But Gideon merely gave a thoughtful hum, his curt nod one of understanding. "Anywhere would be more than lucky to have you."

You practically glowed at this, beaming at him as he squeezed your shoulder. The smile faltered slowly as he reached up to remove his glasses and place them carefully in the cup holder between your seats. He rubbed the bridge of his nose between his fingers. Ok, you clearly hadn't been overthinking; something was *definitely* off. Giving him a more scrutinizing look, you noticed that his antennae were at an oddly steep angle and his wings even looked more rigid. In fact, when you thought more about it, you realized he'd been this sort of gloomy ever since this morning.

"Ok, what's wrong?" You placed your bucket of popcorn between your feet, feeling the fingers on the hand resting on your shoulder twitch as he stiffened slightly. Twisting your torso to be able to look at him more fully, you quirked an eyebrow as you threatened, "You *know* I'll call bullshit if you say 'nothing,' Gideon."

He turned his head, inclining down to look at you. An antenna twitched and you could tell a reprimand at your language was on the tip of his tongue, but he merely sighed. "That is an answer *you* would give, though."

"Which is how I know it's bullshit!" you said cheerfully, patting at his upper arm. You then froze at the impassive look he gave you in return. Uh oh, were you being too pushy? This was so typical *you*, going too far and ruining everything. You winced at your own impulsiveness, twisting in your seat and redirecting your gaze from his face back to the screen. "I can tell something is bothering you. I won't force you to talk about it if you don't want to, but I just thought…"

You felt his arm slide from your shoulder before his fingers curled around your wrist, pulling your hand away from your mouth and into your lap where your other hand was resting. You hadn't even realized you'd been chewing at your thumbnail again. Fingertips were then under your chin, gently guiding it so you could face him again.

"I do not wish for you to worry on my behalf," he said softly, lowering his hand to join its twin in your lap. Both cocooned your hands, squeezing lightly. "You are correct in your observations. There has been much occupying my mind lately."

You chewed your lip for a second, brows knitting together as you studied his face. The light from the projector screen flickered across his skin, causing his features to look much more severe. Even through the harsh shadows, you could recognize a faint dreariness clouding his eyes.

"I had meant to approach this topic with you when the moment was right, but I suppose there is no right or wrong moment." His eyes flickered to the screen, a smile tinged with bitterness playing at the corners of his lips. "Did you know that Frankenstein is often called the modern Prometheus? I could not help but… *appreciate* the coincidence."

"What coincidence?" You *did* know that, but weren't sure how it had anything to do with his brooding mood.

His gaze returned to yours as he shook his head. "No matter." It dropped to your lap to watch his fingertips fiddling with your own as he traced the curvature of each digit carefully with the point of his index finger. "That night in the clearing, I mentioned my grandmother's intentions for me. How she wishes for me to abandon my current career, thinking it frivolous." He studied the pads of your fingers intently, as if trying to engrain the patterns of your skin in his memory. "She has been more insistent lately. I"—he swallowed, his voice suddenly thick—"I do not know what to tell her."

You stared at him, not used to seeing this kind of Gideon. You remembered the same look of uncertainty he had given you that night. She had called him then, too; you had watched his antennae flicker in frustration as he had been forced to excuse himself from the table. You also recalled a similar bitter smile that had tugged at his lips when you had brought up his hobby of fixing motorcycles and old cars during that 3AM conversation at your apartment.

Everything my grandmother hates, he had stated then, his mouth curling around the words as if he didn't like the flavor of them. *My own personal form of rebellion.*

"You don't get along, do you?" you ventured delicately. When he moved to pull his hands away, you held onto them. "It's ok, I don't get along with my parents, either."

His antennae quirked, though he didn't necessarily appear to be surprised. Though this was the first time you'd mentioned them to him, he was intelligent; he probably gathered enough from your very lack of acknowledgement that your relationship with them wasn't necessarily ideal.

"It is... complicated." He allowed his shoulders to settle minutely. "She raised me. My parents died when I was very young. I do not even remember them." He looked up quickly, eyes sharply trained on yours as if scrutinizing them for any traces of pity. When he found none, he more visibly relaxed. He cleared his throat. "She never cared much for my mother. She was extremely disappointed in my father for 'sullying' the bloodline and coupling with a cryptid instead of a fae. Never mind that my mother's family was well of means and well-respected within their community. *New* money, she used to deride them, though."

Your inquiry of how they died was at the tip of your tongue, but you swallowed it down. You gaped at this; though you had every intention of being there to listen to him, you couldn't help but feel a little self-conscious. Would Gideon's grandmother think of your family the same? Social climbers intent on grasping greedily at the chance to be called *new* money?

"That, uh"—you licked your chapped lips, searching for something to say—"sounds a bit judgmental."

You winced. Maybe you shouldn't have landed on *that*. Hopefully he wouldn't take any offense.

Luckily he didn't. He gave another humorless laugh, squeezing your hands. "That is an understatement. For as prominent as the Dulcis family that she married into is, my grandmother comes from an ancient and noble line. For all intents and purposes, I believe she may think she married down by settling for my grandfather." His lips twitched again. "The very last of the old world that she retains is her title. '*Lady* Cordelia Dulcis,' she insists on being addressed, though it means nothing anymore. How utterly nonsensical."

His face contorted, the upturned tip of his nose twitching as he scrunched it in distaste. He reminded you of, well, *you* when he made that expression. You wondered if you had been rubbing off on him as he continued, "Ladyship aside, those who claim to be part of her exclusive inner circle more affectionately, if there is such a thing in her court, call her 'DeeDee,' but she is referred to as 'Duchess' by the ones who could only be content with looking in." He scoffed. "None of that means anything either, of course. Her empty titles were earned less out of respect and more out of fear."

"Is this the part where I sarcastically tell you that she sounds *lovely*?" you tried to joke, wriggling your brows at him. You were pleased to see that the corners of his eyes at least crinkled at this while the tips of his wings quivered, though the glitter silver in the light of the reflective screen you were parked in front of didn't seem to have its usual sheen.

"The very moment," he agreed, going along with your jest. He was still much more tense than usual, but you were glad he seemed to be thawing little by little. You were even more thrilled that he was actually talking all of this out with you. "To her credit, my grandfather was an absolute cad. He left right after the birth of my father. I have never met him." His brow bone scrunched, as if something had pained him. "This is why I told you that I am cursed; this is what I meant about my grandfather and father abandoning their families, by choice or not."

"I still don't think you're cursed, Gideon," you murmured, gripping onto his hands like *you* needed the support. "Even if you *are* thirteenth of your name. Some cultures view thirteen as a lucky number, you know."

"I suppose so," he acquiesced after a moment, his tone still a bit too sullen for your liking.

"She never understood my ambitions. She could not—*cannot*—accept that they may differ from her own, as well as those that she had set for me." He tilted his head, absently looking away from you to peer back at the movie. His next question sounded almost rhetorical, directed more to the air than at you. "What would you say to her, were you in my position?"

Your gaze followed his, looking at the flickering image on the screen. The movie was nearly over, the now much meeker figure of Victor Frankenstein clutching at the captain of the ship he was currently on. Ice clung to the fringes of his hair and his eyelashes while he gasped theatrically, hands trembling as he uttered his last words to the man with a final, rattling breath. *Seek happiness in tranquility and avoid ambition.*

What impeccable timing. And what utter bullshit.

Gideon seemed to flinch at this parting line just as your heart thumped at his question still hanging in the air. This very scenario was one that you knew all too well. The swell of the emotion of your own memory completely washed away any wonder that he was turning to *you* for advice as you felt a fire ignite within you, almost recognizing your past self in him.

You grit your teeth and tugged at his wrists. When he turned back to you, you looked him straight in the eye, stating without hesitation, "I would tell her to fuck right off!"

You would. You *had*.

His jaw went slack at your words, head tilting as they rattled around in his mind. He then seemed to pull himself together right before your very eyes. You could practically see the sparkle return to his wings, the magentas and olives coming alive to fill the space with color again. His antennae returned to their usual angle as the tension in his shoulders dissipated. When his lips quirked in that lopsided way of his smirk, you caught the flash of a single fang. "Well, you can tell her that *yourself*, then."

As you simply gawked at him, he continued by saying a bit ominously, "I have been summoned." He brought your wrist up to his mouth, his breath fanning along the delicate skin there. "I have divulged this *compendium* of sorts to you because I must make my annual visit... and I would like, very much"—he pressed his lips to it without breaking his gaze—"for you to join me."

xviii: a judgement of paris

GIDEON HAD ONCE BROUGHT you to the gates of the Second Circle of Hell, his heady scent wrapping around you as if in greeting. You had enjoyed your time there, feeling as though the slow descent was worth it. Unfortunately, the fall hadn't stopped, and as you gaped at the double doors to the Ninth Circle, you wondered why the flying fuck you had agreed to this in the first place.

The morning had started off splendidly. You had awoken to Gideon's usual antics, opening your eyes in a flash of white just as your lips parted in a silent scream. You had eventually been able to focus on two antennae, realizing his head was between your legs when your blurred vision finally pieced itself together just as you had arched off his silken sheets. Soon, you had been rocking against the ridged nubs of his length, chasing the morning sun just as you chased your next high. Though as the feathered tip flared within you, making you feel like it had been suctioning at your very soul, you couldn't help but feel there was something different about the way he had guided you through your languid release, clawed fingertips carding through your hair while his mouth pressed against the pulse point in your neck. His lips had moved as if whispering apologies into your skin.

He *should* have been apologizing, you thought to yourself, a bit cantankerous as you felt his hand curl around your wrist to prevent you from worriedly chewing your nails down to stubs. You had been forced to sit on your hands in the car on the ride over, knee bouncing sporadically like a possessed jack-in-the box as Gideon's own hands clutched at the steering wheel, grayed knuckles turning white.

When Gideon had first referred to the estate as "Hell on Earth," you had thought he was speaking figuratively. Except as the car had pulled onto the narrow road you would eventually realize to be a private driveway, wrought iron gates parting with a grating screech to seemingly bemoan rather than welcome your entry, you understood his words also rang true in the literal sense; for when the thick blanket of gnarled trees gave way to a clearing, you had found yourself in a world in stasis.

You were half expecting something dark and gloomy in nature, but Dulcis Manor blazed nearly blinding, white and immaculate and more pristine than the untouched snow. This was in acute contrast to the black tiles so dark they seemed to absorb the sun itself, covering the entirety of the roof except for on the front-most tower, whose stunning crimson tiles reminded you of Gideon's eyes.

Vaguely recalling an art history class you had taken in high school, you recognized its architectural elements to be reminiscent of the Victorian era, though you suspected the manor may have even predated that. Pointed finials on the roof pierced the sky, gleaming threateningly against their obsidian backdrop. Projecting bay windows were lined with the same sanguine color as the roof on the tower, thick curtains in the exact shade preventing you from seeing inside. Spindles spun their way between banisters like spider webs, giving the impression that Dulcis Manor proudly wore its wrap around porch like a collar.

Its entire massive facade seemed sharpened with harsh shadows, as if the late morning light had honed into razors rather than diffusing into beams. For all intents and purposes, the structure was hauntingly beautiful, except there was a disconcerting element making it appear that the closer you had drawn to it, the more *alive* it felt. It was nearly oppressive as it loomed above you, and as you stepped out of Gideon's car, unable to keep yourself from staring as he had held your door open for you, the very air seemed to shift. Dulcis Manor had this thick aura of *enduring* about it, as if it was a relic from the past that still refused to be put down or forgotten.

Giving your wrist a comforting squeeze, Gideon stepped forward to wrap his fingers around the brass door knocker. You couldn't help but stare at it, eyes trailing the looping tendrils extending from the ring, wrapping around themselves upwards to disappear into the head of the anguished-looking woman depicted in high relief there. It took you another moment before you realized that those tendrils were snakes and they actually made up the hair of the woman —a Gorgon.

You had been staring straight at the Medusa. It was a wonder you hadn't turned to stone to join the gargoyles that must have been hidden somewhere around the property.

You clung to Gideon's hand as the heavy doors opened with a hollow *creak*, equally parts thrilled and horrified that he wanted you to meet his grandmother. As the doors gave way to reveal a grave man with an expression that suggested he may not know what a smile was, you felt Gideon go tense.

"Master Dulcis." The man's voice was deep and raspy, as if he never had a drop of water in his life. He gave an elegant bow, one arm stiffly pressed to his abdomen while the other curled around his back as he dipped at the waist. Cool in countenance, his regard of Gideon held utmost respect, though when his black eyes lingered on you after he straightened, you felt nothing more than contempt. A sense of déjà vu hit you as he reminded you exactly of the maître d' in Cielo who had harbored the same disdain.

That look suggested that you didn't belong here... that you were merely an outsider that had somehow found her way in, playing a foolish game of pretend while you had picked out your finest dress to wear, brushing off Gideon's offers to take you shopping. This time, though, you didn't shrink away; you lifted your chin, meeting those steely eyes with your own.

"Hello, Gillivray." Gideon's response was curt, voice sounding tight as he squeezed your hand. You felt his thumb sweep up to rub against your wrist in soothing circles, though you weren't sure if the action was for your comfort or for his.

The man — *Gillivray* — opened the doors wider, lifting his arm to extend it horizontally in what you took as a *come in* gesture. You broke your stare as Gideon led you inside, catching the tips of the man's pointed ears as you passed him. He must have been some kind of fae, too.

The doors croaked shut behind you with a resolute *bang*, the sound echoing throughout the open space. Your eyes immediately landed on a dual sweeping staircase, the polished marble and dark iron banisters extending towards you as if meaning to envelope you in a choking hug. A bright red runner spilled down them like a waterfall of blood, the color reflected in the chandelier that hung precariously above your heads.

Your gaze dropped downwards towards your feet. The black and white tiles of the foyer made you feel like you had stepped onto a chess board. You wondered if Gideon felt the same; if he felt like some kind of pawn as you remembered his explanation of his grandmother's ambitions for him. As your eyes slid to his face, you caught a flash of something clouding his features before that mask of indifference clicked into place. It was the same mask he had worn when you had initially met him, you recalled, first noticing the starkness of it when it had slipped after your first kiss.

You squeezed his hand this time, and when he angled his head towards you, you noticed that he was standing perfectly under the chandelier, the angle making it look almost as if the golden monstrosity was some kind of looming crown. That mask may have seemed to suit him back then, but after all this time of learning more about the man behind the diamond facade, you knew it belonged on his face no more than you belonged standing in this manor.

Gideon was then addressing Gillivray in some kind of language you didn't recognize, words flowing out of his mouth like a stream ghosting over a bed of glassy pebbles. The tones were delicate, more like a dance than the result of verbal speech as he continued to speak. Before you could wonder what he was saying, Gillivray gave a short nod and another bow as Gideon was tugging your hand, carting you away into the depths of Dulcis Manor.

His pace was brisk as he guided you through a flurry of rooms, walls covered with rich colors and elaborate brocades of wallpaper. Your head nearly spun, tongue feeling too big in your mouth as you tried to keep up with him. When you finally opened your mouth to ask him where the hell he was taking you, he was pushing open another set of doors. A wash of light enveloped you.

"I have informed Gillivray we will await my grandmother here," he said simply, closing the doors behind him to walk more into the airy space. Gideon seemed to visibly relax when they were shut, as if they acted as some kind of shield to the rest of the manor.

As you walked by his side, you recognized that he had brought you to some kind of greenhouse. In contrast to the almost suffocating interior of the house, *this* space was bright and airy. Pop of vibrant, lush color lined the brick walkways in radiant plumes. Gideon's wings, which had seemed dimmed in the foyer, had come alive again, veins of silver sparkling as the magentas and olives and turquoises scattered like a prism.

"This is beautiful," you managed to say as you slowed to a stop. Gideon's arm outstretched to cradle a milky blossom between his fingers, antennae brushing the petals of its companions as he stooped to smell it. The flower was trumpet-shaped, nearly iridescent against the emerald leaves. A *moonflower*, you recognized after a beat, remembering how they had peppered the meadow he had once brought you to. Your brow furrowed. "I thought they only bloomed at night?"

His response was a hum as his eyes flickered to yours. He straightened, carefully extracting the bloom from its stalk before gently tucking your hair behind an ear. He tenderly slid the flower in place to tuck there. "Nothing a bit of magic cannot help with."

His tone was playful as he brushed his lips against your forehead, toting you along once more to point out various varieties, some of which you recognized, others you definitely didn't. As he spoke, you noticed how alight his eyes were, the flakes of golds and coppers behind the frames of his glasses surfacing as he spoke. He looked absolutely one with these blooms, the shimmering colors in his wings reminding you of an exquisite spun glass garden globe as he continued to relay fact upon fact about each one like an endless encyclopedia of knowledge.

"This is the only thing I miss about this place," he stated finally after he was done with his tour, a bit of a wistful air to his voice. He caressed another bloom with the tip of his finger, the petals seeming to blossom under his mere touch. He looked thoughtful for a moment. "I cultivated them myself. Perhaps we should start a garden together?"

You immediately pictured Gideon in a sunhat and rubber gloves while cradling a pair of shears in his hand, you letting out a string of profanities in frustration as you whacked a bed of soil with a rusty shovel. The absurdity of that imagery made you laugh. His antennae seemed to perk at the abrupt sound as you held up your hands. "Black thumb, remember?"

You blushed the second those words were out of your mouth. He smirked at this, likely recalling just as you were the moment when you had made that very claim after your first tryst in his office when he had referred to you as a convincing Persephone. He opened his mouth to retort before suddenly freezing, back going stiff as he glanced at something over your shoulder.

You spun around to face perhaps the most terrifying creature you would ever come across in your next ten lifetimes.

Gideon's grandmother — *Cordelia Narcissa Dulcis née Eventide*, he had divulged in the car, as if giving you her full name would also grant you some power of protection — stood in front of you both, every bit as regal as her nickname of being a duchess would suggest. She appeared not a day over 60, though you suspected you might be able to tack on another zero to that number and still be understating her age, poised with her head held aloft as if balancing some kind of invisible tiara. Not a single strand of silvery white hair escaped her tidy updo; with the manner she carried herself, you wouldn't be surprised to learn if she had scared any errant strays into submission.

You noticed that she had similar aristocratic features to Gideon's: delicate ears narrowing into pointed tips, high cheekbones, a slightly upturned nose. However, she clearly didn't share Gideon's gray skin color, nor did she appear to have any fuzz on her person or a set of wings. Instead, her skin was so ethereally pale white it nearly glowed, reminding you of some kind of porcelain doll straight out of a set, her black gown dating her to match the Victorian manor she resided over. Rather than a pair of ruby eyes, her own were a startling amethyst, piercing and shrewd like some kind of hawk, making her appear much taller than her slight, slim stature.

This clearly must have been the woman Gideon had inherited his mask from, except where his own was now fraying at the edges, ribbons loose and coming undone, hers was held up by chains that were tethered to her very soul. You would have considered her devastatingly beautiful if not for the completely frigid air that surrounded her. You were nearly shocked that the flowers didn't seem to wilt in her foreboding presence.

Somehow, you found it in yourself to *also* not completely wilt, holding your ground as Gideon let go of you to step forward and place a kiss at the back of her outstretched hand in greeting.

"Grandmother," he acknowledged simply, that odd strain to his tone again, "this is my—"

"Yes, yes. Your human." She waved him off dismissively. Her voice was like a spatter of tinkling bells dipped in honey, though the effect was unnerving rather than soothing. She had the same elegant lilt to her words as Gideon did, although it was much more pronounced. Whereas it lent color to Gideon's accented voice that his preferred wardrobe otherwise lacked, it only made Cordelia's black gown seem that much more severe.

No, not Cordelia, *DeeDee*. Though you weren't part of her inner circle, you would refer to this as such in your head, as if it would diminish her authority in an attempt to make her less intimidating to you.

Her words reminded you of Eden's, how his similar statement had filled the car on your journey into Tenebra City, though it was Gideon's response that had rattled around in your head for the rest of the evening. This time, however, he didn't correct her, only curling an arm around your waist to tuck him into his side rather pointedly as if staking some kind of claim.

Fae can be possessive, you remembered he had said. You may have protested at being somewhat objectified, but this time, you couldn't help but be a little thankful for it.

"Gideon." She wielded his name like a whip and though her voice was nowhere near raised, it somehow seemed to rattle the panes of the greenhouse. "Leave us. Let the women converse."

Normally perfectly composed, even Gideon seemed to falter at this, obviously not expecting for her to send him away. You felt your blood chill, also having not anticipated this; when you agreed to go to Dulcis Manor, you had thought you would be facing the devil together, not in turns.

When he moved to protest, DeeDee only held her hand up, palm facing towards you both to swiftly silence him before he could utter a single syllable. Her eyes narrowed in a way that it instantly became understood there was no use in attempting to dissuade her and as Gideon stood silently, antennae stiffening as you could practically hear the gears in his mind whir into motion, you decided to make the first move.

"I'll see you later?" you offered, patting his forearm and giving him a small smile. He stared at you for a moment, jaw clenching tightly before his chin moved up and down mechanically in a begrudging nod.

He bent to press a chaste kiss at the corner of your mouth. "Behave," he whispered into your ear, lips brushing the shell before he pulled back to touch the flower he had placed there. You tried not to shoot him a helpless look, not wanting to worry him more than you knew he would be as you did your best to put on a brave face.

He gave you one last look, antennae drooping slightly as he drank in your appearance before he quickly bid goodbye to his grandmother, striding back towards those doors he had been so eager to shut behind him. His gait was stiff, the column of his neck as rigid as his wings as he moved forward, disappearing into the maw of the manor without so much of a glance over his shoulders.

Keep your hands at the level of your eyes, you recited to yourself as you were led to a quaint table and a set of chairs, else she might string a noose around your neck and hang you from the eaves of the greenhouse like you had seen in one of the horror movies that Calli had made you sit through. You had nearly ripped out tufts of Greer's hair as your nails bit crescent shapes into his forearms while Effie giggled in the background.

Settling into your seat with Gillivray making a reappearance to fuss over the elaborate china setting that had been laid out, you briefly considered that when you had told your friends what you would be doing today, you also should have warned them to send a search party if they didn't hear from you by dinner.

You fought the urge to grimace at the tinkling sound of Gillivray pouring tea into the fine cups in front of you and DeeDee. *Tea.* Though the man obviously still seemed to have decided he didn't care for you, you still gave him a murmur of thanks, reaching out to drag the saucer towards you. Piercing amethyst eyes watched your movements, narrowing ever so slightly at the sound of the dish scraping across the table.

You froze, though tried to seem nonchalant in your panic. Had that been impolite or something? You cursed to yourself, wishing Gideon had given you a crash course in etiquette prior to your descent here. You pictured him pacing in the foyer, probably wondering if he would ever see you again.

You tried not to wonder the same thing.

"Uh," you started, clearing your throat as you attempted to shatter the thickened silence, "thank you for inviting us." Your lips tightened in a sorry attempt at a polite smile as your fingers played at the thin handle of the cup. "Can I call you Cordelia?"

You weren't sure what the fuck possessed you to ask, but she immediately swooped in on this. "Absolutely not. You may address me as Lady Dulcis."

You thought you heard Gillivray scoff as you gritted your teeth, this very exchange reminiscent of one you had first had with Gideon. "Right. Perfect."

As a distraction, you lifted your cup from its saucer, bringing it carefully to your lips. The steam curled upwards like skeletal hands from a grave as you took a sip, wincing at the heat and the flavor. You felt those eyes on you like daggers the whole time, the weight of them landing on your stubby fingernails, which you knew had seen better days.

When you put your cup gingerly back in the dish, you watched her wave Gillivray away with a short, sharp motion. She then picked her own cup up in a motion much more fluid than your own, holding it in front of her before intoning, "My grandson has told me you do not care for tea."

Ah, so she served it to you already knowing you didn't like it. You silently counted down from ten, not wanting to disappoint Gideon as you tried to rein in your temper as she watched you. This must have been part of some kind of game of hers.

It occurred to you then that this was the caliber of a person that your parents were hell-bent on sitting next to at some kind of high table at the pinnacle of society. You had known it then, but you saw instantly now that they were surely outmatched. DeeDee may have even been in her own class, her craft so honed to perfection that the webs she wove could slice you into ribbons; they weren't made out of fine silk, but *razors*.

"No, I don't, actually," you admitted, having a feeling that she probably detested liars just as much as Gideon did. She lifted her chin slightly at this, but otherwise made no other comment. She pressed the rim of her cup to her ruby lips daintily before setting it back on its plate.

As one of her hands moved towards her side, you noticed that she had brought a cane, her glossy red nails curling over its opal knob. Her fingers tightened over the object as she kept her gaze trained on your face.

"I must admit that when I had requested Gideon's presence," she began, your nose scrunching at the suggestion that it had even been a *choice*, "I was originally not expecting his request to bring you along. However, I believe this may be an opportune moment to offer you some advice." Her pause was foreboding as you steeled yourself, clenching your hands into fists to quell the temptation to chew at your fingers again. "Leave him before he leaves you."

You stiffened at this, remembering Gideon's insistence that he was cursed and how you had brushed it aside. You had wondered then what part DeeDee may have played in the cultivation of that seed, realizing now that she may have been the very one to plant it.

"He won't leave me," you responded, trying to keep your voice steady. To your credit, the statement was made with confidence. You saw her fingers clench the knob of her cane. "Though, please, would you humor me by explaining why you think he will?"

"Gideon is an orphan, as I am sure he must have told you." She stated this flippantly, as if the memory of her own son dying didn't bother her in the slightest. "My own husband was a disappointment, leaving me for some tart after I produced an heir for him. The boy had potential, but he was too much like his father. Weak-willed and feeble-minded."

You chewed the inside of your cheeks as she continued to stare at you, eyes flaming violet behind the facade of the mask she wore. "Do you know how Gideon's fool of a father perished? Protecting his silly little mother from hunters. *Humans.*" The word dripped with vitriol as she said it. "If you were as intelligent as my grandson claims, you will end this *arrangement*"—she fluttered her hand at the open space between the two of you, nose crinkling ever so slightly as if she smelled something she didn't like—"before you live to regret it."

You sat back in your chair, letting her words settle in. The topic of his parents was still obviously a touchy subject that Gideon didn't like to dwell on, yet DeeDee was diminishing their deaths. She was even making it seem like they were at *fault* for them. You folded your arms over your chest.

"Something tells me you don't really care about whether or not I regret anything," you said evenly, arching a brow at her. "Let's drop the pretense and call a spade a spade. I know all about your plans for Gideon. You just want me out of the way, don't you? You think I'm not good enough for him."

Gideon had asked you to behave, but you weren't necessarily *not* behaving. Besides, you wanted to see if DeeDee could take it just as well as she could dish it. Though the features on her face were carefully trained to betray nothing, you saw the way her eyes blazed again. The skin across her knuckles thinned as she clutched her cane.

"My husband's only redeeming quality was his name," she said suddenly, voice holding a bit of malice to it. "The Dulcis name is grand, but I never thought I needed it. The Eventide name is much more impressive; you see, I had both the name *and* money, but unfortunately, I was born a woman."

Her other hand moved to grasp her teacup, guiding the vessel to her lips as she took another sip before continuing, "My husband's *shameful* actions nearly sullied the Dulcis name and by association, the Eventide one. When my own idiotic son married a *cryptid*, he all but drove the nail into his own coffin." A humorless laugh escaped her red lips. "Even as a half-blood, my grandson was the last hope for this family, but it seems like the sins of the men in this family are generational, as diluted as the bloodline may become."

You scrunched your nose at her, feeling more than a bit offended at what she was insinuating. "I'm not sure why you're blaming me for any of this," you stated with a bit of a huff. "It's not like I'm holding Gideon hostage or anything." You then paused, mulling about her words in your head as a pang of realization hit you. "Your husband... he ran off with a human woman, didn't he?"

Her eyes held utter contempt; you pictured her face contorting into a snarl to match the absolute fury there, but her mask seemed to be impenetrable. It was a wonder the opal sphere that tipped her cane didn't shatter under the pressure of her grip.

"That is exactly the trouble with humans," she sniffed, "their lifespans are short, but long enough for them to leave lasting damage."

"That's a bit of a generalization," you retorted, being every bit as stubborn as Gideon knew you could be. "I don't think it's fair to—"

"You would have my grandson give up on his birthright and renege part of his lifespan for you?"

Your brain stuttered as DeeDee abruptly seemed to change tactics, the question slamming the inside of your skull as it jostled around in your mind. Gaping for a moment, you opened and closed your mouth, brows drawing together in utter confusion.

"P-Part of his lifespan?" you asked finally, still baffled at her interruption. You had no idea where this was coming from or what she was even talking about

"Did it ever occur to you, foolish girl, how the life of a human goes by in the mere blink of an eye compared to the fae?" She raised her chin again, voice taking on a more lofty tone. "There is a way with ancient magic for fae to bind themselves to another of divergent lifespan. It may increase the lifespan of their chosen, but at the cost of diminishing their own."

She stopped then, as if wanting to watch the effect of her words sinking in. You chewed on the inside of your cheeks, arms fidgeting where you kept them clasped in front of your chest. Shifting uncomfortably, you then moved to sit on them, the urge to bite at your nails nearly overwhelming.

"He hasn't told me about that yet." You sounded small when you finally spoke to admit this, but did your best to meet her gaze. "But when we talk about it, it will be his choice if he offers it up, just as it will be *mine* to choose if I want to accept."

In that moment, you recalled one of the legends Gideon had taught earlier in the semester. In it, three goddesses had staked their claim for a golden apple meant for the fairest of them all, but it was left to Paris to decide who truly deserved it. He was bribed with titles and skill in war, yet ultimately fell to the lure of the offering of a beautiful woman, culminating in the mythological basis for the Trojan War.

With the way DeeDee looked at you, it felt like your words had spurred a war of their own. If you were Paris, DeeDee was chaos itself, witnessing it all unfold with a glint in her eyes like the very goddess of discord.

"There is never *truly* a choice," she intoned, her tone chillingly cool. You felt the frigidness wrap around you, stealing your breath as if you had just jumped into a vat of ice water. "You cannot have one thing without sacrificing something else. That is the way of the world." She gave you an even look, and though you were able to meet it, you felt yourself falter slightly "Gideon has a destiny to fulfill. It would be cruel of you to force his hand under the false guise of *making a choice*."

Those words echoed through your mind far after your practically untouched tea had gone cold, DeeDee absolutely basking in your stunned silence. Even as some time passed and Gideon led you away from the manor, the warmth of his hand against your back did nothing to stave off your still shivering with the chill of where they had seeped into your very bones, feeling as if Dulcis Manor were now part of you.

And as the car began its journey up the driveway out of the

shadow of the estate, you wondered at how efficiently DeeDee had managed to cut you down to size. You considered, then, that you may have been truly fucked. Gideon may have been the cultivator of the family, but DeeDee was gifted in her own right; ever the wicked gardener, you began to feel a seed of guilt take root.

xix: modern prometheus

THE HOT PINK elephant was back again, neon sign flashing as you and Gideon did your best to ignore it. Not only had it brought its lime green glow-in-the-dark buddy, but that friend had also invited a glittering highlighter blue companion along. You didn't realize this little gathering would become such a party. You should have made it clear that there were no plus ones allowed.

The newest elephants — now plural — in the room had to do with your visit to Dulcis Manor. It was like the lid was closed on the topic just as he had shut your passenger door for you upon your departure, the car ride back to Eventide Falls having been overwhelmingly silent. The both of you had just continued on with your lives together as if you hadn't just escaped from the Ninth Circle of Hell, but from the slight differences in both of your demeanors, you suspected neither of you came out of it completely unscathed.

Gideon didn't necessarily seem *different*, but there was a strange melancholy that clung onto him. His wings even looked duller to you, though you weren't sure if your eyes were just playing tricks on you at this point. You had definitely been more tense in the days following the visit, and though you could easily attribute the stress to your upcoming final exams in your business courses. Luckily, you had already submitted your last paper that Gideon's colleague would read on his behalf in your mythology elective and that was one less thing to worry about, but you would be lying to yourself if you denied that DeeDee's words occupied your mind just as much as the terms *synergy* and *economies of scale* and *oligopoly*.

The sound of your name being called caused you to look up from the textbook you hadn't really been reading, a periwinkle hand coming into your line of sight. You blinked owlishly, realizing Effie had been waving it in your face to get your attention as you zoned off again.

You were at the library attempting to study with your friends after having just given them the 30,000-foot view of the situation and had apparently just zoned off again. You didn't give them the specifics about Gideon's intricate relationship with his grandmother or any of his own insecurities, but mostly just told them your side of things and how you were beginning to feel a bit inadequate and weren't sure what to do about it.

"Don't stress about it too much, lady!" Effie chirped from across the table, pointedly trying to keep her voice lower after some of her earlier screeches had put her on the receiving end of a few glares and *shush*es. The floor you were currently on wasn't *meant* to be a totally silent one, but some people obviously weren't partial to a fairy in full form. "Just talk to him!"

"Seriously," Calli whispered, chiming in. She elbowed Effie playfully, leaning forward to bend over her own open textbook. "You're a total catch! He'd be an idiot not to see that."

You scrunched your nose at both of them, but thanked them with a roll of your eyes. You felt Greer stiffen beside you, having looked more and more sullen as you had basically lamented about your own short fallings. Greer was definitely a lover and not a fighter, but from the way his rounded chocolate eyes had narrowed when your breath had caught during a particular moment, you wouldn't be surprised if he ever tried to put those horns of his to use. You felt a heavy arm circle around your shoulder, squeezing gently to reassure you in that calming way of his.

As cheesy as Effie and Calli could be, they did have a point. You had nearly tipped yourself into a downward spiral in the past by *not* talking it out. You also knew from past experience that just because Gideon wasn't saying anything didn't mean he *actually* thought everything was A-Okay, his more reserved style often just leading him to automatically close off the rest of the world.

You sighed and nodded, giving Greer a grateful smile as you shot Effie and Callie a weak thumbs up, pulling out your phone to check the time.

Gideon would come to collect you in a bit and since he was always punctual, you knew to expect him exactly when he said he would arrive. You felt Greer's arm slide down your upper back to rest on the top of your chair as you stretched, rolling your neck to dissipate some of the tension that had accumulated there from your poor posture. When Effie could barely contain a squeal, jabbing her finger into Callie's arm, you knew the man of the hour must have made his appearance.

You peeked over your shoulder to see Gideon striding towards you, checking his watch with a pinched expression on his face as if he could ever be *late*. A few heads shot up at his presence, students in the library trailing his swift figure with wide-eyed fascination on their faces. It was amazing how Gideon seemed to have such an effect on people and as he stopped at your table, you knew Effie and Calli were among the cohort of gapers as their wings fluttered ever so slightly in excitement.

"Hello, Efficlair. Callista. Greer." He nodded at each of them politely as he said their names, his red eyes lingering on Greer's arm draped over your chair before looking at you. He said your name almost as if it were some kind of secret as he greeted you, the way his lips quirked sending a tingle down your spine while you smiled at him. He quickly stooped to place a kiss on the crown of your head, causing Effie to let out another poorly-contained giggle. He reached down to pick your bag off the floor to help you pack up your belongings.

Gideon may have been a bit possessive, but he knew enough about your friends not to consider them a threat. He had met them a few times before, and while you had stressed about the initial introduction, it had actually been relatively anticlimactic. You had mused about how Greer would give him the handshake test, but realized that it was something that apparently had to be *earned*. You winced internally; you'd have to do a better job at hyping Gideon up to him, else he might not even get the opportunity to take Greer's test.

As Gideon helped you into your coat and settled his scarf around your neck, he led you out of the library, refusing your offer to carry your own bag as you both waved goodbye to your friends. You felt the same eyes that had followed him now land on you as if sizing you up. It was something you were still getting used to, but as time went on, you became less self-conscious about it.

You endured another silent car ride back to his apartment, kneecap bouncing up and down as you sat on your hands again. You wanted to say something, but weren't sure when was exactly the right time to bring it up. Then the silent car ride turned into a silent elevator ride and you were soon standing in his loft, playing with your fingertips as you sat on the edge of his massive bed.

"You are chewing at your nails again." It wasn't a question. You felt Gideon's fingers curl around your wrist as he reappeared from the bathroom, gently prying your hands apart while he bent over you. He slid his fingers in between the gaps in yours.

"I am *not*!" you retorted defensively, cheeks heating in embarrassment. He must have thought you were like a child, unable to kick such an immature habit. Despite your denial, he was right, of course.

And he knew it because your name spilling from his lips was a reprimand as he called your bluff, one antenna arching expectantly as you sighed. "I've... just been *thinking*, I guess."

There was another pause as you saw his wings go rigid. He cocked his head slightly, brow bone furrowing as his jaw clenched.

Then he let out a shaky breath, withdrawing one hand to push his glasses up slightly so he could pinch the bridge of his nose. "About my grandmother, I presume?"

"Well, yeah." You licked your lips, looking down at your joined hands. "She—um—told me a few things and I..."

A torrent of thoughts rushed through your mind as you trailed off, swirling and churning like a maelstrom. You remembered her statement about Gideon considering giving up part of his lifespan for you and everything suddenly felt much more serious. A future with him was something you definitely could see, but at this point in your life, you were focused on crafting three- and five- and ten-year plans; not necessarily *hundred*-year ones.

It was all so incredible; you were some human who just wanted to see more of the world and now you were faced with the possibility of being offered a longer lifespan. You had tried not to think too much about it since DeeDee had revealed that it was even a *thing*, but what seemed more incredible now is the notion that Gideon might deign to even suggest it. Would he still want you if he knew where you came from, if he knew what your parents were? Would he think you were merely trying to climb your way up through the ranks? Would he resent you for it?

An odd pit settled into your stomach. Maybe it was the seed of guilt that you knew would bloom into something ugly and rancid if you didn't stop it. You thought of your near swan dive as a result of bottling everything up in the restaurant as you chewed the inside of your cheek, not wanting that to happen again.

You swallowed thickly, looking back up at him with resolve as your next statement came out in a bit of a rush. "I'm at EFU on a full scholarship. I haven't told anybody this yet. I'm not ashamed, but... my parents cut me off when they learned I wanted to go into business and see more of the world. They wanted me to find a nice man, settle down, and above all, stay in the *human* world."

You squeezed his hand, more to distract yourself. "I haven't spoken to them in a long time," you admitted, shaking your head, "and I'm not sure that I want to. I'm not sure that they want me to." You fidgeted, rubbing your fingertips over his thumbs before looking back up at him. "I... I'm a disappointment to them. They had all these *plans* for me so they could better their station and I wanted—*want*—you to know this"—you inhaled sharply—"in case that it... might impact any of your future decisions with me." Your voice grew softer as you continued. "Gideon, she told me about the whole magical lifespan thing. I don't know if we're ready to have that conversation yet, but... but I wanted to make sure you *knew* before you even considered it for yourself."

He stared at you for a few moments, antennae separating while the tips tweaked slightly as if in surprise. Suddenly he was kneeling in front of you, his other hand coming up so he could clutch at both of them. "I knew all that," he breathed, moving your joined hands so he could tuck them under his chin. "My grandmother is crafty. She had apparently done some... *investigation*"—his mouth contorted in distaste at the word—"and when I had to take her call in the restaurant... that was when she told me."

He maneuvered your hands, kissing your knuckles as if in an apology. "I should have told you then that I knew, but it was your own history to divulge and I did not want to take that opportunity away from you. I wanted you to feel you had the agency to control your own narrative." You looked away in bewilderment, but the sound of your name made you look back at him. "You are your *own* person. I am so immensely proud of you and who you are and what you do. Our situations are not dissimilar in that we have had our paths set for us by our families, and yet... yet *you* have done everything that I cannot."

"Gideon..." Your voice was gentle as you freed a hand from his to lay against his jaw. You'd seen flickers of this vulnerability, but now it was on full display, an eerie, haunted look surfacing within the red of his eyes.

"*Tempus edax rerum*," he muttered suddenly, the words jogging your memory. It was EFU's slogan again. "It was rather clever of them to choose that phrase from *The Metamorphoses*. Kronos was often interpreted as the personification of time. He represented its destructive ravages of time devouring all things. All I have in this world is nothing but time, and yet, like Kronos' sons, it has devoured me."

With a shake of his head, he continued, "If I were stronger"—he rested his palm against the back of the hand you held against his skin—"maybe I could be like *you* and sever these ties. You have accomplished so much more in your short existence than I have been able to manage in a handful of lifetimes. Instead, I have merely been attempting to just reject her expectations of me and distance myself from them." His eyes slid shut. "Do you recall how when we were watching that movie together, I spoke of Prometheus?"

"Yes, but—"

"In the legends, Prometheus steals fire from the gods to gift to mankind and is harshly punished for it for the rest of eternity." There was no lofty air to his voice that suggested he had gone into lecture mode; instead, he seemed to shrink into himself. "Doctor Frankenstein, similarly, steals knowledge from the gods that no human is supposed to possess; the reanimation of life. In doing so, he creates a creature that he ultimately does not know how to control, and like Prometheus, must suffer for it." When Gideon opened his eyes, they looked unfocused, as if he were seeing into some alternate plane. "And I—I fear I have done the same. I have spent my laboriously long existence curating my own interests with such purpose to separate myself from the mold I was meant to be cut from that I do not even know my *true* self."

You were stunned at this admission, mouth going slightly slack as you tried to wrap your head around what he was saying. The term he had used — *mold* — particularly caught your attention as you remembered his curiously pleased expression when you had first stumbled upon his record collection and had been shocked to see hair metal represented there.

And this breaks the mold that you had assigned me to?

It was as though you had been looking at Gideon through a curtain; as time went by, the threads became more and more sheer. Now, it had been tugged away completely, floating to the ground in a whisper of gauze. Gideon had once appeared so maddeningly overconfident to you that it had made your skin crawl. Without the haze between you, you could see how it had only been a front — a method of protection ingrained in him by his grandmother's ruthlessly cynical upbringing and the pressure of living a life in the pressure of the public eye.

"I told you once that my hobby for fixing motorcycles and older vehicles involves things that my grandmother detests... that was the only reason why I had decided to indulge in it. My profession? I told you she thinks it is useless." His lips quirked, but the smile was bitter. "I picked it *because* she believes that. All those doctorates and degrees I told you about were my attempts to search for a field she absolutely abhorred. Ancient mythology was the winning subject."

He moved your palm from his jaw, clasping your hands together to curl his own around. "This is not even my real *fucking* hair color." His voice pitched slightly, but you were more in shock with his use of profanity than the revelation. The curse sounded fake in his lilting accent; too saccharine to be considered biting. "It is naturally white, just like my father's. Just like my grandmother's. But you, little harpy," he said gently, a hint of anguished admiration there, "are so *sure* in your preferences that even when you falter, I watch how you are able to return to who you are. Yet even after that I have done to myself, I cannot help but wonder... is my breeding so deeply ingrained in who I am that it is all for nothing? That this creature I have made of myself may just be destroyed in the end?"

Your jaw was aching from how you were gritting your teeth together, the searing flames of anger licking at your heart. You were furious, not because he had hidden all this from you, but because DeeDee was absolutely, positively, unequivocally, one *downright vile cunt*, thank you and have a nice day. How awful must it have been to live under the constant pressure of her immaculately manicured thumb, so much so that he had felt the need to do all these things in his pursuit to get away from her?

"*Gideon,* you are strong," you insisted stubbornly, extracting your hands from his again to cradle his jaw. You felt his palms rest on your kneecaps as he sagged against your touch, antennae and wings drooping as he rested his weight backwards on his calves. "I've met your grandmother, remember? She's no joke, seriously. It takes guts to stand up to her the way you've done, even if you don't think so. And your hobbies?" You tilted your head to the side, sweeping your thumb against his bottom lip while you smiled. "*Tons* of people get into different hobbies for no good reason other than a distraction. I know you're reluctant to call Eden a friend, but I can tell you care about him from the way you speak of him. Don't give me that look!" —you pecked his lips to stop the scowl that was forming there— "What I'm *trying* to say is that if nothing else, you at least found a friend in it, and isn't that one of the better points of picking up a hobby?"

You pulled back slightly, putting a finger under his chin to tilt his face upwards. This was the first time you'd been in a position like this with him stripped so entirely bare sitting below you while you perched above him on his bed, but he'd picked up your pieces and put them together so many times before that it was finally your turn to care for him. You gently slid his glasses from his face, reaching over to set them on his bedside table. It was night now, so he wouldn't need them.

"As for your profession," you continued, fighting a giggle at the irony that you were actually hyping up mythology, of all things, "you are obviously so passionate about it, it's incredible! Your whole aura changes whenever you speak about it... even *I* found myself paying more attention in your class. And the way you defended it to me in the library when we first met... well, you wouldn't have been so stubborn about it if you didn't actually like it." You reached up to playfully flick the tip of one of his antennae. "I'm not trying to tell you that your fears and anxieties aren't valid, but I do wish you would see from an outsider's perspective. *My* perspective. I'm a harpy, remember? Shrewd and shrill and greedy." You winked. "I definitely wouldn't have stuck around if I hadn't found something I liked so much."

He blinked at you, eyes seeming to glaze over for a moment before his hands slid upwards from your knees to your thighs. He squeezed them lightly, his voice a mere rasp as he uttered, "Thank you."

"We're a pair, you and I, remember? Like scones and hot chocolate!" You rested your forehead against his, relishing in his quiet sigh. "I want to make you feel better. What would make you feel better?"

His expression was so open now, almond eyes so large that you swore you could see another world in them as he stated simply, "You."

His lips were suddenly on yours, frantically moving against them as you clung to him. When he pulled back to give you a hesitant look, you reached forward to weave your fingertips through his hair, pulling him back towards you while you gripped at the leather tie holding the strands in place near the nape of his neck and flung it somewhere into the room. His tongue swept inside your mouth when you parted for him, the taste of bergamot and citrus invading your senses as it curled around yours.

You felt the warmth of his palm pressed to your lower stomach, sliding downwards to dip under the waistband of your leggings. He quickly found your clit, rolling it between his thumb and index finger as his middle finger teased at your opening, delving in further and further when you let out a gasp.

"I'm supposed to be making *you* feel better," you argued feebly as he separated from you to guide you backwards on the mattress. His hand abruptly left your body to join the other in shimmying your leggings downwards as he removed them, not even bothering to fold them as he tossed them to the side. You thanked whatever deity was up there that you had decided against underwear again that morning.

He knocked your knees apart, placing his hands back on your kneecaps to slide upwards, only stopping when they were maddeningly close to where you knew you were already dripping for him. His thumbs pressed into your skin, moving in small, slow circles.

"This *is* making me feel better," he retorted with a near growl, taking the sensitive nub in his mouth and sucking sharply. You let out a high-pitched keen, one hand gripping at his sheets while the other wound its way back into his hair. He hummed at your reaction, the vibrations going straight from your clit up through your core and into your breasts. You felt a tiny pinch on your clit as he teased it with the tip of his fang, the sting liquefying into molten pleasure as he soothed it with his tongue.

Your head fell backwards as he let go of your clit with a *pop* to say, "I need to taste you," before his tongue was pushing into your wet heat, unfurling within you to spiral around your walls. Your thighs trembled as you arched off his bed at the feeling of the prehensile appendage pressing into all the places he knew you liked, vision nearly going white when it bumped against the spongy area near your belly button.

"Oh!" you choked out, word pitching upwards with a moan. You suddenly felt like you might burst into flame, the coil within you dangerously close to snapping. "I-I'm so close…"

You almost sobbed when his tongue retracted, your release dangling over your head like some kind of forbidden apple. "You are so beautiful like this," he crooned, voice slightly husky. "You look radiant. You *taste* even better. I could get off on your delectable little sounds alone." He kissed the inside of your thigh before dragging a fang down it slowly. "Would you like that? To come undone so loudly that I am unable to help my own release?"

You were only able to nod dumbly with a whispered *please*, your grip in his hair gone slack at the feeling of need sizzling through your veins. Though you couldn't find it in you to verbally confirm the way you knew he would want you to, he still gave a pleased hum, spreading your thighs further apart as he delved in once more.

You had been so close that all it took was the bump of his nose on your clit and the long upwards lick across your core before you were shattering around him, hearing him grunt as he lapped at you. His hands held you still while you keened, spine curling off his bed like a woman possessed as you shook and trembled.

Then he was hovering above you, lifting your torso upwards to tug your sweater over your head and unclip your bra before nudging you back down. You blinked to see that his cock had already emerged from its slit — and when the *fuck* had the man even removed his pants? — curving towards you while pearlescent moisture wept from its flared head.

"I have you," he breathed, slotting his mouth against yours to swallow your moan when he slipped into you. You bowed into him, already pebbled nipples brushing against the buttons on the shirt he hadn't bothered to remove, the rough sensation sending another jolt all the way back down to your abdomen. His hands came up to cup your breasts as he continued to sink in, those little ridged nubs bumping against all the right places as they ground against your inner warmth.

You could take him time and time again, and yet the feeling of him being fully seated would always take your breath away, the air being forced into your lungs with panted gasps as you adjusted to his girth. A few shallow thrusts had you moaning again as his hips rolled into you, the head of his cock flaring perfectly to catch your walls, suctioning against you.

Suddenly it felt like the world was spinning, or maybe *you* were just spinning when you found yourself resting against his chest as he was now on his back, his hands no longer on your breasts but rubbing at your back. The silver of his wings splaying over his dark sheets made him look like some kind of angel and you were pleased to see they shimmered again. He stilled, body going so motionless that you could practically feel his heartbeat from where his cock was pressed so deeply within you.

You took another jagged breath to steady yourself, feeling yourself flutter around him almost helplessly just with his sheer size alone. "Gideon?" you were able to ask, reaching with a shaky hand to brush his hair back from his forehead.

He stared up at you, red eyes flickering all over your face as if trying to memorize it before a hand slid up your back to cup against the curve of your neck. He buried his nose in your neck, his words slightly muffled by your own skin. "I would like to remain like this, if just for a moment."

His voice sounded so small that your eyes crinkled. You gave a curt nod, but rearranged yourself so that you could slip downwards to rest your head against his chest. You hissed at the tugging sensation this created, but went lax again when you were finally tucked under his chin. His long fingertips raked through your hair while you slumped against him.

The pressure and tingling sensation still made your breathing slightly labored as you pulsed around him, but you had to admit that the warmth of him just sitting inside you was rather nice. The bulge he created in your lower stomach ghosted against his skin as you listened to the sound of his heartbeat, the fluttering a bit quicker than a human's.

It felt so safe being in his arms like this — so *natural* the way you slotted against him just so. Gideon kept his coremata and claspers away, so there were no distractions to keep you from just being able to *feel* him under you. His heartbeat was like a lullaby as you felt yourself drifting away, your head suddenly feeling fuzzy...

But then he was finally moving again, rocking into you and against you. His pace was tender and slow without any sense of urgency, as if you were in a bubble where time had stood still and there was no beginning or end to it. The way his cock nudged inside you made it feel as though it were trying to mold itself to you, like he, too, had at last found a place where he belonged and he desperately wanted to drown himself in the nostalgia of it.

You felt the heat within you begin to flare again; not a flash in a pan, but a steadily-building inferno as he continued his deep thrusts, pulling nearly fully out of you only to sink completely back in again. He did so with such tender ease that you were barely jostled, your brows knitting together as you pressed your lips into his clothed chest to staunch your gasps. One of his hands continued to rub into your back while the other massaged your scalp, your own hands fisting his shirt helplessly as you whimpered.

Your name tumbled out of his lips in a sigh and you were clenching and quivering, the force of your orgasm nearly taking you by surprise as he steered you through it, the hot warmth of his own coming seconds after yours in a garbled groan. You sagged against him, trying yet again to catch your breath, and though you felt him twitch and spurt within you a few more times, neither of you made any attempts to move as your eyes slid shut.

You must have drifted to sleep with him inside you. The next time you opened your eyes, you woke to find that you were completely clean with the kind of soreness that made your heart swell. From the light filtering in through his expansive windows, you could tell it was morning now. A beam of it fell across his bedside table where you found a note resting by a glass of water.

On a *coaster*, of course.

You peered at it to see his elegant script telling you that he had gone out for breakfast ingredients and basically ordering you to finish the glass. A smile painted your lips at this as you lifted it to bring the rim to your mouth, tilting the cool liquid to trickle over your tongue. The night prior still felt like some kind of dream to you, Gideon's admissions about his doubts and insecurities only making you respect him that much more.

They also only made you respect DeeDee that much *less*.

When you went to place the glass back down on its coaster after taking a few large gulps — maybe it was your *own* act of rebellion that you purposely left a little bit so you didn't quite finish it — you noticed that he had also left his phone on his table. You had a few choice words for DeeDee... how crazy would it be if you were to, oh you didn't know, call her up and demand to speak with her?

You stared at the phone. How crazy, indeed. But just as the seed of guilt she had tried and failed to plant within you had withered and died on Gideon's careful touch, another seed of this idea took its place. You may have had a black thumb, but was this one that you would desperately try to cultivate?

Did you even dare?

You brought your hand down from your mouth, realizing you had been chewing at your fingernail again. You reached forward to grasp his phone, scrolling through his contacts to gawk at her name. It was now or never. Maybe you should just put it down and walk away…

But she had obviously hurt Gideon and that really pissed you off. He may have once been Professor Prick, King of Assholes, Patron Saint of Douchebaggery, but he was *your* Professor Prick, King of Assholes, Patron Saint of Douchebaggery and you'd be damned if anybody ever tried to make him feel like any less than that ever again.

You'd made up your mind. You quickly pressed the call button, knee bouncing up and down as you heard it ring. It stilled when somebody picked up, though you were surprised to hear a masculine voice on the other line rather than DeeDee herself. The posh greeting sounded like it may have been Gillivray.

"Hello," you greeted with as much confidence as you could muster, already picturing the scowl on his face, "I'd like to request an audience with Lady Dulcis."

xx: gorgoneion

OF ALL OF the impulse decisions you'd ever made, this one was probably the most fucked up. Sure, the elephants may have been freed from the room by the talk you had had with Gideon a few days prior, but now you felt them sitting in the backseat of the car you had borrowed from Greer, whooping and hollering while you sped down the would-be scenic route, fighting the urge to scream at the top of your lungs.

If you survived this little mission you'd deigned to take yourself on, you'd need to find a mirror, sit yourself down, and have a little talk about making rash choices after a round of good sex. Your mind must have been mush, else the logical side of you never would have picked up Gideon's phone and dialed it. But then again, the image of the absolutely helpless look in Gideon's ruby eyes made your blood boil, so maybe your logical side would've actually chipped in to convince your impulsive one to kick some ass.

You had known you'd never be able to lie to Gideon — the man could practically *smell* it on you — so when he had asked what your plans for the day were, you'd merely told him that you were *busy* and had a few errands to run. It was the same kind of excuse you'd given to Greer when you had asked to borrow his car, and though both men had given you a matching set of rather cynical looks, neither were the type to pry.

Perhaps the most shocking aspect of this whole thing was that when you had spoken with Gillivray to request an audience with DeeDee, she had actually *agreed*. Maybe she was anticipating that you were on your way to tell her that you were going to back off and leave Gideon be... maybe she thought that she had *won*.

Honey, you wanted to tell her, you've got a big storm coming.

When you drove through those heavy gates and down the long private drive, you started some breathing exercises to prevent yourself from hyperventilating. It was a good thing you had a white-knuckle grip on the steering wheel, otherwise you might've chewed at your fingers all the way down to your wrists. Instead, you bit at the inside of your cheeks, trying to be your own personal hype woman.

Dulcis Manor was exactly as you had left it: imposing and pristine, glinting like the tip of a spear against a bed of freshly-fallen snow. Soon you were standing in front of that Medusa-esque door knocker, being led inside by the stern-looking fae who obviously thought you weren't good enough to even breathe the same air as the estate's inhabitants. It occurred to you when you were back in the black-and-white tiled foyer, stepping back onto the chessboard, that you hadn't really thought this through.

Fuck. Where was your SWOT analysis when you needed it?

Gillivray guided you through a blur of gem-colored rooms, antique after priceless antique catching your eye as he did so. This place was like a treasure trove; you could probably steal a *spoon* from here and be able to pay off the rest of your student loans from undergrad. You were almost sorry you didn't bring a purse.

You almost expected it to be like one of those scenes from a movie where you would settle into a room and DeeDee would come sweeping in a few minutes later with a flourish, so when you stepped through an archway to see her already perched on a high-backed claw foot chair in some kind of sitting room like a queen on her throne, you were a bit taken aback. Gillivray didn't stick around this time, being quickly waved off by her as those amethyst eyes landed on you to pierce your very soul. "You are late."

Your eyes narrowed. If there was *one* thing you were good at, it was being on time. The way you flopped in the matching chair across from her was definitely *not* ladylike, but neither was your glower.

To thine own self be true.

"With all due respect, *Lady Dulcis*," you began, trying to right yourself as you hadn't expected the cushion to be so plush and had immediately sunk in, "I think your clock might be ahead. I assure you I am *perfectly* on time."

She had that cane again, you noticed when her only reaction to your admittedly rude tone was for her fingertips — her pointed nails painted the same bloody red shade — to tighten on the opal gem at the top of it. Full skirts to a similar-looking black gown whispered against the rich carpet as she shifted, her back perfect ramrod straight as her eyes narrowed minutely.

"We may sit here and debate the semantics of the space-time continuum for the rest of the evening," she returned, her words clipped, "but that seems like a terrible waste of time. Would you not agree?" When you shrugged, she continued with, "May I be so bold as to inquire why you have requested my presence?"

You crossed one leg over the other to try and stop your knee from bouncing, folding your hands together to clasp on your thigh. "I think I have a bone to pick with you."

Her fingers clenched again. "Pardon?"

You cleared your throat, unwinding Gideon's scarf from around your neck. There was a fire going and the tiny room was absolutely sweltering; apparently, Gillivray hadn't thought you worthy enough to offer to take your outerwear from you. It may have been the light, but you could have sworn you saw a pair of violet eyes flicker to the material in recognition as you slid it off your shoulders, folding it to drape it over the back of the chair.

"I've been thinking about what you said the other day." You were really calling an audible on this one; for once, you had done the *opposite* of overthinking and you weren't entirely sure what might come of it. For somebody who liked to plan everything down to the second, it was oddly thrilling. "Frankly, I couldn't give a rat's ass whether you like me or not—and I know you don't like me, trust me—but I think you're being a little unfair to Gideon."

"Unfair?" The skin on her already pale knuckles lightened even more. "Who are you to come into my home and criticize how I conduct my affairs with my own grandson?"

"His concerned *girlfriend*!" you retorted, giving her the glare that you know she must have been giving to you underneath that impassive mask of hers. "I spoke with him about that whole lifespan thingy you told me." You waved your hand flippantly, as if the ability to achieve that with magic simultaneously wasn't the coolest thing in the world and also would send you right into an existential crisis if you thought too long and hard about it. "It's not something we're ready to discuss quite yet, but we will discuss it. Oh, also?" You frowned at her. "I heard about the private investigator thing. Kinda low, don't you think?"

Her red lips pursed into a thin line. "I was merely trying to protect—"

"Who, Gideon?" you interrupted, feeling a surge of adrenaline pump through your veins. "Or yourself?" You shrugged. "Look, he didn't ask me to come here. He doesn't even *know* I'm here. I'm probably crossing a lot of lines right now in going behind his back to speak on his behalf, but I just want to make it clear that I have no intention of leaving him. At least not at this stage in our relationship." You fiddled with the fabric of your thick skirt. "I'm pretty rational. I know some things can't last forever, but what we have right now is really good. I can't predict the future, but..."—you looked back up at her—"I'd like to hope that there *is* one with him, at least. Whether you like it or not."

DeeDee stiffened at this, though not even an eyebrow twitched at your statement. She stared at you for a few seconds before looking away, gazing towards the dark mantle of the fireplace. You followed her line of sight to see she was staring at a portrait of a young woman who was dressed in a brilliant purple gown. White hair cascaded over her exposed shoulders, the column of her milky white neck nearly glowing in the light of the fire. Plush red lips pouted under a slightly upturned nose and when your gaze swept upwards, a pair of amethyst eyes gleamed back at you.

Cordelia, the golden plate affixed to the intricate frame read. You saw another inscription under the name: *Vincit qui se vincit.*

"I was like you, once," she said finally. The sound of her voice made you turn back to her, only to see she was now looking at you. "Young and naive." She unclenched her hand from her cane, fingers fanning briefly before settling around the opal sphere again. "I was beautiful, but intelligent enough to know how to use that to my advantage. I obtained a prime education. I could speak multiple languages, was well-versed in the maths and sciences, had a keen eye for business ventures and investments. For all intents and purposes, I was the perfect continuation of the Eventide line. Unfortunately, as I had mentioned to you, I was not a son."

She raised her chin slightly, the angle allowing you to catch a glint of the reflection of the fire roaring violet in her eyes. "I had no desire to marry Gideon's grandfather, yet I did so out of duty. When he left me, which I knew he would, that impudent man, it was the same duty that compelled me to keep the Dulcis name from completely dissolving into tatters. Duty is what keeps our world from disappearing — from being entirely destroyed by the rancor and taint of you *humans*." Her voice was even, though her eyes seemed to blaze as she said the word like an accusation. "Gideon knows this and he will abide by it. It is one thing you cannot defend him from, try as you might."

"That seems like an archaic way of thinking," you muttered in response, nose scrunching. You supposed part of you felt a bit sorry for her, but there were no excuses for being an asshole. "And I don't think that humans want to destroy your world—"

"Responsibility is timeless," she stated, interrupting your protest, "as is the destructive nature of humans. Did I not tell you how Gideon was orphaned because of a human ritual? How my own husband was led astray by a human temptress?"

"Ok, fine, some humans really suck," you acquiesced, holding your hands up with your palms facing her. "We don't have the best history and we are destructive, that's actually a fair statement to make. But most of us are just trying to *endure*"—you recalled your first impression of the mansion's aura—"just like *you* are."

She tilted her head slightly, white hair lit copper in the light of the fire. "If Gideon cannot accept his obligation," she intoned loftily, ignoring your words, "then he is of no use to the Dulcis line, nor the Eventide line."

You lowered your hands slowly, gaping at her as you placed your palms on the arms of your chair. Her eyes never left your face as your mouth dropped slightly open. "You would disown your own *grandson*?" you managed to ask after a beat, completely bewildered. "He-He's all you have left!" You shook your head at your own spluttering, suddenly feeling more sad for him than angry. "Don't you love him?"

"Fae cannot love." Her response was immediate, the temperature in the room seemingly dropping more than a few degrees despite the crackling of the fire.

You scowled at her; your emotions had switched quickly as you felt the fizzle of wrath bubble up once more, the minute sadness evaporating like an ice cube being thrown into a pan. "Fae can't love," you returned harshly, "or *you* can't love?"

The room was silent, save for the sound of the logs continuing to crack and split within the fireplace and your own harsh breathing. You tried to calm yourself as you looked down to play with the hem of your skirt again, wishing yet again that you had come up with some kind of plan other than to just let the floodgates open and speak your mind. This was not a good look for you and when Gideon found out, he would—

"How dare you speak as if you know me?" DeeDee's words sounded like they were forced out between clenched teeth and when you looked up again, you found that the corners of her lips had curled downwards. In that moment, you saw that maybe her mask wasn't as impenetrable as you had originally suspected.

In fact, the more you thought about it, there had been little tells all along. Her fingers clenching on that cane and her eyes blazing in fury were like hairline fractures, the movement of her mouth evidence that an even larger crack was forming. This seemed to be a sore subject, and while you could always walk away now with your tail between your legs, where was the fun in that?

"You're right, I don't know you," you remarked, trying to sound nonchalant, "but it's pretty clear to me that despite all the things you claimed to be gifted at, you still might not know how to love." She seemed to stew at this as you rested your elbows on your knees and leaned forwards eagerly. "Doesn't that enrage you? That I, a mere human, can do something that you *can't*? That I can love?"

"Do not act so proud of it!" she snapped, another crack forming. You mentally smirked at this. It seemed like the Duchess wasn't so steadfast, after all. "Love is a weakness."

"Is it?" you asked, matching her own lofty tone from earlier. "I don't know. I mean, there have been many examples throughout history where love was the only thing that could endure. Some have even compared it to a weapon." You shrugged. "Maybe it's one that *you* just don't know how to wield."

She stood abruptly, cane clattering against the carpet with a *thud* as she slowly stalked towards you. Though she was petite, it felt like there was some kind of invisible, domineering force keeping you planted in your chair, unable to move. You remembered the same kind of oppressive air emanating from the estate itself, but with DeeDee in front of you, amethyst eyes sharper than a whetted sword, it was clear that it had been coming from her all along. She was the heart of this place, the rest of the grounds caught in stasis to mirror the wall of ice she had erected around herself.

"I know how to love," she hissed, stopping in front of you. Your own eyes were wide at the fury that had somehow bloomed between the cracks, rippling over her delicate features to turn them into razors. "I did so once and it nearly cost me everything."

"What—"

"I know your kind," she continued, cutting off the astounded question that almost spilled from the tip of your tongue. "*Intimately.* I was willing to throw it all away for love — for some human woman who somehow decided I was not enough. I gave her everything, yet when I asked for one thing in return, yet again I was reminded that I was nothing more than a pretty face. That I was not a son." Her eyes met yours in a cool, even stare. "Who do you think ran away with my husband?"

You did your best impression of a goldfish as you gawked at her, stunned at the revelation. She then quickly turned away from you, heavy skirts swishing as she moved towards the fire. Clasping her hands tightly in front of her, she resumed looking at the portrait. "Do you know what this means?" She was now staring at the golden plate. "*Vincit qui se vincit.*"

"No," you admitted. Her dry, humorless chuckle at your response reminded you of Gideon.

"*He conquers who conquers himself,*" she recited, still not looking at you. Her skin glowed in her proximity to the fire, but despite the orange tint, there was still no warmth there. "It is a reminder to myself of what my own weakness could have cost me. What it had cost my husband and my son. What it could cost my grandson." When she finally swiveled to address you, her eyes were cold. "For too long, the men of this family have strayed from the paths of their own destinies and have perished for it. Do not tell me I do not love. I am doing this *out* of love."

You swallowed thickly before getting to your feet, clutching the back of your chair as you stood. You didn't move yet, merely stared back at her in the silence that ensued, though her words seemed to linger in the air, seeping into the walls like moisture and dripping down the plum-colored paper that covered them.

You took a measured step, noticing something glinting near her neck. There was a cameo pinned to the collar of her high neckline and you instantly recognized the depiction carved into the ivory as the same one in brass that guarded the front doors. The Medusa.

You remembered one of Gideon's lessons on the Gorgon. Due to her ability to turn man to stone by her mere gaze alone, her head was sought after as a prize, which was eventually won once she was beheaded. But Medusa hadn't always been a monster; she had once been a beautiful mortal woman, only cursed as a result of the discovery of a love affair. She had been an innocent party who was now ridiculed and feared simply because she had loved.

It dawned on you then that perhaps you'd approached it all wrong. Yes, you had come to Dulcis Manor with fire burning in your heart, but were you no better than the humans DeeDee had criticized not ten minutes prior?

You saw it now; how more alike she and Gideon were than either of them — or you — suspected. Where Gideon was doing his best to reject who he was, DeeDee had embraced it, maybe to an extreme degree, though both clearly harbored the same resentment for their stations. You may have not understood DeeDee's methods of showing her love or excuse any of her questionable actions, but you could empathize with the need for self-preservation.

This may never have been about upholding the family name at all. This may have been just a misguided attempt to protect Gideon in the only way she knew how.

You then remembered that "Medusa" meant "guardian," after all.

Your hands sought hers; they were perfectly smooth and unblemished and felt nearly glacial. She could probably crush you with her pinky finger alone, but with that knowledge aside, she felt almost *human*; just as human as the poorly concealed shock that lit up her eyes.

"I do not need your pity," she bit out, moving to pull away from you. But you held on, shaking your head as you remembered Gideon's own scrutiny for your look of pity.

"I'm not pitying you," you said, tightening your fingers around hers. "I'm acknowledging your struggles. It's clear that you did what you had to do in the past to survive, but this is a *new* day and age. Your approach is just pushing him away. I know you care for Gideon, but I do, too." You squeezed her hands. "Gideon is amazing. He's probably the most intelligent person that I know and he's passionate about what he does. He's one of the most well-respected professors on campus."

You offered her a small smile as you continued. "I love his ambitions and his passion for mythology, even if I thought it was kind of silly. I love how his eyes light up; how his wings and antennae seem to freeze, as if suspended in the same moment in time as whatever legend he's talking about. I love how he does this stupid little thing with his finger"—you let go of her hand to hold your arm aloft, index finger pointing towards the coffered ceiling as you'd seen him do time and time again—"and even how he gets into that infuriating *know-it-all* tone of voice when he's correcting me, as much as I want to slap him sometimes. But he's even *more* than that, too. He has so many different interests and hobbies that even *I* was surprised to discover all these things. But I love all of that about him... I love *him* and I'm trying to do my best to support him in any way I can, as long as he'll have me."

You finally let go of DeeDee's hands, though they remained in the same place, hovering in front of her while she stared at you. Where Gideon's ruby eyes held flakes of coppers and golds beneath their surface, DeeDee's amethyst ones had specks of iron and steel, roiling and flickering as she continued to hold your gaze. You watched as her eyebrows, which had lifted closer to her hairline in your soliloquy, slowly descended, while her jaw unclenched. It seemed like the mask was clicking back into place, though you had a feeling it may never be the same again.

"I believe," she stated finally, voice a bit thickened, "that you may have overstayed your welcome."

There seemed to be no ill-intent behind those words. You nodded, moving to collect your scarf from the chair as you heard the ringing of some kind of bell, Gillivray suddenly appearing in the archway. With a muttered thanks back to her, you moved to follow him, but not before glancing over your shoulder one last time. She was staring at the portrait again, though instead of the same smug admiration she had held before, she now looked a bit uncertain. Lost, even.

When you were back in Greer's car, pulling away from the estate to make your way up the driveway, you let out a long, shaky breath. You were somehow alive, and while you hadn't gone in with any kind of plan, the outcome was potentially better than you expected. Maybe you could conduct a proper SWOT analysis once you were safely back in Eventide Falls; the first step was to gather competitive research against your enemy. You knew DeeDee much better now, but something in that very same appraisal told you that maybe she might not be your enemy, after all.

There was so much to unpack that your head spun, but you shoved it all to the corner of your mind. You should have been trying to think of what to tell Gideon next, but you also chose to file that away from now. Those thoughts could chill with the elephants that you'd also banished back there. A singular sentence — your own — kept bouncing around in your head, the realization of its meaning much more potent than the words that had formed it.

All that you could think about was that you had confessed that you loved Gideon.

Gideon detested liars just as much as his grandmother apparently did. And yet DeeDee, like you, could find no dishonesty in your admission.

xxi: ode to demeter

YOU LOVED HIM. The revelation didn't seem as much of a shock to you as much as it was just some kind of surfaced acknowledgement. Somehow, deep down, you'd known this for some time now.

You loved him. You actually *loved* Professor Prick, King of Assholes, Patron Saint of Douchebaggery. He had led you to the gates of the Second Circle of Hell and you had pushed them open yourself, dipping your toe in the pool of want only to rear back and dive headfirst in it. You loved his presence in his life, how he was able to help you hold it all together. You loved how, in business terms, you'd been able to strike the perfect synergy with him — while both of you had obviously survived without each other, you were so much better together.

You loved him... and you'd told his *grandmother*, of all people, before you'd even gotten the chance to tell *him*.

"That's fucked," you grumbled to yourself, gripping at the steering wheel. You imagined the three elephants bobbing their neon heads in agreement where they were holed up in the recesses of your mind.

You cursed to yourself even more as you pulled up to your apartment, driving up to the curb and putting the car into park before turning off the ignition. You would return Greer's car tomorrow, but for now, you needed to figure things out. You loved Gideon and you needed to tell him and his grandmother might disown him—

Oh, fuck. Fuckity fuck. This was a shit sundae with a cherry on fucking top. You had gone to Dulcis Manor and though you had thought you left on somewhat decent terms, DeeDee had at one point before your impasse threatened to disown him and conveniently, you'd never returned to that topic.

Holy Hell. You loved him and you'd gone and gotten him disowned. What kind of a person *did* that?

You, apparently.

Maybe you could get t-shirts made to commemorate the occasion of your momentous fuck up: I traveled to the Ninth Circle of Hell, they would say, and all I got was crippling emotional damage and my boyfriend disowned and cut off from his inheritance.

You clamped your lips shut and let out a high-pitched scream that sounded more like air being let out of a balloon before clambering out of the car, sprinting around it to cross the sidewalk and take the stairs two at a time. By the time you got to your door, you were huffing and puffing, trying to fish your key out of your pocket with shaking hands. You paused just before putting it into the lock, taking a deep breath.

Ok, ok, you had this. You definitely needed to tell Gideon, but you could map this out. Your strategy had been flawed, but all you would need to do now was some damage control. You were pretty sure you had some kind of template in your class notes somewhere for a situation like this. It was going to be fine!

But when the door somehow swung open before you could twist your key, all those half-baked contingency plans flew out the window.

Gideon stood before you, one antenna quirked as he held your front door aloft. It wasn't necessarily a complete shock that he was in your apartment — you had given him a key, after all, and he sometimes waited for you there when you were out — but the *timing* of it was what took you off guard.

Swallowing a squeak, you instead chirped, "Hi!"

His antenna arched even more at your overly-chipper greeting, but he made no comment. Instead, he bent forward to brush his lips against yours, pulling away to tug you inside and begin removing your coat and scarf. "Hello."

He hummed to himself as he did so, as if you weren't standing there internally combusting right in front of his very eyes in your own apartment. As he ushered you onto your couch to sit down once he was finished, you saw that he already had a mug of hot chocolate waiting for you.

On a coaster from the newly-purchased set he had insisted on gifting you, of course.

You felt your couch dip as he sat next to you before two hands were curling around your waist, dragging you on top of his lap. Your brain seemed to refuse to cooperate, unable to produce another thought other than how his firm thighs felt under your own. The weight of his chin resting against your crown made you sink backwards into him.

"How were your errands?" he asked lightly, snaking his arms around you to clasp against your abdomen. You swallowed, brows knitting together.

The fuck was he talking about?

Oh, *errands*. Right... that had been your excuse for being busy. With the way he was holding you, your arms were pinned in your lap, which was probably a good thing because you *really* wanted to chew your nails.

"Just peachy, thanks!" you said after a beat, nearly kicking yourself at the stupid response. You'd given him the same lie when you had tried convincing him you weren't sick. He hummed again, the sound reverberating through his chest as he dragged his chin down to rest on your shoulder. His silky hair brushed against your skin, tickling your cheek.

"You managed to get much accomplished, I presume?" He sounded thoughtful. You could feel his eyes on your profile as you kept still, as if he were some kind of unseeing creature who could only pounce if it detected movement. When he slid a hand downwards to squeeze your thigh lightly to get your attention again, you nodded quickly. "Wonderful. I have been rather preoccupied myself. You see, I received the most *interesting* call earlier..."

He was suddenly swiveling you so you were facing him, arms no longer clasped on your stomach, but against your back as you blinked owlishly at his chest.

You stiffened under his touch, but slowly looked up to peer at his face. Luckily, he didn't *seem* angry. He actually looked kind of amused, the corners of his eyes crinkled ever so slightly while his lips twitched.

Oh, shit. The cat was out of the bag. DeeDee had squealed. That ancient bitch. You should have made some kind of pact with her or something. Didn't the fae like that kind of thing? Or was that demons? Maybe demons.

Definitely demons.

"I got you disowned!" you blurted, the words bypassing your cerebrum completely to spill out of your mouth in a rush. "I mean, well, I don't *know* if you're actually going to be disowned, but..." You squirmed to free your hands where they were trapped against his chest, the movement causing him to go slightly rigid as you clasped at his shoulders. "I fucked up, ok? Wait, let me backtrack... I went to your grandmother's house and then I fucked up! Or I guess going to your grandmother's house was fucking up on its own?"

You shook your head furiously. "Ok, never mind. I was just so *angry* and the sex was *great* and then I was angry again and then I *really* wanted to tell your grandmother off and then all of a sudden I was on the phone and then I had this whole thing planned, see?" You flapped your arms over your head. "Well, not really... I guess that was *another* part where I fucked up because I didn't really have a plan other than going to see her and maybe tell her off... which I did. And that's how I fucked up and got you disowned. Maybe. I'm still not sure if she's going to go through with it..."

Your verbal diarrhea tapered off in a weak garble while you placed your hands back on his shoulders, cheeks heating as you fought the urge to burst into tears. You weren't usually this emotional, but it had been *quite* the day for you. Falling forward, you tucked your face into his immaculately-pressed shirt, sniffling a bit.

"Well, I am glad you enjoyed it," he said simply, hands descending to grip at your bottom. He squeezed. "The sex, I mean."

Your eyes nearly popped out of your skull as you pulled back so quickly that his arms had to shoot up behind your back to keep you from toppling off his lap. A fang glinted at you as he smirked, eyes dancing with mirth.

"You're not mad I got you disowned?" you asked, bewildered. He chuckled, the sound thawing the cold fear that currently had your heart in a vice grip. He shook his head, the tips of his antennae quivering at the motion.

"I will admit I am not so pleased with your crafty omission of the truth," he began, "but no, I am not mad. I am more *impressed* than anything that you somehow managed to keep this from me and that you even went back *there* by yourself." He cleared his throat, cheeks flushing a faint lilac. "I am a tad humbled by it, actually."

"*Seriously?*" You gawked at him, squeezing his shoulders in an attempt to convince yourself that this was the real Gideon and not some imposter. When your grip was met with the same solid expanse of muscle, you manage to snap your mouth shut.

"Seriously," he echoed with a nod, removing a hand from behind your back to place against your jaw. His thumb swiped down to press against your bottom lip, the pointed tip of his nail applying slight pressure to your upper one. "I will never forget the helplessness of leaving you with her, *alone*, in that greenhouse. I will never forget..." He trailed off, placing his hand under your chin to tilt your head up.

"Remember the topic you had chosen for that first essay? The one I had accused you of plagiarizing."

He chuckled as your nose scrunched at the memory. "I suddenly realized how Orpheus must have felt when trying to lead Eurydice back from the depths of the Underworld. Over and over I have read that tale, and yet each time, I have ridiculed Orpheus' weakness. I could never *fathom* how he could not, just for that fleeting moment, resist the temptation. Until *I* was in his shoes and *you* were the one there behind me."

"But you *didn't* look back," you pointed out, remembering the rigidness of his wings as he continued towards the manor, his back as stiff as his forced steps.

"I did not," he agreed, another smile playing at his lips, "because I realized then that *you* were not Eurydice. It would take much more than the gates of the Underworld to contain you." He tipped his head forward to rest his forehead against yours. "Nor, I realized, are you Persephone, as I had earlier suspected."

You blinked, still a bit astounded. You uttered the most eloquent thing that came to mind. "Huh?"

"I read your final paper," he stated, pulling back to tuck a strand of hair behind your ear. You remembered how he had done the same with a moonflower from his greenhouse. You had the blossom sitting on a dish on your bedside table, still as perfect as the day he had plucked it. "My colleague suspected that I may have *assisted* you and when I vehemently denied it, I also requested to read it. I understood why he thought I may have had a hand in it. It was very *insightful*." He cocked his head to the side. "Your particular topic was rather choice, as well."

You blushed slightly at this, having banked on the fact that he wouldn't see the paper. You had chosen to write about the "Ode to Demeter," the Hymneric hymn he once had you read in his office what felt like more than a few lifetimes ago. Despite the manner in which you had first been introduced to it, it was a legend that had stuck with you, making such an impression that you couldn't help but pick that as your subject matter.

"At first, I disagreed with your interpretation, but as I read and reread your words, I could not help but appreciate how astute they were." He tapped your nose, rubbing at the bridge to smooth out where you were scrunching it at him. "In most of the legends, and even in Demeter's ode, Persephone is perceived as being trapped by Hades. It is often depicted that she is tricked into eating the pomegranate seeds, not aware of the implications of such an action. But *you*"—he tapped your nose again—"you argued that this was not the case, that Persephone knew *exactly* what she was doing. That she actually *loved* Hades and her return to bring the beginning of spring was not by choice, but by the doing of her own mother."

He shifted you on his lap, bringing both hands to rest on your waist again as he continued, "You described Demeter as overbearing and controlling, forcing Persephone to return from the life she had chosen in order to fulfill Demeter's *own* aspirations for her. To fulfill the purpose that she believed Persephone should have always been loyal to. It was then that it occurred to me that this could *never* be you. You are too independent; too fierce. *That* is what I was trying to tell you the other night." His next laugh was more breathless as he shook his head in wonder. "It then occurred to me that perhaps, after all, Persephone may have been..."

"You," you finished with a whisper, eyes probably wide as dinner plates as you looked up at him. You placed your hands on his chest, gripping at the expensive fabric of his shirt. "I didn't even realize when I was writing it..." You sounded surprised at your own revelation. "But now the more that I think about it... it's true."

"Ironic, is it not?" he mused, dipping forward to hover over your shoulder. You shivered as he traced the shell of your ear with the pointed tip of his nose. "At the very beginning, I had feared that I would corrupt you. Yet here you are, having trudged back to the Underworld to deliver your own form of justice." You felt his smile against your neck. "Your essay was a perfect example of the purpose of mythology. The art of it is in the ability to between the lines and go deeper than face value to uncover the real lessons the legends attempt to convey."

You tugged at his shirt to get him to withdraw so you could look at him. You put on your best sour face. "Does this mean that you're implying that *I'm* Hades now?"

He tipped his head back to let out another laugh, antennae and wings fluttering as his shoulders shook. He was then looking at you again, the tenderness in his eyes so palpable that it felt like he was hugging your very soul. "You, my love, are a *harpy*," he breathed, dipping to place his lips against the corner of your mouth. "A harpy and a moonflower and just *you*. Never in my life would I have imagined I would be deserving of such a gift."

You drew your hands up his chest to circle around his neck, curling your fingers into his hair just above where it was gathered at the base of his head. Then you tugged him forward, angling his face so his lips were more flush against yours.

He tasted of everything you'd once thought that you would hate — bergamot and citrus, the perfect blend of Earl Grey. The scent of leather and moonflowers accompanied the taste of him, curling around your tongue to invade your senses. When warmth pooled in your abdomen at the prick of his claws against your thighs and the way the heels of his palms pressed into your skin, you somehow knew that you would never be cold again.

Was this the time to tell him that you loved him? You felt drunk on him, recalling how he had called you *my love*. It wasn't *necessarily* a declaration, but you suspected he might have felt the same way you did. But his lips were so *soft* and the way his fangs pricked at yours was so *nice* and it would be such a pity to pull away…

Unfortunately, your stomach seemed to be intent on raining on your parade as it chose that opportune moment to growl, another blush exploding across your cheeks as you separated from Gideon. Both of his antennae twitched at the noise, his lips quirking downwards.

"I, uh, skipped dinner I guess," you admitted, touching the tips of your index fingers together as you looked up at him through your lashes in embarrassment. He sighed disapprovingly, giving you one last kiss before he lifted you off his lap, placing you on the cushion and rising to patter into your kitchenette. You rested your chin on the back of your couch next to a swatch of familiar maroon fabric, watching him open and close various cabinets before rolling his sleeves up to begin cooking for you.

Though Gideon was too fantastic to truly belong in your modest apartment, he looked right at home, confidently opening drawers to get the utensils he required as he knew exactly where everything was now. You were a little disappointed that you hadn't been able to confess your feelings for him, but with the whole topic of being disowned—

Fuck, you'd forgotten about that again.

"Hey, Gideon," you called out hesitantly, ducking behind the couch so only your eyes peeked over the back of it. He paused in what he was doing to turn his head, antennae inclining in question. "About me getting you disowned..."

"My grandmother is not planning to disown me," he said with a playful roll of his eyes. It was a gesture he must've picked up from you, you noted as you watched him chuckle to himself. "Besides, even if she were, I would not be worried."

"Really?" You perked up at his nonchalance, feeling much better about the whole thing. What a relief! You shifted so that your weight was on your knees, allowing you to draw yourself up more to rest your elbows on the back of the couch. "I mean... all those antiques... and the estate! And, well, the inheritance..."

He resumed chopping at the celery he had pulled from your fridge. Your eyes narrowed. You didn't remember buying it, so you suspected he must have stocked your kitchen again.

"Those antiques are priceless, yes, but they are so *gaudy*. And the estate... I told you that the only part of it I missed was the greenhouse. I could put a greenhouse on any piece of property. As for the inheritance..." He trailed off as he picked up his cutting board, holding it over the pot he had put on your stove and using the back of the knife to push the celery into it. "I have dabbled in many subjects, remember? One of them being business ventures." He shrugged, placing the board back on the counter and picking up a carrot. "Another hobby I share with Eden, I suppose. I have many private investments that are quite lucrative."

Yet again, you were staring at him, wondering just who the hell this guy was. Sure, you loved uncovering all the riddles that made up your boyfriend, but was there ever an end to the mystery you had been unwrapping that was coiled around the enigma?

"You mean you could've been tutoring me the *whole* time in my business courses?" you shrieked, launching yourself off the couch to join him in the kitchen. You remembered your 3AM study session and how quickly it seemed he had been able to grasp the material when he had quizzed you; now it all made much more sense. He laughed at your squawking, lightly slapping your wrist with the wooden spoon he now wielded. "You're evil!"

"I am *not*," he retorted, bumping you aside with his hip so he could pull a few more spices out of your cabinet. Spices that you *also* didn't remember buying yourself. "I have seen your marks. You are *quite* capable on your own. You did not require my assistance." He stilled to tap his chin with his finger. "Although I suppose I could have offered my services to you, at a cost of course..."

"What *kind* of cost?" you asked, folding your arms across your chest to pout at him. He was right; you did know your shit, but that didn't mean that you weren't feeling a bit peeved that you could have had some extra tutoring thrown in there.

A single fang flashed as he turned from you, suddenly very interested in what he was boiling in the pot. "I believe I heard somewhere that the *sex* was rather exemplary... "

You let out another squeak as you waved your hands at him, cheeks flushing red. He simply picked you up, placing you out of the way on the counter with ease as if you weighed nothing. He gave you a stern look to stay put before turning back to his stew, his antennae swaying in rhythm as he hummed to himself while he stirred. You kicked your feet back and forth as they dangled, unable to bite back the smile at watching him flit around your kitchen.

It could have been eons before you could fully appraise all the facets that made up Gideon M. Dulcis, but as he was bringing a spoonful of stew towards you to taste, holding a hand underneath it to prevent the steaming liquid from dripping on your floor as he blew on it so you wouldn't burn yourself, you knew you were always up for a good challenge.

Maybe you could start with finding out what the 'M' stood for.

xxii: midas touch

A NERVOUS GIGGLE bubbled through your lips as you looked down at Gideon's semi-prostrate form, the muscles in his shoulders rippling as he bolstered himself up by his forearms while holding his pert ass in the air. Hot damn, you didn't really like yoga, but Gideon's version of the downward dog might be just enough for you to consider joining a couple's class with him.

You licked your lips and shuffled forward, the foreign object dangling between your legs bobbing side-to-side in your movement. This was completely uncharted territory for you — and you were up to *three* corernata now. It had been something you had only recently talked about, saying that it was something you wanted to try, but you hadn't necessarily been expecting him to accept so *eagerly*.

"Did I not say I would indulge your every desire?" he had purred, pressing the tip of a fang into the pulse point at your neck rather greedily.

And now here you were, hovering over him and entirely naked save for the newly-purchased strap on you wore that was nowhere near as pretty as his own cock.

You had already been adequately prepared thanks to his skilled fingers and long, prehensile tongue. When he had helped you ease one of the dildos on the inner portion of the thong into you, it had slid in rather easily while he peppered kisses all over your neck as he fastened the rest of the straps around you. It felt sadly *small* compared to him and didn't contain the ridged nubs or the flared head you loved so much, but this was for him as much as it was for you.

You chewed at your lip, still staring at him anxiously. As you shuffled from foot to foot, you saw his body move as he shifted, looking into ruby eyes while he peeked over his shoulder to see you stalling. An antenna quirked inquisitively. You opened your mouth to blurt, "I'm—uh—kind of nervous about this."

"Would you still like to proceed?" His voice was calm as he turned, rolling his body and moving forward to perch on the edge of the bed. You bit your lip again, but nodded as his arms extended to place his hands on your hips right above the thick band wrapped around them. He rubbed soothing circles into your skin with his thumb. "I am going to need your words, little harpy."

"Yeah, I do," you confirmed, locking eyes with him before peeking back down at the cock between your legs and blushing. His own was straining out of its slit, curving forward and towards you, but Gideon's gaze was still completely focused on your face. "But... what if I'm *bad* at it?"

"You are not bad at *anything*," Gideon insisted in a half-scoff before his voice became more gentle. "You know I will not judge and if you want to stop, we will stop. No pressure. Just you and I, hmm?"

You nodded again, bending forward to place a kiss on his lips as your hands came up to cradle his jaw. "Ok," you breathed against his mouth, straightening again to peer down at him. "Um..." Your brows knit together as you tried to remember what you had seen in some of the *research* you had done prior to this. "Suck?"

"Was that a question or a command, little harpy?" Gideon teased, looping in index fingers in the straps to tug you forward. You flushed again, but tried to give him your best serious expression.

"A *command*," you stated more firmly, taking the dildo in your hand to hold steady as you looked at him with resolve. "Suck."

He smirked at you, but immediately complied, bending forward to take the tip in his mouth. Unlike Gideon's cock, which was mostly gray with a lilac flush towards the tip, the rubbery material of the strap on was a single shade of black. With its mock veins and slight texture, it looked more similar to a human's, aside from the little segments that tapered thinner towards the end. When the first segment disappeared between his plush, pretty lips, you couldn't help but gape a little bit.

Fuck, that was hot. Was that how it looked when you tried to take him, mouth straining and struggling against his girth?

Before long, he was taking more of its length in the back of his throat, maintaining eye contact with you the entire time while he worked it in his mouth. The movement caused the dildo within you to jostle slightly, but you felt much more turned on by just the sight of Gideon deep throating this toy than the faint physical stimulation.

You reached over to the bottle of lube on the nightstand, trying not to move too much while Gideon continued to piston the dildo in and out of his mouth. You gently pushed him back, the object leaving his lips with a wet *pop* that made your core clench as you motioned for him to hold out his hands. He turned his palms upwards as you generously poured the slippery liquid into them.

You could tell from the slight twitch of his antennae and scrunch of his brow bone that he wasn't necessarily thrilled with the mess, but he said nothing, instead rubbing his hands together before pumping them along the toy. He smirked at you again when he noticed your staring, a single fang flashing as he ran his fingers up and down the rubbery length with exaggerated slowness.

Arching a brow at him and feeling a bit bolder, you reached out to push at his shoulder. He tipped backwards, still smirking up at you as he shimmied further up the bed to make room. You placed a knee between his legs on the edge of the mattress right under his actual cock as you reached down, taking his length in your hand and squeezing at the base of it.

Reveling in the falter of his smug look as a sharp hiss escaped between his teeth, you continued your ministrations, squeezing gently as you tugged upwards, your fingertips catching on each bump and nub of his ridges. You stopped just before reaching the flared head of it, which was already weeping with pearlescent moisture. Though you would never be able to fully wrap your hand around his girth, you twisted around it, watching his brow bone crease as he let out a quiet pant. The pastel lilac soon deepened into a more rich eggplant color and when he twitched again in your grip, his antennae going slightly rigid like the rest of his body, you stopped. He let out a frustrated groan.

You grinned at this, knowing *exactly* how he felt. For once, the shoe was on the other foot.

"Turn over," you ordered, much more confident now. He gave you a long, smoldering look before obeying to resume his original position. You still felt the urge to giggle, but swallowed it as you moved forward to kneel on top of the mattress, rubber appendage swaying between your legs as you did so.

You ran your palm over Gideon's ass, the firm expanse of it feeling like satin with the same gray fuzz that covered him all over. Like his lips and his cock, his skin had a faint lilac flush to it. You slid your hand up to rest on the sensitive nubs where his wings splayed out of the mid-section of his back, rubbing them between your fingers as his muscles rippled under you.

It then occurred to you that despite the videos you watched, you still had no idea what to do. You were blanking. You froze again.

"Are you quite alright?" he asked, though with the way his voice strained, you should have been asking *him* that question. You nodded even though he couldn't see you, chewing at your lip as you moved your hand on his back downwards to rest on his ass again.

"Yeah, but..." You cocked your head to the side, nose scrunched in thought. "I'm drawing a blank. A little help here?"

His wings quivered as he chuckled despite his *clearly* aroused state, body shifting to redistribute his weight a bit more comfortably. "Take more of the lubricating liquid," he said, words sounding like they were coming out of clenched teeth, "and use it to work me open a bit more."

Your mouth parted in a small *'O'* as you fought the urge to slap your forehead. *Duh!*

You reached down to pick up the bottle he had placed on the floor, putting more of it on your hands and rubbing them together. Always thinking ahead, he had warmed the bottle earlier in some kind of fancy contraption that had almost resembled a wax melter, so luckily the liquid wasn't shockingly cool against your skin. When you shuffled forward again to place them flat against his ass, he more visibly tensed, wings quivering as if in anticipation.

Holding the small of his back with one hand, you slid the other closer to his entrance, teasing at the puckered rim. The skin was a much darker gray here than the rest of him, feeling more like velvet than satin. From this angle, you could see the twin slits that hid two pairs of coremata, like mirror images to the ones on his front that contained his claspers. Your breath caught at the same time his did when you pushed the tip of a finger in experimentally, slowly pistoning it in and out as he liked to do with your own core. After a few moments of doing this, you added another, working them in tandem in an even, languid rhythm.

"D-Does this feel ok?" you asked, stilling your ministrations to look up at Gideon. His head was dangling slightly, the hair of his ponytail falling over one shoulder. When his only response was a whine escaping from between his lips, you took that as an emphatic *yes*, resuming your earlier pace.

You tried opening and closing your fingers in scissoring motions, still going somewhat slow to get him used to the feeling as much as you were getting used to providing it. Then you were adding a third, spreading the trio apart and curling slightly as the slight resistance you had felt began to ebb. His breath became louder and more jagged as you did so. "Um... is that good enough?"

You heard him audibly swallow, responding in a pinched, "Yes, quite," before you giggled again.

You extracted your fingers from him, relishing in the groan that he made as you dragged them away and bent to put more lube in your hands, pumping the dildo to ensure it was still well-slicked. Then, you knocked his legs a bit further apart so you could settle more comfortably behind him, guiding the first segment of the tip forward as you pressed into him.

He let out a muffled *mmf* sound, head dropping further as he sank more fully into the mattress. His forearms shook in their effort to continue to hold his torso up while the tips of his antennae brushed against his sheets. With your other hand, you cupped his ass, rubbing circles against his skin with your thumb. You bit your lip at the slight sensation of the dildo within you rubbing against your walls, but the hitch of his breath when you began to shallowly thrust was what began to light the match in your core.

His thighs shook when you pressed forward a bit more deeply, the second and third segment disappearing within him. He rasped out a word in that ancient tongue you didn't recognize, the one he had once spoken to Gillivray. From the way it sharply tumbled through his lips, you suspected it may have been a curse.

"Language," you chastised teasingly, going on a whim in your guess that it was *actually* some kind of profanity. He merely let out a grunt in response.

You worked more of the length inside of him, beginning to pant slightly at the exertion. You *really* needed to get into some kind of cardio routine. Still, the dildo within you seemed not able to press against your walls in the way you liked. You missed the feeling of Gideon's ridged nubs grinding within you, the slight tickle of his cock's feathered tip and the suction when it flared within you as he dragged out. But then Gideon did something that could have caused the loosely-wrapped coil within you to immediately snap if not for your complete focus on your movement.

Gideon whimpered.

Oh, that was *really* hot.

You were almost fully seated within him now, the dildo you had chosen for this first time a bit shorter in length compared to the gargantuan ones you had seen in the shop you'd gone to together in Tenebra City. You reached down and around him to grip his cock, rubbing your thumb over its texture, pretending they were bumping against your inner walls rather than your fingertips as you continued to thrust. He stiffened again, letting out a ragged moan as your hand worked up and down his length.

No longer needing your other hand to guide the toy, you splayed it against his lower back, teasing the opening of one of his coremata slits with your fingertips. He let out that same foreign curse again, the area apparently *very* sensitive. You snickered at this and pocketed that discovery for later, the coil within you beginning to wind tighter at his reaction while you moved your palm upwards to caress one of his wings. It quivered under your touch, silky and smooth and delicate as you kept pistoning into him while twisting and tugging around his cock.

Remembering a motion that he liked to make that nearly ended you each time, you abruptly rolled your hips while you gave another deep thrust.

"*Mmph—ah!*" he cried out in response.

Gideon was never usually very vocal, but the noises he was making now were completely intoxicating. It suddenly made sense to you why he always liked to make a point that he wanted to hear you; those sounds were addicting.

Your rhythm was much more fluid now, much more natural. You felt incredibly sexy like this and were extremely glad you could experience this with him. You felt totally in power, imagining the silver veins in those quivering wings turning to gold under your touch like the ancient king of legends. Though Gideon, gasping and panting beneath you, was already your ultimate treasure.

Tossing your hair over your shoulder, you reached out forward to grip at the base of his ponytail, tugging his head gently backwards so his face tilted up. He let out another whine at this as you continued to thrust, the sound pinching off into nothing when you seemed to hit a particularly sensitive spot deep within him. Interesting. You angled yourself again to aim for the same area, getting rewarded with another whimper that made your nipples ache.

Feeling a tickle at your abdomen, you looked down to see the tips of his coremata peeking out from their slits. They were only partially freed, but this was a sure sign that Gideon's usually firm grip on his control was unraveling. They caressed your skin, for once not actually *seeking* anything, just flailing in his pleasure.

You picked up your pace, thrusting in rhythm to the pull of your hand on his cock as you kept a steady grip on his hair. His panting became louder and louder, choking off in grunts as you continued to piston and twist. The coremata brushed against your skin more insistently while your rocking motion evolved into pounding as you found yourself chasing Gideon's release more than your own.

As his grunts picked up in volume, you felt the warmth within you grow hotter and hotter until you were on the edge of a sear. But Gideon was soon coming undone before you could, completely butchering your name in a loud cry as his orgasm crested and crashed over him. His entire body went rigid before he pitched forward; you had to quickly let go of his hair before he yanked his own strands out of his head. You felt his cock go stiff for a split second before it was pulsating, ropes of thick, pearly come painting his dark sheets like gesso on canvas.

He collapsed and you were pulled down with him, careful not to crush his wings against your chest as you stayed buried inside of him. His coremata wriggled their way out from under you, slithering to clasp against your back and tugging you more flush to him like a backwards hug. You fought to catch your breath as he continued to twitch and shake, cock still jerking in your loose grip while you lazily moved your hand up and down to prolong his release.

When the gaps between the spurts grew longer in length and he became more still, you finally removed your hand, feeling his coremata pull away to rest lazily against his mattress. You licked your dry lips, placing an apologetic hand on his ass when the movement of your hips caused him to hiss.

"T-That was pretty fun, huh?" you joked lightly, giving another giggle as he managed to give you a tired huff in response. "I'm going to move now, ok?"

He made another garbled noise that you took as an invitation to continue, the sound pitching again when you slowly withdrew from him. You carefully moved backwards, inching off the bed to place your feet on the floor as you stood in front of him on slightly shaky legs. You paused, giving him another moment to recover before seeing that he was turning over again.

You let out a squeak of surprise when you were suddenly pulled back down, his lips crashing against yours as he tugged you to him. "You are *incredible*," he rasped, the huskiness of his voice sending shivers down your spine as he nipped down the length of your neck. "But you did not—"

"It's ok," you insisted with a giggle as his mouth continued his trail down your shoulders, "you made me come earlier. Twice, actually. Maybe three times?"

"That is not *nearly* enough," he insisted, pulling away from you and giving you one last firm peck on the lips as if his decision was final. He reached around you to undo the strap around your waist, spreading your thighs a bit farther apart so he could carefully extract the toy from you. It slid out as easily as it had gone in, your core already slick as a result of Gideon's pleasure.

Before you could blink you were falling on top of him, scrambling to keep your balance while his legs dangled off the side of his bed. You saw a few coremata hover in the air out of the corners of your eyes, looking down to see one wrapping around his still-hard cock in a spiral, looping three times around the base of it to form that knot you liked so much. You didn't even have time to bite your lip in desire before he had buried himself in you to the hilt, your choked gasp delayed as he did so.

Gideon set a pace that was absolutely feral, pounding within you with wild abandon as his hips lifted savagely off the bed while his hands gripped your waist to hold you in place. His hot breath was suddenly fanning the sensitive skin on your neck while he mouth opened, tongue unfurling to lick against your jugular. You shivered at the feeling before gasping at the abrupt sharp pinch of his tiny fangs sliding into you, latching on while his tongue swept back and forth soothingly as you groaned in bliss.

Just when you thought you were truly coming apart at the seams, you felt two coremata curl around your nipples, tweaking and pulling with a third flicking at your clit. Electricity sizzled up your sensitive nub near your core at the same time twin bolts crackled down the ones on your chest, meeting in the middle of your abdomen to absolutely explode.

You knew nothing but the drag of the ridges of his cock and the suction of that flared head as he continued to pump in and out of you, the feathered tip teasing at your entrance each time he nearly unsheathed himself, only to slam right back in. The bloom of pain from teeth in your neck had dulled to a cloying soreness that caused a deeper ache elsewhere within you. You couldn't even speak at this point, the only noise you could emit being a high-pitched whine that was somewhere between a whimper and a moan. Everything was hot and white and dazzling as you clenched and fluttered around his length, feeling it twitch as it began spurting once again, jumping and jerking as it coated your insides with his molten spend.

When you were nearly certain you must have died, he slowed, thrusts become more sluggish as he pistoned lazily. He withdrew his teeth from you, tenderly lapping at the twin bite marks and the oncoming bruise from his suckling. His hands then guided you down, coremata leaving your cupped breasts to caress your upper back and push your chest on top of his. You felt the pinch of his claspers against your thighs as he shifted from pistoning to merely rolling his hips, the coremata at your clit rubbing circles as you twitched in the aftershocks of your prolonged release.

Finally he stilled, lifting his hips slightly so his coremata could drag against your skin and disappear back into their slits. When he lowered himself again, you felt his claspers release you, your skin aching deliciously from where they had pressed into you. His hands came up from your thighs to stroke your hair, tenderly brushing a few slicked strands back from your sweaty forehead. You felt the soft pad of his thumb brush the sore spot on your neck that was now beginning to throb. "That's my girl."

This was your favorite place in the world, huddled against Gideon while his warmth surrounded you, inside and out. Completely spent, your eyelids began to droop as you heard him hum, the sound and rumbling of his chest combining with the beat of his heart to lull you to sleep. You felt him shift again, hands disappearing from your hair. You grumbled an incoherent protest against his naked torso before they were back, carding through your strands before deftly maneuvering downwards, grabbing new sections to intertwine together. He must have removed the leather tie holding his own hair back to fasten yours, you mused as you felt the new weight of it brush over your shoulder and his lips press into the crown of your head.

Your last coherent thought was how much you had enjoyed this whole experience. Maybe the next time he took you to Tenebra City, you could go back to that shop and peruse their wide assortment of strap ons. Maybe you could even go up a peg in size.

Pun intended.

epilogue: elysian fields

THERE WERE dozens of sayings and expressions about the progression of time that you could pull from, but none quite captured the way you felt when you were with Gideon. In some instances, the days rolled by lazily like honey dripping from a spoon, beading to critical mass before tapering off in thin streams. In others, it felt like you couldn't even catch your breath, minutes and hours stringing together like pearls being threaded on a conveyor belt as the moments flew by in flashes.

You learned to savor the moments with Gideon — the ups and downs, the fasts and the slows. No two seconds were quite the same, which kept your relationship together interesting. As the weeks flickered by and the winter chill thawed into spring, you couldn't help but feel like that future you had envisioned with him was comfortably within your grasp.

Effie's squeal about the two guys she had started seeing simultaneously — both orcs, maybe — pierced the air, causing you to smile and wince at the same time as you heard Calli clap in excitement. You had your phone perched on one of Gideon's shelves while on a group video call with your friends, all of them having gone home for spring break. Just as Gideon had suspected, you aced all your final exams — *and* the final essay for his class, no thanks to him, have a nice day — even beating out that vampire bitch. She could suck it.

Well, not *literally*, you hoped.

After Effie had made her interest in polyamory known to your friends, you had all rallied to try and help her set up the perfect dating profiles, only for her to stumble upon the perfect pair while ordering a scone from your favorite cafe.

You still would never tell her that Gideon's were better, but you digressed.

You had been in the midst of helping him reorganize Gideon's quill collection to make more room when the call had started, your boyfriend having disappeared into the kitchen at some point while Calli and Effie fought to speak over each other, you and Greer snickering while they played their usual game of *who can speak the loudest?* As usual, it was a tossup, the soft, smooth sounds of the jazz record you had put on reduced to nothing but white noise in their verbal barrage. Effie currently had the floor while she described one of the dates she went on recently, gushing to Calli that you all needed to find her a partner so you could finally go on a group date altogether without having an awkward single bystander.

You snorted at this as you picked up a quill, dusting underneath it with your rag before settling it back down gently as you balanced carefully on the ladder you were standing on. Gideon was definitely getting better with crowds and people in general, having spent more time with you in Tenebra City to take in the sights and sounds, and although you had been on a double date with him and Greer, you weren't sure he was ready for the entirety of your group. He would agree if you asked, the stubborn man, but you knew his antennae and wings would be rigid the entire time.

You heard a muffled sound as you turned to see Gideon leaning against a pillar, his knuckles rapping against the concrete to get your attention. He was wearing his usual outfit of dark gray slacks and a white button down, but must have removed his glasses once the sun went down. One ankle was crossed over the other as he looked at you intently. A red kitchen towel was draped over his shoulder.

Cinched around his waist was a cute, frilly apron in a pastel lilac color that said "KISS THE ~~COCK~~ COOK" in dark purple letters. It was definitely self-indulgent as you had remembered your desire to see him in such a getup when he had interrupted your 3AM study session. It had been custom-ordered, and while he had narrowed his eyes disapprovingly at the crossed-out use of profanity, he still wore it whenever he cooked for you.

He even brought it to *your* apartment when you ate there together.

"Dinner is almost ready," he said softly, his lush hair spilling freely around his shoulders. It was no longer sooty gray, but a pure white. After some time deliberating, he had decided to go back to his natural color, which had only been achieved by hours of you sitting on the counter in his bathroom with a color removal kit while he stood in front of one of his sinks. He had scowled while you had giggled, holding the instructions in your hand away from him while he grumbled that you were *doing it wrong*, trying to snatch the leaflet of gibberish out of your grasp.

You were proud of him for wanting to try it out again since he hadn't been back to his natural color in so long. When he had been a bit unsure, you had assured him that he could always dye it again, joking that you could program his phone to put his hair stylist on speed dial. Besides, you had said, the journey of self-discovery wasn't necessarily linear. You knew as well as he did that there could be bumps along the way, but you insisted you would be there to support him all the way.

Alis volat propriis, you mused, recalling the glossy red text that was on Gideon's motorcycle. *He flies with his own wings.*

"What're you making?" Greer's rough voice cut through the squeals of Calli and Effie as you watched Silas' massive green head pop into the frame, ducking slightly so he didn't impale himself on one of Greer's horns. He waved at you, which you returned with a smile.

At some point, Greer had begrudgingly warmed up to Gideon, their mutual love for the culinary arts the straw that had broken the stubborn camel's back. Silas was also apparently a heavy metal fan, so Gideon's deep knowledge in the genre was also a topic of conversation that they were able to bond over.

Gideon walked towards you, holding his hand out and gesturing for your phone. You plucked it off the shelf and handed it to him as Effie and Calli let out a duet of *hello*'s, which he returned while he placed it on his coffee table. Then he returned to you, opening his arms as you descended the ladder to wrap around you in a hug as he spun you in a half-circle, placing you down on the floor with a kiss to the forehead before stooping down to peer at your phone screen.

"Ratatouille," he finally answered Greer, giving you a lopsided smile when you brushed his curtain of snowy hair off his shoulder so you could rest your hand on it. His eyes returned to your phone. "I shall send you the recipe."

"Bye, guys!" you said, picking the phone up and holding it away from you so both of you could wave in the frame. Your friends wished each other a good night before they hung up, Greer managing to exclaim a quick *Don't forget to send it to me!* before your screen went dark.

"You are lucky your friends are sane," Gideon intoned, moving to sit down on one of his accent chairs. He leaned forward with his elbows on his knees in the kind of casual gesture that you never thought would suit him, but the relaxed posture definitely did. You laughed at this with a roll of your eyes, shaking your head.

"Have you *met* Effie and Calli?" you asked, folding an arm across your abdomen while you balance an elbow on your wrist, laying it atop your chest and cupping your chin in the palm of your hand. "I'd say they're only *somewhat* sane, but I love them for it."

Gideon hummed in acknowledgement, ruby eyes darkening. He was by no means an open book, but you knew enough about him now to venture a guess that he might have been thinking about when you had first met Eden in Tenebra City. Gideon had nearly growled, baring his cute little fangs when the incubus had remarked, "She looks delicious."

But when your knees had suddenly gone weak at the abrupt image of both of them tangled around you and writhing against your naked form that had invaded your mind, you practically joined in Gideon's snarl.

Gideon had given Eden a thorough verbal lashing after that, making him promise never to project those kinds of images into your mind ever again as he held your shaking form up by the waist. You remembered the sight of Eden's pointed tail curling between his legs as he scurried away.

"Yes," he said after a moment, his antennae tilting to the side, "you are correct, I suppose."

"Wait a minute!" you exclaimed dramatically, putting your arms in front of you and bending at the knees in a theatrical gesture of shock. You then clasped your hand atop your heart, bringing your other arm up to press the back of your hand against your forehead. "Gideon M. Dulcis is admitting that *I'm* right?" You gave an exaggerated double take, moving the hand over your heart away from your chest and cupping it in a vertical fist as if you were holding a microphone. "Could you please say that again? And maybe in front of a camera this time?"

He bit on a knuckle, but couldn't hide his smirk at your antics. He then leaned back, one arm thrown over the side of his chair as he beckoned to his lap with the crook of a pointed finger, eyes darting down pointedly before returning to yours. You grinned at him, padding across the living room to straddle his strong thighs.

He reached up to touch the necklace that hung between your breasts, tugging at the delicate chain to free the pendant from under your blouse. His fingertip gently brushed one of the petals carved out of moonstone, the gem glowing and shimmering in his touch. He had gifted it to you on the same winter holiday that you had gifted him the apron, the stone carved into the shape of a moonflower. It was imbued with magical properties and glowed at night, reminding you of the way the pinpoints of light dotted the inky grass of the meadow he often took you to now.

The pearly sheen *also* conveniently reminded you of his come and when you caught a twinkle in his eye after you had blushed at the initial realization, you suspected that it was done on purpose.

Along with the necklace, you had received yet *another* surprise — an olive branch from a certain Duchess in the form of a holiday greeting on the back of a card with a formal portrait of her. You supposed this meant that you were at some kind of impasse with DeeDee, and though Gideon had nearly fainted when you had opened it and turned it around to show him, it now hung proudly on your refrigerator.

You still hadn't spoken to your parents, but you could cross that bridge when and if you got there — and this time, you had Gideon by your side. You would start your internship soon, which you had procured all on your own, having basically been in the center of a bidding war between multiple offers. It felt good to be wanted, and though Gideon's smug expression had told you he had known all along it would come to fruition, he had congratulated you in the way he only knew how... with freshly-baked scones, hot chocolate, and a mind-shattering flurry of orgasms that left you practically incoherent and unable to walk for the entirety of the next day.

Well, *nothing* was perfect, but you supposed this was as close as it could get. You had descended with him with the Second Circle, had managed to escape from the Ninth with your life intact, and had met a whole cast of characters along the way. Although you had originally thought mythology was useless, it was incredible how much it actually had ended up applying to your everyday life, as if you could mark all your most important moments like chapters in a book.

And now, you had your own version of Persephone, able to simply bask in each other's comfort, somewhere to the right of Tartarus, out of the darker depths of the Underworld and into the plains of paradise. You pictured yourself and Gideon sprawled atop a picnic blanket in the rolling, lush fields of Elysium, your new nickname for the meadow in the clearing by Eventide Falls. Perched on top of his lap, you were completely content in the sound of his fluttering heartbeat as you pressed your ear against his chest.

When your eyes were about to slide shut, you heard him say your name, causing you to sit back upright. He reached out to tuck a lock of hair behind your ears, tenderly moving the backs of his fingers downwards to caress at the edge of your jaw before he spoke.

"Mason," he said suddenly, sweeping at your cheekbone with his thumb. "*That* is my middle name. My full name is Gideon Mason Dulcis, thirteenth of my name, and apparently the luckiest out of all of them." He smiled at your shock, tugging you forward so he could brush his lips against yours. "I once told you that the fae believe names hold power, but it is useless pretending that any being, living or dead, can hold more power over me than that of which you possess."

"Mason," you repeated, voice breathy with awe. It suited him. You plucked the towel off his shoulder, folding in it the way you knew he liked before setting it aside. Then, you smiled, leaning more against him and tugging at a white strand of hair. Taking a breath, you decided now was as good of a time as ever to say, "Well, I love you, Gideon *Mason* Dulcis."

It was his turn to look shocked, his mouth opening slightly as you grinned at him. He snapped it shut with a *click* before pulling you back towards him, nibbling at your lower lip. He pulled back to cup your chin in his hand, eyes sweeping over your face with such tenderness that you felt as though you could shatter. "And I you."

With a giggle, you melted against him one more, seeking his lips with your own. Just as the taste of bergamot and citrus began to bloom against your tongue, you heard a high-pitched shrilling sound. You swallowed Gideon's gasp as he gently pushed you back, eyes going wide. "My ratatouille!"

He quickly stood, picking you up with him. Swiveling, he placed you gently on the couch before basically sprinting back into the kitchen, wings and antennae fluttering while he moved with impressive speed. You heard him exclaim something in that ancient tongue he knew, the foreign word sounding awfully close to what you had come to learn *was*, in fact, a curse as you tried to muffle your laughter with your fist.

He emerged from the kitchen with a dramatic plume of smoke surrounding him, wisping and curling around his figure in little eddies as they were caught in the slight breeze of his flickering wings. He let out a long sigh, wings and antennae drooping. "Well, dinner is ruined."

"Let's order takeout!" you chirped, clapping your hands at the prospect of junky food. Gideon fed you well — *too* well, maybe — but it had been forever since you'd been able to pig out on garbage. "You can choose?"

His nose scrunched slightly at this — a habit he had clearly picked up from you — tips of his antennae quirking, but he otherwise didn't protest as his wings seemed to perk up a bit. He grumbled something to himself before turning and disappearing back into the kitchen, coming back out a few minutes later. "They said it will take at least an hour."

An hour. That wasn't ideal, but you shrugged. "That's ok," you said, "I'm not super hungry. We can wait."

He hummed at this, striding back into the living room. He stopped with his abdomen pressed against the back of the chair he had situated in as you reached over to pluck a quill off of the side table it had been resting on, twirling the stem between your fingertips.

"I am *starving*," he stated, leaning down. You peeked up at him, the hunger in his eyes suggesting that he was speaking about something other than food. "Now," he began again, his tone expectant. You could hear the suggestion of that future in it, picturing it sprawling before you and cemented even more firmly in your grasp now. "Shall we try for *four*?"

You let out a surprised *eep* at this, quill in your grip snapping in your abrupt shock as you watched his wings quiver with mirth. Tossing the pieces aside, you launched yourself over the back of the chair at him, squawking about how *inappropriate* and *insatiable* he was with your legs clasped around his waist. He merely laughed, twirling you around quickly before slowing to match the tempo of the honeyed voice crooning from his vintage record player.

That *fucker*, you thought, allowing him to continue to twirl you as you moped into his shoulder. He truly was Professor Prick, King of Assholes, Patron Saint of Douchebaggery. No matter what, that would never change, just as you knew for a fact that two *other* things would always remain constant:

One: Gideon was a man of his word.

And two: you always liked a challenge.

bonus content: to a flame

IT STARTED NOT with a flash or a bang, but with a sudden stop.

It is not the impact that will kill you, Gideon remembered from his physics lectures many degrees ago, *but the deceleration.* When you literally crashed into his life, thumping against his chest with as much grace as a minotaur in a china shop, he thought he was dead before you even hit the ground.

Thirteenth of his name, Gideon felt every bit as unlucky as the cursed number would entail. Some higher being had apparently deemed it appropriate to set him directly in the path of a harpy in the form of a human woman, who was chittering and squawking at him after so rudely accosting him. It was not until he realized you were talking about mythology that his antennae twitched in excited recognition, only to deflate when he understood you were not celebrating it, but condemning it. In your eyes it was useless — impractical.

Which was exactly why it had been his final choice after years and years of degrees and doctorates. He tried not to think of his grandmother.

That career is useless, Gideon. You are useless, Gideon.

He knew both those things, which is why he had chosen it in the first place. In that moment when you collided with him, though, he did not feel useless — even while bemoaning his profession, your eyes were wide and shimmering with life, almost imploring him to assist you like some kind of siren. So, while he pointed you in the right direction of where to find those *stupid mythology textbooks*, he relished in the delicious irony that you would be in his class, though you did not seem to know it yet.

Right away he knew that everything about you was too loud — too bright. Not just your eyes, but your voice. Your personality. Your aura. You were too colorful right down from the outfit you wore to your expressive face, nose perpetually scrunched in thought. Gideon knew that his glasses would not even be able to stop the ensuing headache that would plague him for the rest of the semester when you nearly egged a vampire on in class with your snippy attitude during his introduction to *The Metamorphoses*. When he attempted to caution you against doing so in the future, he tried not to think too much about the grisly image you painted in your jest about being found lifeless in an alley.

You may have been giving him an eternal headache, but something told Gideon that the blinding pain of the ensuing darkness without you would be even more severe.

After spending weeks as his assistant after having essentially accused you of plagiarism, Gideon began to notice just how palpable your presence in his life was. There was something about the way you carried yourself, always putting on such a confident front despite the way your brows would crease when you got that faraway look in your eyes and how you sometimes chewed on the inside of your cheek. You were a walking contradiction to him — precariously certain, shimmeringly dour. It was as if Gideon had never considered what three dimensions might look like until he met you and he wondered how long it would be until you snatched the frames from his face to show him yourself.

Gideon did not necessarily *hate* color, but he had always been conditioned against it. Like emotions, color could hurt him, though there were no magically-charmed glasses to protect him from them. It was easier to remain cold and detached; one of his grandmother's earliest lessons to him had been a sermon on the art of locking away his feelings, showing him how to tamp them down and store them in a lead box deep inside himself before throwing away the key.

And then one day in Gideon's black and white world, he saw red.

For as much as he had cursed the gods for putting a harpy in his path that first time, he was ever thankful to them for placing you in his path once again in that accursed maze. You were on one of those *dates* you liked to tell him about when you were alone in the office, his fangs now nearly ground flat with the way he had to clench his teeth to stop himself from betraying his own jealousy. Though it usually thrilled him in a sickening way to hear about your courtship mishaps, he was not at all pleased to find you in the middle of one going wrong. Not because of his own selfish desires, but because you were *scared*. Your normally bubbly personality had been tainted with the sour tang of fear and Gideon, calm, cool, and collected Gideon, was feeling the hot flames of fury.

He imagined clawing the boy's eyes out, plucking them from his skull one-by-one and spearing them on his pointed fingernails like grapes to offer to Dionysus himself, but in typical Gideon fashion, he was useless. *You* were the one talking yourself out of the situation; as much as Gideon could have wallowed in his own inadequacy, he was too thrilled by the current story you were weaving rather theatrically. You were referring to Gideon as your boyfriend, and though it was an act of self-preservation, the tips of his wings could only twitch in pleased flutters as he wrapped his arm around you to keep up the act.

Or so he told himself.

He savored the way your mouth dropped open at the sight of his motorcycle after he insisted on walking you home, more for his own comfort than yours; it delighted him to no end to see that it so obviously shattered the image you had made of him. Gideon himself was not quite sure who he was — he spent his already lengthy lifetime so pointedly rejecting his grandmother's ambitions that he was not certain what his real preferences were, adopting hobbies and careers just because he knew they were what he was not supposed to be doing. Like that mask his grandmother wielded as a weapon, his life was a carefully constructed facade.

But in that moment, basking in the awe-struck wonder of your gaze, he found himself pondering if you had somehow managed to see right through that. And even more extraordinarily... if you liked what you found.

He would have spiraled then and there if not for your comment about the maze being a labyrinth. Though he knew you were joking, Gideon clung to what he knew best, using his vast knowledge of mythology and eagerly launching into an impromptu lecture if only to stop his antennae from vibrating with the pure joy of that look you were still giving him. Bit by bit, he could see your eyes glaze over, and though he felt a pang of insecurity that he was about to scare you away out of sheer boredom, only an act of God could stop him once he got into lesson mode.

But if it started with a sudden stop, it continued with another.

Your lips were suddenly on his. At first, he nearly short-circuited, all the synapses in his brain firing at once as he struggled to comprehend this development, but then he was relaxing into you just as you were melting into him, his wings quivering in the intensity of your kiss as if caught in the winds of the tornado of you.

For a being who was born with said wings, this first kiss with you was the closest he had ever gotten to feeling what flying must be like.

He wanted every bit of you as you dug your hands into his shoulders and he wove his fingers into your hair in return, pressing you closer to him. He could absolutely devour you, a myriad of colors bursting onto his tongue as he nibbled on your lower lip; your delectable little moan of want causing them to flare almost neon.

But then you were pulling away, telling him that it was all a mistake. That you should not have done that. He felt his antennae wilt as the colors bled away again. It was as if you had somehow procured the key for the vault he had locked his emotions away in, but just when you were opening the lid to give him a glimpse, you clapped it shut right before he could touch the warmth of its contents.

You are useless, Gideon.

He tried to gather the pieces of himself that had escaped — to mash them together and shove them back into their prison, but he was too late. Like Pandora's box, the opening of that capsule had only released more curses on his already cursed self. Though he somewhat succeeded in mostly ignoring you when you were alone together in his office, he could not completely overlook you. And when you fell ill, he could *not* be useless again.

Gideon nearly forgot that though Pandora may have released chaos upon the world, only one thing remained after closing the lid of that box: *hope*.

As much as he knew you most likely could take care of yourself with as fiercely independent as you were, the icy grip of concern gnawed at his chest the more he thought of you wasting away without proper medicine in that apartment of yours. Gideon had never received a ticket even since the invention of cars, but risked his perfect record when he drove like a madman all throughout Eventide Falls to find you the best of the best. He even considered calling in a favor to Eden to bring in medicine from those bigger pharmacies in Tenebra City, but managed to somehow talk himself down from the metaphorical ledge as he fought not to drop the vegetables he was examining with shaking hands; nothing but perfection would suffice for the soup he would make you.

When he was finally in your humble living space, staring down at your comforter-clad shivering form, he could not help but revel in the sight of you once more. Your eyes were rimmed with red, your sweaty hair was plastered to your forehead, and the artificial light combined with your illness gave your skin a sickly pallor, but the way your shoulders relaxed minutely when you saw him, as if his presence alone was some kind of panacea, made his wings flutter in rhythm with his heart. When you were tucked at his side, sleepily nuzzling into the tailored shirts he knew may never be perfectly crisp again, he felt needed. He did not feel useless.

He was soaring.

He was finally flying with his own wings.

And then he was plummeting.

Deliciously so.

Despite his warnings that you were making another mistake again; that he was extending you the forbidden fruit and by partaking in it you would be trapped within his Underworld, you were both at the gates of the Second Circle, your hand clasped in his as you pushed them open together. You were fully choosing this — surrounding him, bathing him in the kind of sweet, smoky bliss he never thought he may ever experience. He wanted your every breath, your every moan; in return, he would give you anything and everything you would or could ever want. Not just because of the pure pleasure of the heat of the moment, but because you made him feel like he *deserved* it.

He was *not* useless.

Though Tenebra City was his personal hellscape, he looked forward to indulging you. He wanted the evening to be perfect, pulling a few favors to get a reservation at one of the most exclusive restaurants in the heart of the Diamond District. The darker side of him wanted to absolutely spoil you — to treat you as delicately as the moonflowers he had once painstakingly cultivated in the greenhouse of Dulcis Manor, but he could tell something was off. He could not fathom why *he*, gray and doldrum and plain, still received the usual stares when standing next to the magnificence of *you*, but as the evening progressed, he watched you wilt. He worried he was suffocating you, though he had tried to make it a point to Eden to not appear so possessive.

Then his grandmother called at the worst possible time and he was forced to excuse himself.

Even across the distance, Gideon felt Cordelia's voice wrap around his neck like a vice, her ruby nails digging into the skin of his neck. Instead of flinching under the oppressive nature of her tone, this time, Gideon was beginning to feel the anger build once more. She was saying something about a private investigator, regaling him about your opportunistic parents and warning him that you were only *using* him, but he did not care about any of that.

Then, he did something he had never done before.

He hung up the phone on his grandmother.

Gideon had been determined not to get too attached; he did not want the curse to take root and force you to feel the pain of loss, but as he explained all of this to you in the soft glow of the meadow, something else took root instead. You *saw* him and wanted to see even more; as he revealed more of himself to you, he felt *wanted*. You did not *need* him — Cordelia's revelation about your parents had only confirmed his suspicions that you were fully supporting yourself on your own — yet you still *wanted* him.

Life with you was so intoxicatingly simple. With the soft whispers at the end of the moonbeams of late nights solidifying into slow kisses on the edge of the dawn, Gideon began to thaw. He started to feel as confident in himself as he was in his knowledge of mythology, and though crowds were still intimidating, the weight of your hand in his kept him from flying apart. Even when he felt the doubt creep back in, feeling every bit as grotesque as the creature made by a modern Prometheus, you were there to hold him together.

Bit by bit, pieces of himself fit again. He wanted to be the person you saw in him.

But in a miraculous revelation, he realized he already *was*.

It was completely selfish to ask you to accompany him to Dulcis Manor, but he never would have asked if he had doubted your ability to handle it. When he was younger, he often imagined Dulcis Manor as some kind of looming, monstrous thing, and though it was still oppressive, with you by his side, it was nowhere near as terrifying as he remembered it. His fondest memories were of his time spent in the greenhouse, but even those could not compare to the vision of you walking amongst the blooms.

You always claimed to have a black thumb, but you could not see the way you helped Gideon come alive.

When it was finally time to leave you with Cordelia, though, the streetcar of mirth he found himself on came to a screeching halt. He finally understood what Orpheus must have felt like to lead Eurydice out of the Underworld without looking back until he realized that you were no Eurydice, just like you were no Persephone. You were fully your own person and he loved that about you.

He loved *you*.

There had once been a time when he had refused to give you his middle name for fear it would grant you power over him, but he should have known he was powerless from the very beginning. Cordelia had met her match in you, something Gideon was fully aware of when you began acting rather suspiciously. He had not quite expected you to face off against the Duchess herself on your own, but was not necessarily surprised to learn about this when his grandmother called him after you had left. Though her words were biting when she recounted your insolence to him, Cordelia Narcissa Dulcis *née* Eventide did something she had never done before.

She laughed.

And then you were in front of him again, spluttering about how you had gotten him disowned. You looked so forlorn, wringing your hands together while babbling nonsensically about what you had done just. Though you usually were extremely strategic about things, you had apparently jumped head-on into your visit to Dulcis Manor without thinking.

Because you *cared* for him.

Gideon knew his grandmother was not planning on disowning him, but in that moment, he had never felt closer to his father. Having been orphaned extremely young, he did not clearly remember the man, but was finally able to comprehend the willingness to give everything up for the sake of another. He, too, would die for you if he had to.

Except the knowledge that you would curse him into oblivion for doing so made him smile.

Gideon Mason Dulcis was no Hades or Orpheus just as you were no Persephone or Eurydice. You were your own two people, drawn to each other like twin moths to a flame, though you never let him finish that statement. Even the most mundane moments with you were like an adventure. In between baking scones in his kitchen and dyeing his hair in his bathroom and group outings with your interesting group of friends, Gideon finally felt like he was beginning to know himself and quite spectacularly, just as you did, found that he liked what he saw.

It is not the impact that will kill you, Gideon remembered from his physics lectures many degrees ago, *but the deceleration.*

Maybe Gideon *had* died the day you thumped against his chest — at least, maybe the *old* Gideon did. Except you would tell him that there was no *old* or *new* Gideon; you would tell him that he had always been himself all along, that life was not purely black and white and he had just needed to look within the shades in between to see that.

With you by his side, the carousel of life was beginning to turn, and Gideon's world finally had color.

about the author

A. M. Kore is a monster lover, Mothman's #1 fan, and an enthusiast of *italics* and Second-Person POV. She spends her free time talking about Mothman, thinking of Mothman, and dreaming of Mothman.

Quiver & Quill is her first published work, but she is excited to expand on the world of Eventide Falls and Tenebra City to include more stories about its colorful inhabitants...

Website: www.amkorewrites.com
Discord Server: discord.gg/koresunderworld
Full Links: amkorewrites.carrd.co

twitter.com/amkorewrites
instagram.com/amkorewrites
tiktok.com/@amkorewrites
goodreads.com/amkore
amazon.com/author/amkore
bookbub.com/authors/a-m-kore

also by a. m. kore

Tenebra City Series: Main Content

Quiver & Quill

Sin & Spell

Flame & Fraud

Grinch & Guile: The Duet

Tenebra City Series: Novellas

Grinch & Guile

Hallow & Hew

Tenebra City Series: Anthology Exclusives

"The Mistress of the Labyrinth" (I AM THE FIRE)

thank you!

Thank you so much for reading *Quiver & Quill*!

Please consider leaving a review on Amazon and/or Goodreads — as an indie author, every single review helps tremendously. Thank you again for your continued support of my work!

To stay up-to-date on future releases and general Tenebra City happenings, you can always join my Discord server — or follow me on any of my socials!

Discord Server: discord.gg/koresunderworld
Socials: amkorewrites.carrd.co

special edition content

AN EXCLUSIVE HOLIDAY CHAPTER

the golden bough
(SET BEFORE THE EPILOGUE)

Gideon was going to kill you for this.
    The thought made you snicker to yourself as you draped another handful of tinsel strands on the tree you'd enlisted Greer to help you haul into Gideon's large apartment, stealing furtive glances out of the frosty windowpanes to keep an eye out for his return. It still had the heart-shaped smudge you'd drawn into it with a fingertip while you had waved to him — you could already picture the twitch of his wings at the slight on his otherwise immaculate space — grinning at the roll of his ruby eyes. He had trudged to his car with his antennae drooping as if you were sending him to the gallows, and though you had lent him back his own coal-colored scarf for good luck, wrapping it around and around his neck before pressing a peck to his jaw, you knew an entire day with Eden might as well have been a death sentence in and of itself for him.
    Especially on Christmas Eve.
    One of the things that you and Gideon had bonded over was your mutual anxiety when it came to all things Christmas. For both of you, it came with painful memories of forced time spent with family that only acted as such in name alone, reminders of how thin the

water of the womb really could be. Rather than boughs of holly and *fa-la-la-la*'s, you tended to associate Christmas with sore fingertips and frayed sweaters; the stress of it all always resulted in you biting your nails down to stubs to cope, then pulling apart hems when they were too short to fiddle with. Gideon's preferred method of dealing with his own summons and the Christmas ball DeeDee apparently threw every year at Dulcis Manor was to altogether flee Eventide Falls, many of the quills in his collection obtained on said Christmas trips.

You hadn't spent Christmas with your parents since graduating high school, but the ache remained. The few friends you had made while still in your undergraduate studies had invited you to their own family gatherings, which you had always politely declined, feeling awkward and not wanting to intrude. Since then, your Christmases had primarily been spent torturing yourself with sappy holiday movies with sugar-cookie-sweet happy endings that always made you ugly sob into your carton of takeout, drowning the already too-salty food with your tears.

This year would be decidedly different.

Learning you wouldn't be able to join him on his usual trip due to some last-minute assignments you needed to submit, Gideon had stubbornly decided to stay with you, despite your pleas and reassurances that you would be fine on your own. When he had sniffed at that, antennae going rigid as he turned up his pointed nose and scoffed, you had known from the stiff set of his wings that there was no use arguing with the obstinate man. Instead, you turned to doing what you did best in high-pressure situations: you planned.

Or *plotted*, you supposed was a more apt word for it.

And thus, *Operation: Take Back Christmas* was born.

Being with Gideon was eye-opening in many ways. It showed you that the confidence you had thought you had gained was something you'd had all along, and though you'd always been ambitious, Gideon encouraged you in a way that truly made things feel limitless. You knew Gideon was experiencing a similar *metamorphosis* —

amusingly coincidental, considering the title of his favorite work to teach — little signs such as his return to his natural hair color and the fact that he hadn't absolutely kicked and screamed when you had forced highly encouraged him to take Eden up on his invitation to spend a day in Tenebra City with him proving he was also becoming more comfortable coming out of his shell.

Even if the look of horror on his face at the prospect had made you wish you'd had a camera at the ready so you could have used the picture for next year's Christmas card.

As this was your first Christmas together, you wanted to continue the positive momentum and build new memories with him. Except when it had come time to ponder what to get him, you were left stumped, begging the age-old question: *What did you get the man who already had everything?*

Inspiration had suddenly struck you when you were strolling through the town's winter market — the *agora*, he had once called it — seeing the effort of a crew putting up the traditional giant Christmas tree in the town square. You had immediately ground to a halt, causing Gideon to grumble. With a tug on his hand to get him to stop as well, you'd watched a fairy in a puffer jacket bear-hug a gold star the size of his torso and shakily fly towards the gray winter sky. To the cheers of a small crowd, he managed to gingerly place it at the top.

Giggling at the triumphant raise of the fairy's arms, you had turned back to him to comment on how you'd never seen such a thing before, only to notice he was still staring, puffs of frosty air coming from slightly parted lips as he rubbed a palm over his heart.

While it was in Gideon's nature to love giving gifts, you knew then that a gesture would be much more meaningful to him than any present you could thrust into his fuzzy gray arms. And so, the gears in your mind started turning as you squeezed his hand, smiling at the lilac flush that dusted his cheeks when the far-away look in his eyes had dissipated.

So here you were, sneakily decorating a Christmas tree in his apartment with cheesy holiday songs playing softly in the background while he was most likely being dragged around the glitzy streets of the Diamond District by a certain incubus menace who had been all too thrilled to be an accomplice to your festive scheming. Apparently, Eden's sister had also recently moved back to the city, which had given him more leverage when it had come to goading Gideon into making the trip.

Though you so *wished you could meet Evangeline*, you had gushed into the phone while sitting next to Gideon after having spent the whole morning practicing your response with Eden, you still needed to finish an extra credit assignment for a certain mythology elective.

That had earned you a rather disapproving frown from said professor of this certain mythology elective, but had also cemented your victory. Gideon would never have thought twice about discouraging you from working on your studies, and though he had given you a lengthy lecture on the adverse effects of procrastination on both the quality of work and your overall health, you knew it was well worth it.

Especially since your assignment was long done and submitted to his colleague who graded everything on his behalf, *and* you knew you'd be acing his class, after all.

You snickered again, reaching for another handful of tinsel.

Greer had been equally eager to help you in your venture as Eden had been, accompanying you to a tree farm the day before while you had been under the guise of having a study date. Given Gideon's sensitive nose, the large white pine you'd picked had been perfect due to its low fragrance. While the delicate branches weren't strong enough for heavy embellishments, that was fine with you; you were taking a minimalist approach, opting to decorate in monochromatic hues of silver tinsel and only a strand or two of soft white lights as you didn't want all the colors to hurt his eyes. The ornaments you'd chosen were also light as a feather — literally.

You'd handmade them from various feathers you'd found around campus to make them look like those quills he loved so much.

Gideon hated surprises, though, and while you knew he might want to kill you for it all, you hoped it would distract him enough so you could pull a Heracles and escape from the grips of his Underworld. Actually, this feat would give you a one-up on Heracles... he'd only managed to escape the Underworld *twice*, after all.

You'd lost count of your own running total.

You were putting the finishing touches on the tree when you heard the tell-tale muffled *thump* of a car door closing, causing you to fumble with the feather ornament. Quickly hooking it onto a branch with a muttered curse, you half-sprinted to the window to see Gideon, illuminated by the streetlights like some tragic hero on a stage, beginning to make his way toward the building through a flurry of falling snow. With a glance at the antique clock in the corner of his living room, you saw that you'd completely lost track of time — somehow, you'd worked the entire day to decorate, and now it was well after dinner.

Scrambling to get everything put away, you wiped at the smudged heart on the window with your sleeve to give him one less thing to internally combust about. You took one last look at the tree, a pang of brief worry digging into your chest as something seemed *off*, like it was missing something. But you had no time to either ruminate over this or fix it, moving to quickly flick the switch for the ceiling lights off before situating yourself in front of the tree.

The shallow breaths you fought to control in your excitement sounded thunderous amid the hushed quiet of the low music and the silvery glow emanating from the Christmas tree behind you. It was as if you were an intruder in the still life you had painted, the scream of a floorboard creaking rattling your eardrums when you shifted from foot-to-foot impatiently. As you counted down the seconds in tune with the rhythmic tapping of the fat snowflakes against the windowpanes, you were beginning to wonder just how space-time could have warped like this, stretching the seconds into what felt like eternity.

Maybe you *should* have taken physics.

Finally, the metallic whir of the industrial elevator leading to Gideon's loft shocked the stasis. You wound your arms behind your back, one hand grabbing the opposite wrist to stop yourself from nibbling at your fingertips. As the humming of the elevator's ascent grew louder, the tree behind you seemed to dim while the music faded away; even the snowflakes appeared to still, each element of this cozy scene like actors on a stage preparing for the opening act.

It was quiet once more when the elevator's journey came to an end. You held your breath, your heart thumping audibly from inside your chest. In the minute pause, you couldn't help but think that this was much more exciting than any New Year's ball drop.

Then, the doors began to creak while they slid against each other.

Stepping through the metal curtain, Gideon's presence seemed to be the cue for the magic to truly begin. The dusting of snow against the shoulders of his dark peacoat glistened like diamonds, while the flakes starting to melt into his hair clung to the chiffon strands like the silvery edges of a moonbeam. Behind you, the tree almost flared brighter, the snowflakes outside his expansive windows fluttering again in perfect pace to the tinkling of the music hanging suspended above both of your heads.

He stopped mid-stride; he had apparently removed his glasses at some point, his unobscured cherry eyes widening as his lips parted. You could practically see the neurons in his brain evaporate while he took a stuttering step, stopping again for a moment before slowly making his way toward the tree.

You moved to the side, keeping silent while he pressed forwards and continued to stare. He stood so close to the tree that the delicate branches brushed his chest; when he tilted his head back, his hair rippled across his back like untouched snow on a bare hillside.

A sense of déjà vu hit you as you were reminded of your time in his meadow together. There had been an otherworldly radiance to him within the darkness there, leading you to marvel at how he looked like some kind of constellation. Here, he somehow transcended that, as if his ascension were finally complete.

Draped in the incandescence of the Christmas tree, Gideon's wings did not cast shadows — they cast brilliance, the otherwise unassuming light filtering through them to become so much *more*. Like stained glass, Gideon's wings transformed the pale glare into a myriad of vivid gleams, magentas and teals and olives fracturing through the delicate webs to bathe the room in brilliant color.

In your quest to make the decor as subtle as possible, you hadn't considered that perhaps Gideon's resplendence was what had been missing all along. The prismatic beams stained your skin, the still life you had created for him coming alive in a rush of watercolors, all while he stood motionless, utterly oblivious to the effects his mere presence had on the very air itself.

As the snowflakes dusting his shoulders and hair completely liquified into crystalline pearls, you were beginning to grow worried that you had enormously fucked up. Maybe his reaction hadn't been one of curious wonder, but of disgust, and you had grossly misjudged it. You brought your hands out from behind your back to tug at the bottom of your sweater and looked down at your feet.

"Gideon." You winced at how fractured his name had spilled forth, licking your lips as you tugged at your sweater again. "I just thought—"

"The Ancient Greeks celebrated a similar holiday." His voice was soft. You tensed, wondering if the lecture he was about to launch into was his way of coping with the effects of your royal screw-up. "They celebrated the birth of Dionysus, whom they called a 'Savior' and 'divine infant.' They even sang hymns similar to our modern carols, going to the homes of the rich with olive or laurel branches adorned with wool and different kinds of fruits. The Christmas tree—"

"Gideon," you tried again, interrupting him. With a wince, you curled your fingertips into fists along your hemline. "You don't need to distract me. It's ok if you hate it."

"Hate it?" He sounded shocked, and when you looked up in your own surprise, you saw he had been gazing at you as he murmured, voice thickened with emotion, "It is perfect. *Beautiful*."

You practically melted in relief at this, letting out a soft sigh when he stepped towards you to wrap his arms around your waist. Freeing your hands from being trapped between your chests, you reached up to brush the droplets off his shoulders before gently unwinding his scarf from around his neck. Aware of the weight of his eyes trailing your every move, you tried to sound casual as you remarked, "I got you something."

"Did you?" His brows drew together in puzzlement. "More than this? You should not have—"

"Trust me"—you reached down to grasp the present you'd put under the tree for him, holding it out with a grin—"this was as much for me as it was for you."

A single antenna quirked as he gingerly took the gift from you, careful not to puncture the paper with his claws. He held it awkwardly, as if dealing with something foreign, and you faintly wondered if this was completely unknown to him. Turning the package in his hands, he ran his fingertips along the seams, carefully slicing the tape and peeling the wrapping away rather than tearing it off. When the box was revealed, he folded the paper neatly, settling it in his front pocket like a handkerchief before slowly lifting the lid.

Both antennae flicked at what was nestled between the tissue paper. You dissolved into giggles when he held the lavender fabric up, revealing a frilly apron with "KISS THE COCK COOK" embroidered on the front in dark purple letters.

"Merry Christmas, Gideon!" you exclaimed happily, pressing a kiss to the mouth twisted a bit disapprovingly as his eyes lingered on the profanity you ordered custom-made. The lilac stain dusting across his cheeks caused you to giggle again at the thoroughly offended expression he wore. "Isn't it fun?" You reached up to poke his nose. "Don't worry, I won't force you to wear it, but—"

The warmth of his fingers wrapping around your wrist made you swallow your words, causing you to tilt your head at him. He set the present aside, his hand snaking downwards to disappear into one of his pockets.

"So this is what you have been up to," he mused. An antenna quirked as he cocked his head to the side. "Why did you stop?" He moved his hand from your wrist to rest against your jaw. He then slid his fingertips under your chin, gently tilting your face upwards.

The scent of Earl Grey and moonflower fogged your mind, your eyelids growing heavy at the slight pressure of his thumb slowly sweeping across your skin like a metronome. As tempting as it was to close your eyes and lean in completely to him, you couldn't — not when you were so entranced by the way the light still spilling from his stained glass wings seeped into his profile, caressing his high cheekbones with a brush of watercolor.

"Stop what?" You were finally able to form your own question, gaze flitting back to rest on his lips. A single fang poked out when one corner of them twitched. His chest rumbled, vibrating against yours at his hum.

"Kissing me," he stated simply, antennae flickering. "Is it not tradition to do so when caught in these circumstances?"

The words barely registered when he tipped your head back even farther. Your hooded eyes suddenly went wide, though they automatically slid shut in bliss once his lips abruptly pressed to yours, swallowing your gasp.

But not before you had caught a glimpse of his arm hovering over both of your heads, a bundle of green and red pinched within his gray grip.

You had never been one for tea, but you'd begun to associate Earl Grey with comfort and joy; though the warmth of the liquid could never compare to the security of Gideon's arms encircling you to tuck you into his chest, nor could it hold a candle to how tenderly he cradled your head while ducking into a kiss. Even now, as Gideon pressed the words into your lips that his own would never be able to form, you couldn't help but feel a sense of selfish satisfaction that this particular brew was meant for you and you alone.

"Mistletoe has been featured in many traditions." Gideon's voice was hushed when he finally pulled away, allowing you to take a shuttering breath. There was a whisper of fabric as he shrugged his coat off his shoulders; the way he allowed it to pool on the floor would have shocked you if not for your complete distraction with the steadily growing gleam in his eyes. "Norse mythology speaks of how a weapon made of it was able to slay a god. The Ancient Druids worshipped it, harvesting it with a golden sickle to use in their medicines. Even the Greeks"—he gripped at the hem of your sweater, tugging it above your head swiftly—"used it as the focal point of one of their epics."

A single fingertip traced lightly from the top of your now-bare shoulder up the column of your neck before he splayed his palm against your jaw. "All interesting accounts in their own right. However..." He trailed off to glance at the discarded bundle of mistletoe, settled atop the coffee table he had tossed it on before looking back at you. "I am particularly partial to *this* one, started by the English. I do have one complaint, though."

"Shocking," you remarked teasingly, reaching up to tuck a few strands of his snowy hair behind a delicate ear before slowly unbuttoning his pressed shirt. His chest rumbled underneath your fingertips as he hummed.

"In the original tradition, it was written that a young man should pluck a berry each time he kisses a young girl beneath the hanging plant, and once the berries were gone, the romantic power of the plant would fade." The slight pressure of his hand snaking underneath the waistband of your leggings caused your fingers to pause, your breath hitching when his thumb easily found your clit. You gripped at the edges of his halfway-unbuttoned shirt when he began rubbing small circles, though this didn't seem to deter him as he simply undid the rest of them with the hand that wasn't occupied. "Would you like to guess as to why I find fault in this?"

"N-Not particularly," you replied after a beat, nearly pouting when he withdrew his hand from you to shrug his arm out of his shirt. His lips twitched again, that single fang flashing as he began stalking toward you, forcing you to take small steps backward. When the back of your knees brushed against his couch, he gently pushed at your shoulder, causing you to collapse against the plush leather cushions. All you could do was gape at him as he sank to his knees, settling himself between your legs.

"Oh?" An antenna quirked while he hooked his fingers in your waistband, peeling your leggings down with exaggerated slowness. Gideon's apartment was still stiflingly warm with his fear of you catching cold again, but the tantalizing scratch of his blunted claws against your bare skin left a sea of goosebumps in its wake. He hooked one of your knees over his shoulder, pressing a kiss to a kneecap before doing the same with the other. "Pity." Curling his fingers against your thighs, he tugged you towards him. "I was in the mood for playing a game."

Any retort you could have made promptly died when he dipped his head, bumping his nose against your clit. You gasped at his hot breath fanning against your cunt, shivering again at the prick of his fang while he smirked against your skin. When the vibration of his chuckle caused your head to fall back, opening yourself wider to him, he let out another hum of appreciation.

The pressure of his hands against your thighs increased as he squeezed them, pulling them apart even more while he gave you a long, lascivious lick. "No rules," he stated offhandedly, making you lift your head to see ruby eyes flickering upward from between your legs. "My gift to you." He winked. "Merry Christmas, little harpy."

Merry Christmas, indeed.

Your breath rushed out of you with a *whoosh* as his lips latched on your clit, sparks sizzling through your abdomen when he sucked and pulled. The immediate curse tumbling from your lips at the action made you immediately thankful for his little present to you, but when he released your clit with a faint *pop* only to circle your cunt with the tip of his tongue, you wondered if you'd be borrowing from next year's gift as well.

"Fuck!" you cursed again, bucking your hips as his tongue continued its languid circuit. He merely gripped your skin harder, preventing any additional movement as he continued his maddening ministrations, scarlet eyes locked onto you all the while. They glowed even more brilliantly between the pastel wash of light filtering through his wings, still extended behind him like a stained glass canopy. The tips of them flickered when you whimpered, though he still didn't seem to be in any hurry.

With a shaking arm, you reached out to thread your fingers through his silky hair, head falling back once more when he hummed again. You were careful not to bump too hard against his sensitive antennae, something he apparently seemed to be grateful for, showing his appreciation when he finally flicked the tip of his tongue inside you. The suddenness of it would have made you jump if not for his iron grip on your thighs; though you couldn't see them at the moment, you knew his eyes held just as steadfast on you.

The weight of them on your prone form was almost as sweltering as the pressure that rapidly increased the more and more he fed his long tongue into you, curling it round and round and round to press against every millimeter of space he was currently trying to occupy. One of your hands curled against his scalp while the other managed to find the buttery leather of the couch when you whined at the *almost* fullness, letting out a shallow pant when he pumped the coil of his tongue lazily. The pace was teasing; from the way he was still gripping your skin, ignoring your clit completely as his tongue undulated within you, you knew he was doing so with purpose.

"G-Gideon!" you hissed, cursing those hands as a double-edged sword as they prevented you from shimmying closer to him — prevented you from taking him *deeper*. In response, he coiled his tongue and pressed in sharply, and though it was deepness you had craved, he seemed to be intentionally avoiding that spot that he knew would make you come undone all at once. "Please!"

There was nothing magic in that word when he pulled away, leaving you agonizingly empty. Hand still hovering in the air from where you had gripped his hair, you picked your head up to glare at him, only to see his lips glossy with the precipice of your own release. He made a show of licking them with his tongue, the lavender appendage circling his mouth with the same care he had shown when lapping at your cunt.

"Will you guess now?" he crooned. "Just once?"

It took you a few seconds to remember what he was asking about, your hazy mind struggling to understand the question while it fought with the disappointment of being left on edge as you lowered your hand to the couch. When comprehension finally dawned on you, you licked your own lips, now dry with your shallow panting. "Um." Your eyebrows drew together, forehead wrinkling while you wrestled with yourself to form words. "What do I get if I guess right?"

"Bargaining now, are we?" He leaned down to nip at your kneecap in reprimand, causing you to let out a squeak. "How *naughty* of you."

"This is fucked up!" you exclaimed with a huff, chest still rising and falling with your harsh breathing. "You're telling me that *I'm* the naughty one?"

"Easy, harpy," he warned, tone dry. "This is *my* game we are playing. Remember that." At your glare, he seemed to concede. "If you are correct, I will allow you to come."

That seemed fair. You nodded, though caught yourself halfway. A sudden weariness overtook you as you remembered who you were dealing with. Gideon was half fae, after all, and there was usually some catch. "And..." You could have kicked yourself for inquiring, but ever the curious one, you nonetheless asked, "If I'm wrong?"

"I will still allow you to come." The press of his kiss against your inner thigh felt more like a brand. He looked pleased as punch when he rested his cheek against the pinpoint of heat he had left, blinking lazily at you as he said with scorching sweetness, "But on *my* terms."

"Fine," you responded quickly, just wanting to get it the hell over with. It seemed like a win-win situation for you anyway — coming on *his* terms wasn't necessarily something foreign to you, after all. You cleared your throat, trying to ignore the predatory glint in his eyes as he rose to his feet like a silent specter, moving to undo his belt buckle while gazing intently at you. As the dark fabric slipped against strong gray thighs, revealing the feathered lilac tip of his cock already half-emerged from the slit tucked into a darker thatch of hair between his legs, you swallowed thickly. "Uh..."

Whatever roll you had been on promptly ground to a stop as you were unable to look away, eyelids feeling heavy as you stared. Gideon's cock continued to curl forward, the pointed ridges revealing themselves as his length slipped free from its confines. Your eyes trailed from the lighter purple tip, counting the nubs as they swept down to the darker gray base, only to narrow in confusion when they were met with a shock of silver.

Then they flew wider in realization.

At some point, Gideon's coremata had emerged from behind him, hovering like upside-down icicles in the air. The silver wrapped around his base belonged to one of them as he gripped himself, pumping his cock languidly as he waited for your response. A faint glow from his

"Well?" he asked, his frown suggesting he had been waiting a bit too long. You licked your lips again as he gave another pump, seeing a pearlescent glowing bead gather at the tip, only to stiffen when you heard him scold, "Come now, little harpy. It is not very festive to go against your word."

"Because..." You trailed off as you forced yourself to look up at him, searching for a coherent answer. "Because... uh... it's silly?"

"Silly." The word came out in a huff, as if he thought your attempt was ridiculous. You found the strength to glare at him. It *was* pretty half-assed, but he didn't need to act like it was. He then tilted his head, corema stilling as he considered it further. "Hmm. I suppose you are half correct, actually."

"Half?" You felt a bit hopeful about this, heart thumping when he began to walk towards you once more. "And what do I get for... *half?*"

The brush of two of his coremata against your hipbones quickly doused that hope; another flickered at a pebbled nipple while his hands cradled your jaw as he maneuvered you to lie horizontally across the expansive couch. Despite the myriad of sensations, it was the darkness in his voice that nearly had you jump out of your own skin as he drawled, "I suppose we *both* shall find out."

He hungrily swallowed your satisfied sigh when his feathered tip finally brushed against your cunt, pushing in slowly. You felt every nub and ridge when he gave a few shallow thrusts, delving in deeper and deeper each time as his tongue swept across your teeth. When his legato pumping gave his way to a particularly sharp staccato, you gasped, feeling his lips quirk into a wicked smile against your own as he took the opportunity to curl his tongue against yours.

Gideon was about halfway within you before you could feel the tip of his corema wrapped around his cock, circling it loosely at first before spiraling more tightly towards the base of it to form that clever knot. Though his attentions had made you wet enough that his initial thrusting into you was easy enough, this thickness was met with some resistance. Your brows furrowed at the sudden tightness, the knot feeling much larger than usual as your fingers uncurled from where they had buried themselves in the leather of the couch to grip at his arms instead.

The pistoning of Gideon's hips slowed to more of an experimental roll as he pulled his lips from yours to gauge your expression. Each pass of them pressed more of his cock into you, the pressure causing that coil in your abdomen to twist sharply as you fluttered around him with a grunt. The tips of his hair tickled your forehead, which was still scrunched at the concentration of overwhelming fullness. He was patient, though, continuing to move painstakingly slowly to allow you to take him little by little. Your eyelids eventually slipped shut in concentration as you focused on relaxing, feeling his thumbs stroke your jaw soothingly while two coremata did so similarly against your hipbones.

But with one currently wrapped around his cock inside you, that still left the fourth unaccounted for.

Your eyes snapped open in realization when you felt the unmistakable brush of another corema tip within you.

"T-Two?" Was all you were able to gasp, suddenly understanding why the knot he had created felt gargantuan this time. You shifted your hips, letting out a helpless moan at how it jostled his girth against you.

"Two," he confirmed, flashing you a grin, though it faltered slightly when you winced. Looking a bit guilty now, he seemed more hesitant. "We can stop—"

"No." You squeezed his arm. "I can take it. I *want* to take it." A laugh bubbled forth as you suddenly found the absurdity extremely humorous, though the movement caused you to wince again. "I have to learn how to get to four, remember?"

"Of course." He leaned down to brush his lips against yours, careful not to move your hips again. "Though if there is one thing I learned from my studies pertaining to physics..." Pulling away, he slid his hands downwards to rest at your waist. "It is to let gravity work *for* you."

He was somehow able to roll you out from underneath him to position you atop him, your legs now straddled on either side of his while your kneecaps rested against the edge of the couch. The movement had your mouth falling open in an 'o' of surprised pleasure, this new angle taking the edge off just enough for the fullness of him to melt into throbbing need. Resting your hands on his shoulders for leverage, you felt two of his coremata gripping at your waist to guide you while one of his hands slipped lower to grip the curve of your ass as the other thumbed against your clit.

"Good girl." His breath fanned your shoulder before he sank his teeth in slowly. It wasn't enough to break the skin, but it offered you something else to focus on as you lowered yourself onto him. His thumb rubbing your clit gave you immediate relief, though you still buried your whine into the junction of where his neck met his shoulder, hair tangling in his while you tried to relax around him. You wriggled yourself back and forth, trying to get it to fit just like you knew it could. "Take as much as you need."

I could never have enough of him, you were able to think to yourself, feeling his thighs begin to tremble beneath your own at the strain of not thrusting into you. His thumb began circling your faster, urging the coil of pleasure to twist tighter and tighter. Grasping him harder, you bared down against your knees to pick your hips up a little bit, only to let go and plunge downwards.

The action allowed the knot to finally slip past the juncture of its resistance, slipping completely within you. A simultaneous groan left both of your lips when his cock was fully sheathed; you wrapped your arms around his neck, clinging to him while he began to pump into you.

You felt his chest vibrate against yours as he began to speak again, "The fault in the tradition"—you could barely hear him with the way the blood was rushing in your ears—"is the idea that the 'romantic power' would fade." His hand left your clit to touch your arms, slowly working them from around his neck to push you back so you could look at him. When his face came into view, you realized it was blurry; tears must have been clouding your vision, having pooled in the corners of your eyes from the stimulation. A palm pillowed your jaw as his voice lowered to a hush. "Even if the berries were as numerous as the stars themselves, it would take more than a few heavens for what I feel for you ever to fade."

The taste of your name on his lips was almost as divine as Earl Grey and moonflower as he sighed into you when you captured his mouth in another kiss. You breathed in tandem, your breaths becoming his and his becoming yours as you rocked against each other, the tip of his cock flaring just right as his ridges and nubs traced every part of you that you gave to him. White light began to creep into the edges of your cloudy vision, and while you felt so close and *full*, something still seemed missing.

You hadn't felt a corema leave your hips until it brushed against your ass, flicking lightly against your skin. He pulled back just enough to ask a bit hesitantly, "Would you—"

"Yes," you immediately replied, not even allowing him to finish. "God, yes. *Please.*"

The tip of the corema curled towards your front, gathering the fluids from your weeping cunt before returning to your ass. It was thin enough that the initial push didn't cause much resistance, though Gideon was able to distract you with a roll of your clit between his skillful fingers when the pressure became more pronounced. He slowed the pistoning of his hips in an attempt not to overwhelm you completely, but from the tears that still spilled from the corners of your eyes, you may have been too far gone.

Yet you wanted this. You *needed* this.

"More," you whispered, returning your hands to his shoulders for balance, though you knew he would never let you fall. He complied by pressing the corema into you deeper, the new kind of pinching strain causing your mouth to fall open again as you let out a breathy whine. When you realized his claspers had come out to mold you against him, a sharp pressure on your thighs made you clench.

Your eyes fluttered shut as the bombardment of sensations, though the loss of one sense offered your brain no relief from the onslaught on the others. Though his claspers didn't allow him much room, he began to thrust his hips again in an even, alternating rhythm to the corema pumping in and out of your ass. Even with your eyes shut, that white light began to bleed through again, becoming sharper and sharper with every pistoning movement.

"Open your eyes."

The words that drifted into your head weren't a demand, but a prayer.

Gideon's voice was soft, as delicate as the wings fluttering behind him and the antennae flickering atop his silvery head.

Though you weren't sure if your already fragmented mind could take it, it would have shattered you more not to acquiesce to the gentle plea. When you opened them, struggling to focus through the haze of pleasure and the blur of tears, Gideon's face was hovering in front of you, unguarded and innocent, his own eyes glossy and wide with wonder.

Though Gideon was in your shadow this time, he managed to glow as if lit from within, the tips of his hair spun from moonbeams themselves as his wings stained everything around him in a wash of color. Yet when you realized that the astonished marvel shining in their red incandescence wasn't from the sight of the Christmas tree gleaming behind you, but from *you* hovering atop him, that same color bled into the burst of light that finally overtook you as the coil snapped and you sobbed his name.

His own release followed soon after as he pressed your name into your skin in a flurry of kisses, his hips stuttering before you felt a flush of warmth flood inside you. He continued to rock against you as his claspers pulled you in tighter to him, chanting your name as he guided you down from your orgasm while you could only fall forward to rub your forehead into his shoulder. The corema in your ass slowed and slipped out of you; the movement caused you to clench around him, making Gideon groan as another spurt of liquid heat painted your inner walls.

It took a few moments after he finally stilled for his claspers to retract and his coremata to leave your skin as well. With two hands, he slowly lifted you, carefully loosening the knot he had created on his cock to slip out of you more easily. Both of you groaned at the sensation, and though you were exhausted, you couldn't help but bemoan the loss of him. He gently repositioned you back on the couch, disappearing for a beat, only to return a few moments later with his customary handkerchief.

"Relax." The command was gentle, emphasized by a warm palm splaying over your thigh and the dip of the plush cushion underneath his weight. Music still crooned from the vintage record player you had forgotten about, as muted and tender as his devoted touch while he dutifully worked to clean up the mess both of you had made. Your eyes began to slide shut, but not before you managed to catch a glimpse of a swatch of silk, his monogram now glowing.

He hummed to the music as he worked, which surprised you, given you had assumed that he had rejected all things Christmas. But then again, Gideon knew everything, so you supposed perhaps you had just underestimated him.

How many times had Gideon hummed this very tune in the inky darkness of solitude all those years before?

Your chest suddenly tightened as you tried not to dwell on this too much. In the velveteen luster of the sanctuary you'd managed to create on this Christmas Eve, no Ghost of Christmas Past could haunt you. Not when his hair cascaded around you like a curtain of starlight or when his wings splayed atop of you, twinkling a myriad of colors that could ward off any darkness.

A rustle of tissue paper and the feeling of a light weight settling against your chest forced a bleary blink from you as you struggled to focus back on him. Finished with his task, he kneeled on the floor beside you, two elbows resting on the edge of the couch you were still splayed on.

"In the *Aeneid*," he began, barely above a whisper, "Virgil writes of Aeneas' journey to the Underworld. He is advised by an oracle to obtain a bough of gold prior to making this passage." A gray arm extended towards you, painted magenta and teal and olive in the radiance of his wings. Long fingers curled around the pendant of the necklace you realized he had clasped onto you. "Scholars today believe that this 'Golden Bough' is assumed to be mistletoe. But do you know why it is of such significance in this tale?"

You barely had the strength to shake your head, but you somehow did, mesmerized by the glint of the fang peeking out from his lilac-tinted lips. The delicate curve of the cupid's bow quivered as the corner of his mouth quirked. "The Golden Bough was to be given as a gift to Proserpina, the Roman equivalent of Persephone. It was said to be sacred to her"—the scent of Earl Grey wafted towards you once again as he bent to press a kiss into your bare shoulder—"and though *you* are no Persephone, I am all too happy to embrace the comparison for myself, for I have found my Golden Bough."

His chest shook at his light chuckle. He slowly uncurled his fingers, allowing you to see the pendant he delicately settled back against your skin. "Though it has not taken the form of mistletoe, but of..." When you took in the dainty petals carved out of a moonstone, you immediately recognized the bloom as he breathed, "A moonflower."

Nothing you could have said would have been an adequate response to the complete adoration shining in his hooded eyes. Wordlessly, you simply reached out to him, winding your arms around his neck and burying your face in his hair. When his arms wound around you, pressing you to his chest tightly as his shoulders drooped, you knew this was enough. It was more than enough.

In the faint sparkle of a Christmas tree and the soothing music, you melted into him like the soft pattering of snowflakes into his hair. The last vestiges of wakefulness slipped away as sleep began to claw at you, your eyelids slipping shut again. You gave a soft sigh at the warm brush of his lips against one lid, then the other, as he pressed a promise into your skin.

And when you opened your eyes the following day, the world was new again.

The golden glow of the evening gave way to the silver gleam of Christmas Day as you found yourself cocooned in the dark silk sheets of his bed. Throwing your now pajama-clad legs over the side — ever the gentleman, he had apparently thought you redress you — you spied a glass of water on the side table. You took a few sips before rising, stomach grumbling in protest at your lack of an adequate meal the night prior. The delicate pendant of your new necklace thumped against your chest at your movement.

Quickly taking to the bathroom to brush your teeth, you curled your fingers around the pendant as you padded towards the kitchen, nearly sobbing at the sugary scent of waffles and the sizzling popping sound of bacon cooking. The oven was also preheating, and electronic mixers of various shapes and sizes lined his counters between arrays of meticulously organized cooking pans. It all seemed much too elaborate for just the both of you, but Gideon tended to be rather extravagant.

It was also Christmas, after all.

You were greeted with Gideon situated behind his expansive kitchen island, a large bowl tucked into the crook of his elbow as he stirred batter with a wooden spoon. His snowy hair was tied back as he worked, glasses slipping down to the upturned tip of his nose. Not only was the sight of him making you breakfast enough to melt your heart, but he was shirtless.

And wearing the apron you had gifted him.

You beamed at him as you settled onto one of the high chairs on the other side of the island. "Good morning!"

"Good morning, little harpy," he returned, pausing his stirring to push his glasses up with a knuckle and reach for a spoon. He dipped the tip into his mixture, twirling it to keep the batter from dripping onto his pristine countertops before extending it to you, eying your hand touching his gift. "Taste?"

Letting go of your pendant, you bent forward, letting out an "Mmm," of appreciation around the utensil before he pulled it away. The taste of cinnamon exploded onto your tongue. "Scones?" He nodded at your inquiry, resuming his stirring. "Apple cinnamon?"

"Yes," he confirmed, smirking at your hopeful look. "*And* blueberry." When you merely blinked at him, his smirk only deepened. "They are Efficlair's favorite, are they not?"

You blinked again. "Well, yeah, but—"

"I am so appreciative of the decor," he continued, interrupting you. He gave a nonchalant shrug. "It would have been rather droll to host company on Christmas to a bare apartment, no?"

You leaned forward, cheeks warming in curious excitement. "What do you mean?"

When you had asked your friends what their Christmas plans were, they had given vague answers that they were spending it with family. Gideon may have hated surprises, but apparently also had a few tricks up his sleeve as he retaliated with one of his own. "I extended invitations for your friends to join us for brunch. I have been planning this for the past month."

Giving a happy squeal, you tapped on the countertop with your palms before clapping your hands. "That's amazing!" you exclaimed, unable to stop bouncing in your seat. "Oh!" You suddenly sat ramrod straight, head whipping back and forth in search of the time. "I need to brush my teeth! And get ready! What will I wear—"

"You know," he drawled, still stirring methodically. "You never did let me finish my sermon on the origins of the Christmas tree." Picking his spoon out of the bowl, he held it straight up in the air like he often did with his index finger. As a lump of batter fell back into the bowl with a *clop*, you fought a groan while he ignored your scowl. "The Christmas tree also has roots — excuse the pun — in ancient times. The Ancient Greeks celebrated the epiphany of Dionysus in their festival called the 'Dionysia.' Male-gendered *satyrs* and the female *maenads* were often depicted as part of the god's entourage."

He cleared his throat and you slumped against the counter in response, biting your tongue to stop a complaint from falling out of your mouth. From the performance he gave last night and the fact that he was not only cooking breakfast for you, but for your friends, you supposed the least you could do on Christmas was humor his lecture. Planting an elbow on the glossy surface, you rested your cheek against it while he continued, "This is where the Christmas tree comes in. The pine was a totem plant of Dionysus, both evergreen and"—he returned his spoon to his bowl, giving another stir while he looked down—"*erect*."

When your eyes widened at this, he merely peeked above the rims of his glasses at you. "You see, phallic symbols were extremely important in the Dionysia. The pine tree served as a metaphor for a phallus." He stopped stirring, setting the spoon aside. "Just as its sticky sap was a metaphor for..." He trailed off, dipping the tip of his finger into the batter and bringing it to his mouth. Lips parting slightly, his tongue emerged to lick it off as he finished with, "Semen."

You nearly fell off your high stool as you burst into a fit of laughter at this, Gideon's chuckles accompanying your surprised glee. *Interesting, schminteresting,* you had once called Greek mythology all those months ago when you had first met him. Never would you have been able to guess just how *interesting* Gideon could make it.

"We have a bit of time before I need to put everything in the oven," he remarked offhandedly, setting the bowl down and wiping his hands on the front of his apron. He began to saunter around the island, and when he finally stood in front of you, he had to dart his hands out to keep you from almost falling out of your chair again.

The apron, apparently, was all he had been wearing this whole time.

"O-Oh?" You swallowed thickly, trying not to drool at the way the frilly fabric was beginning to tent in front of him. It traced the outline of him *just* so like a curtain begging to be swept aside. Snaking your arms around his waist, you tugged at the knot he had tied in the back. "Whatever shall we do?"

"You took *three* last night." His voice was slightly huskier, breath catching ever so slightly when you tugged at the knot again. "We—"

The sound of an alarm going off caused both of you to jump. He pulled away abruptly, apron fluttering as he hurried over to the oven. With a scowl, he put on a pair of oven mitts before ducking to open the door, waving at the steam that billowed into the air. You bit back a smile at the lilac blush dusting his flustered face. A pile of envelopes caught your attention just as you heard him groan.

Thumbing through them, you hummed to yourself while he tried his best to salvage whatever he had apparently forgotten about. You had never read his mail before, but when you came across a heavy envelope that was addressed to the both of you, sporting a rather impressive black wax seal with the depiction of a gorgon, your mouth fell open. Pinching the corner, you lifted it and began waving it at him. "Your grandmother sent us a card!"

"Did she?" He still sounded distracted, hovering over the pan he had pulled from the oven. His antennae and the tips of his wings drooped in disappointment while his back was still towards you, which was fine with you as his lack of pants gave you a great view of his ass. He let out a long sigh. "Well, open it, I suppose."

You quickly tore the envelope open, wondering just what Cordelia Narcissa Dulcis *née* Eventide could have possibly sent both of you. When the paper fell away, your shriek had Gideon turning from his burned creation to sprint to your side. Holding it up, you showed him the formal portrait of her seated in front of her fireplace, her signature cameo glaring at you from where it was pinned to the high collar of her black dress. Her impassive expression was in complete contrast to the extravagant scrawl of the embossed ruby script taking up the bottom of the card: *Seasons Greetings*.

"She sent us a *Christmas card?*" Gideon's words wobbled out of his parted lips. The lilac drained from his cheekbones, leaving nothing but pale ash behind. He looked weak, as if he might faint.

"I'm going to just take it as a good sign!" You hopped off your stool, waltzing over to his fridge. Plucking a magnet from it, you affixed DeeDee's card front and center on the door. When you turned back to him with a triumphant smile, he groaned, bumping his glasses upwards to pinch at the bridge of his nose.

"If you so insist." He looked dour, scowling across the kitchen at the oven. The fact that he was still clad only in an apron made you giggle, especially as his arms folded over the scrawl in front of it. "We keep getting interrupted in our pursuit to *four*..."

"Well, you better not pout." You booped his nose with a fingertip before leaning forward to peck him on his sulking mouth. Earl Grey, moonflower, and cinnamon flavored the smile you pressed to his lips. "Let's make that our New Year's resolution."

Made in the USA
Monee, IL
25 January 2023

ce26bb39-55d1-49e0-90d5-97be018219feR01